The

Beleaguered

Prophet

By

Susan Davis Sandberg

SusanDavisSandberg@gmail.com

ISBN-13: 978-1-939577-00-9
ISBN-10: 1939577004

Cover design by John Sandberg
Cover photograph © John Wollwerth, Shutterstock.com

To
My daughter Sara

*Who is too complex, according to her,
to be a character in a book and who
therefore is included in bits and pieces
here and there in the good, the shy
and the beautiful*

Chapter 1

Disaster.

She could feel it in her bones.

She was going to flunk the bar exam and never be able to practice law in Illinois. The fact that she was a licensed attorney in California, which meant that she had passed the bar in that state, did not alter her certainty that she was going to fail tomorrow's test.

Twenty-eight years old, five months pregnant with her first child, Aleta Praetzel sat in her wheelchair staring through the picture window at the bleak landscape typical in Northern Illinois in late February

She knew the apple trees in their orchard were already sending sap up their trunks and that soon buds would swell at the end of the tips of every small branch. She knew that when the time was right, the buds would open. This was a certainty.

She knew that her imprisonment in the chair would end as well. This was also a given.

Passing the bar was not.

Aleta hated uncertainty.

Her one servant-housekeeper, cook and muse combined—approached.

"Ma'am, if you would like, we can walk out to the barn and see the horses," Bertha's soft voice suggested.

"Aren't you in the middle of something?" Aleta asked, wiping her eyes with her one free hand and stifling a sniffle.

"Your needs come first," Bertha said politely.

"You tell me that every day."

"You appear to need reminding, Ma'am."

"Yes, Bertha, a walk would do me good."

That decision would mark the beginning of the change.

"Shall we take the dogs?"

"Of course," Aleta said.   "They'll enjoy an extra outing."

Bertha rolled the chair to the door and opened it. Aleta didn't rise until all five dogs had rushed through the door and they could see them racing past the orchard toward the barn. The walk was always the same—to the barn and back because the ground was hard-packed dirt and flat. It was the only time Aleta was allowed out of her chair.

Bertha helped Aleta to her feet and fastened her long, heavy cape over her shoulders.

Bertha put her arm around Aleta's waist and the two strolled slowly to the barn. The air was near freezing. Light snow flurries brushed their cheeks and settled in their hair.

The unpaved ground alongside the orchard had once been a storage area for tractors and combines and now was merely a huge open area with a few tumbled down sheds on one side behind which was a large wheat field.

Her husband had purchased the property over a decade ago, when the farmer had finally decided to retire. Hubert Praetzel had floated his son a personal loan despite the fact that Stanley was barely seventeen and a college sophomore.

Now as Aleta and Bertha strolled toward the barn renovated by her father as a wedding gift, Aleta thought about the hours he and Ed poured into restoring it to its original state. Stanley had played in that barn as a child and it was the gift he cherished the most.

That this area was fast becoming a cluster of estates was not too difficult to predict, but that Stanley would buy in as a teenager was unusual.

As Aleta and Bertha reached the barn, an old man hobbled toward them. Hubbs had been hired by Stanley to care for the horses.

"The dogs said you was coming. Can you ride yet?" Hubbs asked.

"Not for two more weeks," Aleta said. "Dr. Taekman said the bones haven't healed yet. He wouldn't even do a CAT scan to be sure.

"Dr. Cook agrees with him," Bertha told her.

"He called." Aleta asked, a slight hint of annoyance that she wasn't told.

"He called me to give me instructions."

"Separate from mine?"

"No, Ma'am. He just wanted to be sure I understood that although you're feeling good, you still aren't healed."

"Well, at least I have one arm free to pet the horses," Aleta said reaching toward her sister Jocelyn's horse who was in the first stall.

She withdrew her hand suddenly.

"What is it, Miss Aleta?" Hubbs asked, worry wrinkling his aged face. "He didn't nip you did he?"

Without replying Aleta moved over to pet Sterling, the rescue Morgan Jocelyn had brought home to keep her horse company. Sterling was slated to travel to shows with Jocelyn's show jumper to keep him calm.

Aleta stroked Sterling for several minutes before moving on to her Appaloosa, Shadow, also a rescue horse, a Christmas gift from Stanley who bought a horse for himself, took riding lessons and hired Mr. Hubbs to care for the whole lot.

Aleta started when she touched Shadow. Quickly, she touched Stanley's horse and finally Jezebel, the old mare Mr. Hubbs brought with him when he signed on.

Bertha who'd been watching her carefully, bade her sit down and tell them what was wrong.

Aleta looked at her two servants. She'd never told either of them of her prophetic power. The family was pretty close-mouthed about it even though the recent publicity had identified the three Tri City prophets as Martha Cook, Harriet Locke and Aleta Praetzel. Experienced servants didn't believe the publicity that swirled around their employer's activities.

Aleta eyed the two servants apprehensively. They had to be told. She started by telling them she could foresee tragedies.

"Usually it's a death," she said.

"One of the horses is gonna die?" Hubbs asked.

"Yes," Aleta replied. "Possibly three. I can try to prevent Jocelyn from going riding with Bertha's help, but Hubbs, her horse must not be ridden tomorrow. Neither must Shadow or Minx. I can't see anything except that these horses will be safe only if they stay home."

She took a breath. Neither of her listeners said a word, so she continued, "Stanley is going to be in court. Dad and I are going to be taking the bar exam. Only you two will be here. Both of you have my permission to call the police if anyone tries to remove any of these horses for any reason. In fact, that's an order."

"Yes Ma'am," the two chorused.

On the way back to the house, Aleta was visibly upset. Bertha could think of no way to calm her.

"I wish I could see more. It's so vague. But promise me you'll see that Jocelyn doesn't ride."

"I'll pick her up before her last class ends. I'll have Robert write a note giving me permission. That way she won't slip past me."

"I wish I could safeguard the horses somehow," Aleta said.

"Mr. Hubbs will take care of them," Bertha said.

"I wonder if I should hire someone to help guard them."

"If it will make you feel better, do it."

"Yes, that's what I'll do. You'll help me, won't you, Bertha?"

"Yes, Ma'am."

"You're late," Aleta said when her husband walked through the door.

"Hello, Beautiful," he said coming straight to her and kissing her on the forehead. He brushed his hand lightly on the short auburn brush that had managed to grow since her head had been shaved for the last operation.

"It's going to grow to a respectable length by the time we go on our second honeymoon," he remarked. "I'd hate to have everyone wondering why so handsome a man married a bald-headed woman."

"You're late," she reiterated as he went back to hang his coat on the rack.

"Bertha called and told me when I was in court and told me how upset you were, so I..."

Aleta interrupted, "You were in court?"

"I asked for a recess when she beeped me."

"You allow her to interrupt you in court?"

"She's been told what constitutes an emergency. With you, it's not that you're choking to death."

"She could handle that," Aleta said as he wheeled her to the table.

"So I went to see Dr. Taekman to see what was going on and how much longer you and that wheelchair would be wed."

He took the casserole from the oven and put it on the hot pad Bertha had set in the center of the table as Aleta continued to question him.

"Did you tell him about your... er our... promise?"

"You mean my telling Dr. Cook that I'd be celibate until you were completely healed? It was Cook's suggestion, by the way. I didn't offer to do it. I just said I'd do anything to prevent another relapse."

He took the wine from the ice bucket and poured it into the glasses as he continued his explanation.

"You've got to admit four skull openings is a bit much to go through—anyway, he asked if that included celibacy and I said yes. Aleta, I was worried out of my mind. And afterward, I remembered what I'd said. It was a prayer really."

"I understand," she said. "It's just we haven't been married that long and we..."

"I know. I did ask Dr. Taekman how his married life was," Stanley said plunking a large spoonful of macaroni and cheese on her plate.

"Stanley, you didn't!"

"He's a newlywed."

"Yes, to a ninety-year-old woman."

"Well, he told me," Stanley said, his voice low. He broke Aleta's roll in half and buttered both halves.

"I don't want to know!" Aleta cried. "Martha's a friend. A revered friend. A treasured friend. And she's delicate."

"He said that worried him at first," Stanley said. "He said even if he lost those extra hundred pounds, he'd be too heavy for her."

"I don't even want to think about it," Aleta said.

"He didn't go into any detail. He didn't even give me a general idea."

"Thank heavens!" Aleta said obviously relieved. She took her first bite of food. Stanley began eating as well. After a few moments he broke the silence.

"But their relationship is not platonic. He told me that after talking to Claude, he..."

"He and my grandmother's new husband compared notes?" Aleta gasped setting down her fork.

"Why not? They both just recently married older women," Stanley returned, taking another mouthful.

"Well, I guess that makes sense," she said taking a bite of her roll.

"He said that he and Claude agree that the sexuality is not a gene thing. They figure it's a by-product of being open enough to be a prophet of God."

"You talked to Claude about us?"

"He talked to me about Harriet."

"You listened!" she snapped.

"What was I supposed to do?"

"Not listen," she declared. "She's my grandmother!"

"Anyway Michael..."

"You're calling my doctor Michael, now?" Aleta quipped.

Stanley went on, "He said that Martha was a remarkable woman sexually. She knew how to pleasure a man. He said it was an unexpected bonus."

Aleta scowled angrily. "I told you not to tell me."

"Face it, Aleta. You believe in the truth."

Aleta switched topics. "So how long before we can engage in any sexual activity if and when I ever decide to do it with you again."

"How long will this 'mad' last?" He queried with a slight twinkle in his eye.

"A month at least," she declared.

"That just about fits his prediction of when we can resume normal married life."

"A month!!!" she cried.

"Your bones aren't healing as quickly as they should. It's going to be the long rather than the short end of the spectrum."

"Stanley, I don't know if I can do it," she murmured picking up her fork.

"Sure you can. Tomorrow you're going to take your bar exam and then you're going to start practicing your profession."

"You won't let me go out of the house."

"Aleta, let's not plan for the day after tomorrow," Stanley decided. "Tomorrow needs all your attention. But Martha has a good case for you to sink your teeth into. It will take months to prepare and you'll have months."

Aleta only half-heard him.

"I had a vision," Aleta said abruptly. "It was so brief and so cut up. It involved Jocelyn and the horses."

"You shouldn't be telling me. You should be telling your father."

"Bertha is taking care of that. And I told Hubbs and I hired a security guard."

"Are you still worried?" Stanley asked.

"No more than usual."

"Do you think Hubbs and Bertha believed you?"

"I believe they will do what I asked them to do."

"We could always call Chief Milani and alert him."

"I did tell Bertha and Hubbs to call the police if there was any trouble."

"He likes to be forewarned," Stanley said with certainty. The three police chiefs in the Tri City area had followed a number of warnings by the three women who were considered as a group of prophets. They had never been wrong.

Aleta's spirit remained low even after Stanley hung up the phone and announced that Tom would have patrols check the house every fifteen minutes from three until dark.

"You're tired," he said. "I'll walk the pup and then we'll go to bed."

Aleta nodded, her face blank.

Stanley walked the pup to the barn. He spoke briefly with Hubbs and told him about the patrols.

"Do you have a gun?" he asked the old man.

"Don't like 'em."

"It would bring the police running."

"It'd spook the horses, specially Shadow."

"Sorry, I wasn't thinking," Stanley apologized.

"Miss Aleta give me a phone," Hubbs mentioned.

"Use it," Stanley ordered. "And don't get hurt. There will be a security guard here."

"You taking her serious, huh?"

"Aleta is a real prophet. I always take her seriously."

"So it's true what the papers say."

"Yes."

"She really did save all them lives?"

"Yes."

"And the cops don't think she's nuts?"

"Nope."

"Don't that beat all."

Shortly afterward, Stanley began undressing Aleta which had become habitual ever since she was incapacitated by her first shoulder injury months ago. He carefully removed the sling and then, piece by piece, every item of clothing, folding each item neatly, despite the fact that all were destined to be laundered the next day.

She waited for him to pull a fresh nightgown from the drawer and put in on her. To her surprise, he helped her lay down in bed.

"Tonight," he said, "you get to sleep as you like."

"But..."

"I know I may need to take a cold shower before I even get into bed."

"Stanley, I don't want to put you through that."

"You just lay there and enjoy your freedom."

"It does feel wonderful," she murmured.

"I can manage one night," he said boldly as he began undressing. He turned away as he disrobed. It didn't help. The memory was too vivid.

Aleta had her eyes closed, so she didn't see Stanley step into the shower. She opened her eyes when she heard the water running.

She watched Stanley move about and waited while he put his pajamas on. While she liked to sleep nude, he didn't. However, to her surprise he climbed naked into bed and lay next to her.

"This isn't sexual, but when you're feeling like this, you like the touch of my body next to yours."

"Just having my hand on your thigh is enough," she murmured sleepily.

"Sweet dreams," Stanley said softly.

He waited for her breathing to become regular. He felt her hand slip over and grip his member. The grip was firm but not tight. He was her prisoner until she woke.

"Sweet dreams, my love," he whispered.

Chapter 2

Sixteen-year-old Jocelyn Locke sat down with her friends at lunch and told them she couldn't go riding that afternoon after school.

"But you said you could get us a horse for Winnie," Tiffany complained. "His horse cut its lip and the vet's stitching it up this afternoon."

"You promised I could ride the Appaloosa," Debi Lu added. "You know my horse is lame, so if I can't ride your sister's horse, I can't go."

"Will they let us borrow the horses if you're not with us?" Tiffany asked, smiling coyly at Winnie.

"My sister said something's going to happen that'll spook the horses," Jocelyn reported. "Nobody can ride any of them."

"Your sister? That crazy psychic?" Kevin sneered.

"She's not crazy," Jocelyn declared defensively. "She knows things."

"Maybe Winnie could borrow your horse," Tiffany suggested. "You know he rides well."

"Nobody rides Yudi but me!" Jocelyn declared. "But that's not it. Aleta's not letting any horses off the place."

"So the horses spook at a skunk or a loud noise," Kevin scoffed. "So what? That's happened before. Doesn't your sister know anything about horses?"

"She knows a lot. She's a better rider than I am," Jocelyn countered heatedly.

"Even so, Jocelyn," Wade said. "You've got to admit your sister sounds a bit paranoid. Why didn't she just say no?"

Jocelyn looked at the freckle-faced redhead.

"I didn't ask her," she replied. "I was going to do it last night, but that's when she told me about the explosion and the horses spooking and me getting killed."

"This is ludicrous!" Winnie spoke up, his thick lips trembling slightly. "I'm with Kevin and Wade on this. Your sister's nuts or you are if you think we'll believe that line of crap!"

"Come on, guys. Give me a break. Aleta's serious. She even hired a security guard to watch the horses. Even if I wanted to go with you guys, I couldn't."

"You make me sick!" Kevin spouted. "You're such a pussy. Why don't you go sit somewhere else?"

Jocelyn rose and ran out of the lunchroom.

"That was cold," Lisa scolded.

"Her sister owns the horses," Wanda added. "Whatever her reason, she has the right."

Perry got up quietly. Because he was the tallest of the group, when he moved, they all noticed. Had he spoken, his deep voice would have commanded their attention. He spoke rarely.

"Where are you going?" Kevin asked sharply.

"To find Jocelyn," Perry replied. "You were mean. It's her sister's horse."

"So what. It's a shitty excuse," Winnie said his blue eyes bulging as they did when he was angry.

"Yeah," Tiffany agreed. "She gets to ride and Winnie and Debi Lu don't."

"You didn't listen to her at all, did you?" Perry replied quietly.

He walked off.

"What'd I say?" Tiffany asked Winnie.

"Nothing," Kevin hastily assured her.

Wanda got up. "I'm going to help Perry look for her."

"Me too," Lisa said. "She's probably in the girl's bathroom."

The group watched the cousins walk away.

"Now what?" Winnie asked. "I still don't have a horse."

"I say we go get the horses and meet as planned," Kevin replied.

"What about Wanda and Lisa?" Winnie asked.

"They'll be there," Kevin assured him. "And what are they gonna do when Winnie and Debi Lu ride up on the two horses Jocelyn said they could borrow."

"Yeah, Tiffany agreed. "We all heard her say she'd get Winnie a horse... and Debi Lu too."

"I'm out," freckle-faced Wade said, his redhead ire surfacing. "We know Jocelyn never asked her sister. You can't just go take someone's horse!"

"You believe that shit her sister's spouting?" Kevin snarled.

"No, I don't, but I'm not taking anyone's horse without permission," Wade snapped back. "I'm no horse thief!"

"You're not riding it," Winnie argued, his eyes bulging even more. "I'm riding it. And I say we show Jocelyn her sister's nuts. We'd be doing her a service. Otherwise, every time her sister waves that spooky stuff in front of her, she'll be afraid to move."

"Yeah," Kevin agreed heartily. "We'll be doing her a big favor."

"You're both crazy!" Wade exploded and walked away.

"I'm in," Tiffany said when he was out of earshot.

Debi Lu was quick to agree.

"I'm in. I get the Appaloosa."

"Sure you can handle him?" Winnie asked. "Remember he really spooked once."

"Yeah, but he was shot at," Debi Lu answered. "And I'm a better rider than Jocelyn's sister no matter what Jocelyn says."

"So when do we go?" Tiffany asked.

"Can your horse take double?" Winnie asked.

Tiffany's heart leaped.

"You and me?" she asked. "Yes."

"I can take Debi Lu on my horse," Kevin said. "No one will be looking for us coming in the gate at the back corner of the field."

"I say we skip our last class," Winnie suggested. "Then we'll all be on time to our meeting place."

"Yes!" Debi Lu agreed. "I can't wait to see the look on Wanda and Lisa's faces when they find out we weren't chicken like them."

"Not a word," Kevin hissed at Debi Lu.

"Gotcha!" she responded gaily.

Even though the four teenagers left school before the beginning of the last period, none of them had a car at school that day.

The four decided to hike to Kevin's house which was the closest and take his car to the stable where both Tiffany's and Kevin's horses were boarded. Then they planned to ride double to the Praetzel place to fetch horses for Winnie and Debi Lu.

While the foursome were nearing Kevin's house, Jocelyn was picked up at school in the middle of her last class.

"What's wrong?" she asked as soon as she met Bertha in the hall. "Is Daddy okay?"

"He's fine. He didn't want you to be pressured by your friends after school."

"Too late," Jocelyn replied bitterly.

"They tried to get you to ride after you said you couldn't? Why did they care?"

"I had told them I could maybe get Aleta to loan us Shadow and Minx. Debi Lu's horse is lame and Winnie's has a cut lip."

"You know better," Bertha returned flatly.

"I know. I know. I kept talking about Aleta being in a wheelchair and nobody riding the horses, and their needing exercise and..."

"How would you like it if she loaned your horse to someone?"

"She wouldn't! She knows no one rides him but me."

"And why wouldn't she feel the same way?"

"Shadow's not a show horse," Jocelyn retorted angrily.

"But even though he's not a show horse, he's important to Aleta. And he's her horse."

"Well, I told them they couldn't borrow the horses," Jocelyn said. "Most of them didn't understand at all. They were pissed."

"I'm sorry this turned out badly for you," Bertha said. "But I don't think Aleta would have let your friend ride Shadow. She's not sure he's safe to ride yet."

"Debi Lu bragged she was a better rider than my sister."

"No one rides better than your sister."

"You don't know that."

"That horse was shot, not once, but twice. He was scared beyond control. Not only did your sister hang on despite her injured shoulders, she got that horse back under enough control so he jumped two fences without stumbling and falling. And she rode him all the way to the barn. The horse has been a basket case ever since."

"Mr. Hubbs can ride him."

"At a walk. Around the barn. And he feeds him and grooms him. He's not a stranger. But even he hasn't taken him near the horse path outside the back gate."

"I didn't know that," Jocelyn admitted. "I thought Shadow was okay."

"Now you can explain it to your friends."

"They aren't talking to me," Jocelyn said dispiritedly.

"I think you need new friends."

"Well, that's the only choice I have now, isn't it? All because my sister wouldn't let me ride."

"Are those friends worth the life of your horse?"

"I thought Dad said it was my life," Jocelyn snapped.

"Your horse was injured and had to be put down."

"Yudi was killed?" Jocelyn cried. "Why didn't Dad tell me?"

"I guess he valued you more than your horse."

"He needs to get his priorities straight!" Jocelyn spat out angrily.

"Shadow too."

Jocelyn's face registered her utter dismay.

"Why didn't he tell me? I wouldn't have put Aleta's horse in danger. Honest!"

"Aleta hired a guard for today and the police are checking every fifteen minutes."

"She called the police!" Jocelyn cried. "I'll never be able to face anyone in school again."

"You had nothing to do with it."

"My friends don't know that."

"Maybe they'll see the patrol cars..."

"On the road," Jocelyn snapped. "Who's watching the back gate?"

"Don't worry. We'll be there before your friends," Bertha said. "That's why I took you out of school early."

"Yeah, you're right," Jocelyn said. "They would have had to cut class to beat us. Can we stop for ice cream?"

"We have ice cream at home."

"Old people's flavors."

"Just a cone. In and out," Bertha agreed.

Chapter 3

After completing the essay portion of the bar exam Aleta, whose MBE and MPRE scores were sufficiently high to be eligible for transfer from California, was surprised when she was told the members of the Character and Fitness committee wished to interview her.

While she knew that she would eventually need to pass this committee's scrutiny, this meeting rarely took place on the day of the bar exam. Those with questionable records in other states or involved in legal issues in Illinois were scrutinized before being allowed to take the bar exam.

The men were cordial when introducing themselves, refraining from shaking hands as Aleta's right arm was encased in a sling.

The rigors of writing for hours had strained the part of her arm injured by the bullet. Writing used muscles and tendons in her arm that had been inactive since she had been shot.

She kneaded the muscles in her arm as she waited for the men to begin. It was their interview, not hers.

"Mrs. Praetzel," the distinguished white-haired Judge Roy Lutz began, "we find ourselves in a predicament. Do you have an idea why?"

"Has it to do with my being a prophet?" She asked.

It was the black professor of law, Louis Burrows who replied, "You are far more than merely clairvoyant. Your apparent ability is not merely foresight which many people possess. You evidently can foretell future events with surprising accuracy and you claim that God gives you these visions. Is this true?"

"Yes."

"We read the transcript of your trial," Burrows said. "Your arguments were reasonable and well-constructed. Were they yours?"

"I had help. It was a team effort. But, yes the argument was the one I originally outlined," Aleta replied.

Eugene Powell, the dark-eyed, dark-haired litigator who was planning to run for state office in the near future, took over. "Gentlemen, let's get to the heart of our concern. Mrs. Praetzel, are you a prophet or a lawyer?"

"Are you a lawyer or a politician?"

"Bad response," Powell snapped. "If I'm elected to the State Senate I will be a Senator. Currently, I am a lawyer."

"Sir," Aleta said politely, "your query was faulty, not my response and your answer a political statement which, as usual, was far from the truth."

"Explain further," Burrows said, suddenly taking on the role of professor facing a class of bright minds with opinions almost insulting in their outspokenness.

"People are never wholly one thing or another. A better question would have been: What are my priorities? That's what you gentlemen want to know."

"What we want to know we will ask," Powell declared imperiously.

Burrows stepped in. "What are your priorities? For example, what would you do if you are in court defending a person and you suddenly got a vision?"

"I don't always get visions. Sometimes I just know things," Aleta said, pausing briefly before going on.

A vision stopped her. As usual she had a choice. She could ignore it. Or she could act. She continued speaking.

"For example, I know that you, Professor Burrows, have a cell in your pocket but you forgot to charge it last night. Judge Lutz left without his this morning, but you, Mr. Powell, have a working cell phone in your pocket. And I know that right this minute I need to make a telephone call. Mr. Powell, may I please use your phone?"

"No, you may not!" Powell said. "We are conducting an interview."

"Professor Burrows asked me what I would do if I received a vision. I am presenting my answer. Don't you gentlemen agree that a live demonstration of what I plan to do will provide you with valuable insight on whether or not I have the proper mind-set and moral fiber to meet the standards of the Illinois Supreme Court for any lawyer it deems worthy to argue before them?"

"Give her the phone, Eugene," Judge Lutz said.

Powell put the phone on the table. Burrows rose and handed it to Aleta.

"Thank you," she said as she opened the phone and put in a number and pressed the send button. She then pressed the speaker portion of the phone and placed it on the table, turning the volume to its highest level.

"'Lo," came the voice of an obviously old man.

"Mr. Hubbs, this is Mrs. Praetzel."

"Miss Aleta?"

"Yes. Please listen carefully and do exactly what I ask. You are to take Shadow and Sterling from their stalls immediately. Use halters only. Can you walk them to the house by yourself?"

"Yes, Ma'am."

"Mr. Hubbs it is important you do nothing else first. The horses' lives depend on you doing this now."

"You want I should call the police. I remember how."

"First, get those two horses to the front of the house. The patrol car will see you and come up the drive. If they don't, use the cell phone."

"What about other horses?"

"Tell the guard to watch Yudi and Minx. Shadow and Sterling mustn't be ridden."

"Yes, Ma'am."

"Don't try to ride Shadow. He is going to throw a shoe."

"Yes, Ma'am."

"Do it now."

"Yes, Ma'am. Should I hang up now?"

"Yes. And hurry."

The connection was broken.

"You made a phone call to tell your horseman to move a couple of horses?" Powell asked scornfully.

"Things aren't always what they seem, Gentlemen," Aleta explained. "Some teenagers are about to steal my horses to go joy riding. If they attempt to ride Sterling, his fractured foot will re-break and he will need to be put down. If one of them attempts to ride Shadow he will spook and the rider will be injured. He will break a leg and need to be destroyed. But the real reason for the call is that one of the teenagers will hit Mr. Hubbs on the head with a piece of wood and kill him. I removed Mr. Hubbs from danger."

"Why not just call the police?" Burrows asked.

"That's what I usually do; however, for some reason, I didn't receive this warning early enough. The answer, gentlemen, is that when a person's life is at stake, nothing matters more."

"Smoke and mirrors," Powell claimed. "She's selling us a fantasy. She can't prove any of this."

"Allow me to make one more call," Aleta asked.

"No!" Powell said. "I want no more of this charade."

"As you wish," Aleta said. "I was merely going to ask Chief Milani for a report; however, that is not important at this moment. You have other questions?"

"You have shown no respect for this committee and the seriousness of this meeting," Powell accused.

"On the contrary," Aleta replied. "I have shown you the courtesy of telling the truth. I have not lied about myself or the way I would use my ability in an important situation. This, gentlemen, is one of the most important moments of my career. You have the power to deny me permission to practice a profession I have trained for because I happen to have an ability that even I don't understand. I do not ignore the prophecies when they come. They are often vague. I am given just enough of a glimpse to act in a certain way. Today I could have ignored the warning and a man would have died despite my taking a number of precautions before I left my house. I could have tried to convince myself that I had done everything to prevent his death; however, I would know the truth. Would God forgive me for wanting a career more than a man's life? I believe He would. But now I don't have to go home and kick myself for an old man's death. Now I can go home and see instead the pride in an old man's eyes because he saved two horses from harm."

"Do you know what else happened at your place?" Burrows asked. "I mean, what happened to your other horses?"

"I have no idea."

"Do you know who attempted to do this?"

"I have no idea. I just know they were young people. I see deaths, gentlemen, usually murders, but I never see the perpetrators, for which I am thankful."

"Thankful?" Powell bellowed. "Thankful you can't help the police? What kind of attitude is that?"

"As a lawyer I can tell you that my testimony would not convict anyone. I help the police save lives."

Louis Burrows asked Aleta to present a concise argument for her acceptance to the Illinois Bar.

Aleta raised an eyebrow in silent query. His nod merely confirmed his request.

Her surprise at having to do this caused a brief hesitation, just long enough for Eugene Powell to bark, "We're waiting."

"Gentlemen," she started in a pleasant casual tone, "every lawyer walks into the courtroom with a necklace of ideas, beliefs, convictions, prejudices and experiences that bespeak his character. I am no different. What you want to know is whether any of these will influence my performance as a lawyer. The answer is: they all will. Don't concentrate only on my strong religious conviction and forget that I am a woman or biracial.

"I see from the look on Professor Burrows' face that he didn't know this; but then he probably doesn't have private investigators at his beck and call to uncover secrets. My heritage is not generally known; but, it is there and has been openly used against me; however, it is not blatant prejudice that I fear. It is the prejudice hidden in the hearts of men that stir them to lean away from me as if I am a pariah. Right now it cloaks itself in an openly antagonistic attitude toward my openness in the handling of the prophetic gift I've received.

"I have broken no laws. I have hurt no one unless you want to count the people intent on murder. Them I thwarted; however, doing so has resulted in the scars permanently displayed on my head and arms.

"When I represented my clients in court which as a House Attorney I was allowed to do, I upheld the laws of this state and country and represented my clients honorably. Gentlemen, I rest my case."

When she finished, she saw Burrows smiling, Powell scowling and Lutz deep in thought.

Burrows walked around the table and wheeled Aleta out the door. Her father was waiting in the hall. Aleta introduced him to Professor Burrows, who asked Aleta, "Is he?"

She nodded.

"Sir," the professor, "your daughter was superb. Unfortunately, she nailed one of the committee members to the cross of his own convictions and, unlike our Lord Jesus Christ; he does not forgive or forget. She made a powerful enemy."

Aleta let a small wry smile turn up the corners of her mouth, "You know me, Dad."

"Maybe you were born to be barefoot and pregnant," Robert Locke said. "You'll never be a judge if you don't play the game."

"I disagree," the professor said. "Who you are is impressive. Don't change."

"No chance of that!" her father joshed. "Only Stanley's been able to modify her and he likes her as is."

"Stanley Praetzel? I didn't make the connection until this minute. I guess I had him pegged as a lifetime bachelor. I see he met his match."

"What a nice thing to say," Aleta commented. "Would you like to come to one of my dinner parties? I think you'd like the group."

"Do you always invite people you barely know?"

"Isn't that how one makes friends?" Aleta said.

Professor Burrows laughed. "It's as good as any, I guess."

"You'll be invited no matter what the committee decides," Aleta said. "Tell your wife she'll find a kindred soul in Bessie Dobbins. Your wife won't let you refuse if you tell her that."

"You do your homework, don't you?"

"Professors like you instilled that trait in me."

Professor Burrows reentered the interview room. He found Eugene Powell trying to persuade Roy Lutz to join him in denying Aleta Praetzel admission to the bar.

As he entered Judge Lutz was responding, "Sure, she has a sharp tongue; but, Eugene, she's not done anything to warrant such a decision. I don't want another mess like the 2001 Hale case."

"I'm not a psychiatrist. But in my opinion, if it were real, she wouldn't have been so calm."

"That old man reacted respectfully," the judge observed.

"For God's sake, she's his employer," Powell sneered. "Besides she had him move two horses from their stalls to the house. Why object to that even if it was crazy. Why make trouble for yourself over nothing?"

"So you don't believe she saved his life?" Judge Lutz asked.

"She knows she stuck her foot in her mouth," Professor Burrows inserted.

"Good!" Eugene Powell exclaimed. "She'll be expecting a rejection."

"I don't know," Judge Lutz said. "I'm not happy with voting to deny her admittance to the bar."

"I'll file a strong dissent if you two vote to accept her. Her admittance will be delayed, believe me. I have the political pull to move it my way and to keep someone as dangerous as her from practicing."

Professor Burrows slowly shook his head.

Powell was annoyed at the shake of Burrows' head. "I know you think she's just great because she's part African-American, but you're a fair man. Isn't this prophet thing a bit too esoteric even for you?"

"I thought she explained it very well in her argument in her court case. It's a unique gift from God. Many lawyers hold religious beliefs."

"My point exactly!" Powell burst forth. "She takes her religion one step too far. Her conduct during this interview was bizarre. Who would make so nonsensical a call in the middle of an important interview? Someone who's ridiculing us, gentlemen, that's who. And if she'd thumb her nose up at us, she'll do the same in court. We can't allow her to enter a court room."

"We can't exactly do that," Burrows put in. "She's the Tontine Trust's House Attorney."

"But that limits her access to court," Powell argued. "She's little more than a paper pusher in that job."

"As attorney for the Trust," Judge Lutz put in, "her behavior has been appropriate. Her appearance in court was respectful and her argument sound."

"She collapsed," Powell said scornfully. "Talk about a dramatic concluding statement. She gets to the end and faints."

"It wasn't a trick," Judge Lutz said. "I checked. And I haven't really heard anything today to persuade me she wouldn't be a good, if not a great, lawyer."

"You've been brainwashed. I tell you she's dangerous. She's a Californian, for God's sake, a Berkeley graduate."

Louis Burrows decided that Aleta Praetzel needed Powell to back down. If Eugene fought her admission, he might win. The time to stop him was now.

"You did research on her," Professor Burrows asked casually. "Did your investigators uncover anything that would persuade us we're wrong?"

"She got her job with the Tontine because her grandmother is running the Trust," Eugene Powell said. "She didn't earn her spot."

"You're not too good at making connections are you?"

"What does that mean?"

"You're about to anger a powerful group of people just as you're launching your political career."

"What do you mean?"

"Aleta Praetzel just invited me to one of her dinner parties."

"Well, she knows how to suck up," Powell sneered.

"Whether or not we approve her application or send it to the committee," Burrows responded evenly. "Now when I go to her party, I'm going to be asked about today's interview."

"Our discussions are private!"

"Our decision won't be."

"So what? Who does she know?"

"Her parties are private and very exclusive," Burrows went on. "They are the only private parties Martha Cook attends."

"The Martha Cook of Cook Construction?" Powell asked, surprised.

"And Dr. Michael Taekman..." Burrows continued.

"The famous neurosurgeon? He doesn't go to parties."

"He goes to Aleta Praetzel's parties," Burrows said.

"So what?" Powell snorted. "I go to parties with wealthy people all the time. Nothing much happens except being seen. Nobody discusses anything controversial. If they did, they wouldn't be invited back."

"I only mention the parties because I know you know all the people she listed as references: Judge Davis, Hubert Praetzel, Kurtz West and the three police chiefs. She's been in the state less than a year. These are highly respected members of the law community."

"I have to admit that her references impressed me," Judge Lutz said.

"Come on, Eugene, she raised the race question, so it's on the table. It would be political suicide for you to let a whisper of her accusation be heard outside this room."

"It's false!" Powell shouted banging his fists on the table in a sudden display of anger.

"Does it matter? Lutz asked rhetorically. "Neither Louis nor I are going to repeat it."

Powell scowled fiercely. "I want you to tell me you don't believe her."

"What are we—a bunch of school children taking sides in this?" Lutz snapped angrily.

"You, Louis, did you believe her?"

"Yes," Professor Burrows said quietly.

"See!" Powell proclaimed. "That's why she's dangerous. She's able to twist things around and make people believe what's not true."

"You're making a big mistake, Eugene," Burrows added. "And I'm not voting against her!"

"There's no way I'm going to approve her acceptance to the bar," Powell said through gritted teeth. "No way at all."

"I think we need to refer this to the full committee," Judge Lutz said. Angering Eugene Powell could affect his political career. He was up for reelection in a year.

"How bad was it?" her father said after he and Aleta were on the way home.

"Pretty bad," Aleta said. "I openly hinted to an aspirant to the State Senate that he had discovered I was biracial and that my prophetic ability hampering my ability to function appropriately as a lawyer was a red herring."

"Oh, Aleta," her father sighed.

"What are my chances?" Aleta ventured.

"Not good," Robert said. "The fact that Burrows brought you out tells me he wanted you to know you had a friend in that room but Judge Lutz is an elected official and Powell has a lot of political clout. Lutz will send it to the whole committee."

"Then what?"

"You can call all of us as character references."

"Not you, Dad," Aleta said. "I don't want to jeopardize your future."

"I know you better than anyone else."

"Except Stanley," Aleta grinned. "But you're still not admitted to the Bar. I know you were interviewed."

"Yeah, by one man. Someone who saw that I had been a partner in a big tax law firm in San Francisco and only wanted to know why I was doing it the hard way."

"So what did you tell him?"

"That I wanted to branch out, that I was already helping you study for your exam and that I didn't want my ex-wife to know I was going back to work as a lawyer."

"Did he think you were trying to pull a fast one?"

"He's been through two divorces. I told him I'd given her everything but my future. He understood."

"I could be a good lawyer, Dad."

"You are a good lawyer. And you still have your position as House Attorney."

"Can they take that away?"

"You'd have to do something," her father replied. "Besides in that position, you're not apt to do much more than create legal documents and file tax returns and that's not what they're afraid of."

"I unmasked him, Dad. I didn't get any great insight from God on that. I had looked up his record. It was the numbers."

"You and numbers. You're like your grandmother in your propensity for them."

"You, too, Dad. You were a tax lawyer, after all."

"Whatever made you do it?"

"I saw disgust in his eyes as if I wasn't worthy. I'm not used to that, Dad. Discovering my heritage less than a year ago didn't prepare me for that."

"I'm sorry that happened."

"It wasn't your fault," Aleta returned. "I don't know why I got so angry that I castigated him in front of his peers."

"Prejudice should make you angry."

"But, Dad, if I'd kept my cool, maybe I would have... oh, hell... I did something else too."

"More than accusing a politician of being a racist?"

"I made a phone call."

"You didn't take a phone into the room with you?"

"I borrowed Powell's," Aleta responded and then told her dad the story.

When she finished, her dad said, "You did the right thing."

"I hope everyone is safe," Aleta murmured.

Chapter 4

As soon as Mr. Hubbs hung up the phone he took two halters off the rack, opened Sterling's stall and fit one over the Morgan's head. While the security guard held the halter rope of the crippled Morgan, Hubbs slipped the second one onto Shadow's head and led the Appaloosa out of his stall.

"Want me to walk with you?" the guard asked.

"I kin do it," Hubbs said. "You watch them others. See nobody takes them."

"Sure," the guard said lightly. This was a bogus stint, guarding a couple ordinary horses in a barn. His boss said the lady might hire them for more work if they did a good job.

"Hey, today horses, tomorrow people," his boss had said.

He watched the old man amble down the road at a pace so slow the guard wondered if he'd make the house before nightfall. The two horses accommodated their walk to the old man's slow stride. They were used to it. He often took them out for walks down this road just to get them out of the barn. The plowed fields were too rough for the old man's arthritic joints and the horses didn't care where they walked.

The guard was so busy watching Mr. Hubbs he didn't see the three teenagers open the back gate, cross the field and enter the barn through the back door.

They spotted the guard and stopped.

"What'll we do?" Winnie whispered.

"Lie," Kevin hissed.

Debi Lu scowled. That wouldn't work. She looked around and saw a couple of boards lying in a heap in one corner. She selected a flat board and snuck forward.

By the time Kevin and Winnie realized what she was up to, she was too far away to grab. Neither wanted to yell out, so they just froze.

Debi Lu's footsteps were muffled by the snorting of Yudi in the far stall. He didn't like strangers in his barn. Minx merely shuffled her feet; but, it was enough to mask the footfall of boots on a hay strewn floor.

Debi Lu hopped on a bale of hay and raised the board. Her shortness thus compensated for, she brought the board down hard on the top of the guard's head.

He fell to the ground. Debi Lu hissed at the two who were still standing motionless in the middle of the barn to come move him out of sight.

Both ran forward.

"He's still breathing," Winnie said as he picked up one of the man's arms. Kevin took the other and together they dragged the guard into the barn and out of sight.

"The old man's walking the Appy down by the house," Debi Lu said. "He should be easy."

"We aren't knocking anyone else out," Winnie said. His blue eyes bulged.

"Suppose he turns around? " Debi Lu asked.

"Look at him," Kevin said. "Even if he does, so what? We can have the horses saddled and be out of here before he can make it back to stop us."

Debi Lu glared at Kevin. "In case you haven't noticed, he's got hold of my horse."

"Change your mind," Winnie ordered.

"To what?"

"There are still three horses here," Winnie said, taking the largest saddle off the rack and entering the stall where

Minx was standing, waiting. Kevin slipped the bridle on Minx while Winnie threw the saddle blanket on her back.

"You expect me to ride this broken-down old mare?" Debi Lu asked petulantly, indicating Jezebel.

"If she's your choice," Winnie said, cinching the strap under the bay's belly.

"The only other horse here is Jocelyn's jumper," Debi Lu muttered, obviously distraught.

"You said you were a good rider," Kevin mocked her. "Are you telling us you can't ride as well as Jocelyn?"

"Of course I can!" Debi Lu insisted. "Give me a hand. Yudi is a tall horse."

"We better hurry," Kevin cautioned as he grabbed Yudi's bridle.

The three soon had Yudi saddled. They led both horses around to the back of the barn and mounted up. Winnie and Debi Lu trotted the horses toward the back gate while Kevin hoofed it across the frozen field.

They heard the police sirens as the horses cantered through the open gate where Tiffany waited with Kevin's horse. All four were out of sight by the time the police cars drew up just outside the barn.

Chief Tom Milani was on the scene before the ambulance. Hubbs' call had alerted him minutes before the unit patrolling the area reported that an old man was standing in front of the house with two horses.

Milani talked with Hubbs who told him Aleta had called with instructions to move these two horses out of the barn.

So she knew the thieves were coming, Milani realized. He realized something else. Aleta only saw death. He looked at the bent old man and realized that while a blow on his head might not crush his skull, it might very well break his neck. Still, he wondered why she had him move these two horses. There had to be a reason.

"Anything wrong with these horses?" he asked Hubbs.

"The Morgan has a fractured foot that ain't healed yet. The Appy isn't quite got over being shot, but Aleta says he's gonna throw a shoe."

"Is he?"

"Ain't had a chance to see. I hadda get 'em out."

"What would happen if he did?"

"Nothing much only he shouldn't be rode. With him the way he is now, he could get bothered enough to act up."

"Throw someone?"

"Yeah. That's what I figure is the reason Mrs. Praetzel had me move him."

While the chief was talking to the old man, Bertha drove up the driveway. Jocelyn had her seat belt off and was out while the car was still slowing down. She brushed past the chunky police chief and rushed up to Hubbs.

"Is Yudi okay?"

"Been took."

"Where were you?"

"Here with these two."

"What were you doing here? Why weren't you in the barn?"

"Miss Aleta said..."

"Damn her! She takes care of her horse and she doesn't care about mine."

Chief Milani stepped in. "These two are crippled."

"Sterling is," Jocelyn spat back, "but Shadow isn't. She was just afraid they'd somehow get to those horses and she took hers to safety and left mine."

"Who is the 'they?'" Milani asked. "And where did they go?"

"Bertha, drive me. I'm getting my horse back."

"No, you aren't," Bertha said firmly. "Let Chief Milani find your horse. Now tell him where to look."

"Not unless I get to go along," Jocelyn declared. "I don't want anyone else riding my horse."

"We won't ride them," Milani said. "We'll lead them back."

Jocelyn glared at Hubbs. "They got Minx too? Mr. Praetzel isn't going to like you letting his horse get stolen. You may as well start packing. I'll see you're off the property by nightfall."

"Jocelyn, come inside," Bertha ordered.

Milani turned to Hubbs. "You got any idea where these kids could've gone?"

"Some. But she'd know." He nodded toward the recalcitrant youngster being ushered into the house by the mild-mannered housekeeper. Tom watched Bertha. She just did it. Like a mother. With authority and love mixed together.

"Let's take these two horses back to the barn," the stout police chief suggested. "Then, if she doesn't tell us, I'll have you show me."

Mr. Hubbs began the long trek back to the barn.

"I could go faster on top," Hubbs commented. "But Miss Aleta told me not to."

"You aren't going to be fired," Chief Milani said. "Stanley always wants everyone to do what Aleta says."

"She cares about all them horses."

"I know she does."

"She said these two would get hurt."

"I'm glad you believed her," Milani said heartily.

The old man's head was down. Two other horses entrusted to his care had been stolen.

"Don't know that I did, but she's the boss, and I didn't see no harm."

"There was the security guard, right?" Milani coached.

"Yeah, only he didn't think nothing was gonna happen."

"I guess he was wrong, huh?" Milani said.

"Yeah. Too bad though. I wish he'd been right."

"So do I."

Once inside the house Bertha turned on Jocelyn. "How dare you fire that old man for your mistake!"

"Mine? I wasn't in charge of the horses. He was."

"Whose friends took them? His? Or yours?" Bertha shot back.

"Well, he should've stayed. My horse is valuable."

"There you go again," Bertha said. "I can just see you standing by while they shoot Sterling or Shadow and saying, "Well, at least nobody got to ride my horse.""

"You don't understand," Jocelyn cried. "Besides Aleta said there was going to be an explosion and he..."

Bertha cut in.

"I didn't tell you that."

"Dad must've," Jocelyn snapped, annoyed at being interrupted.

"No, he didn't."

"Then I made it up," Jocelyn spat out.

"You don't make up stories," Bertha said. "How do you know there's going to be an explosion?"

"I just know, and Yudi could be hurt."

"Where were they going to ride?"

"Some new trail," Jocelyn said. "Not new to them, but to me."

"Will you promise not to leave the car if I drive you so you can show the police where to go?"

"I promise!"

"And you'll let the police walk the horses home?"

"I could ride," she started, then paused and continued, "I guess that's the point, huh? I'm not supposed to ride today. But let me help. I can't sit here and do nothing."

"No riding," Bertha said.

Jocelyn knew she was going by the tone of Bertha's query.

"No riding," she repeated. "And I do what you say."

"Are you as good at keeping your word as Aleta?"

"Today, I will be."

As Winnie and Debi Lu, each astride a horse taken from the Praetzel barn, rode toward the meeting point, two small boys were lying under some small trees along a dry creek bed. On the other side was a horse path, little used in the winter when snow hid the rocky terrain.

"I told you nobody comes here now," Davey said.

"I guess," Skip agreed reluctantly. "How long's it been?"

Davey looked at his watch, a gift on his eleventh birthday. "Eight and a half minutes."

"Yeah, we waited long enough."

"So, let's set up the enemy. You got that junk we been saving?"

Skip opened a worn paper sack. "Where we gonna put 'em?"

"On the path over there?"

"That's pretty far," Skip said.

"This is a real grenade," Davey boasted. "It could take out a tank."

"Yeah, okay," Skip said scrambling to his feet and down the short bank to the creek bed. He climbed up on the other side and dumped the sack of broken toys in a heap and ran back.

"They're gonna really fly!" Davey predicted.

Not too far up that path, the four young horsemen arrived at the meeting place and an argument ensued immediately with the three waiting for the group to gather.

"Are you guys nuts?" Perry said, his deep voice rumbling angrily. "You could get in so much trouble if you're caught."

"Cool it, Perry!" Winnie retorted. "It's done. So where's Lisa?"

"Coming," her cousin Wanda replied. She looked at Debi Lu and remarked, "I thought you were going to ride the Appy."

"The old man took him away before we got there."

Wanda stared at Debi Lu's mount.

"That's not Jocelyn's horse, is it?"

"Yeah. It's Yudi," Debi Lu admitted. The responding glare made her shrink a little.

"Jocelyn's gonna be furious. She doesn't let anyone ride him."

Kevin tried to switch the discussion to another topic. "So are we all set to take the old creek trail?"

"Not me," Perry said.

Irked by his self-assured attitude, Kevin scoffed, "You don't believe all that hog wash, do you?"

"I don't take chances," Perry replied. "Jocelyn's sister has a rep for being right."

"Jocelyn was using that as an excuse," Kevin argued. "What's out there? Nothing!"

"Kevin's right," Tiffany agreed. "There's a group of us. We'd scare any wild animal off."

"She said an explosion," Wanda reminded the group.

"That's even sillier," Tiffany said. "What's out there that could explode?"

"Nothing!" Debi Lu declared. "Absolutely nothing."

"Wasn't the whole reason for riding on the old creek trail to show Jocelyn a trail she'd never seen?" Perry said.

His reasonableness vexed Kevin even more. "Well, I for one am not afraid to test Jocelyn's sister's forecast if she even did predict it, which I doubt. Who's with me?"

"I am," Debi Lu said. "I'm not changing our plan because Jocelyn was grounded and spun a tale to cover it up."

"Do you know that?" Perry asked pointedly, his deep voice demanding honesty.

"Well, not exactly. But she's not here. What other reason could there be? Her sister's not her mother, after all."

"I'm with Perry," Wanda said. "I'm not chancing it."

Winnie and Tiffany decided they were going down the old creek trail with Kevin. Wade decided not to.

Lisa rode up, apologizing for being late. Her cousin Wanda cut her off.

"You're coming with us."

Lisa gasped when she saw the horse Debi Lu was riding. "Jocelyn is gonna be pissed!"

"Screw her!" Debi Lu said. "Come on, Kevin, let's go."

"I missed a lot, didn't I?" Lisa commented as she watched the four ride away.

"You don't want to be with them," Wanda said. "I don't think Jocelyn lied to us, so we're taking our usual trail."

"Jocelyn will be frantic," Lisa said. "We've got to call her."

"We can't turn them in," Wade said.

"I don't want to turn anyone in, but that's Jocelyn's horse Debi Lu is riding. And she's a lousy rider."

"How do you know?" Wade asked.

"Same trainer," Lisa responded. "I just want to tell Jocelyn where her horse is. Who knows where Debi Lu will leave it when she's through."

"She'll take it back," Wade said confidently.

"And get caught?" Lisa shot back. "I know her. She'll abandon it somewhere."

"Winnie will see they're returned," Wade declared.

"Debi Lu will talk him out of it," Lisa said. "We can't let her do this to Jocelyn. We'd hate it if she took one of our horses."

"She wouldn't," Wanda gasped.

"She's already proved she would," Perry rumbled. "And the four of them split off from us pretty quick."

Lisa took out her cell.

"Just let me call Jocelyn. If I don't get her, I'll hang up. Okay?"

Jocelyn was in the car with Chief Milani. So was Bertha. She had told Tom that she had promised the entire family that she wouldn't let Jocelyn out of her sight.

Tom had chuckled at her insistence. "You don't trust the chief of police to take care of her?"

"I wouldn't even let her go at all if I didn't trust you; but, I made a promise."

There wasn't room for both in the front, so Bertha and Jocelyn rode in the back. They were close to the meeting place when Jocelyn's cell rang.

"Answer it," Chief Milani said. "Say you're looking for your horse, but don't say whose car you're in."

"Hi, Lisa," Jocelyn said. "Did you know someone stole my horse?"

"Debi Lu. She's taken Yudi on the old creek trail. Do you know where that is?"

"Just a sec." She looked at Milani. "The old creek trail. Do you know where that is?"

He nodded in response.

"Who's riding Minx? Winnie?"

"Yes, but we're not with them. Wanda, Perry, Wade and I are on the trail to the Preserves."

"Thanks, Lisa. You're a real friend."

She disconnected and told Milani everything. As he sped along she worried aloud, "Lisa's not going to be in trouble for telling me, is she?"

"Not if she's not involved."

"I think the group split up over this," Jocelyn said.

"Smart kids," Milani commented. "Stick with that group."

"Oh, I already have," Jocelyn announced with fierce determination. "Can you put Debi Lu in jail?"

"She's a juvenile. They are treated differently."

"She knew what she was doing," Jocelyn declared angrily.

"We're here," Milani said.

"Where?"

"No road from here. Just a dry creek bed and a horse path."

Down half a mile around two bends in the dry creek bed, the two boys stared at the gathering of broken toys from the opposite bank. One of them was fingering the live grenade his uncle had brought home.

"Davey, throw it," Skip said. "There's no one coming."

"Okay, here goes!"

The two young boys watched the grenade sail through the air like a ball being thrown from the outfield in Little League. It landed next to the pile of toys.

"Duck!" Davey shouted.

The two boys covered their ears and squatted down behind a bare bush. They wanted protection but they also wanted to see.

After a few seconds, Skip shouted. "How long?"

Davey shrugged.

After another minute, Davey looked at his watch. "If it don't blow in a minute, we'll go look."

"Is it safe to do that?"

"They either blow right away or they're duds," Davey explained smugly.

"What's a dud?"

"A bomb that don't go off."

"I thought they all go off."

"Don't you know nothing, Skip? Sometimes bombs don't work just like other stuff."

"Is the minute up yet?"

"We got ten seconds more."

"Tell me when it's up."

"Shit. It's close enough," Davey said. "Let's go."

The two boys scrambled down the bank. Skip stopped suddenly.

"Hear that?"

"Yeah. Horses," Davey concluded.

"And people!" Skip added.

"We gotta get outta here," Davey said.

"And leave the grenade?"

"You wanna get caught with it," Davey asked, turning and scrambling back up the bank.

"Not me!" Skip said clambering up the rise behind his friend.

Stanley arrived home minutes before his wife and her father. He saw the police activity around the barn and headed straight for it. Hubbs saw him coming.

"I'm sorry Mr. Praetzel. They done took two of the horses."

"Which two?" Stanley asked, fearing the worst.

"Yudi and Minx. I'm sorry."

"Where's the guard?"

"They took him to the hospital."

"Is he okay?"

"Dunno."

"But you're okay?"

"Yeah, Miss Aleta called and told me to take Shadow and Sterling to the house."

"She called from Chicago?"

"I guess. So I did it. She said it was important."

"You did the right thing."

"I'll be packed and outta here tonight, but can Jezebel stay until I get a new place."

"Why are you leaving?"

"Miss Jocelyn said I was fired."

"Jocelyn can't fire you," Stanley said matter-of-factly. "She was upset about her horse. She hasn't learned how to channel her anger yet."

"It were my fault."

"It was no one's fault. And no one ever gets fired for doing what Aleta says," Stanley proclaimed. "My guess is you saved the lives of those two horses although I have no idea how. Later, we'll ask Aleta."

"Okay."

He was back in time to see Robert helping Aleta into the house. He hurried inside.

"You saved Shadow and Sterling," Stanley announced.

Instead of a smile, Aleta burst into tears.

"She's had a rough day," her father said.

Stanley wrapped his arms around Aleta and she leaned on his shoulder and cried. Stanley looked over her shoulder at Robert who told him what had happened.

"It's not over, Aleta," Stanley said. "And Martha is sending you a case."

The sobbing increased.

"It's a trial case," Stanley said. "And it's all yours."

"I can't...," she sobbed.

"Yes, you can," Stanley said. "You can dive right in. It's a Tontine case. And I'm too busy."

"Dad?" she queried, the spark of hope vanquishing her tears.

"Martha sent it to you," her father said. "It must be a tricky one."

"The Tontine doesn't have any new employees," Aleta mused aloud. "Martha wouldn't send me a case involving a member. Grams would. What's going on?"

Stanley guided her to the couch and sat beside her with his arm around her. "All I know is that Harriet hired a bookkeeper and she rented your office temporarily for her to use."

"Is that why you loaned me your home office?" Aleta asked, vexed that decisions were made without her input.

She pulled away slightly. He gently pulled her back into his embrace.

"Neither of the doctors wants you to leave the house."

"Where's Bertha?" Robert asked abruptly.

"With Jocelyn" Stanley replied. "They're in Milani's car going after the horses. She knows where her friends planned to ride."

"I'm going to check with the cops outside," Robert said.

"You don't have to take this case," Stanley said when Robert left.

"If I don't, who will?"

"Me."

"But you're a child advocate and, as you keep telling me, that's all you want to be," Aleta responded. "So why would I let you take the case? I may be angry with you about this; but, I still love you a little bit."

"How little?" Stanley inquired wryly.

"Try tiny," Aleta snapped.

"That's enough," Stanley smiled.

"You need a new dictionary?" Aleta quipped.

"A minute amount isn't none," Stanley returned. "And you're really upset and angry right now."

"Oh, Stanley. I've worked so hard to be accepted as a lawyer here in Illinois. It's so unfair."

"It's not over," Stanley assured her. "And it's not that you can't practice at all. As a House Attorney you can appear before any court in the state."

"But I need the cases."

"Take this one and show your stuff," Stanley said. "The full committee won't meet until after the results of the essay part of the exam."

"If I fail, they won't have to meet at all," Aleta said. "Wimps!"

"Be grateful. You have six weeks before you have to deal with them."

"Kiss me," Aleta whispered. "Please."

Stanley lifted her chin with his free hand and gently placed his lips on hers. It was a soft, sweet kiss and she wanted it to go on forever.

When their lips parted, Stanley whispered, "Tonight you get to sleep your favorite way."

"I don't want to do that to you."

"Robert's surviving, so I guess I can."

Aleta reared back. "Stanley, I told you not to tell me about the sex lives of my family and friends."

"What sex life?"

"That includes desires as well and you know it," she shot back irritably.

"Okay. I'll be good," he smiled. "I'll even add to your pleasure a bit tonight."

"Then you'll have to take a cold shower in the morning as well," Aleta pointed out, her voice softening.

"Aleta, all my showers have been cold ones since you came home from the hospital."

"My wearing a night gown didn't help?"

"It cut the number in half," Stanley said.

When Robert returned he found the couple kissing.

"I can come back," he said.

Slowly, they parted.

"What's new?" Stanley asked.

"Chief Milani called for more units."

"So they have the horses?"

"Not yet."

As Chief Milani's patrol car crunched across the half-frozen edge of the field onto a farmer's access road, Jocelyn stared out the window, hoping to catch sight of her horse. They rode along for only a few minutes before the road petered out and Milani stopped the car.

"We have to walk it from here," he said.

"We'll never catch them," Jocelyn complained. "Why can't we drive up the creek bed?"

"And wrench my transmission?"

"We'll walk," Bertha said, opening the door.

Jocelyn trotted ahead eager to catch a glimpse of the riders. Fresh horse droppings told her they were on the right course.

All at once, she scrambled down the bank onto the dry creek bed, stood in the center, put two fingers in her mouth and whistled.

Up ahead came an answering neigh.

Yudi stopped, pawed the ground and shook his head as if to rid himself of the bridle and the extra tight hold the light weight girl had on it.

Debi Lu heard the whistle and read the horse's reaction correctly. There was no way she was going to get caught on this horse. She dug her heels into Yudi's flank and urged him forward. Yudi shook his head and snorted. Then he leaped from the narrow path down onto the dry creek bed. He spun around and headed back toward the whistle.

Debi Lu fought for control, yanking the rein hard to her left. Yudi followed the pull all the way around until he again wound up facing the direction from which they'd come. Debi Lu jerked the rein the other way. Yudi spun around to the right, again winding up facing the direction from which the whistle had come. The two were deadlocked, Debi Lu's tight hold on the rein keeping Yudi in place. He pranced angrily snorting and tossing his head.

Kevin eased his horse down onto the creek bed to help Debi Lu regain control of Yudi. He'd heard the whistle but didn't realize it originated with Jocelyn. He believed Yudi spooked at the sound. Jocelyn had said he was high-strung.

Debi Lu began cursing loudly as she pulled back on the reins.

She was near panic when Kevin reached over and took hold of the reins. He walked Yudi back up the creek a few steps before Debi Lu slapped his hand and screamed at him that she didn't need any help.

"This horse will go where I tell it to," she yelled.

Another sharp whistle hit their eardrums. Winnie and Tiffany slowed down waiting for Debi Lu to regain control of Jocelyn's horse.

Just as Debi Lu had turned Yudi once again, the grenade exploded.

The sound electrified the four horses near it.

Yudi reared and twisted around, shaking Debi Lu from the saddle. Thrown hard by the violently twirling horse Debi Lu flew into the air. Her shoulder hit a rock outcropping and collapsed as the rest of her body thrust her sideways into the rock's unyielding surface. Bones broke in her shoulder, arms and chest. Her scream of agony told her companions she was hurt badly.

Kevin, however, whose horse reared straight up, didn't hear her. He had sailed through the air backwards and landed flat on his back. Not a sound emerged.

Tiffany's horse reacted as Yudi had. He reared and twisted away from the sound. Tiffany hung on for a few minutes. Then her horse leaped onto the creek bed from the path that formed one edge. Tiffany was instantly unseated by the jump. Her foot caught in the stirrup and she was dragged several yards before the weight of her body pulled her foot out of her boot and she lay helpless on the ground, badly bruised, her leg and ankle broken in multiple places. Still conscious, her screams joined Debi Lu's and reached Chief Milani and his men immediately after the explosion. Milani radioed for an ambulance as he ran. His men, younger and leaner, outran him and arrived on the scene first.

Winnie was still astride Minx who had merely backed up when the grenade exploded.

Three horses came racing past Jocelyn and Bertha. Jocelyn yelled at Yudi but he kept going.

Bertha came over and put her arm around the youngster who started to cry as she saw her horse race away.

"He'll head home," she assured her. "Let's go get Minx."

Jocelyn paled. "Do you suppose Minx is hurt or dead?"

As soon as Jocelyn said that, she began to run.

Winnie was still sitting in the saddle when Jocelyn ran up.

"Get off my brother's horse, you piece of shit!" Jocelyn screamed.

Without speaking, Winnie dismounted.

"It's all you fault!" Debi Lu yelled at Jocelyn. "If you hadn't whistled, Yudi wouldn't have thrown me."

"There was an explosion!" Jocelyn shot back. "I told you there was going to be an explosion. I told you!"

"Your horse is dangerous!" Debbie shrieked, her anger blocking out her pain. "He should be put down! Wait until my father finds out about the trick you played on me. He'll sue your ass."

"You stole my horse!"

"You gave me permission!"

"Never!"

"Well, you gave me permission to ride your sister's horse," Debi Lu said. "It's the same thing."

"Yudi isn't my sister's horse."

"Some old man took him away." Debi Lu argued. "If I wasn't supposed to ride Yudi, why didn't the old man take him away?"

Jocelyn huffed as she took Minx's reins and led the big bay mare down the creek bed.

When she passed Chief Milani, she said, "Arrest them all! Stanley will press charges. These fools took the wrong man's horse!"

"They did more than that?" Milani said. "Someone knocked the guard unconscious."

"It wasn't me!" Winnie yelled. "I didn't even know she was going to do it! And I stopped her from hitting the old man."

"You sonofabitch!" Debi Lu screeched. "You grabbed the horse you wanted. What was I supposed to do?"

"Where's my horse?" Tiffany asked Jocelyn, her voice full of pain.

"Running loose with mine. Scared out of his wits like mine," Jocelyn snarled. "Both will probably get hit by a truck and killed. And it'll serve you right. I warned you."

"Get him," Tiffany cried. "Please."

"Why should I care about him? Look what you did to mine. You have no heart. All you cared about was whether Winnie could come riding in the group. And you stole my horse to make it possible. If I could, I'd break your other leg. I hope you never ride again."

"You're mean!" Tiffany spat out.

"I learned how from you!" Jocelyn countered furiously. "To hell with you and your horse!"

"To hell with yours!" Tiffany yelled.

Bertha came up and eased Jocelyn away. She didn't reprimand her. The child had the right to be angry.

"Chief," Bertha said, "we're going to walk Minx home. Is that okay?"

"Go on," he said. "A long walk is just what the doctor ordered."

"What doctor?" Jocelyn asked.

"My, you are a new generation, aren't you?" Bertha chuckled.

The two walked silently down the dry creek bed. As they came to the end, Jocelyn saw a horse.

"That's Tiffany's horse," she said. She handed Bertha Minx's reins and slowly approached the horse. He skittered away. She talked to him soothingly and approached him from the side. She stroked his neck as she slowly reached for his rein.

"Come on, boy," she said. "It's okay. Let's go for a walk with Minx. See how calm she is. She knows everything is okay."

Slowly, she urged the horse to walk with her.

Soon the four were walking down the trail that led home. Bertha didn't speak.

"We've got to tell Tiffany her horse is okay," Jocelyn said.

"Call Chief Milani," Bertha said, holding out her cell. "He'll tell her."

"You do it," Jocelyn said, "while I walk on with the horses."

When they reached the gate, Stanley was standing there. "Yudi beat you home. He brought a friend."

"Kevin's horse?"

"Well, somebody's. He had a saddle on, so we figured he belonged to the group. How many more are there?"

"Just these two. The others believed me when I told them about the explosion. They took a different trail."

"Three hurt," Bertha reported. "It was pretty bad. Aleta home yet?"

"In the house resting. She had a bad day."

Stanley took hold of Minx's reins.

Jocelyn's annoyance burst forth. "She had a bad day, did she? She has no idea what a bad day is!"

"The committee didn't approve her," Stanley explained as he started walking.

"What's that mean? She didn't flunk her test, did she? Aleta never flunks anything," Jocelyn said, hurrying to catch up.

"We don't know the test results; but, final approval comes from a group called the Character and Fitness Committee."

"Aleta's only crippled temporarily and her brain works fine," Jocelyn spouted angrily. "Is everyone in this state dumb?"

"Not everyone," Stanley said with a hint of a smile. "But some are."

"The committee can't keep her from being a lawyer, can it?"

"Yes, they can."

"She's got better character than me," Jocelyn said. "You mean I can't be a lawyer?"

"You're not a prophet," Stanley explained.

"Well, that's one thing I'm never going to be," Jocelyn declared. "I don't want my head shaved."

"We've got another guest," Stanley announced as he entered the barn. "Guess you've got more work to do, Robert."

"I'll check on Aleta," Bertha said.

"I ordered dinner," Stanley told her. "It'll be here in twenty minutes.

When Bertha arrived at the house, Aleta was sitting in her wheelchair staring out the window.

Bertha didn't say anything about her leaving her bed unattended. Instead she asked, "Did you know there was going to be an explosion?"

"No, I didn't," Aleta replied, "Why?"

"Jocelyn knew."

That night when Stanley and Aleta were alone in the house, Stanley mentioned casually, "Jocelyn doesn't want to lose her hair."

"Why in the world is Jocelyn worried about losing her hair?"

"She's not," Stanley said.

"Then why bring it up?"

"She thinks that's what happens to prophets."

"Oh, she definitely isn't ready."

Chapter 5

When Aleta woke the next morning, she noted where her hand was. "I did it again, didn't I?"

"If you let up, I can get your bath ready," Stanley suggested softly. "You have a busy day ahead of you."

"Why do you trust me?" Aleta asked as she pulled her hand away.

"I just do," he said leaning over and kissing her lightly.

"So our marriage isn't just sex?"

"Of course it is," Stanley returned with a wry smile. "Otherwise I would have married your father. He's much easier to get along with."

"You know what I mean," Aleta retorted. "I was being serious. I was about to say something nice."

"Go ahead."

"You ruined my mood."

Stanley leaned over again and kissed her lightly on the cheek. "Yes, Aleta, I do love you over and above the sex, but..."

"But what?" Aleta pressed after his pause lengthened and he rose and went into the bathroom.

He started the water then helped her rise. The doctor's had been adamant. Take no chance she could get dizzy and fall, they had said.

"But what?" Aleta reiterated. "You said our marriage wasn't only sex, but..."

"I did?"

"Are you going to tell me what the exception is or not?"

"No."

"You can't do that!"

Stanley helped her into the tub, smiling as he did so. He wanted to see what Aleta's mind would come up with so he bathed her silently. That is, he was silent. Aleta wasn't. Finally, he gave in. He lifted her from the tub and began to dry her.

"All I was going to add was that I was still counting the hours."

"Is that all?" Aleta stormed. "You let me think all sorts of horrible things."

"I know. Your mind is a storehouse of fascinating ideas."

"It is not!" she declared. "It's a perfectly ordinary mind."

"Ordinary?" Stanley scoffed. "That's one thing it's not."

"It's not crazy."

"It's not that either, but it sees permutations no one else's mind would. That, my dear Aleta, is why you are going to be a great trial lawyer."

"I'm never going to be any kind of lawyer," she shot back. "I'm never going to..."

Stanley took her head in his hands. "You are going to be a trial lawyer if we have to move to California to make it happen."

"You would do that?" Aleta gasped. It was unthinkable. His family and friends and practice were here. This was his home. A wife followed her husband as he pursued his dreams; but, the reverse was rare and for a man to give up so much was rarer still.

Stanley was not going to be the first, Aleta decided. She had put her career too high on her list of priorities. A glimpse of the life that would be theirs outside this community of friends made her realize that she would have sacrificed too much.

She tucked her career hopes back where they belonged— below what really mattered.

"No, Stanley," she responded gently, "We won't move. Living here with you is too rich, too full, too satisfying. I'm not giving it up to chase some elusive career goal in California."

"I want you to have your dream," Stanley said earnestly.

"Oh, I will," Aleta declared. "And I already have an open door to walk through. My pink blouse, I think with the brown slacks. After all, I am at home and the dog hair won't show on brown pants."

"Martha said to be prepared to hire Ed Ornstein on this one."

"We've used him on all the others. He loves us," Aleta commented. "We never throw divorce work at him."

"He doesn't do divorce work," Stanley pointed out. "Which is why we've never asked him."

"And we never will. Bald and scarred, I'm yours forever," Aleta declared.

"I'd rather have you with hair," Stanley quipped, "but I'll take you anyway you come."

"We are going to have a great second honeymoon," Aleta predicted.

"Every day I wake up beside you is enough for me."

"Me too," she murmured, not quite able to suppress her desire to have the last word.

Bertha ushered in a neatly dressed woman in her mid forties with large dark eyes framed by long lashes and crowned by heavy untrimmed dark brows. The face was almost more handsome than beautiful partly because the nose and chin were strong and determined.

The woman sat down, brushed the side of her hair with her hand to catch any wayward strands and accepted Bertha's offer of tea.

She introduced herself as Sadah Aloman and Aleta recognized both the name and the accent as Arabian. Her heart sank. This was not a client the committee would look favorably upon.

"You're crippled," the woman stated flatly.

"You're Arabian," Aleta countered. "Now that we have that out of the way, tell me why you took a job as a bookkeeper. You have a college degree?"

"Yes, in accounting."

"A CPA?"

"Yes, but I don't mention that anymore."

"Why not?"

"People are not so afraid if I apply for a lower level position," Sadah explained. "Even then, the fear left over from 9/11 has made me a person of suspicion. Were it not for Mrs. Cook, I would still be looking for work."

"Does Mrs. Locke know?"

"No. And I assume that as my lawyer all I tell you is confidential."

"That is correct. Even if you choose to select another lawyer, all you and I have discussed remains confidential."

"But you have not taken the bar oath in Illinois yet."

"I am a California lawyer and House Attorney for the Tontine Trust. As such, I have taken an oath that protects you. I won't break it."

"My husband has been falsely accused of a crime."

Aleta paused for a long moment. Stanley did not take criminal cases. But then she wasn't his partner yet. She was a House attorney for the Tontine.

She wanted this case not because it was a criminal case and she had chosen to practice corporate law, but because it was this case or no case. She didn't look forward to the potential negative publicity as a defender of an Arabian criminal, but she dreaded the thought of not ever getting to enter a courtroom as a lead attorney again.

She realized then that if she chose to accept Barre's offer, she would probably pass the committee's review because then she would be under the supervision of the head of a large prestigious Chicago firm. But to go back now with the committee verdict pending would drop her down on the corporate ladder a couple of rungs.

Sadah Aloman sat silently. She could tell that the lady lawyer was deep in thought. She had approached several criminal law firms and none would take her case. She wasn't certain if it was because she was Arabian or because she was on the verge of bankruptcy or because the crime her husband was accused of was unspeakable.

Aleta finally spoke.

"The Tontine Trust has two lawyers. The other is a man, my husband, Stanley Praetzel. You are free to elect to have him represent you."

"Why did he not speak to me too?"

"Mr. Praetzel is a child advocate; that is, he represents children almost exclusively. He prefers that area of law."

"So he is not good with adults?"

"Mr. Praetzel is a brilliant lawyer. He can handle any case he finds himself involved in."

"You need to understand, Mrs. Praetzel, that my husband and I have tired to adapt to American ways as well as the rules of our chosen religion. We are now Roman Catholics, but we were raised in Saudi Arabia and old traditions never really die. For us a woman's place is behind a man not confronting him. That does not mean we do not have power; but, we do not overpower. We work differently. A lawyer confronts face to face. It is alien to my deep-seated feelings."

"Then let me assure you that Stanley Praetzel is the finest lawyer bar none. No one would fight more courageously or creatively than he. No one is more honest. No one prepares more meticulously. No one is better at the art of negotiation. He deals with children because they have few who take the time to understand what they want or what they need. He cares about those in the deepest trouble and there is no one better to help you."

"Please," Sadah Aloman said plaintively, "Tell your husband that it is out of great respect for him that I make my choice."

"He will appreciate those words I know," Aleta said. "His secretary will find a good time for you to speak with him."

"You misunderstand," Sadah Aloman said. "I am choosing you because I respect his judgment."

Aleta did a double take. "I don't understand."

"You have great esteem for your husband. It was not just in your words. Your whole face lit up when you spoke of him. He has your love as well as your respect. That tells me you are a woman who can restore my husband to me. You have not only the brain but the heart that is required for this task."

Aleta swallowed hard.

To cover her sudden loss for words, she pulled out a tape recorder and set it on the desk. She then explained that she wanted to be able to review all the facts of the case after the interview was over.

"I could well miss something because I'm thinking of something else you are saying. I don't want to do that. If you are uncomfortable with this, I can take notes. I do have a good memory."

"You are being thorough," Sadah said. "I will accept the recorder."

"Start wherever you like," Aleta said. "You know better than I what factors could have led to your husband's arrest."

"I know very little actually," Sadah said. "Shakir left home three years ago to visit a cousin in Florida. He was arrested and he made one phone call and that is the only time I have heard from him. I called a lawyer in Florida, but he says there is no police record of the arrest. I called another lawyer in Florida. He said the same thing. I waited for another call so I could ask where he was. None came."

"Tell me everything your husband said in the call," Aleta prompted.

"I wasn't home when he called."

"How do you know he called?"

"I have the answering machine tape."

"Do you have it with you?"

"Yes."

Aleta picked up her phone and called Ed Ornstein. "I have a client who has an important message on an answering machine tape. I need to hear the message, but I need a copy and I need you to analyze it and see if you can get some clue where her husband is being held. I'm working out of Stanley's study. Bertha made an apple pie this morning. In fact, I think she made several."

Ed laughed as he replied, "On my way."

"Now, Mrs. Aloman," Aleta said. "Tell me what you heard."

"He said he'd been arrested. They stopped him because he ran a stop sign. They looked at his driver's license, talked to him and then then arrested him. They said he was a Muslim terrorist. He told them he was Catholic. They think he's something called deep-cover."

"Anything more?"

"No."

"Did you go down there to look for him?"

"Forgive me. I was afraid. I had to stay with the children. There is no one else."

"What else was on the tape?' Aleta asked. "I want to know why you didn't go."

"I told you."

"Not the real reason."

"He was cut off forcibly. That frightened me."

"You need to trust me," Aleta said. "I can't be effective if you keep me in the dark."

"I can't. You won't help if I do."

"Is your husband a terrorist?"

A horrified expression exploded on Sadah's face.

"No!" she cried.

"Then I will help no matter what he told you."

"Promise?"

"My word is my promise."

"He cried in Arabic, 'hide'."

"If they had that word translated, that would confirm their suspicions," Aleta said. "Now what I need from you is every legal document you own—birth certificates, citizenship papers, marriage license, driver's licenses going back as far as possible, baptism certificates, mortgage papers…"

"Why?

"I need as long a trail of U.S. citizenship as you can provide. The opposition might call one or two items suspect, ut a plethora of legal documents will provide good substantiation that you two are ordinary citizens and that your husband was plucked from the car because he had an Arabic name and an Arabian accent. Once a person is suspect, everything he says or does is misinterpreted."

A commotion at the front door told Aleta that Ed had arrived with Emma, his black Lab, who was the mother of Scooby, her chocolate Lab pup. To Aleta's surprise, Ed came through the door without Emma.

"Scooby was making such a racket," Ed said, "I thought I'd let Bertha take him and Emma for a romp."

Ed picked up the small tape.

"When do you need to hear this?"

"As soon as you finish making a copy. Since this is a missing person case, you will need to interview Mrs. Aloman yourself. Her husband was arrested in Florida, and after one phone call, he disappeared."

"How long has he been gone?" Ed asked Sadah.

"Three years."

"Is your husband a citizen?"

"Yes."

"Naturalized like you?"

"Yes."

"Muslim?"

"No. We're Roman Catholic."

"I need your priest's name."

"Yes, of course. Father Michael will be glad to help."

"What's your husband's line of work?"

"He fixes computer systems."

"His own business?"

"Yes."

"Got anybody working for him?"

"No."

"Where was he arrested?"

"I don't know."

"Where was he heading?"

"St . Petersburg."

"Did he get there?"

"No."

"Good." Ed said, then seeing the shocked look on Sadah's face, added quickly, "I mean for the search. The smaller the area, the better chance I've got of finding him."

"She consulted two lawyers in Florida," Aleta mentioned.

"Their names?"

"I've got their letters," Sadah said pulling two letters out of her purse. "How do I get hold of you?"

"You don't. You call Aleta."

That evening as Stanley was serving the dinner that Bertha left on the stove, he asked Aleta about the case that came into her office that day.

Aleta, sitting quietly in her wheelchair, began by saying, "I'm so glad we share this client. I need to discuss what I've done and see if there is anything I've forgotten. By the way, she said to tell you that she chose me over you out of respect for you."

"She chose against me because of her respect?" Stanley queried, his forehead wrinkled with puzzlement, his eyes twinkling with amusement and his lip toying with a smile.

Aleta laughed. "I don't get it either. I gave you a glowing recommendation."

"Tongue-in-cheek or real?"

Aleta eyed him askance. "I won't even answer that."

"Then why?"

"It seems my creditability rose when I honestly praised you. If such a worthy lawyer chose to marry me, I must be good. At least I think that's how her reasoning went. It's a bit faulty, because even wonderful, smart, rich men can be fools when it comes to love."

"Not me."

"Of course you," Aleta argued. "You didn't know anything about me."

"I did too. I knew you were gorgeous and kind. What else did I need to know?"

"I wasn't kind. I put that niece of Evelyn's down."

"She deserved it. She was way out of line. Nice boobs though."

"You noticed?" Aleta snapped. "I didn't know you noticed."

"I'd have been blind not to."

"You're never going to get out of that hole."

"Yours are nicer."

"Weak."

"They're natural. I like natural best."

"A little better."

"Hers were out of proportion with the rest of her body."

"You sized her up too!" Aleta charged.

"She was standing between me and you and I couldn't help but notice how perfectly nature packaged you."

"Forgiven," Aleta decided abruptly. "Let's talk about the case."

"I have some good news," Stanley said casually.

"Let's go with that first."

"I had a consultation with Dr. Taekman and Dr. Cook this..."

Aleta charged in. "Without me?"

"Are you going to condemn me before you even hear what it was about?"

"It was about me, wasn't it?" she challenged.

"Not entirely. It was about Martha."

"Oh," Aleta murmured, deflated.

"She gave her new husband an order."

"Martha orders people all the time," Aleta noted.

"This was medical. And it was about you. She told him to do another MRI."

"Did he ask her why?"

"Of course. And, Aleta, you're going to love her response."

"What was it?"

"She said, and I quote, 'because I say so.'"

"The 'mother's response'," Aleta chuckled. "So you told them yes, didn't you?"

"I told them I'd talk to you."

"Why?" she asked puzzled.

"Because the two of them put all kinds of strings on doing it."

"As if we don't have enough?" she griped.

"Here they are," Stanley said. "You promise not to go into the bathroom unattended. You are to do nothing in the kitchen but eat. You are to be in the wheelchair when the dogs are loose. You can go to the office with me but not alone. You won't drive or shop or visit."

"They're afraid of an accident, aren't they?"

"Martha said you were healed.

"Michael called us in to ask us if he should have Martha examined by someone. I explained that he was living with a prophet and, while none of you had ever made such a pronouncement before, that didn't mean it was beyond your ability. After all, your gift of understanding stroke victims surprised us all when it happened. I said I would pay the cost because it means our time of celibacy would be over."

"Can we do it now?"

"Tomorrow morning," Stanley said. "Nine o'clock."

"You couldn't schedule it for seven?"

"I'm in court all day."

"Do you realize how long it's been?"

"Down to the hour," Stanley confessed calmly. "I'll come straight home."

Suddenly, Aleta turned beet red.

Stanley grinned impishly. "You finally remembered what I said."

"You told them we'd been celibate."

"Aleta, you know that they know that."

"There was no reason that I wasn't included in the conference if the subject of sex didn't come up. What part of our sex life was discussed," Aleta demanded.

"You don't want to know."

"I'm already flushed, aren't I? I can feel my face burning. Let's get it over with."

"Martha said I had suffered long enough. It seems I pleased God. They wanted to know what she was alluding to," Stanley said.

"You didn't tell them?"

"I told them it was private and Dr. Cook guessed."

"Why didn't you stop him?"

"Stop his mind from working?" Stanley queried.

"Stop him from telling Taekman about what I do when we sleep."

"He did it before I realized he was going to."

"Didn't he violate something, you know, some confidentiality law?"

"They are both your doctors," Stanley explained, knowing full well Aleta knew that. She was protesting on general principle.

"You did nothing wrong," Stanley said. "And I haven't suffered with what you do, but Aleta, I didn't want to explain that your touch brings me pleasure and that touching me brings you pleasure. That is our private business."

"But you let them think I was a freak."

"No, I told them that I was finding it more and more difficult not to make love to you. I told them that's what Martha meant."

"They believed you?"

"It's true."

"But you think I was the other," Aleta surmised. "That God was pleased because you let me gain comfort from you when it wasn't easy for you?"

"Yes."

"So do I," Aleta observed. "Do you know what this means?"

"Yes, I do. God likes people to keep promises made from the heart."

"We've been so tempted to skirt around that promise," Aleta said thoughtfully, "especially these last couple of days. There were so many times..."

"Let's talk about your case," Stanley suggested.

Aleta told him everything that had transpired. When she stopped, Stanley said, "What happened to Mr. Aloman's car?"

"I guess it was impounded."

"I'd start there. The police may have deleted the records of his arrest, but I bet no one thought about his car."

"You're right. It would have been taken to the impound lot while he was being questioned. After the initial search, it would have been returned to the impound lot and left there. There's been no trial, so the car's just been sitting there, unclaimed."

"Maybe. But police keep computer records of cars impounded."

"I'll call Ed," Aleta decided.

"Now?" Stanley asked.

"Why not now?"

"Go ahead. Get it off your plate."

"You've got dishes to do," Aleta reminded him. "This way Ed can start on that trail first thing in the morning."

Beatrice answered the phone. "Ed flew down to Florida this afternoon. Something about a car."

"He didn't tell me."

"He said I would get a call from you and I could tell you where he went."

"Where exactly did he go?"

"Someplace called Clearwater, Florida," Beatrice said. "And he told me to tell you to ask Mrs. Aloman who her backer is."

"Backer?" Aleta said. "Didn't Martha send her?"

"He didn't say anything else. Ed never wants me to worry so he never tells me much."

"That's okay Beatrice. I'll do as he suggests and go from there.

Stanley looked at her questioningly.

"Mrs. Aloman has a backer only Ed doesn't know who," Aleta reported. "What amazes me is that he knows she even has one."

"My advice," Stanley said, "is to be vague until you do know."

"Lie?"

"Just say Ed is investigating. You really don't know more. If there is someone else in the mix, we don't want to tip Ed's hand."

"Okay. I can wait until I know more," Aleta agreed. "But who else would be in the mix?"

"No idea."

"You aren't going to speculate?"

"I'm going to wait until after you ask Sadah Aloman," Stanley said. "Tonight I'm going to enjoy our last evening as a celibate couple."

"Enjoy?"

"Anticipation is exhilarating." He grinned, and then added, "Tonight we can plan our second honeymoon. Where do you want to go?"

"Somewhere warm."

"That's it?"

"Pretty much. That and a bed."

"We could stay here. I can turn up the thermostat."

"If that's what you want, we can do that," Aleta said politely.

"You're going to make me do it all, aren't you?"

"That's what husbands do."

"Who says?"

"I do," Aleta said.

"You just want to worry about who Sadah's backer is."

"Right."

"Well, nothing's going to happen tonight."

But Stanley was wrong.

Sadah Aloman went to confession after work and Father Michael asked her if Mrs. Praetzel had agreed to be her lawyer yet. She told him that they'd had their first meeting that morning.

"I want you to go to this address," Father Michael said.

"Now?" Sadah asked. "I need to go home to my children."

"I will call Basil and tell him you'll be late," her pastor said.

"Can't this wait?"

Father Michael shook his head. "Please do this. These men have put themselves out to help you. They've been calling me every day. For some reason this is important to them."

"Then I will do it," Sadah determined. "I owe you all much for helping me. It is so good not to be alone."

The building was easy to find, the entrance to the parking garage well lit, parking spaces plentiful. She parked in front of a direct entrance to the third floor and walked across the lighted bridge. The hallway was carpeted and the doors numbered.

She opened the door and entered an empty reception area. Two men emerged from a room behind the reception desk and greeted her warmly.

"Mr. Powell, Mr. Hillers, I am grateful for all you have done for me," she said. "If there is anything I can do, please tell me."

"We wanted to meet with you to find out if Mrs. Aleta Praetzel will be satisfactory," Melvin Hillers said.

"If not," Eugene Powell added, "we will find someone else."

"She is a good choice for me," Sadah said. "She will work hard."

"How much will she charge?" Melvin Hillers asked. He had a sheet of paper on the table in front of him and a pen in his hand.

"She said I will not need to pay."

"What?" the dark-eyed man snapped, his brows knitting together in a fierce scowl.

"It's alright," his tubby partner assured him. "We just write in pro bono. The point is she's dispensing legal advice."

Sadah noticed that Eugene Powell shot a look of annoyance at the fat man with the huge double chin and very little hair on his head. He reminded Sadah of a fat brown toad; but she liked him better than the other one. Handsome and slick, with penetrating dark eyes, Sadah found herself mesmerized by them even as a child she'd once looked into the eyes of a cobra and her fear had paralyzed her.

"Our questions may seem strange to you, but they are necessary," Powell said ingratiatingly. "We just want to be sure everything is being done that can be done."

"She hired an investigator," Sadah offered. "That is more than was done before."

"Good. Good," the snake said soothingly. "Has he made any progress?"

"I think it is too early," she replied warily. She did not like these men prying like this.

"Do you have his phone number?" Hillers asked. "We can call and..."

He stopped when Sadah frowned.

Powell jumped in, "Just to offer our help."

"I can give him your names and tell him you wish to help," Sadah asked with seeming innocence.

"No!" Powell said firmly. "We do not want anyone knowing we are involved."

"Is there something wrong? Have I done something wrong?"

"No, my dear lady," intoned the smooth baritone of the State Senate hopeful, "you have done nothing wrong. Just say nothing and you will have repaid us for our aid."

"As you wish," she said politely.

The questioning continued. They wanted to know everything Aleta Praetzel had said.

Sadah protested. She told them Aleta had told her not to talk about the case with anyone.

"She didn't mean us," Eugene Powell said smoothly.

"I'm sure she did," Sadah countered.

"She is a neophyte lawyer," Eugene Powell explained. "I want to be sure the steps she has taken are good ones."

"Surely, she advised you what to do next," Melvin Hillers posed.

"Yes," Sadah replied, but didn't elaborate.

The questions continued.

Finally when she thought she could stand no more, Melvin Hillers shoved a piece of paper across the table. "Sign this, Mrs. Aloman and we're done."

She took the pen from the fat fingers, anxious to be done. She desperately wanted to go home.

She looked at the paper and saw Aleta Praetzel's name. She tried to read the typed words; but, all she saw were the written words 'pro bono'.

She hesitated. She didn't want to sign anything.

The oily tones of Eugene Powell began explaining that all she was doing was signing a paper saying that Aleta Praetzel had agreed to be her attorney.

"That's all?" she asked. That's what the words seemed to say but she felt it was wrong somehow to sign this document. But she was tired. It had been an emotionally exhausting day. Her mind didn't want to deal with her problems anymore.

She spotted the words pro bono again and asked, "What does pro bono mean?"

"It's a short for pro bono publico which is Latin meaning literally for the public good," Powell pontificated. "It means she has agreed to do this without payment. It's true isn't it?"

"Well, I'm not paying her," Sadah said.

"Is she billing you?"

"No, but I don't think it's this pro bono thing."

"Mrs. Aloman," Eugene Powell said derisively, "you just don't understand. That's all. If you don't pay for a service, we lawyers call that pro bono work."

"Is pro bono a bad thing?" Sadah asked. These men had it wrong.

"No, it's a good thing," Powell said quickly. "It's a kind thing, a generous thing."

"What if someone pays her later?" Sadah asked.

Hillers whispered. "Maybe Martha Cook is funding this?"

"Just sign," Powell decided. "You are not paying. It doesn't matter if someone pays her later. That's what this says."

Sadah, worn down by their relentless pressure, signed her name. She watched the two men sign afterward.

"It is done," Hillers said smiling.

She saw a gleam in Powell's eyes that made her shiver. She felt as if she were watching a cobra spread its hood.

Chapter 6

After Sadah Aloman left the office, Eugene Powell turned to his partner.

"She's not being very cooperative."

"You've got enough," Melvin Hillers assured him. "There's no question she took the case."

"You still think I should wait before filing my report."

"Check things out," Hillers said. "While Aleta might make such an error, I can't see Stanley Praetzel letting her."

"I can," Powell declared. "She doesn't listen to him."

"I think you're wrong."

"He's a child advocate. She's into trial law. This is too juicy a case for her to pass up," Powell argued. "I'll bet he doesn't even know she saw a client. Sadah said she went to her home and that he wasn't even there. Remember we asked her about that."

"I remember." Hiller said, trying to placate his colleague who was becoming agitated. "By the way, that interruption during your committee's interview…"

"Yeah. What about it?"

"I'm surprised you haven't mentioned it, considering it's all about that phone call you told me Aleta Praetzel made in your office."

"Aleta Praetzel discussed what went on?" Eugene gasped.

"Not that. About the horse theft she said was going to happen. It did. Two of the Praetzel horses were stolen by teenagers who rode them out on some unused trail."

"And that made the news?"

"It made the news because a grenade exploded out in the middle of nowhere and the horses spooked and threw their riders," Hiller went on eagerly. "And three of the kids were hurt bad. Two of the horses were stolen from Praetzel's barn. And here's the corker. They were warned there would be an explosion by none other than Aleta Praetzel."

"Another fairy tale."

"But with a twist," Melvin rushed on. "You're going to love this part. One of the injured riders was interviewed at the site and she says she's going to sue Aleta Praetzel and her sister."

"On what grounds."

"She claims that Aleta should have called the police if she knew there was a bomb on the trail."

Eugene Powell leaned back in his chair and stretched. Melvin Hillers waited. Powell was thinking.

"Burrows asked her why she didn't call the police when she called home during our interview and she said that the warning came too late," Eugene mused aloud. "But she also said that she had taken precautions early to safeguard the horses."

"The kids said the sister warned them at lunch."

"So Aleta knew that morning," Powell said. "Who is this kid who wants to sue?"

"Debi Lu Reid. She was hurt really bad. Her father's a lawyer, Lowell Reid."

"Don't know him," Eugene commented.

"Trusts and estates," Melvin said. "I looked him up."

"I want that case," Eugene declared.

"You have an appointment with him at ten tomorrow morning." Hiller said. "I told him you wanted to help him in the Aleta Praetzel case."

"Not represent him?"

"That's you decision, I just wanted you to have the option."

"He isn't a trial lawyer," Powell reasoned aloud. "At least not the kind who can take on Aleta Praetzel."

'I suggest three million. One for expenses. One for trauma. And one for us."

"That's too low," Eugene Powell said. "Let's see if I can stoke the fire a bit."

The next morning when she woke up, Aleta pulled her hand away from its nighttime resting place and tucked it beside her body.

"If you don't think I noticed its presence," Stanley said softly, "then you have a lot to learn about men."

"You're awake!"

"Ready for your big day?"

"You've said that the last three days in a row."

"And I was right, wasn't I?"

"Bet you're going to miss those cold showers."

"Wanna bet?" he asked as he leaned over and kissed her.

"Where are we going on our second honeymoon?"

"Nowhere for a week at least," Stanley said. "This development has caught me unprepared. I can't clear my calendar fast enough to take off sooner."

"I thought....," Aleta sighed.

"I'd already marked off a week next month."

"Spontaneous isn't in your character anywhere?"

"Oh, it's there. I just usually ignore it," Stanley said with a smile.

"We all have our faults," he said as he turned on the water in the tub.

"Some of us overcome ours," Aleta called. "Especially the easy ones."

"Which ones have you overcome?"

"Impatience!" Aleta gloated. "You thought I didn't have an answer, didn't you?"

"You still don't."

"What do you mean?"

"You're still impatient. You want us to drop everything, get in the car and drive somewhere today, right?"

"Why not?"

"To a local motel?"

"No, of course not."

"To a Chicago hotel?"

"That would work for me."

"And have me go to work from there instead of from here?"

"Not to work at all," Aleta said hoping to adjust his thinking.

"You expect me to be a forty minute drive from work and not go?"

"Oh heck! Forget it! You just don't get it."

Stanley helped her from the bed. "No, I guess I don't. But don't despair, Aleta, we will have a super night. That I promise."

Aleta's mood shifted quickly at the thought. She lifted her face up as he was seating her in the tub and he kissed her.

"Yes, we will."

After breakfast, Stanley told Bertha he would help her walk the dogs because he wanted her to take Aleta to the hospital.

Surprised, Aleta asked, "You don't want to know what the result is?"

"The MRI will take an hour. I need to be in court by ten. Besides you want to talk with Sadah Aloman, don't you? Bertha can drive you to the office."

Even though Aleta knew that it was too late to change a court appearance, somehow she had been sure Stanley would have managed it somehow for something as important as this. She sat at the table sipping her second cup of coffee, trying to stem the rising tide of resentment.

He was being reasonable. He was always reasonable. But now when she was so full of anticipation and excitement, she didn't want him to be reasonable. She didn't know what she wanted him to be, but reasonable was not even remotely considered.

But that's not like Stanley, she thought. He takes his duty to his clients seriously. And his clients are children, she reminded herself. Children have no patience.

And why didn't my sitting day after day in the wheelchair count? Tonight he was going to answer that. Tonight he was going to answer for this morning. He knew I wanted him with me. Yes, he was going to answer for that.

After the MRI, Aleta waited for the results.

The two doctors finally came out. Neither looked happy. Aleta's countenance fell. Bertha looked apprehensive.

The doctors seeing the expressions on the faces of the two women hastened to assure them that it was good news.

"Why do you look so upset?" Aleta asked.

"We don't like what we can't explain," Dr. Taekman said. "By rights we should have seen only a small improvement."

"And there was more?" Aleta coached.

"Oh, I'll say," Dr. Cook chimed in. "According to this MRI the bones in the skull and the shoulder are completely healed."

"Not partially," Dr. Taekman said, his voice replete with awe, "but completely."

"We don't understand this at all," Dr. Cook said.

"And we don't trust it," Dr. Taekman added.

"We trust the MRI," Dr. Cook put in. "We just don't trust... oh, hell... I don't exactly know what we don't trust."

"We gave you those rules," Dr. Taekman said. "Could you...would you follow them for a week?"

"No driving, no cooking," Aleta began reciting. "No cleaning, no bathing alone, and no riding my horse. Is that everything?"

"No anything that's dangerous," Dr. Cook added. "Now that's everything."

"So I can walk out of here?" Aleta asked.

"No!" both doctors chorused.

"Don't worry," Aleta said. "Neither Bertha nor I want to carry this chair out of here."

"Didn't we have some other rules?" Dr. Cook asked Dr. Taekman.

"I can't remember any," Dr. Taekman replied numbly. "I need to look at the film again."

A soft buzz caused Dr. Cook to reach into his pocket.

"I thought cell phones weren't allowed," Aleta charged.

"Hospital personnel have phones designed not to interfere with the equipment," Dr. Cook replied stepping away.

"You could loan me yours," Aleta accused.

"Sure," Dr. Cook said holding out the phone. "Here talk to your husband. Tell him you're fine."

Aleta took the phone. "How do I dial out?"

"Try just saying hello."

"Stanley?"

"Hi Beautiful!"

"Did he tell you?"

"He started to and then this woman started yelling at him."

"Oh that!" Aleta said dismissing her behavior as inconsequential. "I'm all healed! Isn't that great?"

"Anything goes?" Stanley asked.

"I thought you were in court."

"I asked for a recess so I could call. I gotta go. See you tonight. May be able to take off a bit early."

Aleta's spirits buoyed up at the last statement.

"He did care," she said aloud to Bertha as she handed the phone back to Dr. Cook.

"Care? He's been bugging us every fifteen minutes. I thought lawyers were pretty much incommunicado when in court."

"They are," Aleta said. "He must've pulled some strings."

"Next time he waits in the waiting room like everyone else."

"I didn't know you carried a cell phone," Aleta commented.

"I usually don't."

"Why today?"

"Stanley insisted. He said he had to be in court all day and so I thought what the heck. Never again."

"Thanks, Wayne," Aleta said.

When Aleta walked into the office, Stanley's secretary, Alice Bergstrom, rose to greet her. "You're done with the wheelchair?"

"Yep!" Aleta said as the two hugged.

"Bet that feels good."

"You have no idea. Is Mrs. Aloman here?"

"She's using your office," Alice said.

Bertha sat down in the chair beside Alice's desk.

When Sadah Aloman saw Aleta, her forehead wrinkled with worry and her greeting was tremulous.

Aleta pulled a chair near the desk and sat down.

"You are well?" Sadah asked, incredulous.

"The doctors decided this morning that my skull is healed," Aleta said. "I wanted to ask you who your backers are."

"Backers?"

"People who have been supporting you, helping you."

"Why?" Sadah asked, her worry now mingled with obvious apprehension.

Aleta leaned forward. "It is not important to me. If you don't want to tell me, don't."

"They said if I do, you won't help my husband."

"Really? You must do what is best for your husband."

"You are best for my husband."

"I've already promised to help him. Did you know I can't pull out now without permission?"

"Whose?"

"If we were in court, it would be the judge. Right now it's the Tontine CEO's call."

"Who is that?"

"The woman who hired you, Harriet Locke," Aleta said. "The Tontine will find you another attorney if you don't believe I'm suitable, but they are paying my salary, so I will try hard to represent your husband well."

"I don't want to lose you from this case, but I'm afraid it's too late to undo what I have done."

"And what is that?"

"What does pro bono mean?"

"Lawyers use it to mean they aren't charging their usual fee. They are working free on a particular case."

"Are you pro bono?"

"No, I'm being paid."

"But I am not paying you."

"The Tontine Trust has lawyers on salary. I am one. We handle any legal problems for the Trust and any of its employees at no cost to the employee. That's you."

"So everyone who works for the Tontine Trust gets this?"

"Everyone."

"How many does that include?"

"Right now—twenty-five. The number is expected to go up when the subsidiaries begin hiring," Aleta said. "We are hiring another attorney in anticipation just as soon as he passes the bar."

Aleta's last comment brought Sadah's fear rushing back. Sadah decided to ask questions about the new attorney. Maybe she would find her answer.

"This new man," she queried, "when will he pass this bar."

"He'll know the results in April, but he won't be allowed to practice until after he's sworn in in May."

"Is it the same for all?"

"There are exceptions."

"Are you one of those?"

"Me?" Aleta uttered with a harsh laugh. "I'm afraid not."

"Please explain. This is important to me."

"Currently, I'm what's called a House Attorney. I came with the Trust from California. As such, the state allows me to appear in any court on any case so long as the person I represent is employed by or otherwise a member of the Tontine. I can legally represent your husband. I would not even have interviewed you if I couldn't. And actually that's the reason I have time to devote to your case. I'm not busy. I was when the Trust first moved here and I will be again soon; but, I have time now."

"Do the courts know this—that you are legal?"

"I have documents to prove I am in case there is a question. They are as good as the bar cards other attorneys produce on demand."

"So everything is okay?"

"Why is this worrying you so?"

"You would not see me for a long while," Sadah said. "Did not Mrs. Cook tell you about me?"

"She said she had a case for me. I told her I couldn't take any cases until I was admitted to the bar."

"But yesterday you saw me."

"When you became an employee of the Tontine, then I could help you legally."

Relief replaced worry on Sadah's face.

"Have you been talking to someone who told you I wasn't legal?"

"It doesn't matter now. I understand."

"I need something from you," Aleta said. "You may keep secret who you are talking with if you want to, but please don't tell them what is happening on your case. This is very important."

"How could it hurt if they are friends?"

"Not knowing who these people are or why they are filling you with doubt, my caution is a general one. Lawyers do not want their cases discussed outside of their office."

"But they want to know about the progress you are making," Sadah protested weakly. "How can that hurt?"

"They are hiding in the shadows," Aleta declared strongly. "I do not trust people afraid of the light."

Sadah bowed her head and Aleta knew she had not won her appeal.

"Have them call me with their questions," she said. "I will know what to tell them that will not hurt your husband's case."

"They want me to tell them," Sadah revealed.

"Then I'm sorry, Sadah. You hired me to help your husband. I represent him now. Since you insist on informing your secret friends of my every move, I will not tell you anything. I will not risk your husband's life."

Sadah's face paled.

"You will stop working?"

"I did not say that. I am going to represent your husband and bring him home, but I am going to do it without some strangers looking over my shoulder second-guessing me. It is going to be a test of your faith in me. You must trust me."

"But I want to know," Sadah declared.

"You made your choice. Now I am making mine. I will tell you nothing. You may request another attorney or you may choose to trust me. Those are the only choices you have right now."

To Aleta's utter amazement, Sadah murmured, "Thank you."

"Are you prepared for me to withhold everything pertaining to this case?"

"Yes."

"I absolutely do not understand your decision," Aleta said with a modicum of hesitation in her tone, "however, so be it."

Aleta rose thus telling Sadah that their meeting was over.

"I will let you get back to work. Did you bring the records I asked for yesterday?"

Sadah took a large brown envelope from the drawer and handed it to Aleta.

"These will be helpful, although not in the way you think," Aleta said. "Did you tell your backers that you gave me these records?"

"I told them you asked for our citizen papers," Sadah said. "They pressed me for information, so I chose the one that seemed the most logical. They asked if you asked for other papers and I said yes but I did not tell them your idea"

"Good." Aleta said. "I may ask for more documents. Please do not throw anything away until this is over. I will put your legal documents in our safe. The court insists that only original documents be presented."

"Sadah nodded.

"May I tell Mrs. Locke about your degree in economics?" Aleta asked.

Again Sadah nodded.

Aleta held out her hand. Sadah took it. The two shook hands. Not another word was spoken. Aleta left the office immediately.

As soon as Aleta arrived home, she headed straight for her office. She plucked her pup from his pen and carried him with her. She dialed Beatrice's number.

"Can you get a message to Ed?" she asked.

"He calls me," she replied.

"That's good enough," Aleta said. "Tell him not to tell Mrs. Aloman anything. Someone not friendly is pressing her for information. I will explain when I see him."

"Is he going to get hurt?" Beatrice asked.

"Not as far as I can tell. I just don't want anything Ed might find out to come back to bite me in court down the road."

"Dean might be in contact with him," Beatrice said.

"I'll call him next," Aleta said. "No, Scooby. Not there!"

She heard Beatrice's laugh as she hung up and scooped up her pup and ran with him to the back door. In the kitchen Bertha, who'd heard her call, came running and opened the outside door. Aleta put the pup down and Bertha gently pushed past Aleta, stepped outside and called her pup to come.

The Chessies all came running and Aleta suddenly remembered the doctor's cautions.

I really can't be trusted, she thought as she returned to her office and called Alice.

"Will Stanley be checking with you before he comes home?"

"He may," Alice hedged.

"Tell him not to say anything to Sadah until he talks to me."

"I will pass along your message," Alice said.

So he is checking back, Aleta thought. She knew he would. He could no more not check back at his office than he could throw his pajamas on the floor.

She heard Bertha come in with the dogs. Scooby joined her in the office while Bertha busied herself with the laundry.   Somewhere in between her scurrying around, Bertha managed to set a sandwich and a glass of milk on Aleta's desk.

Aleta thought it was strange that Bertha didn't check on her at all, then at two o'clock another glass of milk and a plate of cookies appeared at her elbow.   There was a small dog biscuit on the plate with the cookies.

Aleta took a moment to play with Scooby and feed him his biscuit.

Two hours later, Aleta stretched, put the records Sadah had given her in the safe, walked into the kitchen and announced that she was going to the barn.

"Should I accompany you?" Bertha asked.

"Since I'm taking all the dogs, yes."

Bertha grabbed her coat and helped Aleta into her cape. The dogs crowded in front of the door each one vying to be the first one through.

When the door opened, the dogs burst through.   Aleta and Bertha followed.   When Aleta reached the barn, she told Hubbs she would be able to ride in a week's time.

"Shadow will like having you on his back again."

"I won't be riding very far at first," she said.

"Best for him if you don't."

Jocelyn shouted at them as she came running up.   She threw her arms around Aleta.   "I'm so glad you're well!"

Aleta hugged her with one arm.   "Me too."

"So when can you ride?"

"Next week."

"Great!" Jocelyn exclaimed happily.   "We can ride together."

"I can't go far," Aleta said.

"So we'll ride around the field until our horses are ready to go out the gate again," Jocelyn said.

"How's Yudi doing?" Aleta inquired.

"Better than Tiffany and Debi Lu."

"The extra horses are still here."

"Stanley took out a restraining order, nobody can come get them without an appointment with Stanley," Jocelyn said.

"Aren't the boys out on bail?"

"Both are grounded. Kevin's folks are paying Mr. Hubbs to take care of Kevin's horse. Kevin is really pissed about the whole arrangement. He doesn't think he should be punished at all, the jerk!"

"What about Tiffany's horse?"

"Her folks are too worried about Tiffany to worry about her horse. Her leg was busted up pretty bad. Lots of pins in it. She won't be riding for a long, long time."

"What about Debi Lu?"

"Her shoulder is just as messed up. Serves her right! Serves them all right!"

"How many times have you been told to let go of that anger?"

"Not you too!"

The appearance of a car pulling up in front of the house caused the three women to turn. The man who got out saw the three women wave at him and walked toward them.

"Wonder what he wants?" Bertha said, walking toward him.

He stopped and asked a question and Bertha pointed to Aleta. He walked up to her quickly and served her with a summons.

Aleta opened it up and read the short sentence three times.

"What is it?" Jocelyn asked.

"I'm being asked to appear before a judge to answer on the charge of gross negligence resulting in bodily harm to a juvenile."

"What's that mean?"

"It means I'm being blamed for someone being hurt yesterday."

"You?" Jocelyn blurted out.

"I need to call Stanley."

"Aren't you a lawyer?"

"Doctors don't operate on themselves," Aleta returned.

"Ask a simple question and all I ever get is some far out quotation that has nothing at all to do with the question."

"The answer is no," Aleta said.

"You passed the test, didn't you?"

"It's complicated," Aleta said.

"I can do complicated," Jocelyn insisted.

Aleta studied her youngest sister and decided to explain in detail. To her surprise, Jocelyn not only understood the facts, she understood the power play and the hatred. So Aleta went a step further and explained her research into the statistical probability that Powell was not only a racist, but an exceedingly clever and diabolical one. So absorbed was Aleta in her teaching and Jocelyn in learning that the two moved into the barn because it was the closest place where they could sit down. They wound up sitting on two bales of hay while Hubbs took the horses out one by one for a short walk. To the house and down the driveway. The dogs accompanied the old man. Neither Aleta nor Jocelyn noticed when Bertha left them.

Neither saw Stanley drive in and park next to the house, nor did they notice a second man follow him and serve both Stanley and Aleta's father with subpoenas.

Stanley and Robert talked as they loaded Stanley's Lexus.

"I don't want Aleta to know about the suit," Stanley said.

"She received a summons," her father pointed out. "I messed up royally when I talked to Jocelyn. I couldn't risk her disobeying. But I never said anything about an explosion."

"Let's take this one step at a time," Stanley said. "Aleta told me about her vision. There was no explosion."

"Bertha said that Jocelyn told the group there was going to be an explosion and she was going to be killed."

"Four of the group believed that the explosion was going to happen on the old creek trail and rode elsewhere," Robert said. "Her warning must have been strong enough."

"She used Aleta's name," Stanley said.

"I hate to blame Jocelyn," her father said.

"We aren't going to blame her," Stanley said. "She told her group of riding friends about the explosion. Some of them listened to her and some didn't. That's what happens when one prophesies. Jocelyn is not responsible for their choices."

"Are we going to do anything about the suit?"

"Yes," Stanley said. "We're going to file a countersuit. Get my mother to help you with that. She says that as a judge she is always upset when the defendant doesn't countersue."

"You want me to do that?" Robert asked.

"You're named in the suit," Stanley said. "Besides, I don't need the money. You do."

"I'll take care of it."

"We will be back for the hearing. It's a week from today."

"How come it wasn't scheduled immediately?"

"My guess is that that's when Debi Lu is going to be released from the hospital."

"So we know she's behind this?"

"She's the one who threatened to sue when she was interviewed on her way to the hospital. Her father's a lawyer. He knows that the appearance of the victim and her testimony is important."

"I'll take the blame for exaggerating the danger to Jocelyn," Robert said. "But I didn't know about the explosion."

"It appears that Jocelyn got the prophecy this time and stuck Aleta's name on it," Stanley said

In the barn, Aleta finished her dissertation on Powell and said abruptly, "Jocelyn, you need to go see Tiffany. She wants you to buy her horse."

"You don't know that."

"Know what?"

'You said that Tiffany wants me to buy her horse."

"Did I?" Aleta asked, puzzled. "Why does she want to sell him?"

"That's just it. She wouldn't. She loves that horse."

"Go see her and tell her how he's doing," Aleta urged. "Besides, I've got Yudi."

Aleta turned. "Hubbs, can Yudi be ridden in a show again?"

"Wouldn't do it." Hubbs said.

"Why not?" Aleta pressed.

"Sounds bother him more."

"I can't sell Yudi!" Jocelyn cried.

"Retire him," Aleta said. "We've got Sterling and Jezebel now."

"He won't like not being ridden," Jocelyn protested.

"Then ride him," Aleta said. "But if you want to keep on showing, you need another horse."

"Hubbs. Is Royal better than Yudi?"

"Ain't one better than another. They're just different."

"Who's better for jumping?"

"Tiffany's got the better horse."

"How come he knows that?" Jocelyn asked.

"Because he's an expert," Aleta smiled.

"I could go see Tiffany," Jocelyn said thoughtfully. "She's the one I got to yell at. I'm not so mad at her anymore. And I rescued her horse. That made me feel good. It wasn't the horse's fault. I feel sorry for him. Her folks won't care who gets him. He's a good horse. He deserves better."

"Buy him," Aleta said. "It'll be my gift welcoming you to the sisterhood of prophets."

"Buy him?"

"You said once that Tiffany's horse was better."

"I beat him with Yudi."

"Because you're a better rider," Aleta remarked sagely.

The second part of her sister's statement sunk in.

"I'm no prophet."

"You're the only one who saw the explosion and you saw it when you were with the people who would be hurt by it."

"Nobody died."

"Remember I saw horses die. And that was before you were told not to ride."

"So when I didn't go riding that changed things?"

"Yes."

"But Yudi went," Jocelyn reasoned. "Why didn't he get hurt?"

"Because you weren't riding him."

"Debi Lu said that it was my fault that he threw her," Jocelyn recalled. "She said that he tried to come to me. Winnie told me that Yudi kept going around in circles. That's why they weren't closer to the explosion. They were all waiting for Debi Lu to get Yudi under control."

"Later, I saw Hubbs die when the horses were being stolen," Aleta. "I didn't see any horses die that time, but somehow I knew that Shadow was going to throw a shoe. All I could think of was to get the two horses that shouldn't be ridden out of the barn. That's why I chose Shadow and Sterling."

"Debi Lu would have taken Sterling if Shadow weren't there. She's so small that she'd chose the smaller horse even though I told them all that his foot wasn't healed. She has no heart. She is so self-centered."

"And Tiffany?"

"She wouldn't have taken Sterling. In fact, she wouldn't have taken Yudi either."

"Just my horse or Stanley's?" Aleta questioned.

"Yeah, I guess she really had the hots for Winnie that day. She wasn't thinking straight."

"That happens."

"I was so angry with her that day. I said some really nasty stuff. How can I even talk to her?"

"Anger doesn't open too many door, but you can start by telling her about Royal."

"I can apologize," Jocelyn offered. "But will her parents even let me see her?"

"Stanley can arrange that."

Jocelyn stood up and spotted Stanley's car.

"He's here!" she shouted, running toward the car.

Aleta rose slowly and found that she felt steady on her feet. She stretched as she watched her sister pleading with her husband. She saw him open his cell while Jocelyn danced around him excitedly.

When he finished, she threw her arms around him and hugged him. Then she rushed into the house to tell Bertha that she needed her to take her to the hospital to see Tiffany right away.

Aleta stepped up her pace.

"Are you ready?" Stanley asked after she had embraced him.

"For what?"

"Our second honeymoon. I told you I'd come home early."

Robert emerged from the house with two picnic baskets, and Bertha followed with a picnic basket.

Stanley opened the car door and held it for Aleta.

"Where are we going?"

"To my mother's birthplace."

"She was born in Chicago?"

"A little south of Chicago."

"How long will it take us to get there?"

"It's getting longer all the time."

Aleta took the hint and got in.

"Why the picnic basket?" she asked.

"So we can eat as we travel."

"We could have a late supper," Aleta suggested.

"I'm hungry now." Stanley said.

"Okay, we eat while we travel. But tomorrow we dine out."

"Anything you want," Stanley said amiably.

"Who's going to watch the house and the dogs and stuff?"

"All taken care of," Stanley said backing down the driveway. "Now sit back and relax and get ready for a nice surprise."

"You're going the wrong way," Aleta said after Stanley turned north.

"Got to pick up the surprise first."

They drove in silence. All thought of scolding him for not understanding what she wanted disappeared. Chicago, at least, represented a trip. He'd had less than a day to plan this. What did she expect? She had to be sure he didn't notice that Chicago wasn't her favorite city. Even so they would have fun. And he'd bought something as well. And he was in court all day. That took some doing. She imagined Alice actually bought the gift; but, he told her what to buy and that counted.

She nestled down inside her cape and her excitement began to rise. They were going somewhere together. That had been all she wanted the first time. It was really all she wanted this time too.

A few minutes later, she sat up in her seat. "Why are we going to the airport?"

"You don't miss a thing, do you?" Stanley smirked.

"Commercial flights don't leave from here."

"Right again."

"Stop it!"

"Stop what?"

"Enjoying yourself," she shot back.

Stanley laughed. "Oh Aleta. Only you would say that!"

He pulled into one of the parking places facing the field.

"Show me the surprise," Aleta demanded.

"You're looking at it."

"All I see is a group of small planes."

"Which one do you like?"

"Why?" Aleta asked, an edge in her tone.

"The surprise is inside."

Aleta looked around. One small plane was sitting apart from the others. It was shiny like a new car right off the showroom floor.

"You bought us an airplane?"

"Like her?"

"She's gorgeous."

"One person can handle her. We can go anywhere we want by ourselves."

"Where are we going?"

"To the place my mother was born."

"Where's that?"

"Let's get our luggage aboard," he said taking out the suitcases.

"Now I understand the picnic basket," Aleta said picking it up as Stanley locked the car. "How did Bertha ever do it?"

"She said you were buried in work."

"When did you talk to her?"

"When you were buried in your work."

"I didn't hear the phone ring."

"She had her cell on vibrate."

"Can we fly after dark?"

"I can."

The two climbed on board and Stanley went up and sat in the pilot's seat. Aleta sat beside him.

"When did you buy it?"

"I planned to have it delivered a month from now. It's a good thing I'm a planner, huh?" Otherwise I couldn't be spontaneous."

"You win!" Aleta gushed happily. "You win big! I give in. Why did you let me be such a pill all day?"

"You weren't a pill all day. You helped Jocelyn. Sadah said you did what she needed. She said I was blessed to have such a woman. Bertha didn't complain. Hubbs didn't complain. You kept your anger focused on me as was appropriate. I was teasing you. You half knew it and half didn't so you were confused. You get angry when you're confused, but it goes away when you're not."

"Someday I'll figure you out and you won't be able to tease me anymore."

"Don't you wish."

"I'm ready. Let's go," Aleta said. "Can I take off this sling? I put it back on when I began using the arm for too much but..."

"You can take off anything you want."

"That, Mr. Praetzel, is a very suggestive remark."

After they were in the air, Stanley said casually, "This plane has an automatic pilot."

"You mean you won't be watching where it's going?"

"Not if you take off your clothes," he grinned.

"I am not crashing naked!" Aleta declared.

Stanley laughed. "Which are you afraid of—dying in a crash or being found naked after we crash?"

"I'm going to see what Bertha packed us," Aleta determined.

Accordingly, she climbed out of her seat and went back to where the picnic basket was. She opened it up. Then she heard Stanley's voice in her ear.

"Looks good."

Aleta whirled around.

"Who's flying the plane?"

"I'm trying out the automatic pilot."

"Without watching to see if it works."

"I don't like watching people fly."

"That's not people. That's a machine."

"That's even duller."

"Stanley, you've gotta go back!"

"Bribe me."

"I'll bring your food to you."

"Topless?"

"You're kidding."

"Do I sound like I'm kidding?"

"I'm really getting nervous," Aleta said. "You're going to insist, aren't you?"

"I'll take the chicken first," he said returning to the pilot's seat. "And, yes, I am going to insist."

"For heaven's sake, Stanley! You're the one who believes in privacy."

"Do you see anyone else around?"

"That's not the point."

"Well, counselor, you better make a better argument than that if you want to keep the rest of your clothes on."

"You're kidding, aren't you?"

"Where's my chicken. You don't want me to come get it do you?"

"Okay, you win. You just stay in that seat," Aleta said. "I can see this is going to be a wild second honeymoon. Whoever heard of a woman half-naked in a plane serving a meal?"

"Every man's fantasy," Stanley called back.

"What's good for the goose is good for the gander," Aleta said.

"You win that one. You get to put your blouse back on."

"Oh no you don't!" Aleta said. "I win. I get to tell you what to take off."

"Okay, coat, shirt, what?"

"Briefs," Aleta said.

"There's a reason they're called underwear."

"So they are," Aleta smirked. "But that's my choice."

"You minx, you. You know I won't wear pants without briefs."

Aleta grinned. "That's your choice."

"You win. I concede," Stanley said.

"I want your promise you won't leave that seat until after we land. Then I'll accept your concession."

"Yes, Ma'am," Stanley said. "You've got your promise. I can't believe I lost."

"You didn't really lose. You have a half-naked woman serving you dinner."

"There is that," Stanley said. "You are going to get dressed before we land, aren't you?"

Aleta fetched him another piece of chicken.

"Well, aren't you?" he asked as he took it.

"I'm still thinking."

"This is payback, isn't it?" Stanley said.

"Relax. No one should be half-dressed in public," Aleta said as she went back to the basket. "Bertha put in cups of potato salad. It's fresh and cold. It looks great. That's my next choice."

"Sounds great."

"Got to find the spoons... Just a minute... Got 'em."

She handed Stanley a cup and spoon. He noticed she hadn't put her blouse back on when she leaned over from behind his seat.

"Glad you left it off," he commented as he took the cup.

"Thought you would be," Aleta giggled. "As I said no one should be half-naked, so I went the rest of the way."

"And you remember what I said," Stanley countered.

"I remember your promise," she reminded him.

Stanley groaned loudly.

"Aleta, you are a bigger tease than I could ever be!"

"As I said, we're off to a wild start."

"This plane ride is going to be way too long," Stanley sighed.

"Let me finish my potato salad and I'll take care of you," Aleta said softly. "You deserve a reward."

An hour later they landed in Atlanta.

When the plane came to a stop, he kissed her. "Remind me never to tease you again."

"You didn't like your reward?"

"I'm glad the automatic pilot was in good working order."

"You mean you didn't trust it?"

"I mean I didn't expect you to trust it."

Chapter 7

That night Sadah answered the phone and a shiver crawled down her spine when she heard the oily baritone voice.

"You didn't report," he accused.

"I couldn't," she replied, her voice trembling. "I couldn't stay after Alice locked up. I had to buy groceries on the way home. By the time I got home, I thought you'd be gone."

As she talked, her voice gained confidence. Her fear began to seep away. She hadn't told on him and Aleta had made it impossible for her to know anything.

"What's going on?"

"Nothing," she said.

"That's a lie! You said she hired an investigator. He must have given her a preliminary report."

"I won't know anything from now on."

"What does that mean?" he asked angrily.

"She knows someone is asking questions."

"You told her about me?" he snarled.

"She guessed. Or someone else told her. But I would not give her your name so she said she would no longer keep me informed."

"Did you fire her?"

"No."

"Why not?"

"She's going to help my husband."

"I told you I would help find someone else."

"A bird in the hand," Sadah recited. "Do you know that saying? It applies here."

"She is full of empty promises and you will wait in vain."

"We shook hands."

"What does that mean?"

"It is an honor thing. You wouldn't understand."

"Are you calling me dishonorable?"

"No," Sadah replied. "But you are a man."

Partly mollified, Eugene Powell pressed Sadah for the name of the investigator.

"Mrs. Praetzel said you may ask her personally about the case."

"I can't do that," Powell said.

Clever move on her part, he thought. There's no way I'm making it easy for her.

"You mean because she's in Georgia?" Sadah said innocently.

Powell recovered quickly.'

"Yes, because she's there," he agreed heartily. "What I don't know is how long she will be away."

"At least three days. Maybe more."

"Do you know where she's staying?"

"No."

"Can her secretary get a message to her?"

"Maybe on Monday," Sadah said.

"It's important I know where to reach her," Powell said. He had submitted the affidavit along with his recommendation that Aleta Praetzel be denied admission to the bar on the basis that she'd violated the rules. He thought when she'd refused to even speak with Sadah Aloman, he wouldn't be able to catch her in the infraction; but, evidently she believed passing the bar was enough. Professor Burrows must have assured her that she would make it through the committee review. Why else would she act as if she were already admitted? Maybe she thought that preparation on this case didn't count. Maybe she thought that no one would know she'd even taken the case until she appeared in court after being sworn in. The fact that she'd taken no money would have made the violation hard to prove; however, the affidavit from Sadah Aloman sealed her fate.

But Powell wasn't satisfied. He wanted proof that she was actively working on the case.

What the hell was she doing in Georgia?

He tried a new test. "She doesn't seem to be working hard on your case. First thing she does is take time off."

"You would too if you'd just been healed miraculously," Sadah shot back. "She wanted to celebrate. I would have too. I would have taken more than three or four days."

"Healed miraculously?" Powell scoffed. "So she's mesmerized you too."

"What's mesmerized?" Sadah asked.

"Hypnotized. Persuaded you that something is real that isn't."

"Her husband thought it was real. He is not a man easily mesmerized."

"He goes along with her fantasies. He has to. He's married to her."

"The doctors took pictures. Her broken skull is good as new they said."

"Fractures heal."

"I know bones heal. But her head was not healed a couple days before. And now it is healed. It is too fast except for a miracle."

"You believe what you want; but, I can't afford to believe in fairy tales," Powell said his tone laced with derision.

Sadah stayed silent.

"How long did she refuse to even see you?" he lashed out bitterly. "And suddenly you're her best friend. She's using psychology to get you to believe whatever she tells you. She's a snake who'll turn and bite you."

"You are the snake," Sadah blurted out. "Not her."

"You foolish woman. You are putting your faith in the wrong person," Powell ranted his rage taking over his reason. "She's not even going to be admitted to the bar. I'm on the committee that's going to reject her. Your affidavit put the final nail in her coffin."

"Mine?" Sadah stammered. "But it's wrong."

"Too late to take back," Powell said.

"She's legal!" Sadah spouted angrily. "It's you that will look the fool!"

She slammed the receiver down and yanked the plug from the wall. Then she slowly sank down her back against the wall until she was sitting on the floor. She began to cry.

Basil found her there and when he couldn't calm her, he called their priest.

Eugene Powell called his partner.

"The bitch told Sadah she was legal," he shared. "What am I missing?"

"Maybe she was lying," Melvin Hillers replied his tongue thick from the effects of his Friday night indulgence.

"Have you been drinking?"

"It's Friday. No court tomorrow," he responded. "I'm not completely incontinent... incoher... soused, but pretty much."

"I need your help, Melvin. I put in the damn report."

"Told ya to check it out," he stumbled.

"She doesn't lie," Powell said.

"Then she's telling the... telling the..."

Truth," Powell finished. His voice took on a note of desperation. "What do I do?"

"Hope she dies, I guess," Hillers chuckled. "Otherwise you're screwed."

"A lot of help you are."

"You're welcome. Can I go now?"

Powell hung up his phone and called his aide into his office.

"Do we know anyone that does elimination work?"

"We might. Are we talking temporary or permanent work?"

"Permanent."

"I know someone who can find someone; but, it'll be expensive."

"I'll pay it if he's good."

"How soon do you need the job done?"

"Next three days. In Atlanta."

"I'll set up a meet tonight."

In a suite in one of Atlanta's finest hotels, Aleta sat down on the edge of the bed and asked Stanley to undress her. He was half finished when she announced that she wanted him to call room service and order ice cream and a pickle.

"Now?" he queried.

"With whipped cream."

"Anything else?"

"Two flavors."

A banana or nuts or chocolate sauce?"

"Sure all of it," she said. "While we're waiting you can give me my bath."

"Logistically, that's not feasible," he said.

"You could get your clothes wet for once."

"No, I can't. I have a limited wardrobe with me."

"Use a robe to answer the door," she suggested. "It's done all the time."

"Not by me," Stanley declared firmly.

"Okay. First my bath, then we fool around which we are sure to do even if it's not on the program, then you call room service."

"Logistically, that'll work."

After he completed the task of undressing Aleta, carefully folded each garment and stacked it neatly on a chair, Stanley proceeded to undress himself while Aleta lay on the bed and watched. She had come to like his methodical precision in this simple act. And although she didn't ever consider it foreplay previously, this quiet night, it dawned on her that this procedure excited her.

His clothes neatly folded, he scooped her up and carried her into the bathroom. The tub was nearly full when he lowered her in. The temperature was perfect as usual.

The man knew how to draw a bath, she thought. And he knows how to give one.

Afterward he toweled her dry and carried her back to bed. The joining happened soon afterward.

Just as they were coming to climax, she said. "We must stop!"

Startled, he paused. "Stop? Why? Is it the baby?"

She wiggled out from under him, ran to the chair and picked up his stack of clothes. Bewildered, he lay immobile as she did this.

"Hurry!" she said. "Go into the bathroom. Finish up. Get dressed and don't come out until I call."

"Aleta, what's going on?"

"Do as I say and we both live," she said firmly.

"I can't leave you alone!" he cried desperately. "You have no weapon."

"One will be provided," she replied. "I will make it up to you if we survive."

"Survive? Who's coming to kill us?"

"I'm only getting this vision because you're going to die naked. It'll make the papers. Go!"

Stanley took his clothes and went into the bathroom.

"Don't open that door until I call!" she reiterated, slamming the door shut.

A knock on the hall door brought Aleta toward it. She glanced at the robe on the chair in the far corner. Getting Stanley into the bathroom took longer than she expected. He wouldn't stay there long. She had to do this quick.

"Room Service," called the voice outside.

Aleta opened the door and stood half hidden behind it.

"We didn't order any room service," she said.

"Compliments of the management. It comes with the Honeymoon Suite."

"Well, bring it in," Aleta said as she opened the door wider.

The man began to roll the cart in. When his arm was opposite the edge of the door, Aleta slammed it hard into his arm. The gun slipped onto the floor.

Aleta kicked it away with her bare foot. He dove for it. Aleta was quicker. His hand closed on her leg. He looked up the leg and was momentarily startled at the sight of the completely naked body. His hesitation lasted a fraction of a second. Aleta squeezed the trigger in that brief moment and caught him in the shoulder.

"Stanley!" she yelled. "Now!"

Half-dressed Stanley raced into the room.

"Take this," she said, handing him the gun. "If he moves, shoot him."

She looked at her husband. "Glad you broke precedent."

Stanley knew what she meant. He never put his pants on before his shirt.

"Don't watch me," she said. "I'll give you a show later."

She pulled on her pants and felt her cell in the pocket. She opened it and dialed one, Stanley's office. She listened. When she heard the answering machine come on she set the phone on the night stand open.

"You heard the lady," Stanley warned the man on the floor. "I get to shoot you if you twitch."

The man moved his arm anyway. A second shot rang out. The man screamed in pain.

"You freaking asshole. You shot my other arm."

"You only get one warning," Stanley growled. "Aleta are you decent. We have company."

Aleta rushed to the door holding her blouse shut.

"Call the management! Call the police!" she ordered the gathering crowd.

"They shot Room Service," someone said.

"Did anyone make those calls?" Aleta asked.

"I called the police," a man said.

"Thank you," Aleta said. "Knock when they arrive."

Before anyone could protest, she shut the door.

"Stanley, give me back the gun," she ordered.

"Why?"

"So you can search him. You don't think I'm going to put my hand where he's got that extra piece stashed, do you?"

"There?" Stanley questioned, dismayed.

"Yep."

"I don't want to search there either."

"You want to get shot?" Aleta said then added. "Never mind. Let's put it another way. Do you want me to be shot again?"

"Shit!" Stanley said as he reached down the man's pants. "Aleta, there better be... Never mind. I've got it."

"How'd she know?"

"Too bad your boss didn't give you all the facts when he hired you."

"Who says I was hired? I wasn't gonna kill you. I was just gonna rob you."

"That's your story?" Stanley asked.

"So what have we got him on?"

"Attempted armed robbery. Armed assault. Concealed weapon."

"She assaulted me!" the man said.

"I don't like that!" Aleta said. "Puts me in a bad light."

"I say we shoot him dead," Stanley said.

"You ain't serious," the man on the floor said.

"Self-defense," Stanley said. "And then we won't ever have to worry about him coming at us again."

"It won't work. Everybody knows I was alive when you shut the door," the man argued. What was with these two?"

"What's our story?" Aleta asked.

"Easy. He came at us with that second gun."

"Sounds good to me," Aleta said coolly. "You want me to do it?"

"Hey! Let's think about this," the man on the floor begged.

It suddenly occurred to him they could get away with such a story.

"You want money?" the man posed desperation riding on his words.

"How much?" Aleta asked.

"Twenty-five grand," he offered hastily. "It's what I was paid."

"That's all I'm worth?"

She sounded disgusted.

"That's all I got up front," the men explained hurriedly. "I was to get the other half when I finished the job. Ten grand extra if I had to do your husband."

"He's not going to testify," Aleta said calmly as if stating a fact.

"He can't afford to," Stanley returned. "His boss would kill him."

"He's going to stick with that dumb ass story that he came to rob us. If we kill him, we can say he came to kill us. I like that better."

"That's because it's the truth and not some bullshit lie," Stanley said.

"What do you want?" the would-be killer asked.

"What do we want, Aleta?"

"He's got nothing I want."

"The guy you want is from the windy city," their attacker spit out.

"Chicago?" Aleta asked.

"Windy city is all I know."

"Did he tell you why he wanted me killed?" Aleta asked.

"Nobody told me nothing."

"That's a double negative," Aleta observed. "That means someone told you something."

"I was told you couldn't return to Illinois except in a body bag," he spit out. "You must really have pissed someone off."

Aleta put the gun on the bed beside the other one and said, "Open the door, Stanley. The police are here."

As the police entered, guns drawn, Aleta said, "The man on the floor needs an ambulance. I shot him."

"And so did I," Stanley said. "His guns are on the bed. We have no guns. We used his."

"They're lying," the man on the floor said. "They shot me for no reason."

"I warned you," Aleta said. Then she turned to Stanley. "Didn't I warn him to tell the truth or else?"

"The hell with you!" the man said. "You shot me for no reason."

"Call a homicide detective," Aleta said. "On the floor in front of you is the man who shot Al Perrillo and on the bed is the gun he used to do it."

"She's...," the man started.

Aleta eyed him coldly. "Are we testing me?"

The man collapsed. "No. I'm done. I want a lawyer."

Several hours later, settled in their new suite, ice cream sundaes were delivered to their room by the manager himself. On the side were two pickles—one dill, one sweet.

"The pickles are all yours," Stanley commented.

"No one but you knows we're here?" Aleta asked, desperately needing reassurance.

"No one," the manager assured them. "Thank you again for not suing us. And thank you for apprehending him before he killed anyone here."

"Can we use your limousine service to take us to the airport?" Stanley asked.

"He can take you anywhere you want to go. He's yours for the day."

"Show me your mother's old house," Aleta begged.

"I imagine we'll be safe long enough to do that."

"Stay in this room as long as you like," the manager said as he left.

"Have you settled back into a honeymoon mood yet?" Stanley asked as he took a spoonful of ice cream.

"I'm sorry," Aleta said nibbling on a pickle.

"It's okay. I'm still edgy too."

"I'm so sorry to keep bringing danger home. I have no idea what I did."

"It must have something to do with your current case."

"I don't even know anything yet."

"Why did you tell Alice to tell me not to talk with Sadah?"

"Who knew we were coming here?" Aleta asked, her mind on another tract.

"Alice. She made the reservations."

"She wouldn't tell anyone," Aleta concluded. "But Sadah is in my office, and they keep the door open."

"Who would Sadah tell?" Stanley asked.

"She wouldn't tell me who her backers were," Aleta said, "but she asked a lot of questions about whether I was legally able to represent her. And she asked me what pro bono was."

"Why wasn't I supposed to talk with her?"

"When she wouldn't tell me who her backers were, and she told me she would continue to update them, I told her I was cutting off all information about the case. And she thanked me."

"She thanked you?" he reiterated as a query.

"And we shook hands on it."

"What did you make of that reaction?"

"She was being pressured and my ruling relieved the pressure."

"That's my take too."

"Ed told me to check on her backer and I know he didn't mean Martha," Aleta put in. "He was suspicious."

"The trail stops with Martha," Stanley said.

"She trusted the person who told her about Sadah," Aleta said. "No one approaches Martha directly."

"Sadah must have been in direct contact with the man who ordered the hit," Stanley concluded.

"It happened too fast for any other explanation," Aleta agreed.

"Let's go to sleep. If the answer is in our minds somewhere, it will emerge in its own time. If it's not, we wait until we're back home and ask questions."

"I'm cold," Aleta said. She began to shiver.

"You're in shock," Stanley decided. "I need to warm you fast."

He hurried into the bathroom and turned on the water in the tub. He came back and carried Aleta into the bathroom. It was warm. Stanley had turned on the heat lamp. He peeled off Aleta's clothes and dropped them on the floor. Her eyes closed. Gently, he lowered her into the tub.

Her clothes lay in a heap on the floor. As he held her in the tub while the warm water rushed in, he removed his clothes and dropped them on top of hers.

Then he climbed into the tub with her. The water spilled over the edge and he turned off the faucet. The clothes heaped on the floor soaked up the overflow as Stanley lowered himself so that she was sitting on his lap. He put his arms around her and held her close.

Slowly he felt her body warming inside his embrace. She stirred and opened her eyes.

"Are we taking a bath?" she asked.

"We're warming you up," he replied. "You got cold."

She looked over the edge of the tub and gasped when she saw the tangle of wet clothes.

"You got very cold," Stanley said.

"Is your wallet in the pocket of those trousers?"

"I imagine it is."

"We'll have to hang the money up to dry," she noted.

"Your cell phone is in your pants pocket."

"It served its purpose," she said without emotion.

"What purpose?"

"I called your office. We should have everything that was said on tape."

"So that's what we were doing?" Stanley queried. "We said some stupid things."

"I wanted him to tell us who hired the hit."

"So did I," Stanley said. "But no one can listen to that tape."

"We'll get my father to retrieve it," Aleta said.

"I'll call as soon as we get out and dry ourselves."

"We dry the money first!" Aleta said.

The two wound up in the bed without the money being hung up to dry. After they were done, they fell asleep wrapped in each other's arms and didn't awaken until the sunlight streamed in the large window.

"We're still joined," Aleta murmured.

"I know. I woke earlier and...," he paused.

Aleta giggled. "How long before I woke up?"

"A few seconds."

"That long, huh?"

"Shall I stop?"

"Not unless you ordered room service."

"I didn't."

"Good, because our money's all wet."

"You sure woke up in a comic mood."

"I think I'm embarrassed, but I don't know why."

"We can get dressed and start our day," Stanley suggested.

"We've started it," Aleta said. "I rather like the beginning. And the manager said we could stay as long as we like."

"This might take a while."

"Oh, no it won't," Aleta giggled.

Stanley paused. Aleta giggled when she was upset.

"What you did was okay," he stated.

"The robe was so far away."

"I know."

"I was afraid there wasn't time."

"I know."

"I didn't even try."

"You chose well."

"You don't think I'm a..."

"I don't think anything negative about what you did. If it were me, I'd have gone for the robe and we'd both be dead. I am so proud of you!"

"Proud?" she asked, surprise in her tone. "Stanley, I was naked."

"I know," he repeated. "Proud is how I feel. Now are you done beating yourself up over nothing that matters?"

"It does matter!" she protested.

He kissed her tenderly. Slowly, she realized that while his kiss should have been passionate considering the position of their bodies, it wasn't. Passion came from the loins; tenderness from the heart. Ever so gradually, she started to feel forgiven.

"I love you," she whispered during a pause.

"I know," he said and this time his kiss was passionate.

Just as their lovemaking approached a climax she shouted, "I've got it!"

"Not again," he moaned, pausing.

"Don't stop!" she cried.

Afterward, when they lay side by side, Stanley said, "If God keeps interrupting us, we'll never have that second baby."

"It wasn't God. It was me. I thought of something."

"That was no time to be thinking—about anything," Stanley grumbled good-naturedly. "Well, spill it. What world-shaking thought entered that brain of yours?"

"Our attacker said the man was from the windy city. That's Chicago."

"So what?"

"As far as we know neither Frank nor Sergio are mad at me. Isn't Eugene Powell's law office in Chicago?"

"That doesn't prove anything."

"It's a piece of the puzzle. Our first piece. It's a start," Aleta said. "As far as I know I only have one enemy in Illinois—Eugene Powell."

"I don't understand," Stanley said. "What's his motive?"

"My cell phone's on the bathroom floor," Aleta said. "I'll get it. There are some things in there that'll turn your stomach."

"Thanks," Stanley murmured.

Aleta took the pieces of soaked clothes and dropped them into the tub, emptying pockets as she did so. She put the wet wallet and his ring of keys on the counter. She tossed him her phone, saying, "The bathroom's a mess. It's really unusable."

"Bertha packed my electric razor. I'll use it," he said as he opened the phone and punched in his home number.

"Bertha, it's Stanley. Is Robert there?"

A second later, he heard his father-in-law say hello.

"Robert, we were attacked last night and..."

He burst in. "Is Aleta okay?"

"Aleta's fine. So am I. But this is important. Aleta linked this cell phone to my answering machine in the office. I don't know how much of what happened made it onto the tape, but we need you to get the tape and get it to Ed. If he's not back, have Dean do his magic with it."

"I'm on my way. Where are you?"

"Still in Atlanta. We're leaving this morning."

"To where?"

"Even I don't know yet. But I'm getting Aleta out of harm's way."

"Tell him to let Lyle hear the tape," Aleta called from the bathroom.

"I heard that," her father said. "Is the attacker in custody?"

"He is, but he won't talk. Tell Lyle that Sadah Aloman holds the key. She told someone where we were going. If it wasn't her it was Alice. They were the only two that knew besides... Good God."

"Besides who?"

"My mother," Stanley said. "I asked her what places we should visit. Where we were going wasn't a secret except from Aleta."

"Who do you suspect?" Robert asked. He knew Stanley and Aleta would have narrowed the field.

"Eugene Powell."

"He does hate Aleta," Robert said, "but kill her? That's pretty extreme."

"We don't understand it either. Tell Lyle to keep an open mind."

"Keep my little girl safe. Please!"

"I'll try."

When he hung up, Aleta said, "Call the manager. We need his help. We need cash. We can't use our cards. We need breakfast and we need these clothes cleaned."

"We can't wait for that."

"He can arrange to send them home. We can buy new ones wherever we land. And we aren't going to visit your mother's old house. She might have told someone we were going to visit the home she grew up in."

An hour and a half later, they were in the air.

"You filed four flight plans," Aleta said. "Where are we going?"

"You pick."

"A year ago I would have said New Orleans, but today I guess I'd pick Miami."

"We're going to Orlando."

"Why did you have me pick?"

"Because I wanted to see if it was a good red herring."

"Why Orlando?"

"Lots of tourists in Orlando. We can get lost in that city," Stanley said. "And there's lots to do or we can just stay in the hotel and order room service."

"No room service!" she declared.

Stanley laughed. "Not ever?"

Aleta thought for a moment.

"Give me until tonight when I'll want pickles and ice cream again."

Chapter 8

Jocelyn and Bertha were met by Tiffany's parents in the hall outside her room. Mrs. Patson eyed Bertha, dressed in her housekeeper's uniform, with disdain. Both Jocelyn and Bertha noted her scowl of disapproval.

Jocelyn apologized, "I'm sorry my dad couldn't come at the last minute. This is Bertha Carlson, soon to be Bertha Locke and my new mother."

"Your housekeeper?" Mrs. Patson said scornfully.

"My sister's housekeeper, but I live with her because my dad's RV is too small and he says it wouldn't be proper for me not to have my own room. She's housesitting my sister's place but I knew Aleta wouldn't mind if I borrowed her."

Bertha took a modicum of pleasure in Mrs. Patson's dismay that Jocelyn seemed to be unaware that she, Tiffany Patson's mother, was holding Bertha in contempt.

"I'll just wait out here," Bertha said politely.

"No you won't," Jocelyn countered. "I want Tiffany to meet you. I talk about you all the time."

"She is doing the proper thing," Mrs. Patson said with surety.

"But she's not really here as a servant. She's here as my mother."

"But she's not," Mrs. Patson said decisively.

"I don't want to create a problem," Bertha said quietly. "I'll wait here. You go on in."

Mrs. Patson was a bit taken aback by the housekeeper's tone. Quiet as it was, the words were delivered with authority.

"Yes, Ma'am," Jocelyn said politely.

This surprised Mrs. Patson even more. Tiffany never treated her with such deference.

Jocelyn entered and Tiffany's parents followed her into her daughter's room.

"I'm sorry about what I said," Jocelyn started. "I didn't know you were hurt this bad. I thought you'd just sprained an ankle or something. I didn't mean what I said about your horse either."

"We were wrong," Tiffany said. "I would have been mad too if someone took Royal out of his stall and rode him."

"And you'd have good reason," Jocelyn went on. "Royal Wedding is a great horse."

"Yudi is a good horse. You're going to do a lot of winning with him," Tiffany returned.

"I'm afraid not," Jocelyn said, her voice picking up regretful tones. "I have to retire him."

"No!" Tiffany breathed.

"He was already on the edge. I could never be sure when he'd come through for me and when he'd balk at the first jump. The explosion set him back."

"But you have a trainer."

"Aleta and Hubbs agree. He's done as a show jumper. So we've retired him."

"You're going to sell him?"

"Oh, no. He loves the farm and Aleta says he can stay. We have Jezebel and Sterling there now. What's one more retired horse?"

"So what are you going to do?"

"Try to find Royal Wedding's twin," Jocelyn said wistfully.

"You want him?" Tiffany asked.

"If he's for sale, I'd buy him in a heartbeat."

"He's yours," Tiffany said. "You'll take good care of him I know."

"But he's your horse," Jocelyn protested.

"The doctor said I won't ride for a long, long time. Mom and Dad have been telling me I should sell him, but I told them I loved him too much to let him go."

"Why to me?" Jocelyn said.

"Because when you talked about him your face lit up the way it always does when you talk about Yudi."

Mrs. Patson interrupted. "I don't think this will be the most beneficial sale."

Tiffany eyed her mother with contempt. "Jocelyn will pay a fair price; but, more important Jocelyn doesn't discard a horse because something goes wrong."

"He threw you!" her mother lashed out.

"And I'm in a hospital bed," Tiffany shot back. "That fact is not something I've forgotten. But you seem to have forgotten there was an explosion. Kevin's horse threw him too. You don't see him getting rid of his horse."

"He only had the wind knocked out of him," her mother countered angrily.

"So his foot didn't catch in his stirrup," Tiffany shot back. "He was lucky. I wasn't."

"Well, he should get rid of that horse too," Mrs. Patson declared adamantly.

"These horses are not used to grenades going off right in front of their noses, Mrs. Patson," Jocelyn explained.

"Your brother-in-law's horse didn't rear."

"Minx is an exceptionally calm horse," Jocelyn explained.

"That's the kind of horse you should have, Tiffany!" Mrs. Patson said, still irked.

"Minx isn't a jumper," Jocelyn said. "Tiffany is a competitor."

"Not anymore she's not," her mother said. "You think we want a daughter with anymore disfigurements? It's bad enough that leg will never tan evenly and that she'll have to wear slacks the rest of her life but this is where the injuries stop."

"You sound just like my mother!" Jocelyn said angrily.

"That housekeeper? Never!"

"Not her. She'd never say such mean things to a daughter who's been hurt like yours. Bertha would say that the leg didn't matter, that life was what mattered."

"A common woman like her wouldn't understand," Mrs. Patson spit out.

"That's what I keep saying to her," Jocelyn stated.

Mrs. Patson interjected. "So you do understand."

"I understand what love is. Things happen that leave scars. The scars on Tiffany's leg won't be really as hard to live with as the scars caused by your attitude!"

"You can leave now!" Mrs. Patson said.

"No!" Tiffany said. "She stays. Dad, take Mother out of here."

Mr. Patson put his hand on his wife's elbow and guided her out of the room. "You and she are upset. Let's go get a cup of coffee."

"I do love her," his wife murmured. "I don't want her hurt again."

"Neither do I," he agreed.

As they passed Bertha, Mr. Patson said, "Go on in."

Bertha, who'd heard every word, went in. She walked over to the bed and introduced herself. "I just wanted to tell Jocelyn she can stay as long as she wants. I am sorry you are so badly hurt."

"Can Jocelyn afford my horse?" Tiffany asked. "My mother will ask full price. I know her."

Bertha smiled. "Her sister's paying for it. She can afford it. And he's worth every cent. Mr. Hubbs says he's an exceptionally fine animal."

"He is that."

"I'm surprised you want to sell him," Bertha remarked.

"I don't. My mother does. And if I don't do it, she'll do it behind my back. Your coming here was an answer to my prayers."

"That's me!" Jocelyn joshed. "An answer to prayer."

"It's not like I pray or anything," Tiffany hastened to explain. "Mother had this minister come see me after we fought over selling Royal. This isn't our first fight. Boy, was I ever glad she couldn't get her hands on that horse!"

"That was Stanley's idea. He thought we should all cool down." Jocelyn explained.

Tiffany went on. "I asked him to pray for me—you know— pray that my mother wouldn't sell my horse and he said that he didn't pray about stuff like that. I thought that was his job."

"So did you pray?"

"Well, no I didn't really. I didn't really know how. But here you are, so I figure God filled in the words."

"That's exactly what He does," Bertha said. "He reads the heart."

"So how come you're here?" Tiffany asked Jocelyn.

"Aleta told me to come and buy your horse."

"She likes my horse?"

"She says he's a step up from Yudi," Jocelyn confided. "But you and I know he is, don't we?"

"Don't tell my mother. She'll mess up the deal somehow," Tiffany said.

"I'm going for some coffee," Bertha announced. "Do either of you want a drink?"

"Sure," they chorused and Bertha left.

"I need to ask you if you know about Debi Lu suing my father."

"Kevin plans to back her. He says your warning wasn't strong enough," Tiffany reported. "That's not true. It was plenty strong, but I wanted Winnie to ride with us."

"What is Winnie planning to do?"

"Lisa said Winnie isn't talking to anyone in the group. I think his parents told him to stay away from all of us," Tiffany replied. "You know he hasn't even sent a card. I don't know what I saw in him. I only went because I wanted him to have a horse."

"How about the others?"

"Perry sent me those flowers. Wade sent me that miniature horse over there and a nice card. Wanda sent me candy—my favorite. And Lisa calls and lets me know what is happening in school," Tiffany related. "You're my first visitor."

"I'll come again," Jocelyn promised.

"Tell me. Do you think I'll never be able to wear shorts?"

"You've got great thighs. I'd go for a bikini. Nobody will even look at your ankles then."

Tiffany giggled. "I've got one my mother's never seen. I hope it fits this summer."

"Wear it anyway. Bikinis aren't supposed to fit!"

"If it doesn't fit me, you can have it."

"My dad would have a fit!" Jocelyn giggled.

"Yes, he would," Bertha said, walking in with two cola cans and a paper cup of coffee.

"Are you going to tell him?" Jocelyn asked.

"That you're talking about stuff all girls talk about? Why should I? He'd have a fit."

Tiffany and Jocelyn giggled as they opened their cans.

"She's a nurse," Jocelyn said. "She can answer some of our questions about you know what."

"But she's practically your mother," Tiffany objected.

"She won't tell your folks, will you, Bertha?"

"Not if you ask me not to."

Then the questions came pouring out. Bertha answered each with objectivity.

After the two were finished with their questions and Bertha made a pact with the two, Jocelyn said, "I want someone to love me the way Dad loves you."

"Someday that'll happen for both of you."

The talk came to an abrupt halt when Mrs. Patson entered the room and said bluntly, "I hope you haven't been telling Tiffany that she should consider jumping again."

"No, Ma'am, I didn't," Bertha said politely. "I'll be outside, Jocelyn."

"I decided on a price for my horse, Mother," Tiffany said.

Her mother's attention was immediately diverted. "Without consulting me?"

"Do you want to talk about it now?" Tiffany asked.

"When we're alone," her mother said.

"I'll come back and visit tomorrow," Jocelyn said, getting up.

"Are you going to see Debi Lu?"

"Never!"

"I talked her into it, you know," Tiffany confessed. "Not borrowing Yudi, but Shadow."

"Tiffany, be quiet!" her mother ordered.

"Don't worry, Mrs. Patson," Jocelyn said. "She's not telling me anything I don't know. Tiffany has always been the leader of our group."

"Really?" Mrs. Patson responded with a touch of pride.

Jocelyn winked at Tiffany and walked out.

Chapter 9

Outside the city limits of both Arborville and Willow Glen, Ed Ornstein had taken over an old house kiddie-corner behind the tavern that was located next to the firehouse. The exterior of the house, which sat alone on the short side street, was deceptively dilapidated. He'd hired a couple of Cook Construction contractors to shore up the floor, restructure the supports holding up the roof and reroof the building with a dull gray tile that looked old even though it was new. Then he refurbished the whole interior.

He left the outside pretty much alone—gray clapboard siding, dirty windows whose green painted window frames were scarred and chipped. The porch slanted and the railing appeared broken, but it was solid. Weeds sent up tall thin shoots in the spring which dried out in the summer's heat and stood guard from the broken front picket fence to the edge of the porch.

Inside the plumbing was new as was the electrical wiring. A sprinkler system had been installed to protect Ed's massive electrical equipment conglomeration. The walls were insulated and the big workroom enjoyed a constant temperature.

Alan Peets, Oakwood's newest police chief, was the last to arrive. A tall black man, he had a commanding presence.

"Okay, someone tell me why I'm here," he demanded. "Aleta Praetzel lives in Tom's town."

"Oh come off it, Alan," Lyle West said. "We haven't had anything happening in a month. You know you want to be in on the beginning of anything major."

"Aleta's got people after her again?"

"She was attacked in Atlanta."

"What was she doing there?" Peets blurted out.

"Honeymoon," her father said.

"She didn't have one?" Peets asked.

"Second honeymoon," Lyle said. "To celebrate her recovery."

"My wife better not hear about this," Peets said. "Or she'll want one."

"Lauren's already made me promise her one this year," Lyle said.

"Rachael did too," Tom Milani chimed in. "So you'll get no sympathy from us."

Dean turned up the speaker and the three chiefs, Aleta's father and Stanley's father listened in stunned silence.

When the tape was done, Robert took Hubert Praetzel to one side. "Did they break the law?"

"He could say they did and if his attorney ever got hold of this tape, he might have a case," Hubert said somberly. "They tread a mighty thin line."

"There were extenuating circumstances."

"They deliberately toyed with him," Hubert said. "I can't believe Stanley said some of those things with a tape running."

"Maybe he didn't know he was being taped," Aleta's father said.

"Then it would be inadmissible."

"Maybe that's the point. Maybe Aleta just wanted it to be heard by this group who would then have clues to help them figure out who was behind the hitter," Robert said.

"Only Stanley said he and Aleta knew who was behind the attack."

"And who is that?" Lyle asked.

Immediately both fathers realized that although their conversation had been in low tones, the room had fallen silent when they began consulting one another.

Robert looked around. Dean Lundgren was absent.

"Eugene Powell," Robert replied.

"The committee member?" Peets burst out.

"She called him racist in the committee meeting," Robert Locke explained for the benefit of the others. "And it riled him, but I can't believe he'd do this. Another committee is going to review Aleta's qualifications. Why move on her now?"

"He's a politician," Peets said. "What she said in a closed hearing won't hurt him. Even if it slips out, he'd slide around it somehow."

"I've never heard him called that before," Hubert commented. "Surely if it were true his political enemies would have pointed it out."

"She must have found some proof," Robert stated with conviction. "She would never say that unless she could prove it."

"What if she can prove it?" Peets asked.

"Powell would be in trouble," Hubert said, "but she can't do it at the committee hearing. And afterwards it would sound like sour grapes. She has to prove it before."

"There's no time," Peets said.

"What do you mean?" Lyle asked. "None of us have been called as character witnesses yet. The committee gives ample notice when it requires such an appearance."

"Alan," Tom Milani said quietly, "what do you know that we don't?"

"I misspoke," Peets said.

"You have a source," Tom said.

"It's okay to have a friend who tells you things," Lyle said. "We all have those. Just tell us what's going to happen before the five member committee meets."

"I'm sorry," Peets said.

"Okay," Lyle said. "We can get at this another way. We know Aleta has an enemy. She told us this. If he wanted to prevent her from being admitted to the bar what paths are open to him? Mr. Praetzel, help us out here."

"The five man committee is her next hurdle," Hubert said.

"What would take her out before the committee meets," Tom said, "besides committing a felony."

"Breaking any rules laid down for anyone not yet admitted to the bar," Hubert said. "Taking a case would do it."

"Everyone here knows Aleta has a new case, don't they?" Robert Locke questioned.

"Since when?"

"The day after she took the bar."

"But she hasn't been sworn in yet," Lyle said.

"She's representing an employee of the Tontine," Robert said. "She's legal."

"How does that make her legal?" Peets asked.

Robert explained it clearly and concisely and added. "Stanley was already an Illinois attorney but Aleta wasn't. She had to apply. She did that when she first came from California. Until she was accepted, she worked under Stanley."

"I didn't know the Tontine had any employees except for Aleta and Stanley," Lyle said.

"Sadah Aloman was hired as a bookkeeper for the Tontine the day before Aleta interviewed her," Robert replied.

"Where's her office?"

"She has Aleta's office temporarily. Aleta is using Stanley's study. The Tontine has rented the empty office next door to their suite. It's being refurbished."

"Sounds okay," Hubert said. "Is this person a qualified bookkeeper?"

"Aleta told me she has a degree in accounting and economics from Chicago University."

"Why did she take such a low level job?" Lyle asked.

"She hasn't worked in years. She's been a stay-at-home mom." Robert told the group. "After her husband was arrested, she couldn't get work."

"I'm satisfied it's legitimate," Hubert said. "It makes sense for Harriet to hire someone to help her now that she's married."

"But maybe Mr. Powell doesn't know what we know," Chief Milani said.

"If he thinks she broke the law," Peets asked, "why not have her arrested?"

"Because that would mean a trial," Hubert replied. "If it's Powell, he wouldn't want her to accuse him publicly. She'd be allowed to defend herself in a court of law. The committee will seal her fate quietly. From the committee's decision, there is no appeal except for a review. She won't ever see the inside of a courtroom."

"Can the state revoke her license to practice as a House Attorney for the Tontine?" Chief Milani asked.

Hubert and Robert exchanged glances.

"Yes," they chorused.

"That's what he will go for next," Robert predicted. "Aleta said she could feel his hate it was so strong. If she can prove what she accused him of, he will want to shut her down completely."

"If he's found out somehow that he has no case against her for practicing law until she is sworn in," Lyle announced, "to save face he would have to kill Aleta."

"My God!" Robert exclaimed. "You're right."

"He's already submitted the charge," Hubert said. "That's the only explanation."

"That's correct," Peets announced. "The committee has called a special meeting on Monday."

"What will they do if they can't reach Aleta?" Tom Milani asked.

"Postpone until they can," Hubert said. "Or investigate the charges themselves."

"Burrows did the latter," Peets said. "He called me. I had no information. I was sworn to secrecy."

"But you told us," Lyle said.

"I watched your minds work. In a minute you would have figured out that Professor Burrows had called me. Well, wouldn't you?"

Hubert Praetzel was the first to speak. "I already had. Thank you for telling us."

"So if we tell the committee, this will be over," Tom Milani said.

"We will have won the battle," Chief Peets said. "But not the war."

"Suppose we lessen the impact on Eugene Powell," Lyle said. "Keep his mistake within the committee."

"Why would we do that?" Robert said. "He tried to kill my daughter."

"Because we don't want him seeking revenge," Lyle explained.

"He wouldn't dare!" Robert said. "We'd know it was him."

"We know it's him now," Lyle said, "but we can't prove it. What makes you think we could prove it next time?"

"So he's going to get away with this attack."

"Not necessarily," Lyle said. "But I need time and I want Aleta and Stanley to survive long enough for me to nail him."

"Can you?" Robert asked angrily.

"He's the best there is," Tom Milani responded.

"We'll all work with him," Peets said. "We are a good team."

"I want Ed on this too," Robert said.

"Of course," Lyle said. "He loves Tontine work. Harriet pays so well."

"Speaking of Ed," Peets said, "where is he?"

"On a case," Robert said.

"When will he be back?" Peets asked.

"We don't know."

"First things first," Lyle said. "Peets can you call Burrows? Tell him Hubert Praetzel has the answers he's looking for."

"Why don't I tell him?" Peets asked.

"He needs to hear it from a lawyer," Lyle explained. "And he can quote Hubert to the other committee members. It will sound better to Powell. He knows Burrows is on Aleta's side. It will make sense he'd check with a family member. It's a low-profile inquiry and Powell will like that."

"I'll call Burrows as soon as I get home."

Tom Milani clapped Robert Locke on the shoulder. "As soon as Aleta returns, I'll put a guard on her."

Lyle laughed. "She'll hate it!"

"My men like the duty," Milani said. "Bertha makes great rolls and coffee and there's been enough action around Aleta in the past so they find it exciting."

"I'm surprised she doesn't hire private security," Peets said.

Her father smiled. "She always thinks of danger as temporary. I think it's the only way she can cope with it."

"It's actually good for my men," Milani said. "You should see the improvement in their shooting ability."

"No one knows where they are, right?" Peets asked.

"No one!" Robert said.

But he was wrong.

And Professor Burrows had left for a weekend of skiing before the last snow disappeared from the Colorado slopes.

Chapter 10

When their plane landed, Stanley turned to Aleta, "Can you wait until we're in the motel room?"

"Wait for what?"

"You know what," Stanley said somberly. "It's been a couple of hours after all."

"You're teasing me," she guessed.

He grinned. "Partly. But the plane is private and safe. I'm not up for copulating in the back seat of a cab."

"What about the front seat of a rental car?"

"Why do we need to rent a car?"

"So we can drive to Clearwater and check in with Ed."

"Do I get to take a shower and change?"

"Absolutely!" Aleta said. "To save time I'll take one with you."

"That won't save time," Stanley predicted, puzzled.

"Sure it will," Aleta said. "It's quicker than you giving me a bath.

"We have time to fool around?"

"Yes."

"Okay," Stanley said. "You understand that when I rent a car I need to use my own name."

"That's okay," Aleta said. "We're going to sign into the hotel as ourselves too, but I have an idea about that."

"I'm open."

She kissed him. "You're a good guy."

"I love you too. Now what's your idea?"

"We sleep in my grandmother's room tonight."

Stanley's jaw dropped. "Harriet is here?"

"No, but we rent a room for her under her name. A double because she'll have her new husband with her."

"They're not coming?"

"I don't know. Maybe."

"We can't be sleeping in their bed," Stanley protested.

"Why not? We'll have paid for the room."

"Suppose they do come?"

"They'll knock."

"It might not work."

"It's the only idea I have," Aleta confessed.

"We could fly somewhere else."

"Tomorrow we'll do that."

"If we live long enough."

Aleta didn't answer.

Upset at her silence, Stanley pressed for a response. "We are going to live long enough, aren't we?"

"I don't know."

"Why don't you know?"

"Because I don't."

"I don't like living on the edge."

"Everybody is always living on the edge."

"But they don't realize it. I do."

"Exciting, isn't it?"

"I will never go on another honeymoon with you," Stanley stated flatly. "You realize I'm going to be forever traumatized about sleeping in a hotel."

"We don't have to sleep."

"That's no better," Stanley shot back. "We were interrupted and I shot a man."

"I did too," Aleta said softly. "But I didn't kill him. You don't know how good that makes me feel."

"That tape we sent back," Stanley said with a sudden flash of memory. "It didn't record the search did it?"

"Hmmm....," Aleta murmured.

"That's a yes, isn't it? And you told Robert to let Lyle listen."

"I imagine my dad included a few others as well," Aleta said.

"My father?"

"It could be worse."

"How?"

"He might have invited your mother."

"Oh Lord!"

Chapter 11

On the road to Clearwater, Aleta asked, "Feel better now?"

"Much," Stanley responded. "I did find a gun after all."

"Have you been fretting about that for two hours?"

"It just came back to me. I stopped fretting about it when you climbed into the shower."

"So how are we going to find Ed?"

"I'll call Dean," Aleta said flipping open her cell phone.

"Suppose he's not there?"

"Hello, Dean. It's Aleta. Beep Ed and tell him we'll meet him in an hour. Have him pick the place—somewhere we can eat lunch."

She closed her phone and held it in her hand.

"He might not be able to reach Ed," Stanley said.

Aleta opened her phone. "Where's that?"

She was silent when she hung up. Stanley waited for several minutes before he spoke. Then his words burst out impatiently.

"Am I headed in the right direction?"

"Sure," she said. "Clearwater is north of St. Petersburg. When we get to Tampa, we take the turnoff to

Clearwater. We could have flown in. Why didn't I know that?"

"I did. You never asked."

"Why did God want me to rent a car?" she puzzled aloud.

"Don't ask me. Ask Him. You seem to be having regular conversations with Him on our honeymoon," Stanley muttered irritably.

"You didn't expect me to leave Him behind, did you?" Aleta charged.

"Unfortunately for me, God knows that's just what I was hoping."

"We'd be dead if I had."

"I knew you'd bring that up."

"Now let me enjoy my few hours in Florida."

"Do you know yet where we're going tomorrow?"

"Mobile, Alabama. It's almost time for the Azalea Festival."

"So we will live to see tomorrow," Stanley concluded.

"Evidently," Aleta said. No sense telling him that's where she wanted to go. She had no idea if they would be alive tomorrow.

Ed was waiting at a rear table in a small family run Chinese restaurant. It was a dingy place only because it was old and dimly lit. The glasses were sparkling clean.

"The food's good," Ed told them as they sat. "Tell 'em you want the special. It's seven courses."

"Won't that take all day?" Stanley asked.

"Nope. And we need to talk."

"The special," Stanley said to the hostess. She bowed politely and within minutes, bowls of hot clear broth were placed before each of them.

Aleta thanked the waiter in Chinese, and then asked him a question.

The spoons of her two companions stopped in mid-air.

The man replied and Aleta asked another question. Again the answer came in Chinese which she appeared to understand.

Stanley put his spoon back down and stared at his wife. Ed began eating rapidly as if to assure himself this was really happening.

When the waiter left, Aleta said to her companions, "What?"

"I didn't know you spoke Chinese," Stanley said.

"I don't," Aleta said as she sipped the hot soup from her spoon.   "Only a couple phrases.   I had a Chinese roommate in college."

"The conversation was longer than a few words," Stanley accused.

"She was my roommate for a whole year. I have a good ear for spoken language."

"So what did he tell you?"

"People come and talk their secrets."

Stanley frowned. "Why did he tell us?"

"I guess because I spoke to him in Chinese," Aleta said. "This broth is excellent."

"So now what?" Ed asked.

"We eat," Stanley decided.

"And talk," Aleta said. "He said they are never asked questions. So we can talk."

The bowls were removed and a second dish took their place. Ed began to talk.

"Shakir Aloman ran a red light and the cops pulled him over. He's got the same last name as one of the hijackers so the cops called the Feds. He told them he was meeting a cousin and that cinched it."

"How did you find this out?"

"In bits and pieces, Ed replied. "I found his car on the impound list only it ain't in the lot."

"Where is it?" Aleta asked.

"A cop borrows it regularly."

"And no one notices?"

"It makes it back to its spot in time for inventory every month."

"Is Aloman here?"

"Nope."

"Any idea where he is?"

"He ain't dead."

"Why?"

"The car."

"What about the car?"

"If he was dead, they'd tell the widow to come get his stuff, and that includes the car."

"How do you know he's not here?"

"I gave the guard a couple of bills."

"Where is he?"

"The guard couldn't give me that."

"Who can?"

"Someone at the top."

The second course was whipped away and the third arrived, a rice and chicken dish with nuts. Stanley liked it. As far as he was concerned it was the entree. He said so and Aleta asked the waiter if this were so. The waiter smiled at Stanley and held up four fingers.

"That's how many more courses we have coming," she told him. The waiter spoke to her in Chinese and she answered him in Chinese. A long conversation ensued after which Aleta began to eat with obvious relish.

"Are you going to share?" Stanley asked.

"Not this dish. It's delicious!"

"The information," Stanley snapped.

"Patience, my dear Holmes," Aleta chided with a twinkle in her eyes. "We have leverage."

"We do?"

"The cop who uses the car has a mistress in Tampa. That's where he drives the car."

"Who? Where?"

"All he knows is that it's a nice house with four palm trees in the front."

"That's half of Florida," Ed said. "But I'll find it. Then what?"

"I need to know where the Feds have stashed Aloman," Aleta said. "I'm guessing it's a prison. I assume there's no computer trail."

"None."

"Then let's make one."

"How?"

"I want Aloman's car to travel from this impound lot to the impound lot nearest to where Aloman is stashed."

The third course was removed and the fourth set down.

"How long will it take you?" Aleta asked Ed.

"It depends on when our cop visits Tampa."

"Stanley and I are going to Mobile tomorrow," Aleta said. "If anything happens to me, stay on this, will you?"

"Catch me up," Ed said.

Stanley did that including their room arrangement.

"I'll come back with you," Ed said. "I'll stay in your room tonight. You stay in the room you rented for Harriet."

The waiter came over and asked if the dish was alright since none of the diners was eating.

Aleta replied in Chinese that they were worried. The food was fine.

The waiter backed away.

Aleta urged the other two to eat.

"We are being impolite," she said.

"Whoever is after you guys will come to your room first," Ed said. "I'll be ready."

"I don't want you facing him alone," Aleta said.

"I have a stun gun," Ed said. "I'll be okay."

The fifth and sixth courses were eaten more rapidly as Ed discussed moving Aleta's and Stanley's belongings to their alternate room while they went to dinner. He predicted that the hitter wouldn't watch an empty room but would wait in the lobby or follow them.

When the seventh course was served, Aleta smiled and thanked the waiter for his good service.

"You have left your worry behind?" he asked in Chinese.

Aleta nodded, and then told Stanley to give the waiter the largest bill he had in his wallet.

"The largest?"

"He gave us valuable information which may help us save our client's life. The Tontine pays for such information. Tell him to put it in his pocket and hand you the check. That we pay for."

"But we conducting company business," Stanley argued.

"We're on our honeymoon. The Tontine isn't paying for our lunch nor for Ed's. He's our guest."

Stanley smiled.

"Ed, if you figured out her reasoning, you're a smarter man than I am."

"She don't want her gramma to be overcharged."

Chapter 12

At 2:00AM, Aleta and Stanley were startled awake by a single gunshot. Both jumped out of bed and began dressing. For once Aleta was delighted that Stanley's penchant for folding clothes included laying the last ones removed on top of the pile.

That she'd been in a dressy outfit didn't matter. She had no time to hunt for other clothes. It wasn't until she and Stanley were rushing down the stairs to the room located one floor below--the room ostensibly reserved for them--that it occurred to her that being in evening dress made sense at this time of night.

Stanley had, of course, requested that she stay in the room, but she reminded him that if Ed were shot, then their second room would be the next room invaded. In addition, Stanley didn't really want to leave her. He was certain there would be a crowd gathering and the police would be called. It would be safer for her to be with him than sitting alone in their room.

Both of them remembered Ed saying he planned to use a stun gun.

What Stanley couldn't understand was why Aleta hadn't foreseen Ed being shot unless he was only wounded. He hoped that was the explanation.

Aleta's thinking ran parallel to her husband's. On top of those thoughts, her mind was trying to plan how she was going to break the news to Beatrice.

They heard Ed's voice as they were rushing down the hall. He was standing in the doorway holding his badge asking people to return to their rooms saying that the police had been called.

He nodded at Stanley and Aleta to come near.

"Take my car keys," he whispered, slipping the keys into Aleta's hand. "Give me yours."

Stanley handed Ed his keys.

"Now go back to your room," Ed said. "You're safe now."

Stanley took Aleta's arm and guided her away from the two bodies sprawled just inside the room--one unconscious and the other bloody.

"There were two," she commented. "He had to shoot."

"We will stay in our room," Stanley said. "He will call."

For a while both sat in chairs, waiting for Ed's call. Conversation was spasmodic and dull. The shock of their close call hit both of them hard.

After an hour, Aleta's head slumped onto her chest. Stanley rose, lifted her from the chair and laid her on the bed. He removed her clothes, folding each neatly and drew the covers over her nude body. Surprisingly, his senses were too deadened to react. He kissed her lightly on the forehead and sat down in the chair near the window and gazed at his sleeping wife, grateful she was still alive.

He wondered why he was sitting so far away. If a man entered with a gun, she'd be dead before he could leap in its path.

She stirred and reached for him. When her hand didn't find him, she sat up, panicked. He rushed to her and laid her back down. Since she wasn't fully awake, she resumed sleeping at once. The third time this happened in twenty minutes, Stanley realized she'd get no sleep without him beside her. The shooting had rattled her seriously.

To lie beside her fully clothed was an anathema to him. Slowly he began to undress. She woke once and he whispered that he was preparing for bed. Her hand stayed stretched over the empty side of the bed, waiting.

He completed the task of folding his last piece of clothing and looked around for his pajamas. This time Aleta woke even more panicked than previously. He quickly climbed in bed with her and gathered her into his arms. He felt her trembling and held her close.

Eventually her trembling lessened. He pulled up the covers and settled down. She was beginning to relax and he knew he couldn't withdraw for something as minor as putting on pajamas.

Even after he fell asleep, Stanley kept his arms wrapped around his wife. They slept thus until dawn had given way to day. As the sun rose its rays entered through the open drapes, crawled across the floor and hopped onto the bed, hitting Aleta's eyes first. She stirred to escape the bright light and found herself locked in her husband's embrace. She wiggled around and kissed him on his nose.

"Missed," he murmured. "My lips are further down."

"How long have you been awake?"

"It's hard to sleep with a wiggly wife in your arms."

"It's tomorrow," she said gaily.

"It's today," he corrected.

"But today is yesterday's tomorrow. We made it."

"It would seem you are correct unless we're in heaven."

"It sure feels like heaven," Aleta murmured. "I feel happy and warm and loved."

She kissed him again. This time it wasn't on the nose and passion generated its intensity. Stanley responded, his whole body desperate to realize the reality that they were both still alive. Aleta's response, heightened by the same desire brought both of them to a stronger mating than ever before.

When they both lay spent, Aleta murmured, "I didn't know there was another level."

"Don't ask me to move for at least an hour," he responded.

"Give me two," Aleta whispered as she closed her eyes and drifted off into pleasant dreams.

Thirty minutes later a loud knock on the door startled both of them fully awake.

"Who is it?" Stanley called.

"Room service," said the voice.

"We didn't order any," Stanley said reaching for a robe and tossing one to Aleta.

"I did," Ed Ornstein called from outside the door. "Open up so we can have breakfast together. Your treat."

Stanley glanced at Aleta who was up and robed. He opened the door.

"You guys sure slept a long time," Ed said. "I ordered lots 'cause it's your dollar."

The cart was rolled into the room and the steward placed the dishes, napkins and silver on the large table by the window. He lifted the steel covers and presented the various offerings. He poured juice into the glasses and Stanley told him they would serve themselves. Stanley signed the tab and the steward left.

Ed was already seated with a napkin tucked in his collar that covered his shirt and the top edge of his round belly.

"Hope I didn't interrupt anything," Ed chuckled.

"You didn't," Stanley said. "We were sleeping."

"It was that good, huh?" Ed grinned. Stanley's frown made Ed scramble for an explanation. "Hey, it's almost eleven o'clock and everyone knows you two are nutty about each other.

"The breakfast smells good," Aleta said. "And I'm starving."

"How did your night go?" Stanley asked.

"Got a phone call from Dean. I wouldn't come here for no reason."

"About us?" Aleta asked, helping herself to a stack of pancakes.

"Seems the geniuses back home figured out the who, what, and why of these attacks. They got a plan to stop him, but they hit a snag."

"What kind of snag," Aleta asked.

"Somebody named Burrows is out of town and they need him I guess."

"He was on the committee," Aleta explained.

"Yeah. Seems he's gonna get the charge dropped quiet like.

"What charge?" Aleta asked.

"Don't you know?"

Aleta shook her head.

"Don't matter. Nobody wants you to go home yet."

Stanley protested. "I'm due in court on Tuesday."

"Wednesday is when they said. "It seems some hearing has been moved up to Wednesday afternoon."

"Do they think they'll have Powell in custody by then?" Stanley asked.

"They said they were taking away his motive," Ed said. "Milani wants to know when you're coming in on Wednesday. He's gonna meet you."

"You drove down," Aleta said. "Why'd you tell Beatrice you were flying down?"

"She don't like me driving long distances by myself but I had a feeling I was gonna need my equipment. I was right."

"They took your gun, didn't they?"

"That's why I give you my car keys. I got another gun in my car plus a whole lot of other stuff I don't want them messing with. The cops searched your rental car. Thought it were mine."

The men exchanged keys.

"You're on the internet," Ed said. "Hundred grand. That's how they're coming at you so fast."

"How is Powell tracking us?" Aleta queried in response.

"Flight plan is my guess."

"I want to go to Mobile," Aleta said.

"No good," Stanley said.

"Why not?"

"Last August Katrina wreaked havoc in more than New Orleans. Mobile still hasn't recovered."

"Where do you want to go?" Aleta asked Stanley.

"How about Birmingham, Alabama?"

"What's there?"

"It's got a big airport."

"That's its appeal?"

"We're going by plane," Stanley said. "Of course, we could spend the next three days in the air."

"I want a plan with beds and showers."

"Then we go to a quiet city, rent a car, leave the quiet city and stay somewhere even quieter nearby."

"That's your plan?"

"Yep!"

Ed headed for the nicer part of Tampa on the off chance he could find a house with four palm trees in the front and a BMW parked in the drive. He was surprised at how quickly he could scout a block and so he kept going. It was logical that the cop would be here today. It was Saturday and he'd be off.

An hour and a half later he found the combo he was looking for. Four palm trees in the front yard and a tan BMW in the drive.

Ed parked across the street and took photos of the car and the house. The Florida plates didn't fool him.

As he was mulling over his next step, a car drove past the house and then backed up and parked in front of the neighbor's house next door. A young man with a camera got out and ran along the hedge next to the fence.

"A P.I.!" Ed muttered. "Shit!"

He turned on his car engine and made a U-turn and parked across the driveway. Then he walked up to the BMW and leaned on it.

The car alarm sounded and the cop, dressed in swim trunks came running around the corner.

The cop rushed up.

"Did you hit my car?" He bellowed.

Ed straightened up.

"Nope," he said. "But I had to get you out here fast. You're under surveillance. Young guy with a camera. In bushes next door."

As Ed expected, the cop rushed up the hedge row to the back of his neighbor's house. The young P.I. came barreling around the other side of the house and headed straight for his car. Ed was waiting for him.

When the cop caught up to him, the young men had his hands in the air and the tubby man in the flowered shirt and the wrinkled khakis was holding a gun in front of his belly.

"What's going on?" the cop said.

"Get the film," Ed ordered.

The cop, dressed in swim trunks, felt too vulnerable to protest.

The young P.I. opened his camera and took out the film with trembling fingers and dropped it into the outstretched hand of the man in the trunks.

Ed then ordered the young man to get in his car put both hands on the wheel and stay."

"We need to talk," Ed said to the cop moving away from the car

"Who are you working for?" the cop asked.

"Not your wife."

"Who then?"

"A lawyer for Shakir Aloman, the guy who owns this car."

"You see Illinois plates on this car?" the cop charged.

"So you know the man."

"Yeah. So what?"

"Where is he?"

"Gone."

"Where?"

"The Feds took him."

"Where?"

"They didn't tell us. They don't tell us nothing."

"I want you to tell the Feds that someone is asking questions about the car."

"I ain't doing no such thing."

"It ain't a lie. They might even appreciate a heads-up."

"Yeah, they might," he murmured thoughtfully.

"And you probably ought to put that car back," Ed suggested.

"Yeah, I should do that."

"Don't worry about me. I ain't telling your wife nothing."

"Thanks, Man."

"If I was you, I'd tell the Feds to come get their car."

"Or what?"

"Or my boss will subpoena all your records and when she finds out you held a man without a hearing or legal representation, it's you guys who'll be fried."

"What's to stop her from doing that anyway?"

"Her attention is on the car. Move it and her attention moves off you."

"You planning on following the car?"

"Yeah, but what do you care."

"You're right. I don't."

The car was returned to the impound lot that night. Ed breathed a sigh of relief. He went to the motel and went to sleep. He'd been up almost thirty six hours and he was dead tired. He'd leave early in the morning. He set his alarm for four.

While Ed was busy in Tampa, Stanly and Aleta were flying northwest.

"Teach me to fly," she said.

"You're not even supposed to drive," he reminded her. "But, yes I will teach you as soon as the doctor says it's okay."

"Well, give me a lecture then," Aleta said. "What's this for?"

"That controls the flaps."

"What do they do?"

Stanley explained the workings of the flaps, and Aleta pushed him until he'd explained every dial on the board in front of them. Her questions were so rapid fire, that even though he answered each one thoroughly, he assumed that she was moving fast to keep from being bored. When he finished, Aleta announced that she thought she could drive a plane now.

"Fly," he corrected.

"That too," she said.

"What do you mean 'that too'?"

"Don't you drive it down the runway after you land?"

"A plane is taxied down a runway."

"Really?" she said. "Taxies?"

Stanley began to feel apprehensive. She was baiting him. She knew the basic terms.

"So when you roll down the runway to take off, it's not called driving either?"

"No," he snapped. "And if you think that because the doctor used the word 'drive' and not 'fly', you're going to get to do the latter, think again."

"They aren't the same," Aleta argued.

"We'll ask when we get home," Stanley said. "Besides you aren't anywhere near ready to fly."

"You told me about all the stuff," she said.

"How much of it do you remember?"

"All of it," she stated flatly.

"Next step is putting it together. Tell me how you would land this plane."

The accuracy of her response surprised him.

"You've been taking lessons," he accused.

"From my wheelchair?" she mocked.

"You know too much. I didn't tell you some of that stuff."

"And who do you suppose did?"

Stanley chewed on it for several minutes and then burst out. "Your dad!"

"I wanted to impress you, but I went too far," she admitted.

"You've impressed me."

"So do I get to fly?"

"No!" Stanley said firmly. "But you do get to think about what we're going to do after we land."

"I thought that was decided."

"Not where we're going to stay because I already have our reservations under another name, but, what you want to do," Stanley said. "Load Birmingham up on the internet."

"So you think there'll be two people after us like this time?" Aleta asked, opening up the laptop, her mind still ruminating about the danger.

"Three," Stanley said. "If they heard about what happened here."

"They could switch off tailing us and..."

"Ed gave us a little insurance policy."

"What?"

"His stun gun."

As they climbed into their rental car, Aleta said, "I'm scared."

"Your plan's risky, but your reasoning is astute," Stanley commented. "We need to dispose of our tails before we head for our night's lodging."

"Botanical Gardens, here we come," Aleta said with false bravado.

"Tell me about them," Stanley urged, hoping to distract her from her rising apprehension.

"The photos on their website were truly amazing," Aleta began.

"You realize it's only the end of February. There won't be much in bloom."

"Camellias will be," Aleta said. "And to quote their website 'Camellias kick off the flowering season with gusto and pomp'."

"No azaleas? Lilies? Magnolias? Roses?"

"There are woodlands. Can you imagine?"

"We have whole preserves of trees in Illinois," Stanley countered, proud of his state's attention to trees.

"But this is a botanical garden. And each one is different. And there are ponds and even a bog."

Stanley laughed.

"Just what I always wanted to see—a patch of muddy wet ground."

"You're going to love it!" Aleta gushed.

"I'm a bit surprised you didn't pick the zoo."

"That's what we're doing tomorrow. We get there before ten so we can watch them feed the sea lions," Aleta said eagerly. "And they have a green anaconda in the reptile house. I want to see that. And they have a Komodo dragon. Can you imagine that?"

"That's it? We're going to watch sea lions eat, see a snake coiled around a tree limb, and look at a lizard?"

"They have seven hundred forty-seven other exhibits. You'll fall in love with something. I know it."

"I don't dare. You'll want to bring it home."

"Did you know they put food inside puzzles and other stuff to enrich their lives?" Aleta asked. "We'll have fun."

"And we won't take one home, will we?"

"Stop worrying, Stanley. We won't take anything home that's not sold in the souvenir shop."

"I told you before I thought we shouldn't leave the lodge once we get there."

"That's still an option," Aleta said. "I just want you to consider my option."

"Agreed," Stanley said. "We're here."

"Were we followed?"

"Yes."

"How many?"

"At least two."

"I don't like the odds."

Most of the special outdoor gardens were clustered near the main entrance with the various woods scattered along the outskirts of the large elliptical acreage. Aleta and Stanley, map in hand headed straight toward the six-acre Barber Alabama Woodlands which she had ascertained from her web site study contained the landscape they needed to carry out their plan.

They had both expressed concern that perhaps they wouldn't be followed into the gardens. That worry disappeared when two men singly entered the main gate.

Stanley and Aleta walked onto the winding flagstone path leading through the beginning of the display of Alabama's natural forest onto the raised wooden walkway zigzagging through an area of woods mixed with streams and ponds. Halfway down the walkway was a horseshoe circle of benches upon which to sit and enjoy being in the heart of a forest. Aleta sat on the bench her side to the path leading to it.

The angle was wrong unless the assailant took a head shot. Stanley counted on them not being sharpshooters. He

figured they wouldn't carry a rifle into the gardens.
Handguns were better short-range weapons.

The range of their stun gun was twenty-one feet.

Stanley put his arm around Aleta and she laid her head
on his shoulder. Thus they sat and waited with Stanley
kissing her lightly spasmodically as lovers were wont to do
during a private conversation. They were alone, others
preferring the sunnier areas as dusk was closing in.

The first man sauntered up the path alone, dressed in a
business suit, as was appropriate for what he had foreseen as
the obvious first stop, a large hotel in downtown
Birmingham. That the couple didn't go straight to their hotel
surprised him some, but when they drove straight to the
gardens, it made sense. The gardens were huge. One
couldn't do them justice in a few hours. Most out of town
visitors didn't know that.

He expected them to head straight for the Hess
Camellia Garden with its sloping brick promenade leading to
a sunken circular terrace surrounding a splashing fountain
and pool. It was the only garden in full bloom this time of
year but it alone was worth the price of admission.

When he saw them sitting in the woodland area
hugging and occasionally kissing, he knew they were seeking
something besides the colorful display of flowers in this side
journey of theirs.

Perhaps it was peace, he thought. This is as good a
place to find permanent peace as any.

He glanced around. His partner was hovering near the
entrance to the grove, practically out of sight. Before he
disappeared from his view he raised his arm and pointed.

Stanley leaned over slightly and kissed Aleta again
only this time his hand slowly withdrew the stun gun from
under her blouse.

"He's here?" she whispered.

"The gun is in his hand," Stanley whispered back knowing that the sound of their whispering would carry but not the words of their communication.

"I love you, Aleta," he added. "Whatever happens remember that."

"What are you saying?" she asked, no longer whispering. She pushed him away from her as he knew she would. She always did that when she wanted an answer. He stood up and looked at the man coming up the path. He saw the gun in the man's hand follow his movement. It was an automatic response to his quick rise.

He fired the stun gun. The tiny pair of missiles hit the man low in the body where only a single layer of clothing protected his flesh from the penetration of the two small probes. Instantly, the man fell.

Because he was at the edge of the walkway, the weight of his upper body tipped him backward into the water. His gun clattered on the wooden walkway.

The sound of the shot galvanized the assailant's partner into action. His footsteps could be heard running up the flagstone path.

Stanley was reloading the stun gun when Aleta sprang from her seat and dashed toward the gun that had fallen from the assailant's hand.

"No!" Stanley shouted, but his word of admonition only followed her. It didn't stop her.

The second man, gun drawn came up the walkway. Aleta dove for the gun lying on the broad boards and the second man followed her movement with his gun.

Stanley ran toward the pair, the stun gun in his hand. The man saw him coming at him with a gun already aimed and the woman on the ground still reaching for his partner's gun and he raised his gun to take out Stanley.

The two shot simultaneously.

The man went down instantly. Stanley grabbed his side and stumbled backward. His heel caught on the edge of the walkway and he fell backward into the bog.

Aleta's hand already closed over the gun, now released it as she ran toward her husband.

Fearfully she stared over the edge of the walkway.

"Shit!" he exclaimed as he sat up.

"You scared me to death!" she scolded. "I thought he'd killed you."

"Almost did," Stanley said with disgust. "I wish he had. How am I going to walk out of here looking like this?"

"You could just stay there," Aleta said teasingly. "I mean, if not being embarrassed is that important."

"The place is full of people," Stanley said. "This is a most unsatisfactory conclusion."

"So you aren't hurt?"

"Of course, I'm hurt," Stanley shot back. "But I'm such a muddy mess, you can't see that. The problem is, Aleta, you don't see the problem."

"You mean I haven't noticed you're covered in mud?" she giggled.

"So, how do we get out of this place?"

"Let me see. This is a knotty problem," Aleta opened her cell phone.

"What are you doing?"

"Calling the police."

"We don't want the attention."

"What we don't want more is for these two to wake up and finish what they started," Aleta stated flatly.

Thus Stanley left the park on a stretcher.

As the paramedics carried him, Aleta, holding his muddy coat trotted along beside him.

"Get it cleaned immediately," he ordered, "and bring me the pants in my suitcase."

"There'll be time...," she began.

"Do as I say. Be sure to clean out the pockets."

"Stanley...," she began to protest.

"That's an order!" he said quietly.

"Then I'll do it right away," Aleta confirmed.

One of the paramedics raised an eyebrow. The surprise spread to the rest of his face when she asked where the hospital was.

"You aren't following us?" he asked.

"No," she replied, with neither apology nor resentment in her tone, "I have a chore to do."

As soon as he told her, she took off.

"My wife would never have left me," the paramedic commented disparagingly.

"Guess you'll have to work on that," Stanley replied amiably.

Aleta didn't want to leave Stanley. She couldn't understand him sending her off alone. That wasn't like him.

She'd watched the police sergeant take the stun gun from Stanley and bag it. She'd listened to Stanley explaining that he was a deputy from Arborville, Illinois and she'd read the disbelief on the sergeant's face.

"Check," Stanley had said.

The sergeant had nodded perfunctorily and Stanley hadn't pressed the issue. Instead he'd switched his focus to begging for police protection for his wife.

"I assure you," the sergeant said, "this was an isolated mugging. The men are in custody. The danger is over."

As Aleta hurried along, she knew there was no gun in the pockets of the jacket he insisted she carry. His request made no sense to her.

Still, when she reached the car, she searched the pockets. She found a single bullet.

"I need the gun, Stanley," she murmured ruefully.

Suddenly, she knew where it was.

She opened the case and felt along the bottom. She wrapped his pants around the gun and set the bundle on the front seat of the car.

When she pulled out of the lot, she worried about how to carry the gun into the hospital. It was heavier than the stun gun. She wasn't certain the elastic band holding the top of her capris up was strong enough to hold a gun in place.

She had left the parking lot in advance of the ambulance. She had noticed a man sitting in a car not too far away; however, when she left, he stayed in place.

Did Stanley really want the jacket cleaned or did he just want her to find the gun? She wanted to be at the hospital when he arrived.

I could make an assumption he wanted me to find the gun, she reasoned. But, deep inside, she knew he would expect her to follow the order completely. She had absolutely no idea why, but she began looking for a dry cleaner as she drove.

She stopped at the first one she spotted. She was standing at the counter when the ambulance passed by. The siren caused her to turn and watch it speed past. Directly behind it she spotted the car that had been in the parking lot.

Had she been behind the ambulance, it would have been on her tail. Stanley had somehow figured that if she left before the ambulance, she might escape unnoticed. And she did. This man must not have known what car they were in. He was either back-up for the others or he had followed them because he figured they had spotted the quarry at the car rental counter.

I need to keep it that way, she determined.

When she reached the hospital, she parked near the main entrance and wound through the corridors to the emergency section, the gun still buried inside the change of clothes she brought for Stanley.

The nurse directed her to the waiting room, promising her the doctor would call for her when he finished his examination. As she sat there, a man entered the waiting room and glanced around.

Aleta felt a chill of apprehension. He was a rough looking man, dressed casually, with a couple days growth of beard. He carried a folded newspaper in his hand.

Aleta tucked her hand into the stack of Stanley's clothes. The safety on the gun was already off. Hers was the gesture of anticipation. She waited for him to settle in one of the empty seating areas near the door. He didn't. Instead he crossed the room and sat beside her.

Her hand gripped the barrel of the gun. Her finger found the trigger and rested on it.

The man leaned over and Aleta smelled beer on his breath as he whispered. "Look down at the newspaper."

She glanced down and he lifted the newspaper slightly. The gun barrel was elongated by the attachment of the silencer.

"It's aimed straight at your belly," he hissed.

Aleta trembled. She didn't want to kill another person. Why couldn't the police have left her the stun gun? She knew why, but she still thought they shouldn't have left her without protection.

"I want you to get up and leave with me. No fuss. You don't want anyone here hurt, now do you?"

"No, I don't," Aleta said aloud.

Then without fanfare, she yanked the paper away from the gun and stood up, letting Stanley's pants drop to the floor.

In a loud voice, she announced, "I suggest you people leave now. If this man points his gun at any of you, I will kill him."

The old couple rose slowly and, glancing back fearfully, headed for the door. The young woman stayed frozen in her seat until she saw that the elderly people had managed to leave safely, and then she bolted from her seat and rushed for the door.

The gun stayed pointed at Aleta. The man believed Aleta's threat. Her hand was too steady; her eye too steely; her voice too strong. This lady would shoot him. She couldn't miss—not at only three feet away.

He hated that she'd taken control. He should have just shot her. He couldn't remember exactly why he hadn't. His plan had seemed foolproof.

"Drop your gun," she ordered.

At that moment, two police officers appeared, guns drawn.

"Police," they said in unison. "Both of you. Drop your weapons."

"If I do, he will kill me," Aleta protested.

"Then we will kill him," one officer said.

"But I'll be dead," Aleta argued. "He puts his gun down first."

"Both of you. Drop your weapons, or we'll drop you!" the smaller, stockier officer shouted.

"Do it then," Aleta challenged, her voice unwavering. "Better you kill me. He'll shoot me out of greed. You'll do it out of ignorance."

"What's going on here?" came a new voice from behind the two officers standing in the doorway.

"Hello, Sergeant," Aleta said without turning. "You took away our stun gun. You refused me police protection. And now your men plan to kill me because I won't let this man shoot me."

"Put down your weapon and we'll talk," he ordered.

"Are you good at communicating with the dead?" Aleta asked. "There's a hundred thousand dollar contract out on me. You better believe this man has plans to collect."

"If he shoots you, we'll shoot him."

"Shoot both of us now," Aleta said. "It'll be the same result."

"May I?" said a quiet voice.

The sergeant turned. "What the hell?"

The man, dressed only in a hospital gown, IV needle still taped to his forearm, slipped past the sergeant.

"I'm a deputy," Stanley said as everyone noticed that the gunman's eyes flitted between him and the woman. His gun, however, stayed trained on the woman.

"Shoot me and you'll do hard time," Stanley said. "Aleta, did you bring the right pants?"

Aleta nodded.

"Give me my gun and get my badge out of the pocket," Stanley ordered as he came up beside her.

Aleta deftly slipped the gun into her husband's hand and squatted down and picked up the clothes and placed them on a chair. She fished the badge out of a pocket and held it up.

"Police," Stanley said. "Drop your weapon."

"It's fake!" the gunman shouted.

"Drop your weapon and then these officers will listen to you."

"You'll kill me."

"I'm a cop. You're pointing a gun at me. If you don't drop it now, I'll shoot."

"I...," the man began.

A shot rang out. The gun clattered to the floor.

"He's all yours," Stanley said as the uniformed cops rushed in and took both guns.

Stanley put his arm around Aleta. "Come, let's get out of here."

She reached down and swooped up his clothes. Together they went back to the treatment room.

"She has to wait outside," the nurse said tersely.

"No!" Stanley said firmly. "It's not safe out there. As a matter of fact, it's not safe in here. Aleta, gather the sutures and stuff on the tray. You can sew me up."

"Me?" Aleta gasped.

"You can do anything," Stanley assured her as he began to pull on his trousers. Aleta took the corners of the white tray cover and joined them making a knapsack. The instruments clicked as they hit one another.

"You can't steal our supplies," the doctor protested.

Stanley reached into the pocket of his muddy pants and extracted his wallet. He took out a hundred and threw it down on the treatment table.

"That should pay for supplies. Have the hospital and paramedic unit bill me. Here's my card."

He shoved the card into the hand of the doctor who stood slightly bewildered at the swiftness with which this pair moved.

Stanley stuffed his bare feet into his shoes and gathered the rest of his clean clothes in almost a single motion.

"Ready?" he asked his wife.

"Your other clothes?" she asked looking at the pile on the floor. Stanley shook his head.

Aleta spotted a large bottle of antiseptic and a roll of gauze sitting on the counter and grabbed them both as she followed Stanley into the corridor.

"I parked at the front entrance," Aleta said, catching up and leading the way. She found herself running to stay abreast of Stanley.

"Why are we hurrying?"

"I don't want the police to detain us," Stanley said. "They don't have a clue what we're up against."

"But you're hurt."

"All our weapons are gone," Stanley said. "We need to leave now." His voice had a note of desperation Aleta had never heard before. He was clutching a towel against his wound.

She clicked the key fob that unlocked the car door and slipped into the driver's seat. She knew Stanley wanted her to drive.

"Tell me where," she said simply as she drove away from the hospital.

Bending over, he directed her to a highway that led northwest out of town; but, aside from succinct directions, he spoke not a word.

As they wound through the lovely hills, Aleta caught a glimpse of an isolated renaissance-type castle sitting in a small valley surrounded by hills resplendent with early spring blossoms of purple and white and gold.

"Did you register us already?" she asked as they drove toward the main entrance.

"I did. I used the name Stanley."

A short time later, after the bags had been delivered to their suite, Aleta studied Stanley closely. He was still hunched over holding his side. His shirt, clean when they entered the lobby, was now slightly bloody.

"You expect me to sew you up, don't you? You don't have a doctor hidden on the premises, do you?"

"Correct," he grunted.

"And it has to be done, doesn't it?"

"Correct."

"Why didn't we just make nice with the doctor and stay long enough for him to do the job?"

"Too dangerous."

"I have no anesthetic," she pointed out her anxiety growing.

"I'll bite down on a rolled washcloth," he said.

"I'm not sure I can do it," Aleta murmured, her fear beginning to take over. Her voice trembled slightly.

"Then I'll do it and you can assist me," he declared.

"Stanley, you can't!" she wailed.

"Let's do this one step at a time," he said calmly, moving into the bathroom. He stripped then washed his hands.

Silently, Aleta spread out a bath towel on the floor and set the knapsack down. She then fetched the wrapped gauze roll and the bottle of antiseptic. Stanley lay on the cold tile floor. He shivered.

Aleta washed her hands then opened the bottle of antiseptic and poured it on her hands. Stanley asked for a wash cloth. Aleta gave him one and then tucked a towel under his head.

She took a second towel and put it near his wound and then poured antiseptic on the open wound. He stifled a groan.

Aleta apologized.

"Don't," he said. "Remember how they stitched your arm. You were awake."

"I wasn't watching," Aleta confessed. "I looked away."

"Think of me as a turkey and you're sewing the stuffing inside," Stanley grunted.

"I may never be able to stuff a turkey again," Aleta responded ruefully. "Stanley, I don't know what I'm doing."

"Neither did most nineteenth century doctors."

"This is the twenty first century. Maybe I should see if there's a doctor at this resort."

"You see that probe there?" Stanley asked.

"Yes, I see it."

"You need to extract the bullet with it."

"The bullet is still inside?" she gasped horrified at what that meant.

"It has to come out," Stanley said matter-of-factly.

"You didn't tell me I was going to have to extract a bullet!" Aleta exclaimed horrified.

"Aleta, you can do this," Stanley declared.

"It will hurt like hell!" she argued. "I could kill you."

"Yes, it will hurt like hell. No, you won't kill me," he said, his tone quickly becoming persuasive. "Aleta, we need to stay hidden to stay alive. There was a whole network of people after us. Our only chance was to run while they regrouped."

"Suppose there were only three?" Aleta posed.

"I weighed the odds," Stanley said decisively. "I made the choice."

"I'm not a nurse even. I didn't even take a first aid course. I refused to dissect a frog in biology. I am the most unprepared person in the world for this task."

"Yes, I know," Stanley said, "but I trust you."

"My God, Stanley, do you know what you're saying?" Aleta exclaimed, desperation coloring her tone. "I'm squeamish by nature."

"Then you aren't going to like the next part."

"There's more?"

"You're going to need to make a cut deep enough to reach the bullet and pull it out."

Aleta drew in her breath sharply.

"Operate?" she gasped. "You want me to operate?"

"Are you ready?" Stanley said abruptly.

"No, I'm not."

"Take three slow deep breaths, think of how much you want me to live, then close your eyes and feel for the bullet with your fingers. I'll guide you. Then make one cut deep enough to reach it. Pull it out and sew me up."

Aleta tittered nervously. "That's all?"

"Three breaths, Aleta. Focus. Give that brilliant brain of yours freedom to work. And ignore my pain."

Aleta took a huge breath and expelled it slowly. Her mind raced through alternatives. There were none. She couldn't fly him home. She couldn't call for help without alerting everyone to their whereabouts. He was already in too much pain to be able to stand a long drive home, assuming they could even travel unnoticed. If there were a doctor here at the lodge, he would be legally obligated to report a gunshot wound. There were no alternatives.

She slowly expelled the breath and drew in another. Stanley had said to think about her love for him. How great was it? She knew she would die for him. Why then not this?

As she took in her third breath, she found she was relaxing. Dr. Cook did this all the time. How did he do it?"

I guess one takes a dispassionate view of the procedure, she decided. The task at hand required a setting aside of one's personal anathema regarding the laying back of the skin or the spilling of blood or the exposing of the underside of the flesh. To cure sometimes one must cut and remove a deadly object. The body cannot heal if it is left inside.

Aleta knelt beside Stanley. "Prepare yourself. This is going to hurt like hell!"

Stanley put the rolled washcloth in his mouth and nodded.

Aleta picked up the scalpel. Light though it was, the weight of its handle surprised her. It was a perfectly balanced instrument that lent itself to fitting into her hand.

Stanley's finger pointed to the place he knew the bullet laid. Aleta touched the area with enough pressure to locate the hard casing of the bullet.

Stanley moved slightly at her touch.

"Don't move," she said.

Before he could acknowledge her request, he felt the sharp blade of the knife cut through his flesh. Try as he would, he could not completely stifle the scream that rose in his throat.

"Done!" she announced. He saw her put down the scalpel and pick up the forceps.

This he knew would hurt even more. He clapped his hands over his mouth and held them there. Every fiber of his being wanted to tell her to stop. He couldn't stand the pain. He thought he could but he was wrong. They would have to take their chances. He could not, absolutely could not, handle one more second of this pain.

The forceps went into the wound.

Stanley's scream of agony penetrated the gag and the hand blocks. The word 'stop' sprang from his throat. It came to the surface as an unintelligible shout of anguish.

"Pillow!" Aleta said sternly, stopping all movement.

Stanley yanked the towel from under his head and pressed it over his mouth. Part of him was still screaming at her to stop. Part of him hoped she would finish.

She dug deeper with the forceps and this time his screams were sufficiently muffled so they stayed confined inside the bathroom. Aleta heard them; however, she knew she had to complete this part no matter how painful it was for him. If she stopped his agony would continue.

The forceps closed on the metal cylinder and she squeezed it firmly as she carefully withdrew them. It only took seconds for the bullet to make its journey to the surface; but, to Stanley, it seemed as if time had stopped and he was permanently in pain.

And then it was over. The bullet was out. And while the wound bled, the bleeding was minor.

Aleta picked up the suture needle and began to close the wound. Stanley kept the towel over his face. Even though he felt every jab, he managed to curtail his outcries.

Still, he'd suffered too much. He begged Aleta to stop; but, he kept the towel over his mouth so his cries wouldn't be heard outside the room they were in.

To his surprise, she answered him, assuring him she could hear him, telling him she wasn't going to stop unless he could give her a good reason to.

He yelled that he could stand the pain no longer. She continued to insert the needle into his flesh and draw the suture thread in its wake as she replied that that argument wasn't good enough.

"You don't want me to stop part way and finish later, do you?" she asked as she placed another suture in the line.

"I want you to stop, period," he shouted through the cloths covering his mouth.

"And not finish?" she asked, and then added, "I can't do that. You'd never forgive me."

He argued at length that he would forgive her and she told him she'd never forgive herself for letting him down.

He ranted through stitch after stitch and while Aleta talked with him, she continued inserting the needle at regular intervals.

When he felt the sting of the antiseptic wash down the length of the wound, he knew it was over.

Her next words pierced his fog of relief. "It's not over. We have to get you to bed."

"I'll just lie here," he decided, the prospect of moving too horrible to even consider.

"Nonsense!" Aleta snapped. "I'm not spending the night on the bathroom floor."

"You go to bed," he said magnanimously. "I won't mind."

"Don't be silly! I'm not sleeping alone on our honeymoon."

"Aleta, I can't do any more pain tonight," Stanley pleaded. "Please just let me lie here."

"Okay," she said.

He breathed a sigh of relief.

"For as long as it takes me to clean up this mess," she added, "which I guess will be about fifteen minutes."

"Aleta," he moaned, "have pity."

She leaned over and kissed him tenderly. "I do love you. And you will do this."

He heard the steel in her voice and knew he would.

The journey was as painful as he thought it would be. He sat on the edge of the bed gritting his teeth as tears streamed unbidden down his cheeks. His lips were clamped shut to stifle the groans.

She put her hands behind his head and back and he relaxed into them and let her lay him down. She lifted his legs into the bed and pulled the covers up to his groin.

"Farther," he coached.

"Can't. I didn't bandage the wound."

She gently straightened out his torso and while it was uncomfortable to be moved, he knew that it would be far worse if he had to move himself.

She undressed quickly and climbed in beside him and took his hand. Neither said a word.

After a few moments, he moved her hand to the part of his body reserved only for her and she curled her fingers lightly around his member and fell into an exhausted sleep.

Her touch comforted him and he fell asleep moments later.

Chapter 13

Hours earlier, back in Arborville, Chief Lyle West called Chief Alan Peets and told him Stanley had been shot.

"Stanley suspects there may even be a whole network after them," Lyle finished.

"You want me to get hold of Burrows if I have to drive to his house and shake him awake."

"Close enough."

"Maybe they should come home."

"I never got a chance to talk to Stanley. The Birmingham police called to report on his activities and to see if he was a deputy or not. He left the hospital with the bullet still in him. He appears to have turned off or lost his cell. I can't reach him."

"I'll shake Burrows awake," Peets promised.

"As for me," Lyle said, "I'm going to have a talk with Sadah Aloman. She needs to choose sides now."

"Good luck to both of us," Peets said.

Sadah Aloman was settled at her desk listening to Harriet Locke Luther tell her how she was to handle the transfer of the bank CDs that were coming due, when Chief West strode past Alice's desk and into Aleta's office. His face was grim, and Harriet, upon seeing it, stopped mid-sentence.

"Sadah, it is time for you to decide who your friends are," Chief West declared.

Sadah paled visibly.

"What's happened?" Harriet asked.

"Stanley's been shot!"

Harriet sat down hard. Sadah gasped in fear.

"He's alive?" Harriet asked, not daring to believe he wasn't.

Lyle's face was grim. "I don't know. A third man attacked Aleta. Stanley went into hiding with her."

"He must have felt the danger was extreme."

"That's my guess. But I'm here to tell Sadah that she will not speak to Eugene Powell about anything ever again."

Her voice trembling, Sadah protested. "I can't. He has been a friend. You would have him treat him like an enemy."

"Would a friend try to murder your husband's lawyer?"

"That makes no sense. Why would he do that?" she charged.

"We have no other suspects. No one hates Aleta as much as he does. And only three people knew they were going to Georgia—you, Alice and Stanley's mother. Alice told no one. You told Powell they were on their way to Georgia and Stanley's mother told them where in Georgia. Stanley's mother will never speak to the man again. That leaves only you."

"I won't tell them anything about Mr. or Mrs. Praetzel ever again," Sadah said. "I promise."

"That's not good enough," Lyle said icily. "You could say something inadvertently that will fill in a missing piece. If you continue to work here, you will know too much and you won't even know what you know that's not common knowledge, like that slip you made revealing where Aleta and Stanley were going. Powell is a deadly enemy of Aleta's and ultimately you."

"But he's helped me. I don't understand. Why would he do this?"

"To set Aleta up so he could destroy her," Lyle explained. "That paper you signed could have prevented her from ever practicing law in Illinois."

"I would never do that!" she protested vehemently.

"The point is you did."

"But I told him that he was wrong, that Mrs. Praetzel was legal. I told him that it was not pro bono. I told him the truth."

"He had already filed the report based on your affidavit," Lyle went on, his voice still accusatory. "That's the reason he is trying to kill Aleta. You told him he was wrong about her. He needs to kill her so no one finds out the mistake he made."

"I won't do that again. I promise," Sadah said. "He believed me when I told him my husband was not a terrorist. No one else did. I can't turn my back on the only person who believed me and helped me."

"He had an agenda. Helping your husband was a means to an end," Lyle declared. "He is not your friend."

"How can I tell whom to trust?" Sadah lamented.

"I want you to trust us," Lyle pleaded. "Just do this one thing. Don't talk to Eugene Powell at all."

"I know he will stop helping if I don't talk to him," Sadah murmured shamefaced. "He has powerful friends. I am so afraid for my husband."

"Your fear for your husband is blinding you to the kind of man Eugene Powell is. You think about your decision while Mrs. Luther and I talk."

Harriet followed Lyle into Stanley's office. He shut the door.

"Only Tom, Alan and I know what happened yesterday. None of us know where Aleta and Stanley are. Our report came from the Birmingham police. Stanley left the hospital with the bullet still inside him."

"He could die."

"That's my take. This woman cannot let Powell know how vulnerable they are right now."

"Let me talk with Sadah. I have an idea."

Sadah called Eugene Powell at his office and said she had important news. She was put through immediately.

"Aleta Praetzel has been attacked," she said.

"When? Where?" he asked.

"Yesterday. Somewhere in Alabama."

"How badly was she hurt?"

"She's still alive is all I know," Sadah said.

"That's good news," Eugene Powell returned. His voice lacked sincerity.

"I need you to help me find a new lawyer for my husband," Sadah said. "You said you would help me."

"Why?"

"Because she is getting shot at. She could die. Then where would I be?"

"It will take time," Eugene Powell hedged.

"You said you knew of others that could help."

"I didn't say that exactly. I assured you there were others. I didn't want you to feel this person was your only hope. But I think you should stay with Mrs. Praetzel for now."

"I want a new lawyer."

"You don't really have a choice. You must stick with her. You signed a contract."

"I told you I didn't."

"That's right. She's doing it for free. Pro bono."

"I told you it wasn't that," Sadah said angrily.

"You signed an affidavit saying that it was," Powell said. "I don't like being lied to. Have you lied to me about everything? Did you lie to me about your husband being innocent too?"

"I didn't lie," Sadah said her fury rising. "My husband is not a terrorist!"

"That's what you say. But why else would people be shooting your lawyer? Nobody wants a terrorist to be set free," Powell said. "I'm not going to help you find a lawyer. I don't help liars."

With that he hung up.

Sadah sat back and looked at the two people in the room with her.

"What do you want me to do?" she asked quietly. "You are right. He is an enemy."

Harriet patted her on the arm. "You are free of him. It took courage to make that call."

"I didn't lie to him," Sadah said.

"I believe you," Harriet replied.

Lyle spoke up. "You are not to speak to him ever again. This is important. He will twist whatever you say. No matter how angry he makes you, say nothing. Write it down or remember it and tell me. Can you do that?"

"I can," Sadah said with a firm voice. "That I can do. I was raised to respond thus. I can do it."

"Now, can we get back to work," Harriet asked.

"This was work, Harriet. It's called cooperating with the police."

"Am I done cooperating?" Harriet asked tongue in cheek.

Lyle smiled. "I believe you are."

Lyle stopped by Alice's desk. "If Mr. or Mrs. Praetzel contacts you, you are to call Chief Milani or me, no one else."

"Or whomever he tells me to," Alice added.

"No. Nobody but us. I'm giving you our cell phone numbers."

"I don't know if I can do that," Alice said.

"Even though they aren't here," Lyle said, "we consider them both under police protection. If I knew where they were, I'd have them escorted straight back here."

"I'm sorry," Alice said, "but I'll obey Mr. Praetzel's orders whatever they are."

"I thought you'd say that," Lyle said. He spoke into his radio. "Come on up guys. We're doing this the hard way."

"What are you doing?" Alice asked warily.

"Monitoring all incoming calls," Lyle said. "Here's a court order."

"Mr. Praetzel isn't going to like this," Alice said as she began to read the warrant.

"I'm used to that," Lyle said evenly.

"This is signed by his mother!" she exclaimed.

"She's a judge," Lyle grinned. "I dare him to argue with her!"

Monday afternoon the sun was shining in Clearwater and Ed Ornstein wiped his brow with his handkerchief for the dozenth time in an hour. His car was rapidly heating up, but the location was inconspicuous and yet he had a clear view of the police impound lot.

He wasn't sure when the cop would decide what to do about Aloman's car, but he couldn't believe he wouldn't move it. He'd already taken numerous photos with his camera rigged for nighttime shooting. He'd laid that day's paper on the ground to document the date.

Afterward he had breakfast and midmorning he returned to check on the car. It was still there, but it had been moved. He spent the next two hours in the shade. Even though he knew the shade was moving, he had nowhere he could go. He stuck a sunshade on the window and contented himself with watching the gateway through a slit in the window shade.

I need a real surveillance van he told himself. Beatrice would buy him one if he dropped a hint. But if ever he began to ask for big toys, the line he'd drawn when they'd married would become meaningless. It's not as if he wasn't making good money as a PI because he was. But except for a rare occasion like this one, a van would be a luxury.

He reached in the back of the car and snagged a roll of paper towels. His handkerchief had become a soggy mess. As he was leaning back, he saw a truck with a flatbed coming up the road.

Ed yanked his hand back empty, reached for his camera and got three shots of the truck passing and two of it entering the impound yard. He snapped the truck turning around. His view of the back was obstructed by the cars in the lot. He started his car and turned on the air. He pulled out of the parking space and drove to the end of the block. He positioned himself on the cross street so he could move in either direction.

Ed waited until the truck had gone two blocks before tailing him. One of the tracking devices he had planted on the BMW told him the truck was heading north. The other had either been shaken off when the car was loaded onto the truck or it had been discovered. He hoped it wasn't the latter because then the truck wouldn't be taking the car to the same place where Aloman was incarcerated.

He wished he had more coffee He hoped this driver was no more prepared than he was. If he weren't, he'd be stopping after a couple of hours to stoke up. Ed figured he'd do the same thing.

When the truck pulled over for gas, Ed did as well. When Ed saw the amount of food the driver bought, he went back for more. He went to the restroom when the driver left. He wanted it that way.

The tracking device would tell him which way the driver went. He knew now that it wasn't to some dump. The driver had bought too much food.

Once he caught up to the truck, he eased back and fell out of sight of the trucker's rear view mirror.

Four hours after they started they were approaching Atlanta. The truck chose the by-pass around the city and Ed caught up and passed him. He swung off in Marietta and filled his tank. His car didn't have the capacity the truck did. He took care of his personal comfort requirements and bought a handful of candy bars.

He climbed back in the car and turned on his monitor and discovered he was no longer getting a signal.

There were two possibilities. The truck had turned northeast before hitting Marietta in which case it would be out of range or somehow the device had come loose and fallen off the truck in which case the truck was actually still in range and still heading north.

He realized that if the device had fallen off the truck, he had to catch up or he'd never find the car. The other option held hope that he could track it later.

He sped up, hoping to catch sight of the truck. Twenty minutes later, he fretted because he hadn't caught sight of the truck. Up ahead was the Tennessee border. He needed a map in order to figure out which route the trucker might have taken, supposing that he was still traveling north. He didn't want to pass in because he had chosen the wrong highway.

I should have caught up to him by now, Ed reasoned.

He pulled in at a truckers' gas stop in Chattanooga. He filled his tank and then went inside to buy a map. He was studying and saw he had a choice. He walked over to a couple of truckers and asked them which way was the fastest.

"That one's the most direct," said the one.

"But that one's the fastest," the other man put in.

"No slides nor nothing?" asked the first man.

"I just came down that way. Clear sailing." Came the reply.

Ed thanked the men and studied the turns he'd need to make to take the faster route. While he was memorizing the route, he heard the cashier say, "All fixed up?"

"Yeah, I caught a break being so close."

Ed glanced up and then went back to studying the map.

"Is there a good place to eat along here," the man asked the cashier.

"Up the road a piece. Dell's Diner."

Ed folded up his map. He had to go back a couple miles to pick up the highway he wanted. He drove out of the gas station and turned south. He adjusted his rear view mirror and caught a glimpse of a flatbed truck carrying a tan BMW. It was heading north.

"That can't be it," Ed mumbled. "I ain't that bad with numbers. That guy's been here getting a tire changed. It can't be the same guy."

Ed kept driving south

"Besides the driver asked where he could chow down. He bought a ton of stuff before."

Ed looked at the seat beside him. It was full of empty wrappers.

"Hell, yes!" he exclaimed.

He found Dell's Diner with no problem. He fastened two new devices to the car and then he went in and ordered pie and coffee.

Afterward Ed followed close behind the truck. He knew he had planted two new tracking devices, but at night all headlights in the rearview mirror look pretty much the same. Together they drove through Nashville and into Kentucky. Neither stopped until they hit Evansville, Indiana. Ed had to stop. He was out of gas.

To his relief the trucker pulled in as well. The young man ran to the restroom while Ed filled his tank.

We must be close, Ed thought.

An hour later the trucker turned west and entered Central Illinois. Ed Ornstein knew where he was heading. There was only one prison big enough with the segregation protocol in place for dangerous felons. He figured Shakir Aloman would be tagged thus.

It was no place for an innocent man.

Eugene Powell avoided returning Professor Burrow's call until late afternoon when his partner entered his office and told him he should see what the professor wanted.

"But he's on her side," Powell protested.

"We've never walked into court unprepared," Hillers argued. "Why are you walking into this situation blindly?"

"I guess that makes sense," Eugene acquiesced. "Let's hear what he has to say."

Professor Burrows picked up his phone on the first ring.

"Sorry, it took me so long to return your call," Eugene Powell said politely.

"It's about your charge that Aleta Praetzel is practicing law without a license. She isn't."

Eugene Powell suddenly had an idea. He smiled at his partner to show him he was in control. Hillers responded by leaning back in his chair.

"She took a pro bono client," he said. "I know she's not accepting payment, but she can't do pro bono work either."

"She's house attorney for the Tontine Trust. Sadah Aloman works for the Tontine Trust."

"She does?" Eugene responded in mock dismay. "Then Mrs. Praetzel shouldn't be charged. That would be a big mistake."

"I thought maybe you and I and Roy could agree it would be best to drop the whole thing before the committee meets," Burrows offered. "We all make mistakes."

The condescension rankled Powell.

"Especially when we're lied to," he retorted. "I can't begin to tell you how angry I am with Mrs. Aloman. I carefully questioned her, even explained what pro bono meant and not once did she mention that she was receiving legal advice as an employee benefit."

Hillers nodded vigorously to encourage his partner's argument.

"Perhaps she didn't know," Burrows put forth.

"The woman is a college graduate," Powell spit out. "Of course she knew. I don't know what game she is playing, but I won't be part of it anymore. Her husband can rot in jail for all I care."

"I thought you suggested Mrs. Aloman go to Mrs. Praetzel," Burrows said. He was vexed that Powell was shifting the blame and feeling so self-righteous in the process.

"Me? Never!" Powell protested. "Another lie! I would take the woman to court only she doesn't have a dime."

Hillers made a motion with his hand signaling Powell to cut it there.

"I think the whole mess is better dropped," Powell said. "I'll call Roy."

Powell placed the receiver back on the cradle, turned to his partner and smiled.

"He offered to bury it."

"She won't make it back for the hearing, will she?" Melvin Hillers remarked. "That's why you're smiling, isn't it?"

"It'll be a black mark against her, but I'm not counting on that to bury her. In fact, I'm not going to cry foul there because I plan to use her explanation against her. And that's where I'm going to beat her—in a trial, in Superior Court where it counts. Not in some closed hearing in Juvenile Court. "

"The multimillion dollar Debi Lu Reid suit?"

"That's one."

"Will she be lead in that one?"

"Her husband's listed as lead counsel," Powell said. "And her husband has been seriously injured. And the trial date has been set."

"You pulled some strings?"

"I got Judge Hector Zimmitti to find a spot in is calendar next week."

"Will you be ready?"

"Reid is heavily invested in the success of this project." Powell stated. "He's putting his whole firm on it. I need to strike while Stanley Praetzel is out sick. The only other lawyer the Tontine has is Aleta Praetzel."

"You said 'one'. Do you plan on opposing her on two cases?"

"Yes, I can multi-task," Eugene Powell bragged.

"What other case are you taking on?"

"I'm going to ask the D.A. to appoint me Special Prosecutor in the Aloman case."

"That's a big case."

"The work's been done. The Feds have prepared a solid case. All I need to do is argue it."

"If you win, it'll make you the best candidate for State Senator."

"Do you see any problems?"

"No. In fact, the longer the Praetzels stay away, the less prepared either of them will be. He doesn't have a staff to help them with the investigative work on the Aloman case. And the Reid case is a he-said-she-said deal."

After Powell hung up, Burrows called Peets. "It was the most difficult thing I've ever done. The man is an insufferable bigot and he deserved to be castigated in public. And Aleta would have done a magnificent job catching him in such an obvious attempt to discredit her. Remind me why I was even nice to him."

"Because you've been invited to her next party. Without Aleta, there'd be no party."

"Are my motives so trivial?"

"Saving a life is trivial?"

"No, wanting to go to her party."

"The emphasis is on 'her'."

"You're right. She's worth the sacrifice I made."

"It was that bad?" Peets asked sympathetically.

"I wanted to smash my fist in his face."

"Have you figured out what Aleta believes is proof."

"Not a clue," Burrows said. "He often would side with a black applicant that I didn't think should be even allowed to take the exam."

"What kind of lawyers did they make?"

"Almost every one of them flunked the bar."

"A lot of applicants flunk, especially the first exam."

"Yeah, I know," Burrow said. "Powell sure seemed to be willing to go to bat for those guys though. His favorite phrase was, 'Let's give the guy a break. Let's give him a chance to prove he can do it.'"

"That doesn't sound like negative racism. If anything it smacks of the 'affirmative action' mentality overdone. Do you suppose he gets off on seeing blacks flunk the exam?"

"Maybe, but he does give them a chance."

"All of them?"

"That would be too blatant."

"Are his reasons for rejecting blacks consistent?"

"I'm not sure."

"Aleta's a numbers person. She saw percentages," Peets said. "She and her grandmother have this uncanny skill not only to remember numbers, but to put them into meaningful patterns."

"Now I'm intrigued," Professor Burrows said. "I'm pretty fair with statistics myself."

"Let me know what you find," Peets said.

"If Aleta's proof is statistical, I'll see that it's brought to light."

"Tread carefully. Remember Aleta has been attacked every day for the past three days."

Chapter 14

As that conversation was taking place in Illinois, the subject and her husband were lodged near Birmingham, Alabama in an upstairs suite of rooms overlooking green hills sprinkled with spring blooms. Aleta and Stanley woke simultaneously at a quiet knock on the door.

Aleta jumped out of bed, grabbed her robe, and ran to the door.

The soft knock was repeated and a voice said, "Housekeeping."

"Just a minute, please," Aleta called as she slipped into the robe. She heard a grunting behind her. She glanced over her shoulder and saw that Stanley had grabbed the covers and pulled them to his chest. She opened the door. "Just the bathroom today. My husband is recovering from an operation and he had a relapse last night."

"Aleta," Stanley hissed. "The towels?"

The maid turned around.

"Would you leave us an extra set of towels?" Aleta asked quickly as she sat down on the edge of the bed and picked up the phone and ordered breakfast.

"What's with the cream of wheat, tea and toast?" Stanley hissed as the maid ran the water in the bathroom.

"You're post op," Aleta said. "That's what I always got."

"I didn't have an anesthetic," Stanley quipped, "in case you forgot."

"I didn't forget. And you may not know it but your system underwent a major shock," Aleta responded.

"My system has recovered and it's hungry."

"Then the cream of wheat will taste great," Aleta grinned impishly.

"We didn't have supper last night," Stanley argued.

"Well, we'll have it tonight. And today you'll even have lunch."

"I hate to ask what I get for lunch. I'll bet its soup and Jell-O?"

"Of course. That's what my first lunch always was."

"I can't heal if I don't give my body any fuel to use in the regeneration process."

"Stanley, you have a few extra pounds in reserve that your body can draw from."

"No, I haven't!"

"I saw them, remember."

"You couldn't see anything," Stanley insisted. "There was too much..."

Her finger went lightly on his lips and he stopped talking until after the maid left.

When the door closed, Aleta peeled back the covers and looked at the wound in Stanley's side.

"It's swollen," she announced. "Does it hurt?"

"Of course it hurts!" Stanley exclaimed. "What kind of question is that?"

"I don't know if what I'm looking at is normal or not?"

"Take my temperature."

"With what?"

"Just don't touch it."

"I think we should put ice on it," Aleta suggested lightly touching his forehead.

"I think we shouldn't put anything on it," Stanley said.

"Ice. That's what we'll do," she decided. "You have a fever."

"'Nothing' and 'ice' don't sound alike to me. And you can't tell if I have a fever without a thermometer."

"And you don't like pickles with ice cream."

"What's that got to do with anything?"

"It's a terribly long wound," Aleta mused aloud. "I can't believe I made that many stitches."

"I can. I thought you'd never stop."

"I'm glad you didn't ask."

"But I did ask."

"Not really," Aleta said getting up. "I need to get dressed."

"Where are you going?" Stanley asked suspiciously.

"To scare up some ice packs."

"That's what the phone is for."

"I want to see if there's any kind of drugstore downstairs where I could buy a thermometer."

"You ordered room service," Stanley said. "You need to be here."

"You're absolutely right," Aleta agreed. "After breakfast, if you're still hot, I'll give you a cold bath."

"No, you won't."

"Then I'm going out to get a thermometer so I can prove to you that you have a fever," she said with conviction.

He folded.

"Okay, a bath it is."

Breakfast did not go well. Stanley discovered he wasn't as hungry as he thought he was. Aleta saved some of her toast and the unopened juice for later. He ate half his warm cereal and took a few sips of tea.

Aleta drew the bath, just enough cool water to cover his legs and lower hips. She made him put both hands in the water which was deep enough to completely cover half his lower arms. After a few minutes, she left him, telling him she just remembered where in her purse she might have a couple of aspirin.

Once out of sight, she took the car keys from the dresser where she'd laid them and put them in her purse. She unzipped a special pocket in her purse and found a small tin of aspirin.

Let there be some, she prayed. There were three.

She took the three into the bathroom, poured a glass of water and made Stanley take them all.

She felt his head. It seemed cooler.

"It's working," she announced.

"Yeah, now I'm freezing," Stanley complained.

She helped him up, dried him and helped him back into the bed.

"Close your eyes," she said. "Let the aspirin knock your fever down the rest of the way."

"You're going out, aren't you?"

"Yes. I need to get more aspirin."

"Don't tell anyone where we are."

"I won't," she promised. "I need money."

"My wallet's in the top drawer."

She took out a couple of bills and glanced back at Stanley. His eyes were closed. She didn't dare put her hand on his forehead. Suppose the aspirin wasn't working.

Within minutes she was backing the car out of the space in the underground garage. As soon as she emerged, she opened her cell phone and punched a single number.

"Please," she prayed.

"Dr. Cook," said the familiar warm baritone.

"It's me, Aleta. I'm in terrible trouble. Stanley is so sick."

"Get him to a hospital."

"Can't."

"Why not?"

"Last hospital we were in I was almost killed while I was waiting for the doctor to fix Stanley. He had to tear the IV out of his arm and rescue me. The cops were going to shoot me."

"I don't understand why you called me."

"Last night I operated on Stanley and took out the bullet."

"You did what?" he asked shocked.

"We had no choice," Aleta rushed on. "I used clean instruments and antiseptic but I think the wound got infected. He's burning up."

"You need to get the fever down," Dr. Cook said.

"I gave him a cool bath and some aspirin. I'm driving to a pharmacy to get more aspirin. Shouldn't he have an antibiotic?"

"It's standard after surgery," Dr. Cook said. "What did you use for anesthetic?"

"Nothing."

"Good Lord, Aleta! That must have hurt like hell."

"It did. Lots of stitches too."

"You stitched him up?" Awe crept into the doctor's voice.

"We survived three attacks last night before we ran. Believe me, Dr. Cook, I didn't want to do this."

"First of all, Aleta, don't kick yourself. We get infections in hospitals despite our best efforts," Dr. Cook said. "You're doing the right things so far. If you'll have the pharmacist call me, I'll order an antibiotic for Stanley."

"I'm pulling into town. Don't ask the pharmacist where he is. I'll hand him my phone. Will that work?"

"Yes."

"Are you using your name?"

"For this, yes. I don't want you to get in trouble."

"I can write him a prescription for a pain killer. It will make him drowsy."

"If it's a narcotic, I'll have trouble." Aleta decided, "So he'll have to depend on aspirin. Tell me what else I need to know. How about the bandaging? Should I use ice packs on the wound? What should I be feeding him?"

As she drove, Dr. Cook answered all her questions and added a number of instructions of his own.

She kept him on the line as she parked in front of a small drugstore. She walked back to the pharmacy section, told the pharmacist that she was a tourist, that her husband had become ill and that she had her hometown doctor on the phone.

He listened to the doctor's instructions, acting as if this was a normal occurrence. She went through the store selecting the other items Dr. Cook suggested. Shopping was something she rarely did. Comparison shopping was a concept unknown to her, so she picked up the first item of the type she wanted that she spotted. It meant she managed to gather all the items on the list by the time the prescription was ready.

As the pharmacist was ringing up her total and putting the items in a plastic sack, he said casually, "Someone was in here looking for you a little bit ago."

"Really?" she responded casually. "Did he give his name?"

"No, but he seemed to know your husband was sick."

"Do you know which way he went?"

"Sorry."

"That's alright. If it was important, he'd have left a number.

"Oh, he did," the pharmacist said. "I'm to call him if I see you."

"How much?"

"What?"

"How much did he say he'd pay you?"

"Well... I..."

"Someone is stalking us."

"He offered me twenty," the pharmacist said ruefully, placing the prescription in the plastic bag.

"Here's a hundred," Aleta said. "Don't tell him you've seen me."

"Too late," the pharmacist said, tucking the hundred in his pocket. "That's him coming across the street now."

Aleta threw three hundreds on the counter. "Keep the change. Where's your back door?"

He pointed. She grabbed the plastic bag and ran toward the door, but stopped short and ducked into the bathroom instead. She didn't know why she did it; but, when she heard a rough voice raised on the other side of the wall, she knew she'd made a good choice.

Running footsteps came and went and the door slammed. She heard the lock snap into place. You could go out but not come back in. She left the restroom and hurried to the front.

"He saw me ringing up the sale," the pharmacist said. "And he guessed."

"I heard," Aleta said. "Did he take the money?"

"He grabbed it right out of my hand

She reached into her purse and pulled out a hundred. "It's all I have left."

"You didn't steal it. He did."

"You shouldn't be out on my account."

"He said he knew you were here because he saw your car."

"Maybe I can drive away fast enough...," Aleta began as she hurried toward the door.

"Wait!" the pharmacist called. "Nancy, watch the store."

Aleta hesitated. She'd promised Stanley she wouldn't tell anyone. Still, she walked back to the pharmacist. Instinct told her she couldn't outrun her pursuer.

"We'll take my truck. No one will follow me. I make deliveries all the time."

She followed him out the rear door to a five year old truck with the name of the store painted on the white doors. The extended cab gave Aleta an idea. She climbed in back and lay down on the seat, then told the pharmacist to go down the street past her car in the opposite direction from where they were going.

"Where is that?" he asked.

She laid her head back. "You know there's only one place around here whose guests would carry hundred dollar bills in their wallet instead of twenties."

"I know a back road," he said.

However long it takes, Aleta thought. It's essential I get back to Stanley alive and undetected.

As the truck turned onto a bumpy gravel road, Aleta stayed down and out of sight. The pharmacist's truck with him alone in the front seat might be noticed, but that's all. If she were in sight, it would cause gossip.

Stanley is probably beginning to panic, she thought. Wait, Stanley doesn't panic. He'll first try to get up and then he'll try to get dressed so he can go check to see if I took the car. That's what he'll do. That should keep him busy until I return.

Of course, it's possible, he'll trust me to come back safely, she mused. Then she smiled. If he does get up, I'll have something to hang over his head for the next twenty years. It would be just like him to lie there and prove he trusts me beyond all reason. He can be such an exasperating man sometimes. Why does he think I'm such a miracle worker? My ability to prophecy is apart from who I am. It's a gift outside my control. It's not me."

She lay in the back seat as it bounced lightly along the rough road. She had a tight grip on the handles of the plastic bag.

I have to get there in time, she thought. He has to get better. Who else in the world would go through that much pain just to save me from possible danger? It wasn't even real at the time. People will do such things without thinking; but, he made a conscious choice.

She remembered how he begged her to stop. He was in such pain that he couldn't prevent the words from coming out. He had to beg and argue and plead. It was the only way he could survive what was happening to him.

If he'd gotten up while she was gone, she wouldn't hold it over his head. He'd trusted her to cut into him with a scalpel. Talk about trust. He'd trusted her not to stop midway no matter how much at the moment he wanted it. He trusted her to know what he needed her to do. He trusted her enough so he didn't even tell her.

This morning when he asked why she didn't stop when he asked, she thought he was pleased not to know exactly what clued her in to ignoring his request. He didn't want to know if there were magic words that would have stopped her. He never wanted to know.

What stopped her? She smiled as she thought about it. What had stopped her? He would laugh if he knew. He'd told her what to do. She'd agreed. It was a pact. Nothing he'd said had persuaded her to break that pact. She knew it was going to hurt. He was shocked at how much.

But not once did he put his hand on hers to stop her. His hands weren't tied down.

When she opened the door to the room, Stanley's eyes were open. "You've been gone a long time."

"Yes, I have," Aleta admitted. "How are you feeling?"

"You went to Jackson's Pharmacy?"

Aleta looked at the bag. "He drove me home."

"Why?"

"They spotted my car," Aleta said.

"I didn't want you to take such a chance," he remarked calmly.

"How come you aren't angry?"

"Who did you call?"

"Dr. Cook. He told me everything I need to do for you. And the first thing is to take your temperature."

She dumped the contents of the bag on the bed, grabbed the thermometer, unwrapped it, and stuck it in his mouth.

"You just keep your mouth closed and I'll answer all your questions in the next three minutes," she said gaily.

Without further ado, she plunged into her phone conversation with Dr. Cook and then her narrow escape at the pharmacy.

She stared at her watch during her spiel because she didn't want to be stopped by Stanley's possible look of disapproval. Half way through, he took her hand and held it gently, squeezing it occasionally. Still she didn't look at him.

At three minutes, she stopped talking, pulled the thermometer from his mouth and gasped. She felt his head and then hurried into the bathroom.

Stanley picked up the thermometer and read it: 103 degrees. He heard the water running and knew he was in for another cold soak. He reached down the bed covers and picked up the prescription bottle and read the label.

He sighed with relief when he saw the bottle contained a ten day supply. He snagged the other items on the bed one by one. He stretched as far as he could without bending because any torso movement was painful. He snagged a second bottle of prescription pills. Codeine. A three-day supply.

Dr. Cook wasn't raising any red flags.

"I can't give you that until your temp goes down," Aleta announced walking back into the room, removing her clothes as she walked.

"It's not going to go down if you take off your clothes."

"Yes, it will. Hopefully your blood pressure will go up," Aleta said. "And this will tell me if I do indeed have that effect on you."

She opened up a small box Stanley hadn't been able to reach.

"It's a wrist blood pressure cuff—digital, accurate, painless and takes your pulse as well."

Stanley heard the excitement in her voice. She was like a kid with a new toy. If she bought it, she was planning to use it. A dreadful thought occurred to him.

"You didn't get a...," he couldn't spit out the words.

"I'm not giving you an enema," she told him. "I told Dr. Cook I'd feed you prunes instead."

"I hate prunes."

"Then you better hope your intestines don't go on strike."

"There are laxatives, you know."

"I like natural remedies."

"Does what I like matter?"

"Not during your recovery. I'm in charge," she said, smiling impishly as she added, "Dr. Cook's orders."

She fastened the cuff on his wrist and pushed a couple buttons then went into the bathroom and got a glass of water. She noted his pressure on a pad and then had him sit up. She handed him two antibiotic pills and the glass of water. He swallowed them without comment.

She finished undressing, carefully folding each item of clothing as he habitually did. There was no maid to pick up and she was sensitive to his dislike of disorder. The mess on the bed was meant to intrigue him while she prepared his bath.

She left it untouched while she urged him to stand up. She knew he would rather she straightened up first, but she worried that she'd already delayed too long.

"We're on my schedule," she commented. "I'll get to that later."

"It'd only take a few minutes," he said.

"You're hoping the water will warm up, aren't you?" she said. "If it does, I'll just draw more."

"You're enjoying this, aren't you?"

"I am indeed," she admitted, "especially the fact that you're making such a fuss over being mildly uncomfortable after last night."

"Aren't you going to tell me how brave I was," he grunted as she helped him sit down in the cold water. To his surprise she stepped into the tub and sat down facing him.

"This could be fun," she said. "It's a bit cold."

"It's freezing," Stanley said.

"That's because you have a fever," Aleta responded.

"How long?" Stanley asked, trembling from the cold.

"Until I say we're done," Aleta said quietly. "Afterward I will give you a codeine pill and bandage your wound."

"I don't like the sound of that."

"We need to fight the infection externally as well as internally," Aleta said. "I know some of what I am going to do will be unpleasant."

"That's too mild a term," Stanley protested.

"Horrible?" Aleta offered.

"Detestable!" Stanley countered.

"Awful?"

"Abominable!"

"You win," Aleta laughed. "Your words are better than mine."

"Can we get out now?"

"After we play two more games," Aleta said.

"Games?" Stanley protested. "Aleta, I'm freezing."

"Good! If your brain is frozen I might win one," Aleta said excitedly. "First, twenty questions."

"I'm not up for this," Stanley fussed.

"You win two games in a row and we're out of here," Aleta promised. "I'm thinking 'animal'."

He guessed it after eighteen questions.

"One down, one to go," Aleta announced gleefully. "Four letters, six guesses."

"A new game?"

"Why not?"

They played six games before Stanley won two in a row. Immediately, Aleta stepped out and gave Stanley her hand. Stiff from the cold, he got up slowly.

She toweled him dry gently.

He guided her into a standing position, cupped her chin in his hand and kissed her tenderly. Aleta resisted the temptation to ask for more; but she lingered as long as his lips were near hers. It was a reawakening.

Dr. Cook had said the antibiotic would work quickly. He'd also told her that once Stanley's temperature came down, he'd feel better.

She knew the next step was one Stanley would hate; but, Dr. Cook had told her it was necessary. She helped him back in bed, carefully avoiding his wound.

She spent a few minutes putting the scattered supplies in the top drawer. Stanley watched her hoping she had forgotten the wound cleaning. When she disappeared into the bathroom and reappeared with a towel, washcloth, cotton and antiseptic, he knew she hadn't forgotten.

"I'm feeling better," he said optimistically.

"I know," she replied matter-of-factly. Stanley recognized the nurse-mode at once.

"Maybe we could order lunch," he asked hopefully.

"As soon as I finish. I don't want to be rushed."

"You don't think we could skip this part?"

"No."

"Even if I ask you to? Even if I say I'm willing to take the consequences of my decision?"

"No."

"Even if I say I don't think I can handle any more pain?"

"No," Aleta said decisively. She handed him the washcloth. "Use the pillow under your head to stifle your screams. It's important that no one hear you."

"This is important?"

"Yes."

"This is the only time?"

"No. We do this daily until the wound heals," she informed him.

"What if I say no?"

"You won't," Aleta declared staunchly.

The wound cleansing was as painful as he had anticipated. He used both arms to keep the pillow over his face. Breathing was not a priority. He half-hoped he would pass out. That, however, didn't happen. He stayed wide awake and acutely aware during the entire proceeding.

The pain had been less severe, but he was more apprehensive than the night before. It felt the same. Eventually, it ended.

"I thought you were going to give me something to ease the pain," Stanley admonished.

"You didn't ask for it."

"I can't go through this again," Stanley declared.

"Tomorrow I'll ask," Aleta said. "The one thing I have to block out is the pain I'm causing you or I can't do what needs to be done."

"You can block it out?" he inquired, surprised.

"Stanley, I am so sorry. I feel so helpless when it comes to assuaging your pain that the only way I can handle it is to turn my back on it."

"But you don't," Stanley assured her. "Your touch is always gentle. I am injured. Pain is part of that."

"After lunch," Aleta said, "I will show you how much pleasure I can give you."

Stanley's countenance grew grim. "I don't think you understand."

"Dr. Cook prescribed it as therapy. You will like it."

"You talked with Dr. Cook about that?" Stanley gasped, reddening.

"Not in person," she hastened to explain. "Over the phone."

"That's in person," Stanley exclaimed.

"Not really. He's hundreds of miles away."

"In person means you and he talked one on one."

"Oh, that 'in person'," she quipped. "Yes, I did. He was very helpful. He said you taught him a lot."

Stanley groaned. "I want our love life to be private—very private."

"He's a doctor. He's used to discussing sex."

"No, he's not," Stanley declared. "Nobody asks their doctor about sex."

"You want me to ask your mother?"

"Heaven sake, no! Never! Never! Never!"

"That's how I feel too."

Stanley sighed. "Dr. Cook doesn't know how badly I'm hurt."

"Sure he does. He asked very specific questions," Aleta said. "And that was to the fat layer I cut through."

Stanley's mind jumped back to the main topic of conversation.

"I can't, Aleta. I'm sorry, but I can't."

"Oh, you aren't to move," Aleta said. "You are to just enjoy."

"I'm not sure I can even do that," he said regretfully.

"You'll have the power to say 'stop'," Aleta said sagely.

Stanley stopped protesting.

Lunch for Stanley was soup and Jell-O. Aleta wasn't giving up her nursing duty, he realized. They were on her schedule. He hoped there were no more cold baths on that schedule. The lack of food he could live with, but sitting in cold water was something else.

Sitting up wasn't easy; but, Aleta insisted that he needed to move a bit on a regular basis. She ignored every complaint he made about movement being painful. He desperately wanted her to baby him. To soothe him. To feel sorry for him. He wanted her to mother him.

Before the steward cleared the lunch dishes, she settled him back in bed. After the steward left, Aleta undressed and crawled in bed beside her husband.

"Now for your dessert," she said. "Close your eyes and relax."

She kissed him tenderly on his lips. It was a brief kiss. When she withdrew she whispered, "Remember, you have the power now."

He wanted to say something about her saying that meant she was still in charge. The problem was she wasn't mothering him. She was nursing him. He didn't want a nurse. He wanted to be coddled. He wanted to feel loved.

She kissed him on the mouth again. Then with a touch as light as the brush of a butterfly wing she kissed his cheek, then his shoulder. Her lovemaking slowly progressed, each touch as light as the last. He felt his whole body beginning to respond. And he didn't stop responding. Aleta never stopped her ministrations until he'd reached the end he thought he couldn't reach, injured as he was.

How she had managed to elicit such completion without hurting him he didn't know. What she had done was greater than the physical satisfaction she'd given him. She had loved him as only a wife can. She gave him love as a woman gives a man. He didn't know it could be richer than a mother's love, but it was.

Late that afternoon when Stanley woke, he saw that Aleta was dressed. She was heading toward the door.

He looked down and realized he was covered.

Was it supper time, he wondered. He was certainly hungry enough.

She took the towels from the maid and closed the door. More towels could only mean one thing. He was beginning to feel good. A bit warm, perhaps, but otherwise fine.

She returned, stuck a thermometer in his mouth, put the blood pressure cuff on his wrist and jotted both readings on her pad.

"Well?" he said, his tone demanding a report.

"Blood pressure is a little low, but not bad. Your temperature is over 102. You are going to have another bath," she said beginning to strip.

"Why are you always taking off your clothes?"

"I only have one clean outfit left. This one has to last."

"How about an aspirin instead of a bath," he asked hopefully.

"You're getting both."

He lay quietly and reminded himself that even though she was going overboard in her regime of care, because she was, he was probably going to recover. Even though there were times when that goal seemed less important, there was no stopping Aleta.

He wondered what she would do if he refused to take a bath. She couldn't carry him. He decided to try. The antibiotic was already working he knew. Another cold bath was superfluous. Aspirin was all he needed. He could take a stand on this issue. He smiled at the prospect.

She turned off the water and reentered the bedroom.

"Why are you smiling like a Cheshire cat?" she asked. "Do you think you're going to refuse to take this bath?"

His smiled broadened. "Uh-uh."

She threw off his sheet. "Then I'll wash one part at a time, beginning with this one."

What she grabbed sparked immediate compliance.

"You don't play fair," he grumbled as she led him into the bathroom.

She let go of his member and stepped into the tub first.

"Come, join me," she said.

Reluctantly, he stepped into the tub.

She drew him to her and kissed him. He felt a tingle of excitement stir his heart into beating faster. Nothing was ever the same with Aleta.

Her body felt cool against his. She was right. He had a fever. Slowly, he sat down and she came with him.

Without warning, he splashed water on her upper body.

"You're still angry about the penis thing, aren't you?"

He splashed her again. She shivered but she didn't splash back.

"Why don't you splash me?" he asked, knowing full well she wouldn't. Keeping his wound dry was a sacred trust with her. Suddenly, he was ashamed of himself. He reached over and wiped the drops of cold water from her body. "I'm sorry. I acted like a child."

"You are having a rough time," she responded sympathetically. "I'm sorry I can't skip any procedures Dr. Cook laid out. Too much is at stake. If you relapse, we'll be in big trouble."

"I had forgotten all that," Stanley said. "I was so focused on eliminating any more pain that I didn't think about what might happen if I got my way. You're right. We can't afford to take chances."

"We're already taking a chance staying here," Aleta said. "Our car's sitting on the main street in downtown Hoover."

"Then we need to move it," Stanley said, "so whoever's after us will think we're gone."

"We can't send anyone for it."

"Yes, we can."

"They'll follow it to here."

"We call the rental agency and say the car's parked in Hoover and we're not able to return it."

"You can do that?"

"Offer to pay to have someone pick it up," Stanley said. "And apologize."

"As soon as we finish, I'll call," Aleta said.

"Do it now," Stanley said. "I'll stay put."

Chapter 15

The next day Stanley felt stronger. The cold baths were discontinued. The wound cleaning he elected to endure without codeine. He didn't want to be woozy in case there was trouble.

Hours folded into days. Aleta rarely left the room, using the phone to order everything. She spent most of the day naked by choice. He found that his robe belt hit his wound, so he decided that since they were alone, he might as well opt for comfort.

Aleta never seemed to tire of giving him sexual pleasure. He wished fervently he could reciprocate but the wound limited his movement.

Somehow she sensed his desire; however, she refused to let him participate telling him that he might mess up his stitches and she wasn't going to redo them. The thought quickly cooled his desire to reciprocate.

Each day she examined the wound and announced, "We need to stay one more day."

She never worried aloud about when they were going to be able to leave for home. Somehow they both knew that the infection had set back the healing process. There was nothing to do but wait and hope no one would find them. He couldn't fly them home. On the fourth day, he suggested they drive home.

"You can barely sit long enough to eat," she pointed out.

"I could lay down on the rear seat," he proposed.

"While the car bounced along," she snapped. "There's no way we're doing that! Period!"

He didn't bring up the idea again.

Back in Illinois, Lyle West was the first to voice an opinion in the group that had gathered to discuss the situation.

"It's been six days since anyone's heard anything," Lyle West said. "We have got to find them."

"The car was returned four days ago," Ed Ornstein put in. I've checked every hotel register in a fifty mile radius of Hoover. There is no Stanley Praetzel or Aleta Locke in any of them. I checked both names misspelled, plus Luther and Davis, in case one of them had either Harriet's credit card or Lydia's."

"He must have paid cash," Stanley's father said.

The group was gathered at Aleta and Stanley's house. Bertha served coffee and fresh cinnamon rolls. It was early morning. Hubert had a late court appearance. Robert just didn't go in. Alice would field the calls. There wasn't much he could do without Stanley.

Claude and Harriet had come over when Lyle called.

Both Milani and Peets were there. Milani had stationed men at the airport day and night. Peets had reported that Burrows sensed that Powell was still incensed.

While Ed had shut down the website, he couldn't guarantee that no one was still tracking the couple.

Harriet spoke up. "Let's put our heads together and come up with the most likely choices the two of them would make."

"That'll be hard," Hubert said. "I would never have believed Stanley would have left the hospital before the bullet was removed."

"But he did," Harriet said. "So what would they do first?"

"Get him medical help," Hubert proposed.

"Aleta would have insisted upon it," Robert said.

"I checked every hospital and emergency room in the area," Ed reported. "I've checked every gunshot wound reported."

"So it wasn't reported," Harriet said. "That leaves three options. Either it was never removed or it was removed by a doctor that Stanley bribed not to report it or..."

"Aleta wouldn't let him suffer for six days," Robert said. "It was removed."

"Stanley wouldn't bribe a doctor to do something illegal," Hubert said.

"That leaves the third option," Harriet said.

"What third option?" Peets asked.

"Would she do that?" Hubert asked Robert.

"Do what?" Peets pressed.

"She hates the sight of blood," Aleta's father replied.

"Does anyone have another explanation?" Harriet queried.

"She operated on him," Lyle surmised. "Without anesthetic! My God!"

"She would never have volunteered," Robert put in.

"Stanley would have chosen that route," Lyle said. "She wouldn't have done it otherwise."

"He would do anything to protect her," Hubert said.

"Suppose something went wrong?" Robert said.

"Who would she call?" Harriet asked.

"Dr. Cook!" Lyle concluded. "Let me call him."

Fifteen minutes later Dr. Cook arrived. When he saw the group, he knew why he'd been summoned.

"She took out the bullet, didn't she?" Harriet asked.

"I'm sorry I can't discuss this with you."

"He's my son!" Hubert exclaimed.

"She's my daughter!" Robert put in.

"It's privileged."

"We need to find them, Wayne," Lyle said.

"You're on your own," Dr. Cook replied. "Anything else?"

"Do you know where they are? That's not privileged."

"No, I don't."

"Did either of them say anything about their location?" Lyle pressed.

"Not to me."

"Where was she when she called?" Lyle asked.

"I didn't say she called," Dr. Cook said. "Now if you'll excuse me, I'll get back to the hospital."

"Thank you, Dr. Cook," Harriet said. "You've told us what we wanted to know."

"I've told you nothing," Dr. Cook protested.

"Exactly. Only a doctor that's involved would be so non-communicative," Harriet said. "I'm glad she called you."

After he left, Harriet said, "What's the most common problem following surgery?"

"Infection," Claude said. "Stanley would need antibiotics."

"Dr. Cook prescribed them," Lyle said. "All he had to do was call the pharmacy, give them his number and the prescription would have been made up."

"She wouldn't have gone too far," Harriet said. "Not with Stanley so sick she'd risk a call."

"You're thinking she was frightened into abandoning the car," Lyle said. "That means they're near Hoover. Ed did you bring the lists?"

"On my laptop," he said, opening it on the table.

"Try the most exclusive first," Harriet suggested. "Select for the guests that arrived six days ago."

"Done," Ed said. "Four couples. As I said before, no Praetzels."

"Read the names," Lyle said.

"Porth, Coleman, Stanley and Bechard," Ed read.

"Of course!" Lyle exclaimed. "Stanley."

"See if they are still there," Harriet said.

"They're still on the list," Ed announced.

"They're taking a terrible chance," Lyle said. "They wouldn't still be there if they could leave."

"Stanley's not well enough to pilot a plane," Harriet said. "And Aleta can't. For some reason she won't drive either."

"We need to go get them," Hubert said.

"We need at least three pilots," Robert said. "One of us needs to bring their plane home."

"Take Dr. Cook with you," Harriet said. "How many can your plane carry, Hubert?"

"Claude's big one carries more," Hubert suggested.

"It's being worked on," Claude remarked.

"My plane can carry eight," Hubert said.

"Six can go," Harriet said.

"No eight," Claude corrected her. "Two of us can fly Stanley's plane back."

"Six," Harriet reiterated. "We can't count on Stanley's plane being there."

"We're not going to a foreign country," Claude said. "We're flying to Alabama."

Harriet eyed him coolly.

"Okay, six," he agreed.

"And you are all going as my deputies," Lyle announced. "That way you'll all know I'm the leader."

"Who's the sixth person?" Hubert asked.

"Harriet. She's the best shot here," Lyle proclaimed. "And she's a prophet. We need all the help we can muster."

"Do you anticipate trouble?" Robert asked.

"I can't believe we won't be noticed," Lyle remarked.

At the resort hotel near Hoover, the morning had been rainy.

"Not a nice day to be out," Aleta said standing at the window.

"Are we going somewhere?"

"I just have a feeling."

"What kind of feeling?"

"It's nothing," Aleta said brushing away the statement. "I think I'm just a bit homesick."

"Tired of being on a honeymoon?" Stanley inquired knowing full well she wasn't.

"Never!" she exclaimed, half-turning.

"My temperature is rising," Stanley announced as he feasted on the silhouette of his pregnant wife standing naked in the dull light of the rain spotted window.

"Your temperature is not what I affect. It's your blood pressure and it was low enough a few minutes ago to rise a bit and still be healthy."

"It's that time of the morning."

"I'm on a schedule?"

"You've had me on a schedule and my body expects certain pleasures at certain times," he said watching her carefully. If she had received a vision, she would respond differently or not at all.

To his delight, she came over, crept quietly into the bed and kissed him. The only difference was that this time the kiss was passionate.

"Does this mean I'm well?" he asked. Only she could assess his wound. He couldn't twist around enough to see it. When he went into the bathroom where there was a mirror, all he saw was the bandage. He didn't dare remove it. Once it had gotten wet. That day his wound was cleaned twice.

Aleta drew back. "No, you aren't well. You're just irresistible."

"Am I well enough to reciprocate?"

"Nope," she said firmly.

He thought about the kiss as he lay back and released himself into her care. The kiss had been different.

Something was going to happen. Perhaps even she didn't know what.

As her ministrations continued, he forgot about his budding concern. This was too delicious not to savor. He couldn't believe she could bring him to satisfaction so often.

They slept lightly afterward, her hand in its usual place. Her grip tightened slightly. The pressure woke him.

He tried to think about what they could do; but, as he had no idea what was about to happen, he couldn't plan. Before Aleta woke up, he decided to observe and not question. Perhaps her actions would tell him what to do.

The first thing he noticed was that she didn't put on the outfit she had worn since they arrived. Instead she donned the one clean outfit she had left.

"Maybe I should try getting dressed again," he suggested.

"We could try your pajama bottoms," she suggested. "It has a soft band."

He wanted to put on his regular clothes, but he had to agree, starting with pajamas was a reasonable first step.

After I have tried pajamas, I can suggest regular clothes, he reasoned.

Unfortunately, when Aleta pulled the band up, even though it wasn't touching his wound, he immediately pushed it further down on his hips.

"The whole area is still sensitive, isn't it?" she inquired. "Perhaps we should take them off and wait a day."

"No!" he said a bit more stridently than he intended.

"Don't worry. I can put them right here on the bed where you can reach them."

He let her remove them.

I'm overreacting, he thought. I'm seeing shadows where there aren't any. Just because she decided to change clothes was no reason to panic. After all, she hadn't packed or made any other movements that would indicate that today was going to be a day of change.

When Aleta removed her clothes and climbed in bed beside him, he relaxed and fell asleep. He didn't awaken when twenty minutes later she slowly removed her hand and left the bed. He didn't stir when she carefully pulled up the sheet so it covered him.

Aleta went downstairs and requested her bill be prepared.

When her grandmother entered the lobby accompanied by Dr. Cook and Chief Lyle West, Aleta quickly signed the hotel bill and rushed to meet them.

She hugged her grandmother and then led the threesome to her room.

"I didn't know who was coming," she said as they took the elevator up. "Stanley is asleep."

"What do you mean you didn't know who?" Lyle asked.

"Friend or foe," she replied. "I'm not packed. Stanley's not dressed. His wound is too sensitive still."

"We brought an ambulance with us," Dr. Cook said. "He won't need to dress. He's going straight from here to the hospital."

"I followed all your instructions," Aleta said, "but he's taking so long to heal. I think I messed up somehow."

They entered the room.

"Lyle, the bullet's in the top drawer with all the surgical instruments," Aleta said. "I didn't clean them."

Stanley opened his eyes at the sound of Aleta's voice. Startled at the sight of the crowd his hands reached for the sheet.

Dr. Cook strode over to the bed, took the edge of it and lowered it just enough to expose the bandage. He took hold of one end.

"Can't you wait?" Stanley said. "She just cleaned it."

Dr. Cook smiled as he yanked it off. "Doctors don't wait."

"Wow!" Lyle exclaimed. "That bullet really tore you up."

"Neat surgery line though," Dr. Cook said. "Nice job, Aleta."

Aleta flushed with pleasure as she watched Dr. Cook's fingers gently probing the area around the wound.

Harriet turned her eyes away. One glance was enough. She opened the suitcase and began to pack.

"Does he still have a temperature?" Dr. Cook asked.

"Yes," Aleta said.

"When did the antibiotic kick in?"

"First day. The fever came down the second," Aleta said. "I kept a record."

"Can he be moved?" Chief West asked Dr. Cook.

"As soon as I clean this wound," Dr. Cook replied.

Stanley groaned.

Suddenly, Aleta said, "There's no time. He can't even wait for the paramedics to get up the stairs. We have to go right this minute."

"The bullet!" Lyle said.

"Packed," Harriet replied snapping the lock on the suitcase.

Lyle grabbed the case and radioed the group waiting below.

"My pants!" Stanley said. Aleta grabbed the pajama bottoms and quickly helped him slip them on. She and Dr. Cook lifted him to his feet. She grabbed the top but didn't help him into it until they were in the elevator.

It was then she noticed that both Lyle and her grandmother had their guns drawn.

"The bill?" Stanley asked.

"Paid," Aleta replied.

"You knew."

"Only partly," Aleta said.

"She was surprised to see us," Harriet said.

Stanley knew immediately what she had done.

"You were going to sacrifice yourself?" he scolded.

The elevator doors opened.

"Be alert!" Lyle ordered.

To Aleta's amazement, her father and Stanley's were waiting in full body armor, guns drawn. They fell in on each side.

Claude was at the door.

The ambulance was backed up to the entrance. Its doors were open. Dr. Cook helped Stanley in and climbed in after him. Hubert Praetzel climbed in front.

Claude and Harriet ran to the car parked at the side of the ambulance. Harriet reached inside and pulled out a rifle. Lyle threw the suitcase in the open trunk.

The first shot rang out as Robert escorted his daughter from the building to the car Harriet and Claude were guarding.

Harriet spotted the shooter and fired back. There was no returning volley.

Another shot came from even farther away.

Lyle ordered the ambulance away as he joined Robert in shielding Aleta.

Harriet fired again. Again there was silence.

"Get in!" Lyle ordered. "Change of plans. I'm riding with you."

He climbed into the rear seat with Aleta and Robert. Claude had the wheels rolling before all the doors were closed.

Lyle radioed the police unit left sitting in front of the resort. "See no one follows us."

He heard the man reporting the shooting and calling for back-up. The ambulance put on its siren and sped toward the airport. The police car followed, its lights flashing and siren screaming.

A police guard was waiting at the airport. Hubert guided the ambulance driver to his plane. Claude drew up beside the ambulance.

Stanley was carried on board. Harriet opened the suitcase and gave Lyle the towel with the bullet. He handed it to the police chief.

"This should convict the man," West said.

"Why didn't you tell me how important those people were?" the police chief asked.

"My interest should have told you that," Lyle replied.

"Do you know Claude Luther?" the chief asked.

"He's one of my deputies," Lyle responded.

"Whoever killed those men in the field is an expert marksman."

"That was his wife."

"Damn! I was hoping it was a cop."

"She's a deputy," Lyle said calmly.

"Can I just say one of your deputies nailed two assailants?"

"Go ahead. She doesn't want a rep as a sharpshooter."

"Why bring amateurs with you?" the chief asked.

"They own the plane and they're cool under fire."

"This isn't the first time?"

Lyle sighed.

"And it won't be the last."

"Glad I'm not you."

"I'm glad I am me. My whole force is sharp thanks to the challenges these people present. Stanley would never have fled from my hospital in such a condition with three of my officers on the scene. One of them would have done the right thing."

"They followed protocol," the chief said defensively.

"They almost got Aleta killed and they still don't know what they did was wrong."

"What would your guys have done?"

"Noticed that one gun had a silencer," Lyle shot back.

Chapter 16

Dr. Cook told Aleta that he was keeping Stanley in the hospital until the change in antibiotics killed the secondary bacterial infection and his temperature had been normal for a full day. Aleta didn't want to leave his side, but her father told her that the hearing was scheduled for ten the next day. She had no choice.

"Stanley is my lawyer," she protested.

"So, whom do you want to take his place?" her father asked.

"I don't need anyone," Aleta said. "But Jocelyn does. Judge Jacobi will insist upon it."

"Ezra Finch is a good man," Stanley said from the bed. "Call him."

"You will need a lawyer, Dad," Aleta said.

"Hubert volunteered."

"Then I guess we're ready."

"Aleta," Stanley interjected. "I need to see Lyle immediately. It's important and private."

"From me?"

"Aleta, you have enough on your plate without being concerned about everything I'm concerned about."

"But..." she protested.

"Let go, Aleta. Please." Stanley pleaded. "Think about the hearing and the suit and Aloman's trial. All three need your full attention."

Aleta smirked. "Not possible to give three…"

"You are an exasperating woman!" Stanley lashed out.

Aleta immediately changed her approach.

"Oh, Stanley, I am so sorry. How helpless you must be feeling," Aleta said contritely. "Tell me how to handle the hearing and I will do it exactly as you want me to."

Surprised at her about turn, Stanley decided to do just that.

"Just tell the truth. Don't try to explain Jocelyn's words or your father's. They have lawyers capable of defending them. Let Norma Jacobi sort through the mess. She likes to do that. Honor her fantastic brain."

"Honor her," Aleta mused aloud. "I can do that."

"Remember that Powell doesn't."

Aleta leaned over and kissed her husband, and whispered, "Can you sleep by yourself tonight?

Stanley laughed.

"I'll manage. Don't stay up past ten," he said. "That's an order."

Aleta met Lyle on the way out and told him that Stanley had a job for him. Then she giggled.

Lyle was scowling as he walked into Stanley's hospital room.

"What do you mean you have a job for me?"

Stanley realized that Aleta had teased him.

"I have a request," Stanley corrected. "Aleta is angry because I said I wanted to talk with you privately."

"She giggled." Lyle said. "That was disconcerting."

"She gave you both barrels, didn't she?" Stanley noted. "She must really be upset with me. Usually when I want to speak to someone privately, I simply take them into my office and shut the door. I can't do that."

"Ask away," Lyle said. "You restored my mood."

"Tomorrow I need you to do something for me."

At ten o'clock the next morning Judge Norma Jacobi opened by having all those present in the court identify themselves. Lyle West presented himself as amicus curiae.

Debi Lu was sworn in first.

"Tell us what happened at lunch the day of the ride where you wound up so grievously injured," Powell said.

"Jocelyn told us that her sister had predicted that there was going to be an explosion on the trail and she was going to be killed and that was why she wasn't going riding."

"But you took that trail anyway. Why?"

"Excuse me, Counselor; does the witness have an attorney?"

"I am acting as her attorney," Eugene Powell said tersely. "I identified myself as such earlier."

"Then I suggest you act like one," Judge Jacobi scolded. "I will question the witness."

"But he has all the questions written out and my answers too," Debi Lu protested.

"I want to know the reason you told your friends that you didn't believe Jocelyn's story."

Debi Lu relaxed.

"I thought Jocelyn was lying because she was grounded."

"You must have had a reason to believe that, right?"

"If there was a bomb... I mean, if there was a real bomb... her sister would have called the police."

"After you were hurt what did you say to the first person that appeared?

"I yelled at Jocelyn because she whistled to her horse to come and that's the reason I was thrown. The horse wasn't minding me. He was twirling around and fighting me and I got dizzy and when he reared, it was impossible to hang on. She didn't tell me her horse would spook at a little noise. He's a show horse. They are supposed to be used to loud noises. He surprised me. That's what happened. I'm a good rider, but he went wild when she whistled."

"Did the horse throw you before or after the grenade exploded?"

"After."

"That is all, Debi Lu," Judge Jacobi said.

"Don't you want to know how bad I was hurt?"

"I can see that," Judge Jacobi said. "And I'm sorry."

Debi Lu went back to her seat.

Chief West, I will hear you now."

Lyle stood up.

"The police were called," he began. "But not about the explosion. Aleta Praetzel had a vision of two of her horses being put down with broken legs. She didn't know how the legs were broken. Her visions are fragmentary and brief. She told Chief Tom Milani exactly what she had envisioned. Then she guessed that the horses would be in danger if they were taken on the trail. I think her glimpse showed them being shot in some unfamiliar spot.

"Chief Milani arranged to have patrols pass by the Praetzel farm every fifteen minutes. They were to drive up the driveway if anything appeared unusual.

"Hubbs had been given a cell phone. Mrs. Praetzel had a vision of Hubbs dying as she was meeting with the committee of which Mr. Powell is a member. She borrowed his phone and called Hubbs and told him to take two horses out of the barn and walk them to the house. They were two of the horses that would be hurt if anyone rode them.

"Mrs. Praetzel had a hired a private security guard to watch the horses. Mr. Hubbs told him to watch the two remaining horses while he walked to the house with the other two.

"The guard was struck over the head and rendered unconscious. Two witnesses have already given sworn statements that Debi Lu Reid alone attacked the guard.

"Two horses were stolen. Four teenagers were involved.

"Later those four met up with four others with whom they normally rode. The four thieves chose to ride on the old creek trail. The other four decided not to take a chance since Jocelyn's sister had a good track record as far as predicting danger.

"Had Aleta Praetzel known there was a bomb on the trail, she would have told the police. She always informs us of any possible threat no matter how vague. And we follow through.   Jocelyn Locke has never to our knowledge prophesied; however, had she called us, we would have investigated."

"Thank you, Chief West." Judge Jacobi said. "Jocelyn, please come up here and answer a few questions. Clerk, swear her in."

Judge Jacobi started right in.

"Where were you when you horse was being stolen?"

"Getting ice cream," Jocelyn admitted sheepishly. "Bertha had picked me up early at school, so I could be there to help watch the horses, but I figured that we'd make it in time…how was I to know that they'd cut the last class."

"So you didn't take your sister's prediction seriously?"

"Dad told me I was going to be killed," Jocelyn said. "I didn't believe him."

"Why not?" Judge Jacobi asked.

"Because he almost never lies, so when he does, I can tell. He was lying. For some reason he didn't want to tell me the truth. So I was stuck with the fact that Aleta had warned Bertha who had warned him and somewhere along the line, the truth had been twisted. So I told my friends what I believed was the truth—that there was going to be an explosion and I was going to be killed. I found out later that what Aleta saw was my horse being put down because he was injured."

"Did you Dad tell you why he lied?"

"He said he wanted to be sure I didn't go riding."

"And what would you have done if he had told you the truth."

"I would have gone home right away to protect my horse and Aleta's horse. I would have known that Debi Lu and Winnie were planning to borrow them. But I was fooled by the lie. I thought the danger was just to me and I wasn't going riding, so why not get a treat. I really like ice cream."

"One more question, Jocelyn," Judge Jacobi said. "Did you give Debi Lu permission to ride your horse?"

"Nobody rides Yudi but me!" Jocelyn exclaimed. "All my friends know that."

"Thank you, Jocelyn. I'm ready to rule."

Eugene Powell sat mute. The fact that he hadn't been allowed to cross-examine would work to his advantage during the trial. He knew exactly where the weaknesses were.

"First of all, Jocelyn, your friends didn't have your permission to ride your horse, so the term is not "borrow", it is steal. And if they didn't have permission to ride your sister's horse, then the term is still steal even though yours is a show horse and hers is not. He is still her private property.

"Now, as to Aleta Praetzel's actions with regard to safeguarding the horses and trying to prevent an accident, she actually took more than the normal precautions with regard to the danger she saw. She saw two horses being put down as a result of an accident. She did not see the accident; hence she had no reason to call the police. She called them anyway because she noticed that they were being put down someplace away from home, so she guessed correctly that they were about to be stolen. She hired a guard to watch the horses. Had he done his job, none of the Praetzel horses would have left the property and we would not be here.

"Debi Lu, your actions brought about your injury. You didn't have a horse to ride on the trail where you were told there was going to be an explosion. You say that Aleta Praetzel should have warned you and called the police. Aleta Praetzel did not know about the grenade going off. Jocelyn predicted it, so you got the warning straight from the mouth of a prophet and you ignored her advice and took the trail anyway. The question is why didn't you call the police? You were told there was going to be an explosion on a trail you intended to use. Why didn't you call the police and ask them to check it out? Four of your friends elected not to use that trail. They made a wise choice. You chose to prove Jocelyn wrong. You gambled and you lost.

"The court finds no evidence of negligence on the part of Aleta Praetzel. Further, because Jocelyn Locke shared her vision with all those that would possibly be hurt by it, the court deems her not guilty of negligence as well.

"Finally, Debi Lu Reid, please stand before the court."

Debi Lu looked at her attorney as if to ask his permission. He rose and bade her come with him. She stood beside him and faced the judge.

"Debi Lu Reid, this court finds you guilty of grand theft. You took Jocelyn's horse without her permission and rode him on a trail that she said was dangerous. This much you admitted under oath before a judge.

"I sentence to five years to be spent in the appropriate juvenile facility until your twenty-first birthday at which time you will enter the state prison for the remainder of your term. Any subsequent charge resulting from your actions during the theft will be served in addition to, not consecutively with, the sentencing handed down today by this court.

"Bailiff, take Miss Reid into custody. Court adjourned."

Powell rose as soon as the judge had left the courtroom and hissed at Debi Lu's father not to speak until they were alone.

Aleta turned to Lyle and scowled at him.

He smiled at her. "It was Stanley's idea, not mine."

"I didn't get to say a word." Aleta protested.

"He's going to be so pleased."

Dr. Cook sent Stanley home on the fourth day. His wound had closed and the area around it was no longer sensitive to the touch although the scar itself was. It might remain that way for a long time.

As soon as they arrived home, Aleta took Stanley into the bedroom. She closed the door and said, "It's payback time."

Stanley laughed. "Payback for what? The pain or the pleasure?"

She giggled. "For all of it."

His eyes twinkled as he pulled her close. His lovemaking was passionate and left Aleta breathless.

"That," Stanley said, "was for operating on me."

"You hated every second."

"It was one of the most horrible experiences of my life," Stanley remembered. "I don't think I'll ever forget a single moment. But I'll never forget that you did it. I owe you my life."

"Do I get more payback tonight?" she teased.

"As often as you want," Stanley said soberly. "Whenever and wherever you want."

"Then tonight it is. Same place. Seven o'clock."

"Deal," he said.

Aleta smiled. Suddenly, Stanley knew he'd gotten himself into something. He couldn't guess what; but that particular smile meant she was up to some sort of mischief.

"I don't like surprises, Aleta," he said before they sat down to eat that evening.

"Yes, I know."

"I'm wondering why no one came by today."

"Because I told them not to. I said they could visit you tomorrow."

During supper, Stanley reiterated, "I don't like surprises."

"Is being alone a bad surprise?" she asked.

"Well, no. I guess not. In fact, I rather like it."

"Okay, then enjoy it. I can't pull this off any old night I want to you know," Aleta commented.

Aleta began to talk about the parties that were being planned in the near future and Stanley protested because all of them were going to be held at their house.

"I like being alone with you, Aleta," he said.

"It's almost seven o'clock," Aleta noted.

"We haven't had dessert," Stanley protested.

"Afterward," Aleta said. "We had a deal."

"What are you doing?"

"Sticking the dishes in the dishwasher. You don't know how long I've missed using my hands."

Stanley eyed her suspiciously. She never did the dishes.

"Leave them," he said.

"When we come back for dessert, I don't want to see them," she replied. "Do you?"

She won the argument.

"Okay. I'll help," Stanley said. "A deal's a deal."

At exactly seven, Stanley and Aleta entered their bedroom. Aleta locked the door.

"Why did you do that?"

"Have you forgotten we have police on guard around the house?" Aleta said.

"They don't come in."

"I'm taking no chances."

Stanley hesitated, a lingering suspicion that Aleta was planning something. Then she began taking off her clothes, dropping them in a heap as she always did at home. It was so normal an action he found himself relaxing. Whatever she was planning, it wasn't going to happen tonight.

She came over and started undressing him. Knowing his penchant for folding his clothes, she handed him each one. It was an odd beginning to lovemaking. With Aleta, there was always variation. He had never been sexually stimulated while folding his own clothes. Usually she just watched. Of course, she hadn't had the use of both arms for months. She had had no choice.

Thus aroused, Stanley's lovemaking evolved quickly into a passionate exchange that left both of them exhausted and fulfilled.

"It's been so long," Aleta whispered, kissing him. "I'm not a celibate person by nature."

"For that I'm grateful," Stanley murmured. "You don't know how grateful."

Aleta laughed. "Oh I think I know... Wait, did you hear that?"

"What?"

"I heard something," Aleta said. "I think the puppy's loose and into something. Go see."

"Why isn't he in here?"

"Bertha moved him closer to the guest room when we were gone.

Stanley groaned. "Can't you go?"

"Naked?"

"Put on some clothes," Stanley countered. "That's what I'll have to do."

"Mine are a tangled mess. I didn't plan on wearing them again."

Stanley grunted as he pulled on his trousers. "You're punishing me for being neat."

"I'm not punishing you at all," Aleta said. "Don't you want me to stay this way?"

"Yes, I do," Stanley said.

"Put on your slippers. You don't want to step in anything," Aleta said.

Stanley opened the door. "Aleta, didn't you leave a light on?"

Suddenly, Scooby jumped on him.

He knelt down and ruffled the dog's ears. "So you didn't like sleeping all alone in the kitchen. I don't blame you. Let's see what damage you did."

Stanley stood up.

"Aleta, it's Scooby. He got out of his pen."

"I let him out," came a familiar rough feminine voice.

Startled, Stanley stopped dead and blurted out,

"Aleta, we've got company!"

"I know. I want Grams to see my work."

"Your work?"

"Sure," came Aleta's voice. "Dr. Cook said I did a good job. He showed all his interns."

"That was different!" Stanley protested.

"Don't worry, Stanley, we'll stand here in the dark while you put on your shirt," Harriet said.

"We?"

"Claude drove me over and your parents are here too."

"Oh, for Heaven's sake! Aleta!"

"Coming!" she called.

"I'm not a side show!"

"I'm bringing your shirt. Hang on and be nice!"

"I'm always nice," Stanley quipped. "If anyone turns on a light, I'll shoot him."

"Stanley, don't try to bluff your mother," came Lydia's authoritative voice from close by. "Harriet, turn on the flashlight."

"You have a flashlight?" Stanley inquired.

"There's no light in here," Harriet said.

"You came prepared?" Stanley gasped. "Aleta! Get out here! This is your idea. You handle it!"

The door opened and Aleta walked toward Stanley, shirt in hand. She'd turned off the lights in the bedroom so it was still dark.

Scooby jumped on her and she bent over to pet him. She held out the shirt and Hubert took it and helped Stanley slip into it.

"Thanks, Dad," Stanley said, quickly buttoning it.

"You win, Aleta," Hubert announced.

"What do you mean she won?" Stanley demanded angrily.

"She bet none of us would get even a glimpse of her work."

"She bet on me?"

"We thought you wouldn't win if pitted against Harriet and your mother. I'm still not sure how you did; but, even I couldn't trample over your sensitivities. I think she counted on our good taste to hold us back. She's a very astute judge of character."

"She won?"

"Yes. Unless, of course, you'll let your mother see your scar."

"Just the scar," his mother said. "That's why the flashlight. I just want to see what Aleta did."

"She's so proud of the job she did," Harriet put in. "We're sorry if you feel invaded. It was just such a feat."

"Boy, you guys are good!" Stanley remarked. "But you're wrong. Aleta isn't proud of the job she did although she should be. She did indeed manage to operate, remove a bullet and sew me up while I was screaming at her to stop. She persisted and she saved my life. She isn't proud of her accomplishment. She is still too upset over having caused me so much pain. She doesn't see that I am grateful that she had the guts to save my life. I will never forget the agony of that night. Nor will I ever forget her bravery. And that's as much a glimpse of our ordeal as you are going to get. Aleta deserves to win!"

"One thing," Aleta interposed quickly, "before we turn on the lights. Stanley makes light of what he did that night. When I was threatened and the police were no help, he left the hospital, the doctor, the anesthetic behind and whisked me off to a remote resort. Then he told me I had to operate. He is a master persuader. But while I did the surgery, he did the suffering. Yes, he yelled at me to stop. But not once did he put his hand on mine to stop me or roll away. He laid still and let me work. But that wasn't all. Infection set in and I had to clean the wound every day. That was no less agonizing than the surgery. He could have decided he needed better care than I was giving him. At every turn he put my safety above his own suffering. I know it seems silly to Stanley for me to show off his scar. The truth is I wanted you to see the scar to see how brave he was."

The clapping startled Stanley. "Just how many people did you invite over to see my scar?"

"Everybody!" Aleta laughed. "Lights."

"You are both spellbinding!" Professor Burrows said coming forward, extending his hand. "I had heard your parties were different. I'll admit I was totally unprepared for your definition of different."

Stanley shook the black hand numbly. "Welcome, Professor Burrows. Believe me; our parties aren't usually this bizarre."

"Don't believe him," Alan Peets said. "They pack a surprise in each one. My first time here, I found out my wife was pregnant."

Dr. Chesney came up. "I was looking forward to seeing Aleta's work after Wayne told me about it. I missed you at the hospital."

"Oh, for Pete's sake," Stanley said suddenly yanking up his shirt.

"Wow!" Dr. Chesney breathed. "She did a hellava job!"

Stanley drew Aleta to him with his free hand and kissed her.

"You lose," he whispered.

"I love you," she replied. "Now while you're showing off your scar, I'll help Lauren set out the food."

"Aleta, I'm not... oh, hell..."

His mother put her arm around him. "I'm so proud of you, son."

Dr. Taekman leaned over and examined the scar. "She did it just right. Wayne, I thought you said she called you afterward."

"She did."

"How did she know how much pressure to use?"

"I have no idea; but, I wish she were one of my interns," Dr. Cook said. "She's a natural."

Dr. Taekman eyed Stanley curiously, "And you stayed still while she did this?"

"She had a knife in her hand," Stanley said with a straight face, "and she told me to."

"Remarkable!" Dr. Taekman said. "Truly remarkable."

"It was worth the trip, wasn't it, Michael?" Dr. Cook asked.

"As if Martha would let me stay home."

"My grandmother has an adventurous spirit," Wayne remarked.

"But there is no way I'd ever let her operate on me," Michael added.

"I'm with you there," Wayne said.

Lauren clapped her hands and everyone's attention turned toward the archway where Lauren stood holding two hats. Everyone grabbed a number. She then had them find their partners for the evening. Couples who happened to pull the same number were separated immediately. Lauren had worked it all out in advance.

Maryanne Burrows looked distressed. Hubert who was her partner assured her she'd have a good time.

"All the wives are in the same boat," he confided. "We can sit at the same table as your husband if you like."

"I'm sorry," she said. "I'm being rude. I've been to a number of parties; but none like this one."

"Which is why everyone comes," Hubert commented. "Aleta knows how to celebrate life."

"I find the mix intriguing."

"Haven't figured out what unifies this group yet?"

"What does?"

"Aleta," Hubert said. "Now who haven't you met that you would like to?"

"Martha Cook."

"You were talking with her earlier," Hubert said.

"I talked with Dr. Taekman's wife, Martha." Suddenly her face showed comprehension.

"Who else?" Hubert asked smiling.

"Harriet Locke."

"The professor's wife?"

Again comprehension showed in Maryanne's face.

"I didn't read about their marriages," she said.

"We are all quite circumspect. The weddings were very private. My wife and I were the only witnesses when Claude and Harriet exchanged their vows. They'd met on a hunting trip my wife gave me as a Christmas present. I introduced them. Claude thought I was setting him up so he was barely civil to her. Then I insisted on Harriet as my hunting partner. She came home with more birds than anyone but Lyle. Claude snatched her and her dog as his partners on the second day. And they fell in love in the duck blind."

"What a delightful story!" Maryanne exclaimed. "Any more weddings coming up?"

"Two weddings, four babies. Aleta is going to have a party to celebrate each event plus her dad's admission to the bar."

"Not hers?"

"That's still problematic."

"What will she do if she doesn't pass the committee's review?"

"Continue as House Attorney for the Tontine, give birth, train her Lab to hunt, go riding with Stanley, and give parties to celebrate life."

"She's a remarkable woman, isn't she?"

"We'd better get in line. We're going to get the last two empty places. I guess you'll meet whoever's there."

She wound up at a table with Dr. Cook, Bessie Dobbins, Ed Ornstein and Harriet Locke. After the introductions, she asked Bessie a telling question about her technique. The two artists began an exchange that fascinated the rest of the guests at their table.

Toward the end of the meal, Aleta stood up and called to Stanley. She uttered one word: "Now." He rose from his place, excused himself, promised to return shortly and urged everyone to continue eating. He then followed his wife to their bedroom.

Maryanne's wrinkled brow showed her puzzlement.

Harriet looked at Hubert.

"A new deal," she posed.

"It would seem so," he responded matter-of-factly.

"What sort of deals do they have?" Maryanne Burrows asked.

Harriet smiled. "We all know about the first one. When they were married, Stanley uttered the usual vow but Aleta didn't. She said simply, 'I promise to obey you.' She told me later it was the only meaningful gift she could give to express her love."

Maryanne shrugged. "I don't see the importance."

"That's because you don't know Aleta," Dr. Cook put in. "If Stanley tells her to do something, she does it."

"Remember the wheelchair incident?" Hubert asked.

Several people at the table chuckled.

Hubert explained to Maryanne. "It was when Aleta came home from the hospital with both arms in slings and her dad had bought her a wheelchair. Dr. Cook didn't want her to fall. Aleta refused to even sit in the chair. No one would physically force her for fear of hurting her."

Harriet took over the tale. "Her father and I reasoned with her. She didn't argue our logic at all. She simply refused. Then Stanley pushed the chair behind her and said, 'sit', and she sat."

"And she was pleasant in her compliance," Hubert added. "If he gives her an order, she doesn't pout."

"But this time," Maryanne pointed out, "she told him what to do."

"Well," Hubert said, "that wedding vow was the beginning. None of us understands the deal with these two; but, things change the rules after every major trauma."

"Setting that aside for a minute," Maryanne said, "are you telling me he ordered her to operate and she did it?"

"Stanley would never do that!" Hubert exclaimed.

"Always he orders her to do things for her own protection," Harriet said. "Actually I know he didn't order her to operate. He talked her into it. Once she decided to do it, he trusted her to carry through."

"You two seem to know these two pretty well," Maryanne concluded. "Surely you have some idea what this is about. Could she have persuaded him to let her off the hook on that promise to obey?"

"Never!" the two chorused.

"I hope that never happens!" Dr. Cook put in.

Maryanne's surprised look prompted the doctor to explain. "Stanley told her to obey all my orders and she does."

"How do you know?"

"I ask her."

"And she tells you?" Maryanne questioned with obvious skepticism.

"Aleta doesn't lie. She says God wouldn't like it."

"We all know that; but, we do it anyway."

"Aleta has a special relationship with God."

"Louis told me about her so-called vision," Maryanne said. "Of course, I don't..."

Harriet interrupted her to call to a nearby table, "Martha, are you getting anything?"

Perplexed, Maryanne sought out Dr. Cook but it was Hubert who leaned over and whispered. "Harriet and Martha are prophets too. None of them can see danger to themselves, only to others."

When Stanley closed the bedroom door, he half scolded Aleta. "I said anytime; but, Aleta really. You want to do it now?"

"I don't understand the urge myself," Aleta confessed moving in front of the window. "Maybe all I need is for you to hug me and tell me you aren't angry."

Stanley took her in his arms. "I'm not angry. I don't like surprise parties; but, I must admit you did a terrific job with this one."

"Scooby out was a neat touch, huh?"

He lifted her chin. "We aren't here to talk about Scooby."

He kissed her tenderly.

"I love you, Aleta," he said softly.

"Just keep holding me, Stanley," Aleta said.

"What's going on?"

"Right here, right now I feel safe."

"We're in front of the window."

"The glass is bullet proof," Aleta said. "The walls aren't."

"What do you know?"

"Nothing. That answer just popped into my head."

"We aren't here to have sex, are we?"

"What I planned to do was see if you would, kiss you and then have both of us return to our party."

"And now?"

"Now, I feel we are to stand here and kiss."

"I can do that," Stanley said. "At least I can keep my clothes on."

Aleta was silent.

"I can keep my clothes on, can't I?"

She still didn't respond.

"Please, Aleta, don't tease me," he begged. Then remembering what she had said, he tilted her chin up slightly and kissed her. The kiss started out tentative, but as she responded, he returned her escalating passion. One kiss led to another with no words between. It was as if nothing else mattered.

The bullets hit the glass where their heads were.

Aleta's kiss held Stanley in place.

The sound of rifle fire brought Milani, West and Peets to their feet.

"Everyone stay in here!" West ordered as Milani radioed his men. Peets ran to the front door with Milani close behind. Scooby ran after them barking. He shoved past them out the door.

"Wayne, come with me," Lyle ordered as he headed for the bedroom. West shouted into his radio, "French, Operation roadblock. Aleta. Now. Milani's men are on site. Perps are still here."

West rattled the knob of the bedroom door.

"We're okay," Stanley shouted. "Aleta says we can't move.

"Don't let Mr. Hubbs get killed!" Aleta shouted.

Cook reported back to the assembled guests that both Stanley and Aleta were okay and explained that Aleta said they weren't to move.

"Some psychic," Maryanne commented sarcastically.

"Yes she is," Harriet stated flatly.

"She walked right into danger," Maryanne pointed out.

"She pulled it away from us," Harriet remarked.

"She took her husband."

"He would have followed. This way she could control where he was."

Martha intervened in the verbal exchange. "She used the window."

"What does that mean?" Maryanne questioned.

"It's bullet proof glass," Martha explained. "She would seem vulnerable but not be."

"Why are they still in there?"

"As long as they stay there," Ed put forth, "we're safe in here."

Aleta clung to her husband. "Powell is never going to stop is he?"

"You are his accuser."

"But won't killing me substantiate my accusation?"

"He probably plans to blame your death on anti-terrorists. They're almost as bad as anti-abortionists only instead of killing doctors, they'll go after lawyers."

"But Aloman is innocent."

"He's Arabian, therefore he's guilty."

"Why did this happen during my party?" Aleta moaned.

"Lucky for us."

"Lucky? How?"

"The police are already here."

"I see your point," Aleta admitted.

Peets and West returned to tell the group that Milani's men had arrested five suspects. West announced that his roadblocks were taking names and addresses of everyone driving away from the area and no one should be surprised if they are stopped on their way home. He knocked on the bedroom door and told Aleta and Stanley it was safe for them to come out.

"Who'd Aleta anger this time," Bessie asked. The group looked at her with surprise. Bessie had never spoken up in the larger group before.

"Some lawyer," Stanley replied vaguely.

"A crook?" Bessie asked.

"Aren't all lawyers crooks?" Hubert joshed.

Bessie read between the lines. "So he's a crooked crook."

"That sums it up," Hubert said.

"So if you know who he is, why isn't he in jail?"

"Because he hires these hit men through the internet. Ed's on it," Stanley said. "He shut down the first web site he used."

"He's not on the internet no more," Ed said. "He's back to local contacts is my guess. He does lawyer for criminals you know."

"Where's the money coming from?" Hubert said. "Claude, you guys did a background check on him. Does he have that kind of money?"

"You guys?" Aleta asked.

Harriet stepped in. "Claude is on the Democratic National Committee. Aleta's nemesis is someone the party is looking at as an up and coming political figure. Aleta has accused him of racial prejudice."

"Why hasn't anyone else seen it?" Bessie asked.

"Because he's very clever," Aleta said.

"Tell us what you know," Bessie urged. "We're your friends. Let us help."

"Yes, tell us," chorused others.

"It's just a theory," Aleta said.

"Go ahead, Aleta," Claude urged. "Tell everyone your theory. I say that the attacks on your life say you have hold of the truth and he's scared to death of you. Let your friends help."

"Please do," Professor Burrows said. "I need to hear your argument from you personally. I couldn't find what you found."

As Aleta slowly began to explain her theory, chairs were scooted closer. She had every fact and figure at her fingertips. She began to talk to the group as if it were a jury, leading them step by step into how her mind arranged the facts into a devastating pattern of prejudice disguised as affirmative action. She explained how Eugene Powell presented himself on the Character and Fitness Committee as a tireless advocate of the African American applicant but in reality only chose to argue for those whose performance in the study of law predicted the probability that they would be unable to pass the bar exam. On the other hand Eugene Powell worked hard at barring from taking the bar exam any Afro American whose law school record predicted that they would pass.

She summed up her theory stating that Eugene Powell based his decisions not on the seriousness of the legal problems facing the applicants but on whether or not he judged them capable of passing the bar. Those he deemed capable, he rejected. Those he thought would flunk, he found acceptable. It didn't matter if the problem were major or minor. He overlooked major problems in those black candidates he found unacceptable in white candidates. On the other hand, intelligent black candidates with identical minor legal irregularities as their white counter parts were rejected while their white counterparts were allowed to sit for the exam.

Professor Burrows interrupted her there. "I found that, but, a significant number passed the bar.

"That's because not all blacks come before the review committee before the exam takes place. And Powell has no control over those not appearing before the committee. I made those my control group."

"That never occurred to me," Professor Burrows admitted. "Go on."

"Because he was so strong an advocate for the majority of the black applicants, the committee followed his lead when he voted to reject a black candidate.

When Aleta finished, the room was silent.

Professor Burrows heaved a huge sigh. "No wonder Powell is afraid of you."

Claude Luther added his take, "If I could argue your theory as well as you, Powell's political ambitions might well bite the dust; however, I need more."

"I know this Eugene Powell," Bessie put in. "I believe he's that kind of scum bag. Look what he did to that lovely young lawyer he hired."

"What did he do?" Claude asked.

"He fired her." Bessie related. "It happened the day I went to ask him to take my case. You remember, Aleta, I told you lots of lawyers turned me down."

"Did you witness the firing?" Claude asked.

"No, but after Mr. Powell turned down my case, I went to the ladies room to, er... wash my hands and there she was, crying her eyes out. I gave her a ride home. I was so mad and she was so mad, we both vented, but she got the worse deal. He said he'd see she didn't ever work in a law firm in Chicago again."

"Did she tell you why she was fired?"

"You need to remember I was upset by his rejection of my case, so while I was listening, I wasn't really."

"Did it have anything to do with discrimination of any kind?"

"I'm sorry. I don't remember. It was unfair though. That much I remember. Something about tokenism. I couldn't figure out what tokens had to do with anything so that stuck. I'm sorry."

"Do you remember her name?" Claude asked.

"No," Bessie said.

"Oh," came the disappointed response.

"How about where she lived," Ed asked taking out a notebook.

"I remember she had me drive down Chicago Avenue to Cicero. I thought I was in Cicero. I'd heard bad things about that town. She said no, we were still in Chicago. She lived a block from there."

"Think she's still there?" Ed asked as he jotted down the street names.

"It's her mother's house. It was a small gray house. I met her mother. Nice lady. No way she would've raised a bad daughter. Most of the street was brick two flats. Pretty rundown neighborhood. She was planning to move her mother out in a year or two. She was saving all her money, riding the El to work, packing a lunch. I told them where I lived and they said it sounded nice."

"Why would he tell her he'd see she never worked in any Chicago law firm?" Hubert pondered aloud. "Why would he care where she found a job?"

Lyle's father jumped in. "What did she do that made him that angry? If it were illegal, he would have had her up on charges."

"Tokenism implies prejudice," Stanley offered. "Bessie, was the woman black or Asian?"

"No," Bessie replied. "Neither of those. Had high cheekbones. I asked if she was part Indian. Her mom said she was mostly Swedish with a little English mixed in. I'm always interested in facial characteristics."

"Ed, look into this," Harriet said.

"First thing tomorrow."

Bessie spoke up.

"I don't want to make trouble for her."

"Don't worry, Bessie," Ed said. "I ain't out to hurt her."

"She was really scared of Powell," Bessie said.

"I ain't gonna tell Powell," Ed assured her.

Late that night, when they were alone, Aleta asked Stanley if he planned to go to work in the morning.

"It's time, don't you think?"

"I guess," she said sadly.

"It was a great party," Stanley assured her.

"We were attacked."

"Hubbs is okay."

"Will he stay?"

"Of course, he'll stay. He loves it here. He loves our horses. They're his children," Stanley said. "Besides I'm installing a security system in the barn. That'll make him feel better. He doesn't want anything to happen to the horses."

"Will you make love to me tonight?" Aleta asked. "And stay home tomorrow all day?"

"Aleta, what's wrong?"

"There were five men out there intent on killing me. That's a lot of hate."

"That's a lot of greed. They don't even know you."

"Powell is still gunning for me. I thought he'd be relieved that we made it possible for him to save face with the committee. On top of that, in that hearing with Debi Lu, I didn't say a word. Judge Jacobi took charge and there was no stopping her. Why is Powell still mad at me?"

"Reid dropped his suit," Stanley mentioned.

"Why?"

"Powell walked away from it."

"Why?"

"Judge Jacobi threw a monkey wrench in the works when she found Debi Lu guilty of grand theft and then sentenced her on the spot."

"That shocked me," Aleta said.

"Norma has a strict code of justice. Debi Lu was not only guilty, she was blaming everyone but herself. Norma doesn't like that."

"She absolved Jocelyn of all blame," Aleta mentioned.

"She knew that's where Powell would go next."

Stanley embraced his wife.

"I know this last attack has been hard on you. I'll work from home tomorrow. And we can go riding and play with Scooby and make love whenever you want."

In response to his offer, Aleta began to cry. He held her close until the sobbing lessened.

Aleta asked for reassurance, "You will stay home tomorrow?"

"I won't leave you at all. Two can work in the study. You have a case pending," he said as he removed her blouse and carefully folded it.

"I don't feel like working," she said, comforted by his habit of folding clothes destined for the laundry.

"Just let Ed give you his report. He's been busy since he got back from Florida. Hawk has gone over the car. Ed's working some angles. All he needs you to do is hear his report and tell him where you want him to dig deeper," he said as he continued to undress her.

"Just that?"

"No more," Stanley said firmly. "You'll have time to mull over what he tells you if you need to do that. Harriet gave him an assignment so he'll appreciate a break to do what she wants."

"What about Powell and his political ambitions?" she asked.

"Harriet told me that she and Claude would deal with that. She understood every word you said. She sees what you see. Let her take it from here. She knows this last attack left its mark on you."

"She told you that?"

"Your grandmother is very perceptive," Stanley said. "I can work from home for a couple of days. Alice will tell my clients I'm still recovering. If you need me longer, I will make arrangements."

Aleta lay down on the bed. He hadn't offered to put on her nightgown. He meant to make love to her. She watched him as he stacked both sets of clothes on the chair.

She giggled. "Bertha will know who took off my clothes tonight."

Chapter 17

Scooby's barking woke Aleta and Stanley up. Aleta glanced at the clock.

"Bertha's here," Aleta exclaimed. "Your alarm didn't go off."

Stanley rolled over and got out of bed.

"I didn't set it. I'm not driving in today."

"We didn't leave her a note not to make breakfast."

"So we eat cold eggs," Stanley said. "Come and take a warm shower with me. Be a nice change from those icy baths."

"Those were a week ago!"

"I have a long memory. How about erasing a bit of it this morning?"

Aleta climbed out of bed. "Showering together will be faster, I guess."

Stanley's eyes twinkled. "Wanna bet?"

Harriet and Claude entered without knocking. They held the door open for Ed who'd driven in behind them.

"Something smells great," Ed said.

"Glad you're here," Bertha said. "The bacon and eggs are done."

"I'll eat 'em," Ed said.

"There's enough for two," Bertha commented.

Claude sat down. Bertha poured coffee and took the rolls out of the oven. The men dug in. Bertha put more bacon on the grill.

"Are they even up?" Harriet asked, taking a roll and buttering it.

"Yes Ma'am, they are."

"Silly question," Harriet asked. "You fixed breakfast."

"I assume they've been delayed, Ma'am."

"I gather Stanley's not going in today," Harriet said.

"I don't know, Ma'am."

"I'll take two eggs scrambled," Harriet said. "And some orange juice."

Stanley and Aleta came out just as the three were finishing. After some banter, Harriet asked Stanley why he was still home.

"I'm working out of the house for a few days," he replied evenly.

"Then I can fly to Carbondale with Claude," Harriet said. "I didn't want Aleta to be alone after last night."

"Bertha is here," Aleta shot back, obviously vexed. "I'm not a baby that needs to be sat with!"

"Your grandmother knows you need special care, Ma'am," Bertha punched in. "You need more than me, Ma'am."

Stanley asked Claude why he was going to Carbondale and the focus of the discussion changed.

"I have some grad students working on the Powell problem," Claude said. "I think I need to talk with them personally."

Harriet coughed.

"Er... Harriet needs to tell them what to do next," Claude remarked. "I have to admit she does have a good idea how to dig out the figures to prove that he's prejudiced against blacks. And she knows what the committee will listen to."

Aleta and Stanley sat down and Bertha set down warm plates with just the portions of each offering that each one preferred.

"The lawyer Bessie talked with was Kay Rivers," Ed said. "Guess where she wound up?"

"Not in Chicago, right?" Aleta said, breaking her roll.

"Lake County prosecutor's office," Ed said. "I get to see her at eleven today. Now about the Aloman case…"

"Perhaps we should go into the office," Aleta said.

"You got more eating to do," Ed said. "Who don't you want to hear this?"

Aleta looked around.

"No one."

Ed started right in, "Shakir Aloman went from Clearwater, Florida to Minard. He's got no name no more, just a number. I got it down to three guys.

"So we've hit a blank wall." Aleta concluded.

"Not so," Ed returned. "Dean took a mini-camera down to the prison. He found a guard in that section and you paid three hundred bucks a shot.

Ed took out nine photos, all enlarged, and spread them out on the table.

"I thought you said three," Stanley said.

"I told Dean to ask for extra so the guard wouldn't know who we was after."

"This guy's got a full beard," Aleta said. "I can't really see his face. Aloman doesn't have a beard."

"Which guy you think is a Muslim?" Ed asked sharply.

"Him," Aleta said pointing to the man with the full beard."

"Sure looks like one, don't he?"

Aleta's countenance reflected her understanding.

"He'll be convicted on looks alone."

"He's gotta get a shave before anyone sees him or you're sunk," Ed predicted.

"I've only got one shot at this," Aleta said. "I can't make a mistake."

"What makes you think you got a shot?" Ed asked. "If you ask to see Aloman, they'll throw him in solitary."

"He gets to see his lawyer."

"Not if he don't know you," Ed said. "Before you argue your way in, he'll be somewhere else."

"Why?"

"'Cause they don't got a case."

"Then he should be free," Aleta declared.

"The Feds don't want to be wrong."

"Let's not go Federal," Claude suggested. "Let's go state."

"What?" Aleta and Ed chorused.

"He's in a state prison," Claude explained. "The governor has power over what happens in the state prisons. And since nobody in Illinois arrested him and he's a Federal prisoner, no state government heads will roll."

"The Feds will get wind of it and he will disappear." Ed cautioned.

"We need the media help," Aleta decided. "Can we get the governor to move him secretly to a Northern Illinois jail to await trial?"

"Why move him?" Claude asked. "And why secretly?"

"So we can involve the press," Aleta explained. "If it's not a secret, the press won't care."

"If the TV flashes him on the screen with that beard, he's toast," Ed said.

"What we need is our friend Justin Conway," Aleta proposed. "We promise him an exclusive TV interview after we clean our man up. But, the story breaks in print."

"Justin is gonna want a picture," Ed said.

"We give him a family photo. An old one when the kids were little," Aleta said. "We need to stir up some sympathy."

"Some will hunt down his family and take photos," Stanley said. "That could backfire."

"You're right," Aleta agreed. "We give Justin a recent photo and run them side by side. That would be even better."

"How are you gonna get him tried here?" Ed asked.

"The Feds moved him to Illinois," Aleta said. "We can assume that they meant to try him here. At least that's what we claim publically."

"Then what?"

"We demand a jury trial."

"That may not be possible," Stanley said. "He was arrested in Florida. A Florida judge needs to order a change of venue."

"We start with publicity. We absolutely don't want Shakir Aloman to disappear into the prison system somewhere else."

"How soon do you want to do this?" Claude asked.

"Immediately," Aleta determined.

"Harriet, I hope you packed my good suit," Claude said.

"I even packed mine," Harriet smiled. "We'll leave Justin Conway to you, Aleta. Claude and I will take care of the governor.

"What prison?" Claude asked.

"No prison," Aleta declared. "People don't go to prison until they're convicted and sentenced. He gets transferred to a jail just like any other prisoner accused of a crime."

"The governor may not go for that," Claude cautioned.

"You two must convince him," Aleta said. "I need him where I can talk to him at length. I need him nearby. I need him where he can see his family again and begin to feel like an American citizen again. And we begin by reestablishing his innocence."

"What jail could handle such a transfer?"

"Not jail. Jailor. Chief West has the knowledge to see that Aloman is treated correctly. His men are experienced and honest. And he doesn't have the task of trying to keep me alive. In addition, it's closest to the courthouse."

"Should she come with us, Harriet?" Claude asked.

"I can't. I have a brief to prepare to see if I can get his case moved to Illinois."

The Luthers left followed by Ed.

After two hours, Stanley stood up and stretched.

"Time for our ride. Chief Milani gave us an officer that can ride."

"I'm not sure Yudi is stable enough."

"He brought his own horse."

"Just in case we went riding?"

"To protect Hubbs and watch over Jocelyn just in case some fool thinks she's you. Right now he's saddled up, ready to accompany us."

"Our horses are ready too?"

"One of my calls was to Hubbs. I told him we'd want the horses at eleven."

"I made an appointment with Lyle West."

"I told him we'd be riding."

"You changed my appointment?"

"Actually, he changed it. He called me on my cell since our phone was busy," Stanley said. "So let's go. It looks like rain, by the way."

"You win. We ride."

"You need to learn how to let go of your focus when that's called for," Stanley remarked.

"I'm able to do that."

"Only when you're not upset. Then you escape into a project and refuse to be interrupted."

"You interrupted me."

"Do you have any idea how many arguments I had to come up with? Everything from the horses saddled to an incoming storm."

"I exhausted your arguments?" she asked cocking her head coyly.

"I had one more," Stanley admitted.

"Save it," Aleta said. "Are we going off the farm?"

"I told Hubbs to put halters on Sterling and Yudi so we could exercise then while we rode around the farm."

"You really planned this, didn't you?"

"Hubbs planned it. He said the two needed to go out with the others once in a while," Stanley responded, and then asked, "Aren't you going to ask me if it was safe."

"You check out that too?"

"Lyle said that his men picked up one more man in the road block. It was a clean sweep. Today we'll be safe."

Aleta hugged her husband impetuously. "I do love you. Never change."

"Aleta, every day with you changes me."

"I'm glad I saved your life. It was a good choice."

"You were considering another option?" he asked not entirely facetiously.

Aleta laughed. "You are so easy."

"Okay, you're in a silly mood," Stanley commented. "Let's go. Come on Scooby. Time to stretch those legs of yours."

An hour later the rain started. When Aleta felt the first drops, she turned to Stanley and gaily challenged him to a race back to the barn. He told her to go ahead without him.

"Go," he urged her. "You can beat the downpour."

The police guard with them was torn. Stanley urged him to accompany Aleta.

"I just need to take it slow," Stanley said. "A little water won't hurt me."

Aleta had Shadow trot back to Stanley's side. "Water won't hurt me either."

While their police guard didn't want to be caught in the upcoming downpour, he was relieved when his two charges stayed together. He studied the man in front of him and realized he was having trouble maintaining his seat. They had perhaps done too much riding for the first outing, but Aleta had been excited at being back on her horse. But it wasn't his job to monitor the length of the ride, just to guard both of them.

When the three reached the barn, the officer told the couple to go straight to the house. He and Hubbs would rub down the horses. He explained that he hadn't anything else to do.

Aleta noticed that Stanley walked slightly hunched over, but the heavy rain made that seem reasonable. He seemed okay as he left his wet outer clothes in the laundry room and sat down with her to eat lunch.

After they finished eating, he announced that he and Aleta were going to take a nap. Aleta took one look at his face and quickly agreed that she needed one.

She plucked his wet jeans from his hand and dropped them in the tub with hers. Then she insisted he give her the remainder of his clothing, all damp. She handed him clean pajamas.

"I thought...," he said.

"After our nap," she whispered as she scooted into bed beside him, completely naked as usual.

"I am tired," he admitted.

She rolled on her side and cuddled against her husband. She put her hand on his chest and felt his heart beating faster than usual. She closed her eyes and relaxed. If Stanley knew she was worried, he would fight sleep.

Stanley was comforted by having her beside him. She said she was tired. It made sense. They'd had a long day yesterday replete with change and excitement with a chunk of terror thrown in. They hadn't rested much today.

He decided his suddenly appearing weakness was nothing more serious than plain old tiredness. Sleep is what he needed. He put his hand on hers and closed his eyes. He fell asleep shortly afterward.

Aleta, who'd planned to get up and call Dr. Cook, found out that he stirred every time she tried to withdraw her hand from under his. Eventually, she gave up and let sleep overtake her.

Lyle West called the Praetzel house and Bertha answered and told him that both were asleep.

"Have Aleta call me on my cell when she wakes," he said.

He turned to the two chiefs waiting for him to complete his call which he had told them he had to make because Aleta had something important she needed to tell him.

"They're asleep," he reported.

Both his companions chuckled.

"It's not funny. Something's wrong."

"You want there to be something wrong," Tom joshed. "Otherwise it'll look like Aleta has you jumping through hoops."

"Has she ever called any of us when it hasn't been important?" he retorted.

"I guess I could check on my men," Tom said. "Come on Peets, we can have our meeting at their house and wait for Aleta to wake up. And maybe Bertha will have some homemade rolls lying around."

"I can always count of your stomach to lead us," Lyle joshed.

"Waiting for her to wake up could take a long time," Peets said.

"I don't think so. She was pretty agitated," Lyle responded. "Stanley won't sleep long if at all. And he'll know what's going on."

"Okay," Peets acquiesced.

Bertha greeted the three chief's warmly, told them they'd have plenty of privacy in the family room, served them warm homemade rolls and coffee and busied herself cleaning the guest room.

When they were alone, they began to piece together every scrap of information each of the three had garnered talking to the men in their custody. Peets having arrested two personally, took those two back to his jail. The man caught in the road block was in the Arborville jail and the remaining three taken from the Praetzel place were incarcerated in Willow Glen's jail.

Peets had extracted the most information. No one knew how he did that. He never gave them anything. He wasn't even a friendly interrogator, just a demanding one.

All three had done computer searches on their men. Every one of them had a history of armed assault or armed robbery charges most of which had been dismissed.

Technical foul-ups had been the forte of their lawyers, none of whom were public defenders and three of whom were associates in Eugene Powell's law firm. That was not surprising as his firm serviced many felons.

The three chiefs checked and double checked each other from arrest through interrogation. Tapes were listened to and discussed. They had these men cold. There was no reason to worry.

"I want them put away," Lyle said. "How about we offer the five the same deal: minimum for full confession including naming the others, maximum if we go to trial."

"We could sell it," Peets said. "If we could drop a charge."

"Absolutely need the conspiracy charge to stay," Lyle said. "It's all I have on my perp and I don't want him to walk unless he gives us Powell."

"Any real chance of that?" Tom asked.

"Not really."

"I bet Peets could work him."

"His lawyer would be all over us if I transferred him for no reason," Lyle commented.

"All we need is to have one take the deal. The others will fall in line," Tom concluded.

"If we're done," Lyle said, "I'll wait here. I can't do anything until one of you gets someone to fold."

Chapter 18

It was almost two o'clock before Aleta woke up. She pulled her hand from under Stanley's hand and he didn't stir. Quickly, she rose and dressed. She hurried into the living room and spotted Lyle sitting in a chair reading.

"What are you doing here?" she exclaimed.

"Waiting for you."

She looked startled and then realized what she'd forgotten.

"Oh my God!" she blurted out. "Bertha, were there any calls for me?"

"Yes, Ma'am," Bertha reported. "Chief Lyle West called.

"Not Grams?"

"No, Ma'am."

"I need to call Dr. Cook," Aleta said.

Seeing her worried expression, Lyle urged her to do that first.

He listened to her anxious query about Stanley's sudden near collapse. He saw her nodding as she murmured faint yeses to Dr. Cook's questions. Finally, she was back.

"What did the doctor say?" Lyle asked.

"If Stanley doesn't wake up by three thirty, I'm to call him back." Aleta responded without any real thought. Her mind was still worrying over what could be wrong.

Lyle West decided whatever she had meant to tell him was not as important at this moment as Aleta's distress. People don't get over an attack like the one visited upon her the prior evening instantly even if they are not injured. And this one had happened to her when she was in her own home.

It's too much too rapidly, Lyle thought. The woman needs some peace. Today was supposedly a time to recover and now Stanley had folded.

"How'd the ride go?" Lyle asked.

"I didn't realize until I talked with Dr. Cook that he was supposed to take it easy."

"So why are you feeling guilty?"

"You sound like Stanley," she accused irritably.

"Is that bad?"

Aleta's lips turned up into a hint of a smile. "No, that's not bad."

"Don't you think he just over did it?"

"Most of me thinks that. But a piece of me is worried it's more serious."

"And at the point when a doctor would be needed, one has promised to come."

"I'm to call."

"Lay you even money, he'll be on your doorstep at three-thirty," Lyle said. "Perhaps you'd better tell me why you called me so you can go back to fretting for the next hour."

"A prisoner is going to be transferred from Minard this afternoon.

"How does this affect me?"

"He's coming to your jail."

"That's not possible."

"Claude and Grams took care of that end." Aleta said. "The governor is sending him straight to you."

Lyle was genuinely taken aback. "The governor is sending a prisoner to me?'

"To your jail. I told Harriet that Shakir Aloman could not be a prison to prison transfer because he hadn't been convicted of any crime. He's going to be treated like an innocent man. But, Lyle, this is important. No one sees him until he gets a shave and a haircut. And I don't want anyone to know that he's there just yet."

Lyle nodded his understanding. He opened his cell.

"Peets, I need to transfer my prisoner to your jail as soon as possible. Can you pick him up? I'll have French put him in interrogation until you arrive."

"I'm in the middle of negotiations. Can Tom take him?"

"We both were wishing earlier that you could be in the room with him," Lyle said. "I now have a legitimate reason for the move. I'm expecting a prisoner who needs to be isolated."

"Flattery will get you what you want," Peets chuckled. "I'll send a couple of men over immediately."

Chief West's next call was to Peter French. "We are transferring our prisoner to Oakwood. We are receiving a transfer."

After Lyle left, Aleta reentered the bedroom, sat down on the bed and stroked her husband's hand gently. He didn't acknowledge her touch at all. Now she was more frightened than ever.

She couldn't bring herself to try and awaken him. She was afraid she wouldn't be able to. She assured herself that she was wrong. He was just tired and she shouldn't interrupt his sleep. He'd force himself to stay awake to allay her fears. He'd already done more for her than his body was physically able to do she realized now.

She left the bedroom and sat where Lyle had been sitting. Scooby came over and tried to climb in her lap. All he could manage to fit were his front legs. He licked her chin and she began to pet him and talk to him. His brown eyes fixed on her face while his brows did dances above them depending upon the inflections of her voice. Whenever she inserted his name his tail would wag.

She wasn't sure when he backed off and just let his head rest in her lap nor when she stopped stroking his head and he backed off her lap and lay at her feet nor when her eyes closed and she fell asleep. It all happened gradually.

Bertha had entered the room, heard her worrying aloud to Scooby and quietly began making rolls. There were going to be visitors again soon.

Dr. Cook spoke to Stanley softly but received no response. He began his examination, talking as he did each procedure. Then he asked Bertha what Mr. Praetzel had been doing.

"Doesn't he know the meaning of the words, 'take it easy'?" Dr. Cook perturbed.

"He was tending to Mrs. Praetzel's needs," Bertha said. "She has been close to a psychological collapse."

"So they've been acting as if everything is normal, have they?"

"Yes, Doctor."

"Well, I'm not ready to take them back to the hospital since the type of nurse they need already in house."

"I will follow any orders you give."

"I'm going to give you a schedule," Dr. Cook said. "No deviation. I'll write out the schedule while you prepare Mrs. Praetzel for bed."

Strangely, Aleta didn't protest. The rain had darkened the sky and Aleta thought it was later than it actually was. Being roused from so sound a sleep disoriented her, and Bertha undressed her in the same manner she had numerous times. Vaguely Aleta remembered that Stanley was ill. It was difficult to remember that she no longer was.

When Bertha dressed her in pajamas, Aleta's protest was mild.

"The doctor may want to examine you," Bertha said. "This will make it easier."

Aleta's mind was too befuddled to mount an argument. She lay back in bed, reached over for Stanley and gripping his hand fell back to sleep.

Dr. Cook handed Bertha the schedule. "They aren't going to like this. The party was exhausting for the rest of us, but Stanley was less than a day out of the hospital. Those infections drained his body of strength. He wasn't really for a full day of activity."

"Yes, Doctor. I can explain that."

"As for Aleta, Stanley and you have recognized how devastated Aleta was by this latest attack. She needs Stanley's company more than any other type of therapy, but she doesn't need to be his nurse. Do you understand what I'm saying?"

"That she's sick too," Bertha replied.

"She will obey my orders. Stanley will do so if he believes by doing so he will help Aleta."

"You believe Stanley will waken by six?"

"If he doesn't, call me," Dr. Cook said. "In fact, if there is any change, call me."

"Yes, Doctor," Bertha said then asked, "What about visitors?"

"None tonight. Tomorrow, but only short visits, ten minutes or less," Dr. Cook said. "No TV no phone calls. Call me with any question you may have."

"They are going to want to ask... er, well, you know."

"They may do anything they want so long as they stay in bed. In fact, some foolishness in bed may be just the ticket for them both."

"I will tell them that," Bertha said, the corners of her mouth twitching.

"It's hard to maintain decorum with these two, isn't it?"

"Very hard."

"I can send a nurse to take over at six."

"No need. I'll stay overnight," Bertha replied.

"Don't hesitate to call if Aleta takes a turn for the worse."

"Do you believe she will?"

"I believe she's the sickest of the two."

Ed Ornstein showed up at four. Bertha told him he would need to return the next day.

"But only with good news," she admonished.

"She's that bad?"

"Yes," Bertha said bluntly.

"Well, it's good news I've got. And it'll keep."

Ed had no sooner left than Chief West called and asked to speak with Aleta. Bertha told him what she'd told Ed.

"I knew Aleta was on the edge. I hated leaving her."

"I heard her tell you to go," Bertha said. "If you hadn't, that might have agitated her even more."

"Is Dr. Cook keeping a watch on her?"

"He is," Bertha said, then softening her tone, added, "The two can have visitors for short periods."

"Dr. Cook is concerned, isn't he?"

"Yes, Sir, he is."

Chapter 19

It was close to six o'clock when Stanley opened his eyes.

"Bertha!" he heard his father-in-law shout. "Stanley's awake."

His shout brought Aleta awake instantly.

"They're both awake!" he called out.

"What are you doing here?" Stanley demanded.

"Do you have any idea how long you've been sleeping?" Robert asked.

"Several hours. But why are you here?" he demanded.

"Dr. Cook's orders," Robert replied.

"Dr. Cook?" Stanley questioned.

"I called him," Aleta admitted. Suddenly, she realized she was in bed too and in pajamas. "I remember sitting in the chair in the living room waiting."

Bertha appeared. "Dr. Cook came at three thirty. You, Stanley, were asleep. He ordered me to put you, Aleta, to bed. He left orders as well."

"For Stanley," Aleta presumed.

"For both of you," Bertha said.

Robert went over and kissed his daughter on the forehead. "You obey Bertha. She's in charge."

"But there's nothing wrong with me!" Aleta protested.

"Bertha will explain," Robert said. "I'm going to check on Jocelyn who thinks she has an excuse not to do her homework."

When Robert left, Bertha read from the schedule and then told Aleta why Stanley needed to adhere to it.

Aleta nodded her head. She didn't want a repeat of today's collapse.

Then Bertha told Stanley why Aleta needed to be his companion and Aleta immediately objected. "I'm fine. The past is over. I'm over it."

"Dr. Cook says you aren't," Bertha said matter-of-factly. "And he told me that I was to tell Mr. Praetzel it was important that you take time to recover from last night's attack."

"Nonsense!" Aleta exploded. "Stanley's recovered. So am I. I was just tired, like Stanley."

"You were tired because your spirit was as exhausted as Mr. Praetzel's body," Bertha explained. "He said Mr. Praetzel would be able to provide the appropriate therapy but only if you are under Mr. Praetzel's care, and since he is confined to bed, so are you. And that is that."

"Therapy? Hah! What kind of therapy ever happens in bed?"

"The kind only a husband can provide," Bertha said. "If you give me any trouble, Dr. Cook will hospitalize both of you in separate wards."

Her voice carried a warning as her eyes fixed on Aleta's, "You will be locked in the psychiatric ward. Their doors are locked."

"I'm not crazy!" Aleta cried. "He wouldn't do that!"

"No, you are not crazy. You've been deeply traumatized," Bertha said. "And Mr. Praetzel knows it. Dr. Cook said that every time the two of you are together and outside pressures are removed, you are both healed emotionally. This time he believes the process can be done here because I'm here."

The last phrase had a bit of pride embedded in it.

"Does anyone else know about this?"

"Yes, Ma'am," Bertha replied. "Ed stopped by with good news. Lyle called. Both will have ten minutes visitation tomorrow."

"I want to talk with them now," Aleta declared.

Bertha ignored her protest and continued with listing the changes. "No phone calls. No television. Robert already disabled the set in here and the one in the family room."

Aleta's hand went to her nightstand.

"You took our cell phones?" she gasped.

"Yes Ma'am," Bertha said. "Are you ready for supper?"

"Do we get to eat at the table?" Aleta asked petulantly.

"No, Ma'am," Bertha replied. "And I'll be here all night if you need anything."

"We'll have supper in here then," Stanley said. "Give Mrs. Praetzel ten minutes to adjust to this imposed confinement."

"As you wish, Sir," Bertha said and departed.

"Stanley, this is ridiculous!" Aleta declared as the door closed.

"Dr. Cook has always been there for us. The least we can do is obey him."

"I have a client in jail. I need to talk with him. I have a trial to prepare for. I have to call Justin and give him a heads up. I can't loll around in bed for three or four days being psychoanalyzed by my husband!"

"I don't think that's what Dr. Cook had in mind."

"Of course it is," she insisted.

"He said I was to do what only a husband can do." Stanley reminded her. "Any good doctor can be a therapist. But none of them can give you the therapy I can."

"He wouldn't tell Bertha that!" Aleta exclaimed.

"I think he couched the concept with great care."

"But she knows!"

"Oh, for Heaven's sake, Aleta. Put two healthy people who love each other in bed for several days and, of course, that's what's going to happen. That and a lot of frank talk."

"I don't understand completely."

"I need to stay in bed because I'm not as strong as I need to be to keep pace with you."

"I can function on my own."

"I know that, but can't you wait for me?" His eyes pleaded with her to acquiesce.

Aleta's arguments folded at that moment.

Why wouldn't she wait for him, she wondered. Then a new concept encroached upon her resentful thoughts.

Stanley had been with her through all the shootings. He'd been the one shot. He must've been affected equally by the attack in their own home. It wasn't her alone who was the target. They as a pair had been profoundly affected by the events of the past two weeks, each differently. Dr. Cook had seen that. They needed to heal together. Why hadn't she seen that?

Never mind, she told herself, I see it now.

She leaned over and kissed him. "I'm sorry I was so obstreperous earlier."

"We all understand," Stanley assured her. "What pleases me is that you didn't jump out of bed to prove your independence. Instead you obeyed Dr. Cook's order. He didn't tell you not to get angry, just to stay in bed."

"I did that, didn't I?"

"You honored me by your action."

"You always see me in a good light," she said, kissing him again.

Bertha's knock interrupted them.

"Come on in!" Stanley said. "We're ready to eat."

When Robert and Bertha left after delivering the trays, Robert commented, "Aleta seems more relaxed."

"Stanley has that effect on her," Bertha responded.

"She's been through a lot," Robert said. "And he's stuck with her through it all."

"He loves her," Bertha said. "But I agree. He's been tested."

"He said to tell you that you can sleep tonight. They won't wander if you'll serve Aleta ice cream and a pickle around nine o'clock."

"I hope I won't interrupt anything."

"Stanley will be sure you don't."

"We can't lie in bed and make love all the time," Aleta commented after the trays were removed.

"We could sleep too," Stanley joked.

"And talk, I guess," Aleta added.

"I opt for sex and sleep."

"That's not therapy!"

"It'll work wonders for me. I guarantee it."

"You aren't sick."

"Neither are you!" Stanley shot back, knowing that was what Aleta needed to hear.

"We'll do it your way," Aleta said lightly leaning over to kiss him. "At least no one knows we're confined to bed, except for Ed and Lyle and who would they tell?"

The next morning Bertha told her who had been told.

"Lauren has arranged for lunches and dinners for a week plus lots of desserts. I told her it would be too much food. She said I could freeze the dinner leftovers. She was sure you would be getting enough company so there wouldn't be any treats left to freeze. She said the frozen dinners would come in handy when Robert and I are on our honeymoon."

"She knows I don't cook," Aleta said. "She's a good friend."

"Sounds as if she's not alone," Stanley said as Bertha left the two to eat and talk.

"Why is it I keep needing to be reminded?" Aleta fretted.

"Eventually, you won't. These are new friends," Stanley explained patiently. "You've known most of them as long as you've known me—just seven months. That none of them have fallen away is partly the result of them recognizing what a good person you are and partly the result of your terrific ability to discern who is worthy of your love and trust."

"Next you're going to say I have terrific taste in husbands as well."

"Well, don't you?"

"When did Bertha say we could shower and change?"

"Immediately after breakfast. She plans to make the bed and pick up our laundry. You do realize that we need to be circumspect."

"The door will be closed," Aleta countered.

"You're really into this therapy idea of Dr. Cook's, aren't you?"

"And you aren't?" she quipped.

"So we're like-minded," Stanley observed.

"I hate to be so predictable!" Aleta exclaimed.

"I'll bet he thought we'd get a lot of sleep," Stanley said.

"He doesn't know us at all, does he?" Aleta grinned.

"Not at all!" Stanley agreed.

"Have you ever had sex while you shaved?" Aleta asked impulsively.

"You should know," Stanley returned.

At ten the next morning, they heard someone enter the front door.

"It's Lyle," Stanley said.

"We can't entertain in our bedroom!" Aleta gasped.

"If we don't, we won't be able to see anyone."

"I don't care. It's too personal a place," Aleta remarked.

"He's been in our hospital rooms countless times."

"But we're in our bedroom," Aleta wailed.

"Do you want me to send him away?"

"No. No. Don't do that. Bertha's been in and out. My dad was here late night. Why not Lyle?" She sighed heavily.

Lyle entered. "I came bearing gifts."

"You didn't knock," Aleta said.

"I made noise enough to wake an elephant," Lyle said lightly. "You weren't sleeping were you? Bertha was sure you weren't."

"What gift?" Aleta asked abruptly.

"Homemade chocolate fudge from Evelyn," Lyle said. "Bernard Chesney told her of your fondness for chocolate. Lauren has designated me as her delivery boy again. Milani has tightened the restrictions regarding who can visit you."

"Did the transfer take place?" Aleta asked.

"Shakir Aloman is safe in my jail."

"Is he anxious to see me?"

"Actually, he was so happy to have a shave and a haircut and homemade food, he didn't dare tempt his good fortune, so he's not asked for anything."

"Will you tell him about me?" Aleta said. "I am working on his case. I already have petitions ready to file, but I have to get out of here first. The children are in school. I'd like him to see his wife. That should give him hope. Her too. Warn her that if she tells anyone, it could jeopardize not only her husband's life but mine as well."

"I'll escort her to the jail personally. That way she won't need to sign in."

"Thank you," Aleta said, her manner indicating she was still worried.

"We can keep his presence a secret," Lyle assured her. "You just relax. That's your job right now."

A knock on the door told Lyle his time was up. "I'll check in with you tomorrow. I brought lunch, compliments of Lauren. Ed will be by this afternoon with dinner. Bertha is only allowing you two visitors today."

"No family?" Aleta asked.

"I imagine your dad will stop by tonight. I understand he helped Bertha serve you dinner last night."

Stanley saw an anxious frown appear on Aleta's brow. He spoke up.

"Don't worry, Aleta. My family can wait."

When Ed arrived at five, he found Scooby lying in the middle of the bed with Aleta on one side and Stanley on the other. The pup stood up and wagged his tail hitting both the people sitting up in bed in the face.

"Sit!" ordered both at the same time. Scooby bounced off the bed and sat at Ed's feet and gazed up at him hoping for some sort of reward. Ed bent down and stroked him gently.

"Better late than never," Aleta laughed.

"I got better news than we hoped."

"Better?" Aleta queried hopefully. "Kay Rivers will testify against Powell?"

"Yeah, and so will the gal who was fired before she came. I saw her too."

"What about her?"

"Top of the class too. Same rotten deal," Ed reported. "They gave me more names. You want me to keep on? It'll take time. Most got outta Chicago."

"Yes, keep going. Two isn't a significant number. I'm speaking statistically, not personally. I'm convinced."

"Some might wanna let the past stay buried."

"Just get their stories. Ask them if they'd speak to one man."

"Professor Luther?"

"He's down in Carbondale. His grad students are researching Powell. Combining what both of you discover may be enough."

"For what, Aleta?" Stanley asked.

"I'm not sure. I haven't enough facts to bring him before the disciplinary committee. I'm hoping I have enough to enable Claude to take him off the Democratic ticket."

"If you succeed in either of those endeavors before Lyle can tie him to the attacks on us, we'll be in more danger than we are now."

"You give me an idea," Ed said abruptly. "I'll be in touch."

After Ed left, Stanley sat quietly thinking for several minutes. Aleta waited. Finally he said, "We need to talk."

"I thought you said no talk, just sex and sleep."

"Not that kind of talk," Stanley said. "A serious talk."

"Oh, well, okay then, as long as it's not frivolous," she joshed.

Stanley decided it would be best just to plunge in.

"How important is being sworn this year to you?"

Aleta sobered instantly.

"Why?"

"You're almost six months pregnant."

"I know that."

"If we could keep you safe for another couple of months, the baby would have a good chance of survival."

"Connect the dots, please," Aleta said, still unsure where Stanley was going.

"If you begged off appearing before the five man committee for six months, maybe Powell would back off."

"And my reason?"

"Pregnancy complications."

"And the Aloman case?"

"You hand it to me," Stanley replied. "The publicity could generate public anger and Powell might get away with killing you because there would be others with motives to lay the blame on."

"It's my case!"

"And it's your decision," Stanley declared firmly. "I'm only suggesting this course because I think sidestepping might be called for here."

Aleta frowned.

"I may never get another chance to handle such a major case," she pointed out.

"This might be our only child," Stanley returned somberly.

Stunned by Stanley's words, Aleta fell silent.

Stanley wisely fell silent as well.

When Bertha and Robert arrived with that evening's dinner, Stanley greeted them with an admonition not to chat as Aleta was pondering an important decision.

Both were a bit surprised at the announcement; but, neither said anything. They set down the trays and left.

"Not much of a visit, Robert," Bertha commented.

"It's all I need—just to see her."

"I didn't sense that anything was wrong," Bertha said.

"When she concentrates on a problem, she barely notices anything that's going on around her. She didn't really notice my giving her the tray."

"She will eat, won't she?"

"Without even knowing she's doing it," Robert said, smiling. "I remember how this tendency of hers used to disturb her mother. I can still remember Marian saying, 'Aleta, pay attention to the dinner and to us.' But Aleta never did. She couldn't. Her mind was locked into solving whatever puzzle had intrigued her."

"What do you suppose she's thinking about?" Bertha asked. She had switched from the servant role to the future step-mother role.

"Some question Stanley asked," Robert replied.

"And just how do you know that?" she challenged.

"Because he would have explained otherwise," Robert answered. "He is only circumspect about private matters. Aleta, on the other hand, isn't circumspect at all."

"She can be," Bertha noted. "But she likes things out in the open. I like that about her. I always know exactly where I stand. She's an easy person to work for."

"She expects a lot," Robert put in.

"But she knows it."

"She thinks the world of you," Robert said taking Bertha's chubby hand and drawing her into an embrace, "as do I."

"Will we be as happy as they are?"

"Don't worry," Robert whispered. "It runs in the family."

An hour after the dinner trays were removed, Aleta was still deep in thought.

"Ask me some questions," Stanley suggested. "It'll help you decide."

"If I don't decide to take the route you suggested, will you order me to?"

"No."

"But you feel I'm in danger."

"I feel it. And my reason tells me my feelings are correct. But, I'm not a prophet. You are. Whatever you feel God wants you to do, I will support wholeheartedly."

Aleta smiled. "God wants me to put the baby first."

"You were praying?"

"Which direction to take was beyond my ability to discern, so I prayed. And what came into my thinking over and over were your last words."

"I didn't mean to frighten you," Stanley apologized.

"Yes, you did. And your words rattled me. What if this was to be our one and only child? How would I decide? What was more important—my desire to try this case? No. My desire to uncloak Eugene Powell? No. My desire to be sworn in this May? Well, that one was tough, but no. Nothing was more important. So let's plan how we're going to safeguard this baby."

"You're sure this is what you want?"

"Absolutely. This is the baby's time. If I'm meant to practice law in Illinois, it will happen. I know I passed the bar. I can do it again if I have to."

"The Aloman case."

"I thought about that. It's a complex case. The first round may be mine but it will only be one battle. The war could erupt full-blown the last month. It could, in fact, stress me enough to precipitate a premature birth. You aren't pregnant. And you don't fold under pressure."

Her voice showed a determination as she continued, "And I'll be here to draft the replies to whatever briefs the government files. I'll work at home. You'll be the face on this case."

"You won't get any credit," Stanley cautioned.

"You'll know."

"And that will be enough?"

"Earlier today I would have said no," Aleta declared, "but, strangely, what I want most is your respect."

"That you already have."

"There's another consideration. My pregnancy could interfere with my handling this case properly as could having Eugene Powell bent on killing me. It's already a tough case. I can't do my best with those two pressures. You aren't pregnant and you aren't hated by Powell as I am. On top of that you will represent Aloman brilliantly."

"So you can set aside being admitted to the bar. You can hand the Aloman case to me. What about Eugene Powell?"

"I've said what I have to say in that committee hearing," Aleta responded. "I don't take the next step."

"The next step has already been taken," Stanley said.

"I'll have Ed report his findings to Claude. I won't take Powell before the disciplinary committee and, Stanley, you won't either. If Claude wants to drop it, it's dropped."

"You mentioned working at home," Stanley tendered. "Does that mean you will stay at home for the next three months?"

"That's exactly what it means," Aleta said. "And I will ride Shadow only with a police escort and I will do everything Milani asks, except live somewhere other than here."

"Staying home will be difficult for you," Stanley cautioned.

"Yes, it will be; but, I am determined to protect this baby," she declared staunchly.

"I hear voices," Stanley said. "It sounds as if my parents are here."

"Let's take Bertha off the hook," Aleta suggested. "Have her call Dr. Cook and ask if we can talk to our parents this evening, and I'm including Bertha."

Stanley frowned. There was no intercom system. There hadn't been a need until this moment.

"We need a better system than just yelling," he complained as he shouted Bertha's name.

Dr. Cook insisted on examining Aleta first. Bertha waited in the living room with the other parents. Robert put his arm around her and assured her she'd done nothing wrong.

"I think it's good news," he added.

Hubert, who'd been pacing the floor, stopped.

Robert's eyes met his. "Aleta's been thinking for hours, maybe even praying. That's not out of the ordinary for her. It drove her mother nuts."

"Does she do this frequently?" Hubert asked.

"Not since she married Stanley."

"Why now?"

"I don't know," Robert said.

Bertha interjected, "You said before that Stanley must have asked Aleta a question."

Stanley's mother worried aloud, "Maybe they want to be in separate rooms."

"That's hardly something Stanley would announce," Hubert countered gently. "Why don't we stop speculating?"

"But Dr. Cook's been in there so long."

"He does have two patients to checkout," Bertha reminded her.

The four waited in silence, but no one relaxed.

When Dr. Cook emerged, he was smiling. Immediately the tension in the room dissipated.

"I've never seen the like," he said. "Put those two in a room together and shut off the outside world and they heal each other. Works every time!"

"So they're okay now?" Lydia asked hopefully.

"They both must take it easy for a week; but, they've both made major strides toward complete recovery."

"What exactly is wrong with them?" Lydia persisted.

"Emotional exhaustion. That led to physical exhaustion. That operation Stanley went through and the aftermath was fraught with pain and fear. Then the attack on them after they thought they were safe..."

"Do I drop the schedule?" Bertha asked.

"Cross off the next three days and go from there."

"Will they be okay with that?"

"They are both being terribly cooperative. That in itself is almost a miracle," Dr. Cook commented.

Robert laughed. "It is indeed!"

"Of course, each one is cooperating for the sake of the other," Dr. Cook remarked. "They plan to get well together."

"Interesting attitude," Hubert commented.

"They do come up with strange attitudes as a couple," Lydia added. "That's not a derogatory comment. I rather like their unique way of handling life."

"I'm rather proud of both of them," Robert said.

"Can we go in to see them?" Hubert asked. "My curiosity over what they want to tell us is becoming quite overwhelming."

"I've given them permission to receive all future visitors out here," Dr. Cook said. "And they can take their meals in the kitchen from now on."

"Do you know what they are going to tell us?" Lydia asked.

"That's privileged, Judge, and you know it," Dr. Cook replied.

Lydia smiled. "I like to be a step ahead."

"Goodnight," Dr. Cook said and left.

The bedroom door opened and Aleta and Stanley emerged, both wearing robes over their pajamas. Aleta sensed the tensions in the room. She smiled. "It's good news, guys."

The two sat on the couch and Aleta took Stanley's hand.

"We've decided to make some serious changes in the direction our lives are going in the next few months."

"First," Stanley said, "I'm taking over the Aloman case. There may be some public outcry by people who are presuming guilt rather than innocence. We want Aleta away from any danger for the baby's sake."

"What about you?" his mother asked anxiously.

"There are ways to handle such an outcry as long as it doesn't get mixed up with Powell's single-minded determination to kill Aleta."

"With that in mind," Aleta interposed, "I'm not going to appear before the five-man committee."

"Powell will believe he has won!" her father protested.

"He has," Aleta conceded. "But Stanley and I want our baby to be born alive and healthy. Right now that is our prime consideration. I believe we both thought that once we arrived home the attacks would stop. It was that hope that kept us going. When we were attacked here... well..."

Aleta hesitated for only a moment before finishing. "We want to protect this baby. I will do whatever it takes. I don't intend to leave this house until our son is born."

"Aleta!" her father gasped. "You can't!"

"Your father's right," Lydia said. "You will hate this house if you take that path."

"I would if I were forced to stay here or ordered to stay here but..."

"You weren't ordered?" Lydia questioned, her assumption obvious.

"Stanley would never do that," Aleta declared. "I never even consulted him about this. It's solely my idea. Since it's my choice, the house will not be a prison. A prison is a place you can't leave when you want to. I will always be able to leave. I just won't."

"All that may not be enough," Hubert commented. "That statement you made in front of the committee was a serious charge. It won't be easily forgotten. And it will spread like wild fire because you've been attacked."

"Powell is certain that you will expose him someday," Lydia added. "He's an astute politician. He knows how the game is played."

"We have two women ready to come forward on gender bias charges," Stanley reported. "Are they in danger?"

"Not as long as Powell doesn't know," Hubert ventured. "But any hint of new charges will just make him more determined. He will see Aleta as the king pin."

A feeling of uneasiness filled the minds of the people in the room. Lydia decided to ease the tension.

"What will you do with your time, Aleta?" Lydia asked.

"I still have the Tontine legal work and I'll help Stanley with the Aloman case from home. And I'll train Scooby."

Lydia chuckled. "For a moment I had visions of you taking over the housework and cooking."

"Me?" Aleta laughed. "Never!"

"What will you do when Bertha goes on her honeymoon?" Lydia pressed.

"Let the house get dirty, the laundry pile up and order take out," Aleta replied without hesitation.

"You'd let the dishes pile up?" Stanley teased.

"I would, but you won't," Aleta responded. "And you'll do the laundry too I expect."

"And you won't help?"

"I'll keep you company."

At that response the whole group laughed.

The visitors prepared to depart on that note.

As Lydia and Bertha lingered a moment to chat, Hubert took Robert aside. "We have to do something about Powell."

"This last group were pros," Robert said. "They won't crack in interrogation."

"They may not even know who hired them," Hubert noted dourly. "Still the police are better equipped to squeeze information out of them than we are. That's not what I had in mind."

"You have a plan?" Robert queried.

"Can you find out who the person is whose bulldog Aleta shows?"

"I guess, but why?"

"He works for one of the Families in Chicago."

"What good will that do?"

"He's intervened before when Aleta was in danger."

"I'm not sure you wouldn't be better at this."

"You're her father," Hubert returned. "You can stumble and even ask for help badly and be forgiven."

"What will you be doing?"

"Contacting a few of my clients who owe me a favor."

"Isn't Powell a criminal attorney too?" Robert asked.

"That's where he's coming up with the men," Hubert said. "Two can play that game."

"What are we asking for?"

"Them to put out the word that Aleta Praetzel is off-limits."

"Can we do that?"

"We're the only ones who can get away with it."

"I wish we could bring Powell before the disciplinary committee."

"When Claude and Ed report in, then the four of us can decide the next step," Hubert said. "But Stanley and Aleta aren't to know about any of this."

"Agreed."

When the family had departed, Aleta suggested tentatively that their proposed changes appeared to be well received. Stanley nodded in agreement.

"But you are worried."

"This case could take all of my time," Stanley said. "I'm basically a child advocate which is what I want to be."

Aleta's eyes lit up. "That's what makes you so perfect for this."

"I don't follow."

"They will underestimate you for one. Second, they will believe you will be too busy to properly prepare the case. But, Dad and I won't be. You can concentrate on your own work and we'll prepare the petitions and whatever briefs are required. Remember, we aren't law students or legal aides. We're both lawyers."

"And good ones," Stanley concurred. "It could work to our advantage; but, my secretary won't be able to keep up."

"We're being paid handsomely by the Tontine. We can afford another secretary," Aleta proposed. "In a couple of months Dad will need one, so we can let him select her. That way you won't appear to be gearing up for the Aloman case."

"I appreciate your grasp of the subtleties."

"That's not the only thing I grasp brilliantly," Aleta teased.

"Ready to play, are you?" Stanley rejoined, moving closer.

"Doctor's orders!" Aleta said gaily.

Chapter 20

Three days later, when Aleta and Stanley woke up, Aleta rolled over and said, "Today you go back to work. I guess our second honeymoon is over."

"Are you going to be okay when I leave for work?"

"I'll be fine," Aleta said with forced bravado. "It's only for half a day. Grams promised to come over and help me start Scooby's training."

"Remember Dr. Cook said not to worry if you have feelings of profound sadness. You have the right to grieve over your loss."

"It's only my dream!" Aleta scoffed. "Not my life."

"Dreams are what make us unique."

Harriet arrived an hour later.

"Where is she?" she asked Bertha.

"Bedroom," Bertha replied. "I'm glad you're here, Ma'am."

Harriet burst through the door. "Aleta, the dogs need a walk and we need to talk."

Aleta rose. It was obvious she'd been weeping.

"I don't need a lecture," she admonished.

"You're not getting one. I have something important to tell you, and it's private."

Within minutes they were walking toward the barn with the dogs bounding in front of them. Her grandmother remained silent. Perturbed, Aleta complained that her grandmother's words had been a ruse.

Still there was no reply

They entered the barn and Aleta greeted Mr. Hubbs and then the horses.

Matt asked her if she was going riding and she looked at her grandmother who signaled her to do it.

"We can exercise Sterling and Yudi."

The dogs raced alongside the four horses, heedful of the trotting hooves. While such a ride might be too confining at another time, it wasn't on this day. The small of fresh green grass lightened Aleta's mood.

After numerous trips around the property and past the house, Aleta drew up at the barn door and dismounted. Hubbs took Shadow's reins and bade Aleta to leave the horses to him.

Her tiredness surprised her.

"Yes, please," she said. Turning to her grandmother, she talked on, "Grams, I don't think I'm up to training today."

Harriet chuckled. "Have you looked at the dogs? You wore them out. Very good conditioning, I'd say. Mine needed a good run to get their wind back."

"Did you have something to tell me?" Aleta asked.

"Yes, I did and I still do," Harriet replied.

"Is it a message from God?"

"Yes," Harriet replied, stopping on the road between the barn and the house. It was a place where they could talk undisturbed.

"I came to tell you God is pleased with your choices. God wants you to trust Him."

"Exactly what does that mean?"

"He wants you to let go of your grief," Harriet replied.

"Grams, they're only dreams, not people, that died. And Stanley assures me they aren't really dead, only postponed."

"You believe they're dead though, don't you?"

"Yes, I do."

"Why?" Harriet asked.

"Powell still wields power in that committee. Lyle said the police can't tie Powell to the attacks. Claude said his students are stumbling over how to present my theory clearly. There are so many other factors they don't believe I've considered. They're bogged down in trying to explain the exceptions. Ed said that none of the other women that Powell fired wants to relive that experience. And I don't blame them, especially with Kay out of the picture."

"Kay is out of the picture?" Harriet questioned.

"Of course she is," Aleta declared. "It's one more reason that I need to let my dream die. It's the only way I can prevent Powell from robbing Stanley of his. People have many dreams. Some are bigger than others; but, like children, the loss of one of them is devastating."

"Let's go back to why I'm here," Harriet said. "God wants you to pay attention."

"Are you telling me He sent me a message?" Aleta pondered.

"Apparently."

"You are mistaken," Aleta proclaimed. "Nothing happened. We got up, dressed, ate breakfast and Stanley left. The TV on. I wasn't in any mood for the news, so I turned it off. It was on just long enough for me to hear about Kay Rivers' death."

"I thought your television set wasn't working."

"Dad must have fixed it."

"Did you see him do it?"

"No."

"So God sent you a message via a disconnected television set."

"Nonsense! I would have known somehow."

"Really?" Harriet asked.

"Besides she died as the result of an accident. She wasn't murdered."

"You're sure?"

"I remember the reporter's words exactly. 'This morning Kay Rivers, Assistant Prosecutor for Lake County, died of multiple wounds received in a hit-and-run accident at noon yesterday.'"

"Suppose today is yesterday."

"Was I that obtuse?" Aleta fretted. "I'm no use to God either."

"For heaven's sake, Aleta. He didn't send me over to fire you as a prophet. He sent me over to help you discover His message."

Aleta glanced at her watch.

"We have to contact Kay right away."

"Not the police?"

"No time. She's getting ready to leave now."

"Use my cell," Harriet offered.

"I don't have her number."

Harriet punched a speed dial number.

"Aleta needs Kay Rivers' cell number."

"Why her cell phone?" Aleta asked.

"It's private," Harriet replied.

As soon as she had the number she disconnected and punched in a new number. The number was ringing when Harriet handed the phone to her granddaughter.

Aleta assumed she was connected to Kay Rivers.

"My name is Aleta Praetzel. Please listen until you reach your car."

"How did you know...?"

"You are in grave danger," Aleta continued. "You have my name. The cell phone I'm calling from belongs to my grandmother. It will be in your phone's memory banks. I'm only saying this so you will know this is legitimate."

"What kind of danger?"

"An accident is being planned. You are the intended victim.   You will die of multiple injuries tomorrow morning."

"I don't like this conversation.   Threatening a prosecutor is illegal."

"I'm not threatening. I'm a prophet. I know you've read about me. I know you don't believe me. Is there any way I can persuade you to return to your office?"

"No."

"Someone has offered you important information about a case you are prosecuting."

"How did you know?"

"That was a guess; otherwise you would turn around to check me out."

"You are correct. I can't be dissuaded to miss this meeting."

"Please do the following three things for me: first, do not fasten your seat belt; second, memorize the license plate numbers of the two cars blocking you; third, when you find yourself stopped in the middle of an intersection, move immediately into the passenger's seat."

'Those are crazy."

"Let me tell you why," Aleta said. The urgency in her tone captivated Kay's attention.

"You won't be able to move fast enough if your seat belt is fastened. You will wish you had the license plate numbers after the accident. Finally, if you don't move, you will die. The driver's side will be crushed."

"I don't believe a word of this!" Kay declared.

"Remember, move!" Aleta urged.

The phone went dead.

"She disconnected," Aleta said. "She said she didn't believe me. Why is God punishing me?"

"He's not," Harriet said adamantly.

"He's all-knowing," Aleta argued. "He knew I would be too distracted to pay attention to the prophecy."

"He sent me over," Harriet mentioned.

"Why did you wait so long?"

"My mind went blank?"

"Blank?"

"I forgot."

"You didn't tell me that."

"I was ashamed," Harriet confessed. "Old age sometimes monkeys with the memory. I'd been rather proud I'd retained my faculties. I guess I was supposed to learn a lesson too. One cannot help one's brain's failing despite all the media hype telling you to exercise your mental powers. When you are robbed of the speed you enjoyed in your youth, you blame yourself as if you had the power to affect the complex factors that keep your brain fully functioning."

"You seem fine now?" Aleta said.

"I was praying," Harriet admitted. "I was asking God to help me remember before it was too late."

"Why did He wait so long?"

"He has reasons," Harriet said. "All I know is He is using both of us still, flawed as we are."

"Why would anyone want to kill her?"

"She is a prosecutor."

"I'd say it was Powell, but then I'm blaming him for everything these days."

"I think it is him."

"But why?"

"He's afraid of a class action suit."

"Kay wouldn't threaten him with that."

"She has a lawyer. He's investigating her claim."

"Who's her lawyer?"

"Jean-Peter Cachet."

"How do you know all this?"

"I gave Ed permission to work for him."

"Ed asks your permission now?"

"Only on this case since I'd paid for his research into Powell. I told him he could share any information gathered thus far."

"Claude's students didn't find anything."

"The key word is 'students.' Ed is an experienced investigator."

"Powell is very clever. Discovery could take a long time," Aleta said. "I don't think Kay has the money."

"Someone is backing her financially."

"Who?"

"Ed wouldn't tell me."

Chapter 21

Kay Rivers was a tall, bony woman. Descended from practical stock, she hadn't believed the newspaper stories of the three prophetesses who resided in the nearby Tri City area. She had to admit, however, that this Aleta Praetzel sounded rational. She hadn't expected a voice as young as her own speaking to her in a clear, sensible and logical manner. The woman actually presented reasons for the behaviors she asked of her.

She climbed into her car and fastened her seat belt automatically. She glanced over at the passenger seat and chuckled. It was loaded with papers and books. Her bulging briefcase sat on the floor.

I couldn't move over even if I wanted to she realized.

She inserted the key in the ignition and then hesitated.

Utter nonsense, she reminded herself.

Her mind challenged her inaction. How much trouble would it be to transfer the stuff to the back? Suppose her informant wanted to talk inside her car?"

She unfastened her seat belt and plucked her briefcase from the floor and threw it behind her seat. In an orderly fashion she stacked the books behind the passenger seat. She heaped the papers on top of the rear seat. Then a glance at her watch told her she was going to be late.

Quickly, she turned the key in the ignition, shoved the gearshift into drive and left the parking garage. Her seat belt was still unfastened.

Two cars sped up behind her, both passing her. She would not have taken note of them if the one hadn't moved over in front of her and the second hadn't drawn abreast of the first and stayed even with it through two intersections.

"Memorize," the prophetess had said.

Inside her mind a debate raged as to whether she should follow directions she felt were ludicrous or not.

"It's a valuable exercise," she rationalized.

She broke the numbers and letters into groups and memorized the pair as a single plate. It took three tries before she had the two committed to memory accurately.

The two cars in front of her entered the fourth intersection and she followed immediately behind them. Both slowed to a stop just as their bumpers came in line with the curb on the far side of the intersection.

Kay found herself stuck in the middle of the intersection. There was little traffic in the area, which made the halting of the two cars unwarranted.

Kay heard the roar of the huge engine and even as she turned to look, she propelled herself from the driver's side to the passenger's side. The truck racing toward her was monstrous.

Her mind was so taken with impending doom it froze. However, her limbs completed the trajectory she had begun before the sight of the truck gave her fear a face. And the face was huge and composed of a chrome upper lip and a broad expense of steel forming a gigantic grinning mouth.

Her last thought was that this truck was rigged for ramming.

The impact was violent. The last sound Kay heard was the screeching of metal. Her car caved in under the impact thus removing the metal armor it had provided around her fragile flesh. Both airbags popped up as the side of the front door and fender were crushed by the bigger vehicle. Glass shattered; the steering wheel snapped; the roof folded, and the driver's seat collapsed from the weight of the door driven into it by the truck's massive bumper.

The truck backed up, moved around the crash and sped away. The two cars which had begun moving when the truck was nearly on top of Kay Rivers' car leaped forward as the truck rammed into the sedan crushing the driver's side totally. The cars were long gone before anyone's eyes could tear themselves from the sudden collapse of one metal vehicle by another.

Shortly afterward, Kay Rivers was rushed to the hospital where her injuries were found to be minor. The doctor kept her overnight to watch for a possible concussion.

Witnesses told the police that the truck had rammed her while she was stuck in the intersection behind two cars that weren't moving. They would have chalked it up to a strange accident, had Kay not regained consciousness and claimed she was attacked.

Kay didn't mention the phone call from a prophetess.

Chapter 22

To Stanley's amazement, when he came home late for lunch he found Aleta in a perky mood.

"You took advantage of the fact that I couldn't come and fetch you," she scolded lightly. "You have to behave or I won't let you go to work at all tomorrow."

"So you had a good morning?"

"I had a strange one," Aleta responded. "Come have lunch. Then it's nap time for you."

"I'm not tired," Stanley protested.

"I'm giving you no choice," Aleta said. "I need a nap and I'm not taking one by myself."

"Oh, that kind of nap," he smirked.

"No, not that kind. You're going to lay down and sleep."

"I'm not tired," Stanley reiterated.

"It doesn't matter. You are taking a nap."

"I gather you are practicing being a mother right now."

"If I were, I might punctuate my words with the..."

Stanley rushed in. "Aleta, you wouldn't hit our son?"

Astonished, Aleta stared at Stanley. "You didn't let me finish. I was about to say with the threat of no television. I can't use that on you because you never watch it anyway."

"And our TV has been disconnected," Stanley added.

"That too," Aleta said after a minute hesitation.

Stanley looked askance at his wife. He saw her eyes flick away and while she recovered quickly, he had become aware that to catch Aleta hiding anything, he needed to pay attention to the littlest signal.

"What aren't you telling me?"

"After you nap nicely, I'll tell you about my morning."

"I'd like to know now."

"That's not going to happen."

Stanley decided to let her win this round. She was after all going to tell him. The lunch had come compliments of Madge Tobias. Professor Burrow's wife, Maryanne, had sent over a chocolate marble pudding cake which Robert had already tasted and pronounced delicious.

"Why did Dad manage to get here on time and you didn't?"

"Back to that are we?" Stanley returned.

"I couldn't even call you. I need to be able to use a phone again."

"When does the schedule allow it?"

"Not for a week!" Aleta exclaimed.

"Then a week it is."

"You were late."

"I was in with Justin Conway and Shakir Aloman. It took more time than I thought."

Aleta scowled.

"Aleta, you need to trust me. I am as committed to the schedule as you are, but emergencies arise. They will need to be handled when they do. Afterward we go back to the schedule. We don't throw it out."

Aleta just smiled slyly and Stanley wondered what he'd given her permission to do. He was about to lecture about manufactured emergencies, but instinctive caution when it came to lecturing Aleta bade him wait.

In the bedroom, Stanley saw two sets of pajamas laid out on the bed. Aleta anticipated his query.

"Just in case we have company," she explained.

"In our bedroom?"

"Why are you fussing?" Aleta asked.

Stanley was uncomfortable when Aleta changed things. She always had a reason. She rarely told him at the outset.

She undressed and redressed so quickly, Stanley realized she did intend to take a nap. He changed his clothes methodically folding each item as usual. By the time he climbed into bed, she was asleep.

He touched her gently and kissed her lightly on the mouth. She stirred but didn't wake. Her hand, however, found its usual resting place. Her grip soothed him and slowly he let sleep gather him up. His eyes closed and he was soon dreaming.

He woke several hours later and, while they lay in bed, she told him about her morning in complete detail.

"And you don't know if Kay Rivers is dead or alive?"

"That's why I want a phone."

"I brought work home for you."

Aleta wouldn't let go her desire for a phone despite her pleasure in the prospect of legal work.

"What if God sends me another vision?"

"Then He will send you a means to communicate it," Stanley said rising. "Let's go riding while there's still some light and Matt's still here to accompany us."

He saw Aleta glance at the television set.

"Are you expecting it to talk to you?"

"It might."

"Not with me here it won't" Stanley surmised.

He saw Aleta visibly relax. Later he would ask Robert to help him move it to another room.

The two saw Lyle arrive as they rode alongside the front of the property. Scooby and King ran to the fence and barked at the car coming down the long drive.

Lyle parked and greeted the bounding dogs immediately. He held up a box tied with string and asked them to guess what was inside.

"Cookies?" Stanley guessed.

"Scottish shortbread, baked by none other than Bessie Dobbins," Lyle announced. "She called Lauren. She said she felt left out the last time."

He opened the box. "Try one. They're delicious!"

"You already ate one?" Aleta queried reaching for one.

Aleta held the cookie in her hand. The two men stared at her. Her eyes were focused on the cookie and her horse snorted and moved sideways.

Aleta swayed with Shadow automatically.

"Aleta, what is it?" Stanley asked as Lyle grabbed the reins. Aleta dismounted silently.

Matt moved in. "I'll walk the horse back to the barn."

Stanley dismounted and handed Matt the reins to his horse. Matt rode off.

Lyle and Stanley took Aleta into the house. Bertha hurried toward the group as they entered. Lyle went to hand her the box when Aleta told him to give it to her.

She sat down at the table and set the box on top of it. Then slowly she put her hands on the box. After a few seconds, she handed the box to Bertha.

"It's no use," she said. "I'm not getting any more than I got when I first touched the cookie. I hate these fragmentary visions. I feel so unprepared."

Lyle exchanged glances with Stanley who told him she'd had one earlier involving Kay Rivers' accident.

"Attempted murder," Lyle corrected.

"Then she's alive?" Stanley breathed gratefully.

"There's an APB out on the cars," Lyle said. "What accident victim remembers the license plate numbers of the cars she's following in traffic? I suspected she was forewarned."

"Then she did listen," Aleta exclaimed. "Lyle, I need to call her."

"She's in the hospital," Lyle said. "What's wrong?"

Instead of answering, Aleta burst out, "Of course! That's why I saw her being grabbed at the entrance to a hospital. Only I didn't know which hospital. Or even who."

"You're making no sense," Stanley admonished her. "Kay made it into the hospital."

"Not Kay, her mother. I saw an older, stout lady being grabbed. Lyle, you have to stop it from happening!"

"We're into kidnapping now?"

"I can't see the end result," Aleta responded, "but, I would guess it ends in death."

Lyle opened his cell. "French, find out what hospital Kay Rivers is in and who has jurisdiction."

"Lakeside Hospital," Lyle repeated. "Lake County Sheriff. I have his private number."

As he punched in the number, Lyle asked Aleta what she knew.

Aleta closed her eyes. "Emergency entrance. She gets out of a cab. After she pays the driver two men grab her and drag her to a car parked in back of the cab."

"Time?"

"It's dark."

"Chief Lyle West here," they heard him say as he moved out of earshot.

Since Lyle never raised his voice, neither Stanley nor Aleta heard a word until the very end when he moved toward them, obviously ready to disconnect.

"How should I know?" he spat out.

Aleta quickly interjected a suggestion. "I have a place where Mrs. Rivers will be safe. Have him tell Kay..."

Lyle handed her the phone.

"Sheriff Patterson, this is Aleta Praetzel. Tell Kay Rivers her mother is in danger and that I have a safe place for her to stay."

Lyle waited while the sheriff spoke to Aleta. He worried that maybe he had made an error in handing the phone to her.

"No. I don't expect you to believe me, but I suggest you check with Kay Rivers."

When she disconnected, Aleta said, "Let's eat. You're invited, Lyle. Since you have to wait for the call, you may as well be doing something productive."

"Eating is productive?" Lyle laughed.

"Just get the food you brought," Stanley ordered. "We'll argue after we eat."

"By the way," Lyle said as he headed for the door, "where am I hiding Mrs. Rivers?"

"With the Scottish shortbread maker," Aleta said. "The two know each other; but, no one outside our group knows that."

"Are you sure?" Lyle asked. "I hate to put two old ladies together outside my jurisdiction."

"Go get the food," Aleta said. "That's where God wants her."

"I'm not telling Patterson that!" Lyle muttered.

Noon the following day Kay Rivers showed up at the entrance to the Praetzel driveway and was stopped by the police guard. After presenting her identification, she assumed she would be allowed through; however, she was made to wait until Chief Lyle West turned into the drive and identified her personally.

She was visibly upset by the delay and said so as soon as she left her car.

"Pretty paranoid," she said.

Lyle West responded coldly. "We take no chances."

"Don't you think so much police presence labels the house Aleta Praetzel is in?"

"That's already known," Lyle said. "And the last attack almost cost Milani two officers. Only the alertness of a couple of others resulted in the capture of the perpetrators without bloodshed. The men know this is not a one-man assignment."

"No one in their right mind would drive up the driveway and attack!" Kay declared.

"It's happened."

"How often has she been attacked?"

"Five times in the last month."

Kay scowled. "So my mother's not really safe here, is she?" she challenged.

"She's not here."

"Not here?"

"Too dangerous," Lyle commented, "as you have observed."

"Where is she?"

"As soon as I've delivered lunch, I'll take you to her."

Kay gasped, "You deliver meals personally?"

"No delivery men are allowed on the grounds. There is a short visitors list. Aleta's friends send over meals to let her know they're thinking of her."

"They could call."

"No phone. Doctor's orders."

"She called me."

"On her grandmother's phone."

"Her grandmother lives here?"

"No. She was visiting."

"How lucky for me!"

"Luck was not involved. Harriet came over because she was told to. She is a prophet as well."

"You're just loaded with prophets, aren't you?"

"Actually, I have only one. Tom Milani has the other two in his jurisdiction."

"Why are you here? I thought police chiefs were pretty territorial."

"Not in the tri cities. We work together."

"And you two believe that these women are prophets?" she asked disdainfully.

"There are three chiefs in this area and we all believe. The three are too accurate in their predictions not to believe."

"What makes these psychics different from countless others?"

"They aren't psychics. They are prophets and they can only foresee murder. Unfortunately, none of them sees the perpetrator."

"Not much use then are they?" Kay scoffed.

"You're alive, aren't you?"

"Why are we standing here?" Kay asked angrily.

"Because unless you drop that attitude, you can't go in."

"What attitude?"

"That somehow Aleta is to blame for all your trouble."

"That's because I am," Aleta said from the open doorway. "Lyle, we're starving in here. Come on in, Kay, so I can apologize properly."

Taken aback by the young woman's conciliatory approach, Kay entered the house without her anger.

"Your mother's with a friend," Aleta said. "I thought she might need someone to talk with."

"She doesn't have any friends here."

"She has one."

"Will she be safe there?"

"As long as you tell no one."

At lunch, the talk turned to their common enemy.

"Why has he come after me?" Kay asked. "I haven't enough evidence to mount a suit."

"He must believe you can get it if you dig deep enough," Lyle said. "If he thought you couldn't win, he wouldn't try to kill you."

"You may need to go at this statistically," Aleta commented.

"Statistically?" Kay asked.

"You will need to hire a statistician," Aleta said. "However, if you will give me the facts I ask for I could do a preliminary workup for you."

"You'd do that?"

"I have a way with numbers. I enjoy playing with them. It could be fun."

"Aren't you busy with a case of your own?"

"There are three of us on that one," Aleta said. "I have the time and, I might add, the inclination to help you."

"What will Stanley say?" Lyle asked.

Aleta looked around.

"Speaking of Stanley, where is he?"

"In court," her father replied.

"Is he going to find some excuse every day?"

"He's there on your case," Robert said defensively.

"It's his case now."

"Your name's still on it."

"I gave it to him."

"I'm sure he had his reasons," her father returned.

"He still has to come home on time," Aleta said perturbed. "He needs to schedule his time better.

During this exchange, Kay's mouth had dropped open. Lyle, seeing this, chuckled.

Aleta, noting their reactions, spouted out her defense. "He's not fully recovered from the complications from the gunshot wound.

"He was shot?" Kay gasped.

"They meant to kill me," Aleta said. "He interfered."

"He tried to protect you, you mean," Lyle put in.

"He wasn't supposed to get hurt doing it," she shot back.

"I'll be sure to tell him that when I see him," Lyle retorted. "But how he's supposed to do that I don't know."

"He's a clever man. He can figure it out," Aleta declared.

Lyle's laugh ended the exchange.

Chapter 23

Aleta was alone in the study when Stanley arrived home.

"I thought you weren't supposed to work after lunch," he commented. The minute the words were out, he realized he'd made a mistake. Aleta's scowl confirmed it.

The first words out of her mouth surprised him however.

"What do you mean this is still my case?"

"It was easier just to add my name."

"Easier for whom?"

"For our clients, for one."

"So that leaves me still on Eugene Powell's hit list."

"He has other plans for you," Stanley announced.

"Oh?" she queried, curious, but not frightened.

"He plans to take you on. He's managed to get himself into the role of special prosecutor," Stanley said. "This case could be a political stepping stone for him."

"The Feds are going to arraign Aloman in our court?" Aleta asked aghast. "He was arrested in Florida. That's unprecedented."

"He's being arraigned in Florida by closed circuit television this afternoon. I want you there. I got Dr. Cook's permission."

"But our decision?"

"Still stands. I faxed your petition for change of venue to the Florida judge. There was no time to redraft it or the brief. The brief was superb, by the way."

"Why are we changing our plans?"

"Because Eugene Powell threw us a curve. He intends to beat you in court. His is a personal vendetta. But, as long as this lasts, you'll be safe from him. Our baby will be safe."

"I don't trust him."

"Nor do I, but let's take this one day at a time," Stanley said. "You've already begged off appearing before the committee due to pregnancy complications. Your court appearances can be both brief and infrequent for the same reason. They can be nonexistent if you want; however, I don't want Powell withdrawing, and he just might if he thinks I'm on the case rather than you."

"What time are we scheduled to appear?"

"Three o'clock our time. Four o'clock Florida time. We are the last item on today's docket."

"You didn't give me much time to get ready," Aleta fretted.

"You look fine to me."

"You're lucky my hair's short."

"It's practically non-existent."

"It's almost two inches long. Some women wear it that short."

"But you're letting it grow, right?"

Aleta merely smiled.

"Help me pick out my suit," she said. "I think my turquoise one would look nice on television."

"This will be closed circuit television," Stanley reminded her. "It's not going to be broadcast on CBS."

"Isn't it?" Aleta returned mysteriously. "Don't be too sure."

Aleta readied herself quickly enough so that she and Stanley were the first to arrive. Justin Conway was directing the camera crew.

"These X's on the floor are where we stand?" Aleta asked, taking a position furthest removed from where Eugene Powell would stand. After a few moments of consideration, she moved to the spot closest to him.

Powell arrived with only moments to spare. Shakir Aloman had already been directed to the spot between his two lawyers. Dressed in his best suit which hung loosely on his now thin frame, he looked like an ordinary, forty-year-old business man. It was a good image.

All the cameras began transmitting the images simultaneously.

"The clerk's voice was heard reading the name of the accused and the charges.

"How do you plead?" the judge asked.

"Not guilty," Shakir Aloman said, "except to the traffic violation. I plead guilty to that."

"Sentence is five days," the judge declared, rapping his gravel. "Time served."

"We recommend the accused be held without bail," Powell said.

The judge waited a moment.

"That is satisfactory with the defense, Your Honor," Aleta announced.

The camera caught a flicker of surprise on Powell's face. He recovered quickly with only a hint of a smirk. That was her first error.

"Mr. Aloman," the judge said, "Do you wish me to set bail?"

"No, Your Honor. My lawyer, Mrs. Praetzel, has represented my wishes in this matter."

"Don't you want to go home while waiting for your trial to commence?"

Aleta leaned over and albeit softly, nevertheless loudly enough for the television sound system to capture, "Explain to the judge."

Shakir Aloman straightened up. "Respectfully, Your Honor, I do not wish to return home until I am exonerated and can again take my place as head of my family."

"Mr. Aloman is to be held without bail," the judge ruled.

"If Your Honor pleases," Aleta said. "At this time we would like to petition the court for a change of venue."

"I have read your brief," the judge said. "While your arguments would fit a civil case, this is a criminal case."

Aleta realized at once that the judge wanted her argument recorded. This was a ground breaking precedent and he wanted his to be a solid ruling.

Aleta took a deep breath and began.

"First, the remaining charges are all Federal and no crime was actually committed in the State of Florida. Our argument therefore rests on convenience. To hold this trial in Florida will pose an undue hardship on the defense.

"Only two witnesses reside in Florida, the arresting officers. The interrogators who are Federal agents have been transferred to Texas and Ohio since the arrest. The defendant himself was transferred by the Federal government to a prison in Illinois. All defense witnesses reside in Northern Illinois as does defense counsel and the Federal prosecutor.

"In addition, the evidence is currently being held in an impound lot in Illinois. It has not yet undergone an analysis by a forensic expert, so the use of a local expert seems reasonable at this point.

"There is no question in the mind of the defense that Mr. Aloman would receive a fair trial in your court, Your Honor. That is not the basis for our petition. Rather it rests on the matter of convenience to all parties concerned."

Aleta hesitated for a moment, and then continued. "It is no small matter, Your Honor, that given the advanced and precarious state of my pregnancy, this is a matter of considerable personal concern to me as lead counsel. I will not be allowed to fly during the latter months which could seriously hamper my effectiveness should the trial take place in Florida."

"You have a co-counsel on this case," the judge pointed out.

"I do, Your Honor," Aleta said simply.

"Mr. Powell, I'll hear your recommendation now," the judge said.

"I would appreciate the opportunity to try this case, Your Honor, and I would like to concur with the request for a change of venue. May I add that Mr. Aloman deserves what he believes will be his best legal representation as the possible penalties are grave."

Aleta was impressed with Powell's presentation.

He is going to come off so magnanimous, she thought, and I'm not going to come off so well. I wish I hadn't gotten personal. I don't think the judge liked it. Whatever made me decide to make that last remark? I know Stanley wanted me to push for the change in venue; but I had done that. I have got to keep my personal feelings under better control.

When the judge began his response, Aleta barely heard him. In her mind's eye she'd done exactly what Powell was hoping she'd do—become emotional and personal.

She felt a hand touch her elbow and glanced over at Stanley. His attention was on the monitor. His touch woke her to the present.

The judge was summing up. She vaguely heard him say that the court traditionally positions itself in not placing an undue burden on the defense in civil cases should certainly be applied in a case as singular as this one where the charges leveled were national, not state-related. He cited the location of the witnesses and the legal representatives from both sides were Illinois residents. To transport so many to Florida bordered on the ludicrous.

He concluded by saying, "The arrest phase is completed. The trial phase has its own requirements. Said requirements will be better served in Illinois than in Florida. Accordingly, I approve defense's petition to change the venue to a federal court in Northern Illinois."

After the judge announced that court was adjourned, the television cameras were turned off. Justin Conway approached Eugene Powell who greeted him with a smile and thanked him for his help in setting this up.

"You came off quite well," Justin said. "You have an excellent public presence. Are the rumors true that you plan to run for the state senate?"

"I haven't decided that yet," Powell smiled. "Right now my attention is on this trial."

"Mrs. Praetzel was personal in her appeal. Care to comment?"

"Inexperienced lawyers make errors like that one."

"You think her lack of experience will hurt her client?"

"It won't help."

"Her co-counsel is experienced."

"Yes, he is. He is a fine child advocate. But this is criminal law. It simply isn't his area of expertise."

Lyle West was removing the prisoner while this exchange was taking place.

"Don't worry," he said to Shakir Aloman as he led him away.

The man smiled in response. "I'm not."

Stanley wanted to escort Aleta out of the room; however, she chose to stay. Justin moved to her next.

"Do you think you have the experience to try a case of this magnitude?"

"Absolutely not!" Aleta replied evenly.

Justin grinned. He could always count on Aleta Praetzel not to say the politically correct thing.

"However, sometimes experience isn't the most necessary quality in a lawyer. Women see things differently than men. Some men have a problem with that. That's my edge."

With that she smiled enigmatically and moved away.

When they were alone in their car, Aleta bemoaned her lapse into her personal situation.

"I have no idea why you did it," Stanley responded, "but it was a brilliant move. Your change of venue argument didn't need it; but, you not only verified your reason for not appearing before the committee, you set the stage for your absence from court."

"You weren't embarrassed by my statement?"

"No," Stanley assured her. "And that comment to Justin was priceless!"

"I did enjoy today. Thank you for including me."

"Aleta, you are a born trial lawyer. You think on multiple levels instinctively. By the way, when did you find out about the two Federal agents?"

"You told me."

"I didn't know," Stanley said, puzzled. "Let's go home. I promised Dr. Cook we would only do the arraignment."

"I'm feeling pretty good actually," Aleta confessed.

"So am I, but a promise is a promise."

"Let's celebrate!"

"How?" Stanley asked. "We're confined to the house."

As they rounded the bend, Aleta caught her breath. "What are all those cars doing in our driveway?"

"Your father's, my father's, Claude's, Lyle's," Stanley enumerated. "All family except for Lyle and he's bringing dinner."

"Something must have happened," Aleta assumed. "They know the rules."

When they opened the door, savory smells from the kitchen clued them into the fact that whatever happened called for a celebration. The living room, however, was devoid of people. Lauren turned when the door opened.

"What's going on?" Stanley asked walking toward the kitchen.

"You two are on national TV," she replied excitedly. "You're famous!"

"That's not possible," Aleta said. "We just left the courthouse."

"We're taping it," Robert said. "Hush? Here's where you respond to Justin."

Aleta stared at her image on the television screen. Her hand went to her head.

My hair is really short, she thought. Stanley is right. I need to let it grow.

Lydia turned. "I thought you'd turned the case over to Stanley."

"I did... but..."

"I asked her to defend her petition," Stanley explained. "And we figured that if Powell believes Aleta is handling the case, she'll be safe until the end of the trial."

"Why did he take the case?" Lydia asked. "Now he can't attack Aleta."

"Oh, he already has," Aleta said.

"You mean that comment about your so-called mistake?" Lydia asked.

Aleta nodded.

"It wasn't a mistake," Lydia said. "You didn't hurt your case with it. As a judge, I sometimes appreciate a touch of the personal in an argument. It did set you up to turn the reins over to Stanley. I assume that was your intention."

"An unconscious one," Aleta replied.

"Stay with your instincts. They're good ones."

Hubert interjected, "Your client came across well. Nice prep work."

Robert and Claude set up the folding tables and Aleta asked who rented them.

"We own them," Stanley said. "You're planning half a dozen parties at least in the next couple months. It seemed a reasonable purchase."

Bertha shook out two folded cloths and Lauren, Lydia and Harriet set the table.

"Dr. Cook gave us two hours for our celebration," Harriet told Aleta. "He saw you on television. He said he felt you could handle a little party—just family. We voted Lyle and Lauren into the family for the evening."

"Where's Jocelyn?" Aleta asked.

"At a friend's," her father replied. "We invited her but she said 'no, thank you!' in a very definite tone. She didn't want to party with a bunch of old folks."

Lauren and Aleta laughed.

"I guess to a sixteen year old, anyone past nineteen is old," Aleta commented.

"Hey we are old," Robert quipped. "Half the people in this room are about to become grandparents and the other half parents. That's so far removed from Jocelyn's world she can't even relate."

"I guess I'd have chosen dinner with friends over dinner with the family at her age," Aleta commented.

"You did it all the time!" her father exclaimed.

"Well, then, she's going to turn out just fine, isn't she?" Aleta returned smiling.

The party went well.

Later that night, Aleta remarked, "Everyone was extraordinarily kind to me this evening."

"Everyone is extremely proud of you," Stanley returned, "including me."

"My hair is way too short."

"A fact I've mentioned."

"I took my eyes off the judge."

"Which you corrected."

"And I got personal when it wasn't necessary no matter how nice a coating your mother put on it."

"I think God had a hand in that," Stanley observed. "He is more interested in your welfare than your perfection."

"You're saying that so I'll stop beating myself up."

"You don't believe He was there?"

"Of course, He was there. He's everywhere."

"You don't believe He interferes in the lives of men?"

"Of course, He does. He sent Jesus to us. That was the greatest interference of all time. Jesus changed the world."

"So who do you suppose told you about the Federal agents?"

"Ed."

"After you prepared the brief and before the arraignment?"

"Yes."

"I was with you every moment. We had no phone during that time. So how come you knew and I didn't?"

"I guessed?"

"No, you didn't. I asked you. You knew."

"Suppose I'm wrong."

"Justin checked. You weren't."

"Why did he do that?"

"Because Powell's face registered surprise when you made that remark. Justin knows enough about law to know a lawyer can't lie in court. He could sense Powell's animosity toward you."

"How do you know this?"

"Justin had Lyle check," Stanley said. "He thought maybe it was something about to happen and he wanted to use it if it was."

"So how long ago were they transferred?"

"They received their orders at three o'clock today."

"I don't want that known."

"Lyle told Justin to sit on it and promised him a TV interview with the prisoner in exchange."

"Lyle didn't ask me," Aleta said.

"He had no time. Justin planned to go on the air with it immediately."

"I was only a phone call away."

"We still don't have our phones, remember," Stanley said. "However, Justin did promise that we could review the footage and he'd edit out anything we didn't like."

Aleta breathed a huge sigh of relief.

"I think you need to take a couple days off. Let me handle the case. I can set the trial date. I assume we are waiving a preliminary hearing and going straight to trial."

"I'd like to see what Powell's got."

"He won't show us all the stuff he plans to hit us with in trial. He'll mislead us."

"You're right. We'll go with discovery and the witness list. He's got something. I think maybe it's time I talk with our client."

"No," Stanley said. "It's time for you to back off and let me handle some of this case. I'm very good at getting children to reveal what they are afraid to talk about. This man is thoroughly frightened. This is where I can truly help."

Aleta pondered his words. He was the expert here. A good attorney used experts.

"He's all yours," she said.

Chapter 24

Stanley visited Shakir Aloman first thing the following morning. Shakir's face showed his pleasure at seeing Stanley.

"Is your wife well?" he asked politely.

"She is well. I am making her follow her doctor's orders, so she will work from home for the next few days."

Shakir smiled. "You can make her?"

Stanley returned his smile. "I see you've appraised my wife correctly. No one can make her do anything; however, when we took our marriage vows, she promised me only one thing. It was the most priceless gift she could give me. She promised to obey me."

"She is truly a remarkable woman to promise such a thing."

"She is that," Stanley said. "Now tell me how you felt the arraignment went."

"She got the trial moved here. I didn't believe she would be able to do that."

"There were forces at work that we are not completely aware of."

"The prosecutor means to humiliate her in this trial."

"You are an astute judge of people," Stanley said. "Did you know that he sent your wife to Aleta to trap Aleta into illegally representing you? She has not yet been admitted to the Illinois bar."

"Is she a lawyer?"

"Yes, she is. She's from California where she was a practicing attorney."

"So she could represent me because the charges are federal?"

"She is what we call a House Attorney. She is permitted to represent members of the Tontine Trust and its employees in all legal matters in this state. Your wife's new position as bookkeeper entitles her and her family to representation at no charge. Aleta and I are both Tontine Trust lawyers. Together we worked to transfer the Trust from California to Illinois and that's how we met."

"So who will represent me in court?"

"We both will."

"I heard Powell say you are a child advocate. What's that?"

"A lawyer who represents children."

"Why do children need you? Do they commit many crimes?"

"They need someone to protect their interests in custody battles, cases of abuse and when they are without parents to advise them, as well as when they have broken the law."

"You have questions for me?" Shakir asked.

"I told Aleta I was used to talking with children and I'm afraid I completely misjudged you."

"I have found that the appearance of fright serves me better than bravado."

"So why did you change your approach?"

"Respect."

"Then let me talk to you as a man speaks with a man," Stanley said. "The entrance of Eugene Powell into this leads me to believe he is holding all the aces. I absolutely must know not only everything that happened but every question you had when it occurred."

"My questions? How could that help?"

"It means you observed something that puzzled you at the time. That is where we will find out clues as to the basis for their case."

"Don't they have to tell you what evidence they have?"

"Yes, they do," Stanley said. "Now let's clear up one thing. Everything you tell Aleta or me is privileged. We can't reveal anything you tell us without your permission. In order to defend you properly, we must know the truth. If we are surprised in court, you will lose. I can almost guarantee that. If you are caught in a lie, the jury will convict you on that alone, especially considering the charge."

"You think I am lying when I say I'm not a terrorist?"

"What I think is not important. I am committed to defending you. If you only tell me what you think I want to hear, we won't be able to defend you."

"I do not lie," Shakir declared.

"Of course, you do," Stanley countered roughly, "we all do when we are protecting those we love."

"Who am I protecting?"

"Your son."

"He is guilty of nothing!" Shakir declared.

"The Koran found in the trunk of your car is his, is it not?"

"No, it's mine."

"I told you that you would lie to protect a loved one."

"You cannot prove it isn't."

"My guess is that Powell already knows that the book is his and plans to trip you up with that lie."

"I will warn my son."

"It is too late."

"Why do you say that?"

"He had long conversations with your wife when he was pretending to help her. If he mentioned to police seeing the book as the reason for their suspicion; what would her response have been?"

"She would have said that the book wasn't mine but Basil's. She would have thought that would clear up the matter."

"Do you see why I need the truth?"

"I will lie rather than see Basil imprisoned as I was."

"I know," Stanley said. "But I can see that absolutely doesn't happen. He was thirteen at the time he was reading the Koran. Thirteen-year-olds are curious by nature. One of your relatives sent it to him, didn't they?"

"His uncle. I couldn't tell Basil not to accept it."

"A wise decision," Stanley said. "Now let's go over every moment following the police pulling you over. This I'm going to record. Aleta is very astute. She many discern something upon reflection that I might miss."

"Two minds are better than one," Shakir remarked.

"Especially when Aleta's is one of them," Stanley said as he turned on the recorder.

Stanley listened carefully without interruption. His attention and frequent head nods encouraged Shakir to give every detail he could remember.

He described the arrest and the first interrogation, and then he talked about the new men in suits.

"There were three," he said. "I didn't like the third one. He didn't speak; but, the other two kept looking to him for approval. He's the one who gave me the papers. I hated that he wore gloves, you know, the kind doctors use, as if touching me would give him some disease."

Stanley made a note on his pad.

"I'd never seen most of the stuff before. It was a poorly printed manifesto from some radical terrorist group. I shoved it back at him and that made him angry. He nodded at one of the men and he hit me hard.

"He demanded that I read every word. It was in Arabic, but I had no trouble doing as he asked. "I had to hold it in my hands as I was sitting in a chair in the middle of the room.

"It took a long time. It was many pages of fine script. I hated reading such viperous material; however, I was fearful that if I stopped I would be beaten. I thought that the scowling man might ask me questions about what I read and, if I got the answers wrong, I'd be beaten."

"Go on," Stanley urged when Shakir began trembling at the memory.

"I dropped it about two pages from the end. He was quite angry and my apology fell on deaf ears. I brushed some of the dirt off but stopped when I heard him growl an order to keep reading.

"My fear, which at that time was real, seemed to ameliorate his attitude toward me."

"You have quite a vocabulary for a person of foreign birth," Stanley observed.

"I wanted my children to be fluent in both languages, so we encouraged them to enter spelling bees when they were older. They had to study a wide assortment of English words. It is not something one does entirely alone. The whole family enters in."

Shakir continued the tale of his incarceration and his movement to the prison in Illinois. When he finished Stanley began asking questions.

"When you were shown the Koran, whose did you say it was?"

"I lied at first. I said I didn't know. I may have said it wasn't mine. I'm not sure. Anyway, it doesn't matter. They said my fingerprints were on it, so then I admitted that it was mine."

"A second lie on top of the first," Stanley observed.

"I couldn't say it belonged to my thirteen-year-old son," Shakir said. "The inscription was in Arabic. They couldn't read it."

"They will have had it translated," Stanley said. "We'll have to work on how to handle those lies. They weren't under oath were they?"

"No."

"Remember when you're under oath..."

"Don't lie," Shakir finished.

"And don't explain unless I ask you to."

"But....," Shakir started.

"You may ruin a point I am trying to make and, believe me, I would have done it better. Give me my due."

Shakir nodded. "I will trust you."

After a few more instructions, Stanley left.

Late afternoon, Stanley arrived home, passed the guard at the door and saw another patrolling the grounds. Milani wasn't convinced that the danger had been lessened by Powell's taking the case. Stanley found his wife in the study.

"How did your day go?" It was not a casual question which Aleta knew when he stood silently and waited for an answer.

"Claude and Grams came over soon after you left," Aleta said. "We trained dogs."

"And then?" Stanley asked, sensing more had happened.

"Kay Rivers came by," Aleta said with a grin. "She was upset at not being recognized. Lyle had to vouch for her again."

"At least we know Milani's men aren't letting just anyone through."

"They let you through."

"I live here."

"One wouldn't know it considering how little you're here."

"I won't leave you so long tomorrow," he promised. "Besides we have Shakir's tape to go over."

"Tonight?"

"Tomorrow would be better for me," Stanley said. "I'm very tired. I may have overdone it again."

"Let's eat early and go to bed," Aleta suggested.

"We could have company."

"I'll see we don't," Aleta said, rising and leaving the room.

He knew she was telling Bertha he was overtired. He wanted to stop her; but, it was true. He sat for a few minutes and dozed. When his dropping head caused him to awaken, he rose and walked into the kitchen. It was amazing how quickly his energy had left him.

Aleta was standing in the kitchen with a tall glass of some brown stuff. "It's a chocolate shake. Bertha put in lots of ice cream so it's thick."

"I'm really too tired," he mumbled.

"Drink," Aleta ordered, "or I'll call Dr. Cook and he'll put you back three days on the schedule."

Stanley took the glass and began to drink. Halfway through, he stopped. "Can't do more."

"Do you want Bertha to hold the glass for you while I undress you?"

"Aleta!" he said sharply.

"Drink half," she said.

Stanley took several more swallows and handed her the glass.

"Enough," he said.

Aleta took the glass and put it in the refrigerator while Stanley moved toward the bedroom.

"Call Dr. Cook," Aleta told Bertha. "I'll help him into bed."

"I'll stay the night, Ma'am."

"Thank you, Bertha," was all she said. She had no idea what orders to give.

He couldn't be sick. He'd be unable to leave the house. Aleta hadn't thought about that contingency when she made her decision to work exclusively from home. She had assumed that Stanley would be well. He hadn't even spent a full day at the office. Could he handle the rigors of a trial?"

Stanley was asleep when Dr. Cook arrived. This time Aleta was awake and opened the door for him.

When Dr. Cook took his pulse, Stanley woke up. "I'm not sick enough for a house call. I'm just tired."

"Would you ladies step outside please?"

"I don't need an examination," Stanley protested. "I need sleep."

Dr. Cook shoved a thermometer in his mouth. Stanley took it out to voice his protest anew.

Dr. Cook scowled.

"Do you want me to take it anally?"

Stanley put the thermometer back into his mouth.

Dr. Cook's fingers explored his neck and moved to his abdomen and down to his groin. Stanley grunted a few times to indicate sensitivity to touch. When the doctor finished, he plucked the thermometer from Stanley's mouth and grunted.

"So have I got some contagious disease and need to be quarantined and confined to bed for months, or can I go to work tomorrow?"

Dr. Cook drew out a syringe.

"What are you doing with that?" Stanley asked folding his arms closed.

"I need to test your blood."

"I'm not anemic."

"You're not well either. I believe you have mono."

"I'm thirty years old. That's a teenager's disease."

"The blood test will confirm it."

"It's contagious."

"Infectious. If you don't kiss your wife for a month, you won't give it to her."

"How'd I get it?"

"Obviously not by kissing you wife because she's not sick."

"Wayne! Be serious!"

"I don't know. It's caused by a virus. Usually by your age the body has encountered the virus and dispatched it.

But your immune system isn't normal yet. It's a malady of the immune system reacting to a virus of a certain type."

"How long?"

"Bed rest for a month. You'll be too tired to do much anyway."

"I can't. I have a trial coming up."

"You have no choice," Dr. Cook said. "Now are you going to unfold your arms and let me draw blood?"

"Do I have a choice?" Stanley asked ruefully, extending his arm.

The two women were waiting in the kitchen when Dr. Cook finished his examination.

"He stays in bed for a month at least," Dr. Cook explained. "Bertha, call me if the swelling of his lymph nodes increases or you see any symptom of jaundice."

"Visitors?" Aleta asked.

"As many as he'll allow into the bedroom," Dr. Cook smiled. "Only two or three at a time. Short visits."

"He has a trial....," Aleta mulled over in a soft voice.

Dr. Cook heard her.

"Out of the question!" he pronounced. "Can't it be postponed?"

"I'm considered lead council; but, Stanley has other clients depending on him."

"If you overdo it, I'll put you to bed too," Dr. Cook warned.

Later that evening, Aleta presented the problem to the family in the living room. Both sets of parents were present, Bertha now being considered a member of the family as well as Claude and Harriet. The first to respond to Aleta's announcement was her father.

"Two months from now I could fill in for Stanley," Robert said regretfully. "I can help prepare the cases, but child advocacy work requires a lot of counseling and court time which I can't do. I hate to send Stanley's clients elsewhere."

Hubert eyed Robert thoughtfully. "Is it an area you're interested in?"

"I'm considering it. I've enjoyed the work immensely and working with your son has been stimulating. He has a terrific mind."

"If that's the case, I think we can get you admitted to the bar early. I'm certain you passed the exam and the character and fitness committee has already approved your application. And I know a judge who'll swear you in. This is an emergency and there is a contingency for such. I'll get on it tomorrow."

Aleta spoke up excitedly. "I know you can do it, Dad. Stanley's brain still works fine. It's not as fatigued as the rest of him."

"But who will help you?" Robert objected. "Stanley's cases will take all my time."

"I'll help Aleta," Hubert offered. "I have no major cases pending. My partners can handle any new work. And I can enlist the help of several associates. I'm assuming the Tontine will pay for their time. My services are free."

Harriet nodded. "We will pay for your services as well. We are not a pro bono client. This is a situation where Aleta would find it necessary to seek help from an outside firm. There's no question we would pay. I don't see the difference, except that we are hiring the best. And Aleta will feel less pressure with your support than a stranger's. And that's important."

"I'll have a contract drawn up in the morning," Hubert said. "My partners will be ecstatic."

"And Aleta, Stanley is still on salary," Harriet noted. "I know he will be advising you on this case; but, officially he's on sick leave."

Aleta smiled. "How much sick leave do we get each year? It seems as if we've used up a decade's worth already."

"The Tontine considers itself fortunate you haven't asked for hazardous duty pay. You would certainly have been entitled to it."

"I'm wondering if we should hire a new attorney for the Tontine. Stanley really wants to devote his time to his practice. It's work he enjoys. And I don't want to rope Dad into the Tontine work. It's too close to what he just left."

"You have someone in mind?"

"I was thinking of Kay Rivers. Her insight into how Powell thinks could be valuable on the Aloman case."

"She has a point, Harriet," Hubert added. "She's a brilliant prosecutor; however, I doubt she'll want to take the Tontine job. I think it's a bad fit. However, we do have an opening for an associate. She has a lot experience in criminal law. She'd be perfect for us."

"That still leaves the Tontine work," Harriet said.

"I know a young lawyer that could handle it temporarily," Hubert said. "Stanley could oversee his work if you want. You won't mind that he's black, will you?"

Harriet was the first but not the only one to laugh.

"Sounds perfect!" Aleta said.

When Stanley woke later that night as Aleta was getting ready for bed, she relayed all that had been decided.

"You have your cell phone back. It's your intercom," Aleta said. "I'm one. Bertha is two. I will be here most of the time and you aren't absolutely confined to bed; but, if you want to know where either of us is, don't come looking, call."

"Where will you be going?" Stanley asked.

"Riding. Training Scooby. And when the trial starts, I'll make one trip to court a day. Milani is supplying a car and three men to escort me. There and back."

"When was that arrangement made?"

"It's one that will be made in the morning."

"What about our client?"

"Hubert will prep him for me," Aleta said. "I am determined to leave this house only for court appearances. Hubert will take care of deposing the prosecution witnesses and other such matters."

"This is going to be a frustrating month for me," Stanley said.

"You'll be lonely, won't you?" Aleta queried sympathetically.

"I expect so."

She slipped into her satin nightgown and crawled into bed and took Stanley's hand. "I don't want you to feel that way.

"Some things can't be avoided," Stanley sighed.

Aleta kissed his hand and turned toward him.

"I could move a table in here and work," she suggested, her eyes watching his expression.

"That's not necessary," he said.

"I heard you. And I agree. It's not necessary, but would you mind? I like working near you."

"No, I don't mind," Stanley replied, a lightness in his tone.

She kissed him full on the mouth.

He pushed her away. "Aleta!"

"I've had mono. I got my diseases out of the way at the appropriate ages. I didn't save any for adulthood."

"You could get it again."

"I don't think so," Aleta said.

"No more kissing," he ordered.

"On the mouth," she added.

"Okay, on the mouth," he acquiesced.

She kissed him on the cheek.

"You can kiss me too, you know," Aleta prodded.

"If you insist," he conceded, kissing her hand.

"Where only a husband can," she prompted.

And he complied.

Chapter 25

The next morning, Stanley woke to find Aleta fully dressed and standing beside him. "If you are awake, Bertha and I will move the table in here now."

"Are we allowed to do what we did last night?" he said circumspectly.

"Bertha's in the kitchen," Aleta informed him. "And Dr. Cook knows us. He would have said something to one of us."

"Chances are you've already passed the virus to me. Either I'll get mono or I won't," Aleta determined. "So let me enjoy the fact that I have you available any time I want to indulge myself."

"I'm supposed to rest."

"It would be best if you'd program your naps to coincide with when I'm gone."

"Program my naps? You've got to be kidding."

She looked at him with a straight face. "That doesn't sound reasonable?"

"You can't program naps!" he exclaimed.

"Of course, you can."

Stanley conceded defeat.

"Bring in your table. I'll try to program my naps. But honestly, Aleta, you have got to be the world's most demanding woman."

Aleta smiled when she left. If he slept when she was gone, his loneliness would be much less. She decided to order her day to accommodate his need for periodic sleep.

Hubert Praetzel showed up mid-afternoon. Aleta was just finishing her ride. He watched her ride to the barn. Matt dismounted and led both horses away. By now Aleta realized that Hubbs liked rubbing down the horses after they'd been ridden and stopped offering to relieve him of that chore.

"How's Stanley?" his father asked. "Did he approve of our decisions?"

"He's resting," Aleta said as the two moved toward the house. "He's supposed to nap when I'm gone. I've moved my workstation into our bedroom so he won't be alone all day. It's hard for me to stop working periodically, but he needs naps, so I do. He should be waking up soon. I'm sure he'll want us to talk in the bedroom instead of the living room."

She opened her cell phone. "Stanley, your dad's here. Are you up to talking about the case?"

Aleta nodded to signal his affirmative reply.

"We'll stop off in the kitchen and bring you a snack," she said.

"Kay Rivers gave notice today," Hubert said. "She joins our firm in ten days unless they tell her she's free before then."

"You moved fast," Aleta said.

"Nothing like the announcement that one of our young associates was going to be busy with Tontine contracts on the same day I announced that we were being asked to assist in a Tontine criminal case. They were ecstatic over getting a piece of such a plum."

He opened the front door for Aleta and she entered and called to Bertha that they were going to take a snack to Mr. Praetzel.

Aleta studied her father-in-law when she asked, "They understand I'm lead, don't they?"

"They are satisfied with being associated with this case. It's a high profile case. That's worth more than money."

"Let's go ask Stanley what problems he sees us facing," she said. "Bertha, we'll take our coffee in the bedroom."

"You haven't talked about the case?" Hubert asked as they moved toward the bedroom.

"We listened to the tape of his interview with Shakir Aloman, but we didn't talk about it. He fell asleep toward the end," Aleta said, opening the door.

The room had lost some of its bedroom atmosphere with the addition of the worktable and two chairs. Stanley's position in bed completed the circle around the large round table which took up almost the whole area in front of the picture window.

Hubert smiled when he saw the scattering of papers on the table's top. Stanley was so orderly. He must have wanted Aleta near him so much, he had forced himself to cast a blind eye toward the mess or else he loved even that part of his wife's character.

Hubert half expected his son to apologize for the mess; but, instead Stanley welcomed him warmly.

Aleta plunged right in. "What do we need to work on?"

"The manifesto," Stanley said. "They purposely had him read every page so his fingerprints would be on more than the cover. It's not his."

"That would be impossible to prove," Hubert said.

"He dropped it on the floor of the interrogation room," Stanley said. "Some of the dirt may still be on the manifesto. What we need are samples from various interrogation rooms."

"We'll need a court order," Hubert said. "That could alert Powell."

"We can send Ed," Aleta said. "He knows one of the cops down there."

"It's a long shot," Hubert said.

"We can have Hawk teach Ed how to take a sample," Aleta said. "It'll be so low profile; we may avoid raising any red flags."

Stanley moved on. "Shakir had the Koran with him to continue what he was doing for his son."

"Catch me up," Hubert requested.

"He was marking passages in the Koran that were like those in his Bible," Aleta explained. "He was teaching his son that both religions offered similar advice to believers."

"A tutorial in comparative religion," Hubert commented. "Why not? The man is a university graduate. That's what a scholar would do."

"We need to have someone translate all the marked passages," Aleta said. "We need to know if any could be used against us."

"Check Shakir's Bible too," Stanley said. "If we're lucky, he may have marked the similar passages there."

"He was going to see his cousin," Stanley said. "We need to know everything there is to know about him. I understand he was arrested. He was probably deported. I assume he had Shakir's name and address on him."

"I believe Ed took a copy of the arrest report off the computer at police headquarters in Florida," Aleta said.

"Can't use it," Hubert said. "We can't even know it exists."

"How do you think we found our man?" Aleta said. "It's going to come up. The point is we didn't take it. We didn't even know that's what he planned to do. He was supposedly searching for the car. And interestingly, the car was impounded and never signed off the lot. How did the Feds get hold of a manifesto from the car? The arresting officers only removed the Koran according to the police report."

"I need to go down there," Hubert said. "I will take Ed with me."

"Take Kay Rivers with you," Aleta said.

"She may not be free," Hubert said.

"She's free," Aleta declared. "As a former prosecutor, she will turn out to be invaluable."

"Former?"

"They cut her loose an hour ago."

Stanley looked shocked. "You're predicting transfers now. First the two Feds and now Kay."

Aleta turned to Hubert. "Please call her from the living room. I'd use her cell number."

When her father-in-law departed, Aleta scowled. "Don't broadcast what I can do."

"It's my father!" Stanley protested. "Besides you yourself, in case you forgot, spilled the beans about Kay right here a few seconds ago."

"I did, didn't I?" Aleta confirmed embarrassed. "Well, don't you say anything! Do you understand?"

"Why are you so upset?"

"Because I wasn't in control," Aleta shot back.

"You're never in control of your prophecies."

"This wasn't a prophecy. This had already happened. This is a whole new area and I'm not happy about it. It's as if my brain isn't my own. I just insert facts that I don't know and treat them as if I do. I don't like it."

"You said that," Stanley responded softly. "Aleta, come here."

Too upset and angry to even protest, Aleta went over and sat beside him. He put his arms around her and embraced her. "There's no reason to be upset. God would never have you lie. You can trust in that."

She buried her face in his shoulder and began to cry.

Hubert returned and was completely bewildered by the sight of Aleta sobbing.

"She's upset with her new ability," Stanley said. "She would appreciate it if you didn't say anything to anyone."

"Don't worry, Aleta, I won't. But let me tell you what happened. It seems the reception to Kay's announcement that she was moving on was met with acrimony and she was told that they'd taken her in when no one else would touch her and her leaving was an ungrateful act."

Aleta, who'd stopped feeling sorry for herself midway through Hubert's recitation of Kay's departure trauma, murmured, "Poor Kay."

"I told Kay you suggested she accompany us on a trip to the arrest site in Florida. I told her there'd be five of us."

"Five?"

"I need to get back," Hubert said, "so Claude's coming along as co-pilot and Harriet's coming along because they're still on their honeymoon she says."

"You did all of that arranging in three minutes?"

"I'm afraid it was longer than three minutes," Stanley apprised his wife. "You were very upset."

"The bottom line is that Kay's thrilled to be an integral part of this case right from the start," Hubert said. "You turned her day around, Aleta."

"One more thing, Dad," Stanley said. "Shakir said there were three interrogators. The third is the one who handed him the manifesto. See if any of the city police know who the third man was."

"At the rate you're piling on the work, I may not get back tomorrow."

"What's tomorrow?"

"The second most important event in my life, your birthday being the first."

"Your birthday is in June," Stanley said.

"And your mother's is in May," Hubert responded. "So what's in April? You know it's okay if you forget mine, but you'll never live it down if you forget yours."

Stanley looked blank.

"It's their wedding anniversary," Aleta whispered. "And when's ours?"

"It's marked on the calendar," Stanley said.   "It's sometime between August and September."

"You can't remember," Aleta huffed. "How could you not remember? We even had two weddings? That would have made an impression on most men."

"I'm hard to impress," Stanley smirked.

"You're teasing me."

"You're so easy," Stanley said. "Dad, divide the tasks. Harriet and Claude can help."

Chapter 26

While Hubert and Claude piloted the plane, Harriet, Ed
and Lydia chatted with Kay in the back. Mid-way Hubert
left his seat and came back to discuss the tasks that needed
doing.

Kay was assigned to interview the two arresting
officers. It was something she had done frequently in her
former job. She was pleased she had an important
assignment

To Kay's surprise and delight, the six enjoyed a fine
dinner at a nice restaurant and she was told it was to celebrate
her joining Hubert Praetzel's law firm. For her this was an
exciting finish to a day of mixed emotions. All awkwardness
she felt had vanished by the meal's end and she was eager to
prove herself the next day.

Meanwhile, back in Willow Glen Aleta fretted over not
being able to travel with the group. Stanley listened as she
talked but could think of no words of comfort. He was
feeling left out as well.

"Why not join me?" he said.

"Join you? How?"

"Put on your pajamas and your robe and we can
commiserate over supper like a pair of shut-ins."

"If we eat at the kitchen table," Aleta said, "you have to promise me you won't fall asleep over supper. I sent Bertha home. You're too big for me to lug back to bed."

"I know it will be difficult," Stanley grinned, "but I'll try not to fall face first into my soup."

"We aren't having soup."

"Then I guess I'll stay awake."

"What if they don't get done?" Aleta said.

"Dad took Mother just for that reason. He was certain they wouldn't. He wanted to complete his investigation before Powell would guess he'd even begun."

"I can't believe Powell doesn't know. Your mother cancelled her court calendar tomorrow."

"He can't do anything," Stanley decided.

"He must be having a frustrating evening as well."

With that idea floating between them, their mood lightened and they enjoyed their meal.

When Aleta cleared the table, she noticed the rusty red truck pause on the road that ran past the front of the house.

She turned.

"You know, Stanley," she began when the sharp staccato beat of as assault weapon being discharged abruptly interrupted her. When the rounds hit the house, the plate slipped from her hand. She shrieked and dropped onto the floor.

A series of single shots followed.

Stanley leaped from his seat and rushed to check on his wife. The front door opened.

The guard called out. "Are you okay?"

"Yes," Stanley returned.

"It was a red truck," Aleta shouted.

"We have them, Ma'am," the cop said. "Our man at the gate shot out their tires and wounded the driver. The shooter gave up."

Sirens could be heard in the distance.

Aleta nestled inside her husband's arms. "Why is he still coming after us?"

"Do you want to think about this now or do you just want to go sit in the living room by the fire."

"We have no fire."

"Someone's going to start one," Stanley said as he led her to the couch."

"Who?"

"Whichever one of us is strong enough to strike a match. Bertha always sets up the fireplace after cleaning it. Haven't you noticed?"

"I guess I never have," Aleta confessed, picking up the match holder and striking a match.

"Who did you think built the fire?" he asked.

"The Fire Fairy?"

"Well, at least you believe in fairies."

"If you don't, you never get the silver dollar the tooth fairy leaves."

"You got a dollar? All I ever got was a quarter."

"My dad said he used to get a dime," Aleta said, "but I didn't believe him."

"Well, believe him. Both my parents said in their day, a dime was the going rate."

"We have to give silver dollars you know."

"We couldn't compromise and give two quarters. Kids like multiples."

"Two dollars then."

"You're going the wrong way."

"Why is Powell still coming after us?" Aleta said suddenly somber.

"It was a carelessly planned attempt."

"Do you think this attack was a red herring?"

"Possibly," Stanley responded. "But consider the timing."

"We're alone?"

"Where's our team?" Stanley went on.

"Florida."

"What might Powell be hoping?"

"They'd fly back before they're finished," Aleta said.

"

"So, we don't tell them."

"Someone else might," Stanley said.

"We need to tell them then," Aleta decided.

"Tell them what?"

"That we're okay."

"They won't believe that," Stanley remarked. "They're our parents. They'll believe we're putting on a brave front."

"Which is the truth," Aleta said. "Powell is a devilishly clever man. He's distracting us from the case."

"What could sink our case?" Stanley questioned, accepting her hypothesis.

"If they had a witness that said Shakir admitted he was a terrorist."

"He was alone in his cell. I asked," Stanley said.

"But if their jail is anything like the jails here, sometimes there are only bars between cells"

"Assuming he has a witness," Stanley contemplated aloud, "he'd have to put him on the witness list. We wouldn't miss some strange name on the list."

"Cops sometimes pretend to be prisoners. They make better witnesses than real criminals. They probably used one of their own men. It's what Lyle would do," Aleta asserted.

"Powell will list every cop on the force. We wouldn't have the time to investigate every name. He'd probably throw in the name of everyone else in the jail at that time."

"That's the key," Aleta proclaimed. "We hunt down the fellow prisoners. They might tell us what we need to know about what went on between interrogations."

"That we can call them with," Stanley said. "And then, when we say that the attack was a bogus attempt to rattle us, they'll believe us."

"Who'll believe what?" Lyle said entering the house.

"Don't you ever knock?" Aleta asked.

"It's a crime scene," he said. "Did any of the rounds penetrate?"

"If they did, they're inside the cabinets," Stanley said. "Excuse me I need to make a phone call."

"Tell your dad I'm here," Lyle said. "Tom took his wife to dinner and a show."

"It was a rusty red truck," Aleta said. "I just turned to tell Stanley that I thought... never mind. I can't ask you to do that."

"Close off the road?" Lyle said. "It's being done. The only two houses affected are yours and Stanley's parents' place. It's going to be a semi-permanent blockade and it'll take in that rise in the road that runs alongside your other neighbor's fence line. He'll still have access to his driveway. Everyone else along this road will have to take a little detour on their way home."

"The neighbors will complain," Aleta lamented.

"Tom says crime in this area is way down. The men at the gate note every license number that passes. The word got around," Lyle responded. "Now what's bogus?"

"It was a stupid attempt," Aleta said. "We think it was meant to distract us from the case."

"We police don't take kindly to people using automatic weapons as a distraction. Since Milani's men patrol the grounds around the house, and as it was night, I'm adding attempted murder of a police officer to the charges," Lyle informed Aleta as he sat down opposite her. "By the way, since it was dark, how did you see the color of the truck?"

"Oncoming headlights."

"The men who were looking at it from the outside of the house couldn't tell the color at all."

To Lyle's amazement, Aleta began to cry.

"What did I say?" he asked perturbed.

"That she knew the color and no one else did," Stanley said entering the room.

"Short phone call."

"They were at dinner," Stanley said as he sat beside his wife and gathered her in his arms.

"Why is Aleta upset?"

"It seems Aleta knows things she shouldn't know. It's a new gift and it's proved to be very upsetting."

And she's pregnant," Lyle said. "Lauren has been doing the same thing lately."

"And how do you handle it?"

"Same as you. I just hold her," Lyle replied. "And, Aleta, you won't have to testify. Four officers saw the shooting. I'm on my way down to the hospital. That extra charge just might loosen the tongue of the man who was driving."

He rose and started toward the door. "No one else will disturb you tonight."

He then left them in a close embrace watching the fire in the fireplace.

Hubert's cell phone rang just as they were starting dessert. When he saw who it was, he excused himself and took the call in the foyer.

When he returned, his face reflected his anxiety.'

"They were shot at," he announced without preamble. Stanley assessed it as a bogus attempt, meant to rattle us. The two of them figure Powell plans to surprise us with a devastating witness from here."

"What kind of witness?" Claude asked.

"One who was with him in jail and said he confessed," Kay replied. "A plant. It would be difficult to discredit a cop. Of course it could be a jailhouse snitch, but it's been three years. I'm betting on the cop, someone still on the force."

"How do we want to approach this?" Hubert asked.

"It won't be anyone on duty at the time Aloman was arrested," Kay said. "In fact, they'd want to use someone none of the other prisoners knows is a cop."

"Wouldn't that be practically impossible?"

"A new man," Kay suggested. "Or one coming back from sick leave, preferably detective grade or higher, someone most of the small time hoods wouldn't know."

"How do we zero in?" Hubert asked.

"Payroll records. Time sheets." Harriet offered.

"I think we should interview those who were in the jail at the time," Lydia proposed, intrigued by the investigative process she had been thrown into.

"I'll go back to the arresting officers," Kay said. "Don't overlook the men at the impound lot or in the evidence room. They are good resources for the movement of evidence."

"Check back with me on regular intervals," Hubert said. "Your reports will dictate our next step."

"Do Stanley and Aleta need us?" Harriet asked.

"It was his suggestion that we take another day or two as long as we're here," Hubert said.

"Suppose we don't get the cooperation we need?" Harriet asked.

"That's where Lydia comes in."

"Me?"

"You will see we are granted whatever access we need."

"I have my limits."

"We will need you to creatively expand those limits."

Chapter 27

The following morning Stanley woke to find Aleta standing beside him dressed for court.

"You didn't wake me," he scolded.

"Remember the feeling," she retorted, "in case you ever decide I don't want you to wake me when you get up."

"I don't like to interrupt your sleep," he explained. "You need your sleep."

"And you don't believe that reasoning applies to you?"

"Are you going to be alright?"

"Milani gave me four guards. He's notified the court bailiff the courtroom is to be clear of spectators."

Stanley returned to his real query rising on one elbow, "I mean are you going to be alright?"

"God restored my soul," Aleta announced with a winsome smile, "as usual, through you."

Stanley laid his head back satisfied. One of the characteristics that made Aleta easy to live with is she was so open. Her feedback to his efforts was a solace when he was in doubt as to whether his efforts to help her had done so.

"Have a nice nap," she said as she leaned over and kissed him.

"I haven't had breakfast," he complained.

"You only need to call Bertha when you're ready," she advised him. "And if you want her to feed you, she'll do that."

"I'm not a helpless invalid!" he protested.

"Rest your brain. I may need to pick it when I get home."

"Promise you'll wake me," he requested.

"I promise," she said. As she closed the door she saw his eyes close.

"He's resting," she told Bertha. "Last night was hard on him."

"On both of you," Bertha noted.

"He expended a lot of energy comforting me," Aleta said. "I won't be in court long, but if I am, check on him in a couple of hours."

"Yes, Ma'am."

Judge Aramis Heard entered a nearly empty courtroom. On one side were Eugene Powell and one of the assistant DA's; on the other, Aleta Praetzel and her client who looked like an ordinary forty-year-old businessman. Eugene Powell he knew. Aleta Praetzel he didn't.

His eyes rested on her close-cropped hair which he didn't like. It made her look a trifle mannish. Aleta realized at once that her trim business suit needed a different blouse.

She smiled demurely and saw approval in the blue eyes under the bushy gray brows. She was thankful she'd worn the skirt rather than the pants.

"The first order of business," the judge said, "is to set a date for the preliminary hearing."

"We can be ready in a week," Powell said rising.

Aleta rose as well and moved away from the table so the judge could see her short skirt, stockings and soft black leather high heels. What Judge Heard saw was a pair of lovely slim legs and her very pregnant belly.

"The prosecution has had three years to prepare its case," Aleta stated matter-of-factly. "The defense moves to go immediately to trial."

"You are waiving a preliminary hearing?" the judge asked. This was a green lawyer. This was a mistake. Where was her co-counsel?

"We are, Your Honor," Aleta said. "And since the prosecution has had three years to gather its evidence and witnesses, we request that the witness list and evidence be dusted off and made available to the defense this afternoon."

"But, Your Honor," Powell protested. "We need more time."

"I'll take the witness list this afternoon and the forensic report Monday afternoon," Aleta stated.

Powell wanted to protest, but the judge's look warned him not to. He didn't dare reveal that his bluff had been called.

"So ordered," the judge ruled.

"How long does the defense need to prepare for trial?"

"We will take the earliest date Your Honor chooses. Our client has spent an unconscionable amount of time in prison," Aleta said, and then noting the frown closing the bushy brows, quickly added, "However, the defense has no intention of mentioning that again. I believe Your Honor is aware that he has waited a long time for his day in court."

"I note that you have another reason for wanting to move this along. Perhaps later would be better."

"We can be ready to select the jury in two weeks," Aleta said. "Later is not an option for my client."

"That will not give us enough time to depose the defense witnesses."

"You've had three years to depose my client," Aleta contended. "He's been interrogated ad infinitum. Your Honor, the defense requests that my client be subjected to no more interrogations.

"The prosecution has a right to depose your witness," the judge said almost kindly.

"It is a delaying tactic," Aleta asserted. "As well as an exercise in abuse. The prosecution means to hammer at my client some more. He has already endured days of such interrogation by three of the federal government's best men. The prosecution has those interviews on tape."

"You have made a good point," Judge Heard declared. "I'll accept a brief on the matter in the morning. I'll make a ruling then."

Aleta went to her briefcase and pulled out a neatly bound sheaf of papers.

"My brief, Your Honor," she said handing it to the clerk who handed it to the judge.

Judge Heard was openly impressed. He began to view this young lawyer in a new light.

"What about her other witnesses, Your Honor?" Powell pressed. His ire was evident.

"I have no other witnesses," Aleta stated evenly.

"I have a long list," Powell said. "Mrs. Praetzel will need time to depose them."

"I don't intend to depose any of the prosecution's witnesses," Aleta said. "However, I do want a list, and if the names of all three interrogators who questioned my client are not on his list, then I want the third interrogator added to the defense's witness list."

"That is an irregular request," Judge Heard said. "You don't happen to have a brief supporting it on you, do you?"

"I do, Your Honor," Aleta said opening her briefcase and selecting a more slender brief.

"Hand it to the clerk," Judge Heard said amusement causing his mouth to twitch as he saw Powell's befuddled exasperation.

"I object!" Powell said, at a loss as to how to explain that he wasn't aware there was a third interrogator.

"I'll expect your brief in the morning," the judge said. "Jury selection will begin two weeks from next Wednesday. Court adjourned."

Once back in his chambers, Judge Heard asked the three men, "Did you hear it all?"

"She was ready with the briefs," said the tallest of the three.

"A remarkable feat," Judge Heard commented. "That woman was prepared for Powell at every turn."

"Didn't you find that suspicious?" the same man persisted.

"Suspicious of what? Hard work? Overzealousness?"

"How did she know what brief you would request?"

"She knew what rulings she was going to ask for," the judge replied. "She had several more in her briefcase. I think she was prepared for a number of contingencies."

"Why prepare briefs in advance?" the rotund man inquired.

Heard laughed.

"Well, to impress the judge for one. She certainly impressed me."

"You found her arguments rational?" asked the third man.

"I'd say so. Different, but reasonable," Heard responded. "My guess is she was at the top of her class."

"Anything you didn't like?" the tallest man asked.

"Her haircut!" Judge Heard exclaimed. "Why do smart women so often insist upon looking like a man?"

"Don't you know?" said the rotund man.

"Know what?"

"She has had four brain operations. They shaved her head each time. I was told she used to wear her hair quite long."

"Now it all makes sense," Heard commented. "The hair didn't fit the rest of her."

"That was your only problem?" the tallest one pressed.

"So far," Judge Heard responded. "You'll be able to watch her from the courtroom two weeks from Wednesday."

Aleta rushed into the bedroom upon arriving home and woke Stanley.

"Hold me!" she demanded.

"It didn't go well?"

"It went better than I'd hoped. Powell was furious."

"So that's why you're shaking."

"Yes," she said burying her head into his shoulder.

"Did you waive the prelim?"

"Yes."

"Did you ask for the witness list?"

"The judge ordered it delivered this afternoon."

"And the evidence?"

"Monday."

"How many briefs did you need to submit?"

"Two."

"How long have we got?"

"I had them ready."

"You guessed?"

"Is that bad?"

"It's brilliant!" he exclaimed.

"One was on them not deposing Shakir," Stanley said. "What was the other on?"

"Adding the name of the third government interviewer to our witness list if he wasn't on the prosecution's," Aleta said. "That one shook Powell."

"When's the trial?"

"We began jury selection two weeks from Wednesday."

"You need to be there. You have great instincts."

"Maybe we should use a jury consultant."

"Pick the ones you think will listen to you," Stanley said.

"I don't know if I'll be closing."

"You will make your case when you question the witnesses."

"The judge ordered the tapes of the interrogations be delivered this afternoon. If there are three days of tapes, I don't know if I have time to listen to every word."

"Alice can transcribe them," Stanley suggested.

"Good!" Aleta responded.

"I can preview them for you," Stanley offered.

Aleta heard the hesitation in his voice. He didn't want to intrude. He needed to sleep and rest; but his brain yearned for work.

"It could be dull work," she responded, "but I would be so grateful. You won't miss anything important."

She watched his face light up.

"I'll try to keep you up-to-date," she added. "I know I have your father; but, I need you too."

"I wish I could have been there," Stanley said with regret.

"Just keep holding me," Aleta said.

Stanley picked up his cell phone. "Bertha, Mrs. Praetzel is exhausted. We're taking a long nap. No visitors."

"Yes, Sir," she said. "I'll see you're not disturbed. Send Scooby out here or he'll wake you when he gets hungry."

"Aleta, tell Scooby to go get lunch."

"It's early."

"Bertha doesn't want to disturb us."

"Scooby, go to Bertha. Bertha, give him a cookie."

"We have a phone so we don't have to yell," Stanley reminded her.

"Scooby understands the words 'Bertha' and 'cookie'. I yelled for his benefit."

"Come here and let me help you get ready for your nap."

"You're sick."

"I'm not so sick I can't handle talking off a woman's clothes."

Aleta confessed shyly, "I feel guilt asking you to help me; but, I love having you touch me."

"Well, then we're going to have a pleasant time before we sleep."

Robert arrived for lunch. "How'd it go for Aleta?"

"She made a beeline for Stanley and they talked and then told me they were going to nap. Last night's attack took its toll on both of them."

"So, no one knows I was sworn in this morning," he commented as he sat at the table.

"I'm sorry I couldn't be there," Bertha said setting a plate of chicken and rice in front of him.

"It wasn't much of a ceremony. Me, the judge and a couple of witnesses."

"Anybody I know?"

"Kurtz West and Lyle."

"Lyle?"

"He was waiting outside Aleta's courtroom and I asked him to come."

"You didn't pop in on Aleta?"

"There were guards at the door."

Bertha joined him at the table.

"So you're a lawyer again," she said. She slipped a small box beside his plate.

"A gift?"

"I hope you like it," Bertha said shyly. "Go on. Open it."

Robert slipped off the ribbon and opened the small square box. Inside nestled in cotton was a gold pocket watch. He opened it and read the inscription.

"To My Beloved, on the occasion of his admission to the Illinois bar, Bertha."

"We can add the date at the bottom," Bertha said. "Do you like it?"

"I'm speechless," Robert stammered. "It's the nicest present anyone's ever given me."

Bertha giggled girlishly. "Don't let your mother hear you say that."

Robert stood up and drew her to him. "I'm touched. It's a perfect gift. I do love you."

His kiss was, without a doubt, the most loving Bertha had ever received. When they parted, she saw the tears in his eyes.

"My life has been a celebration since I met you," he said softly. "Thank you."

"May I tell the children when they wake up from their naps?"

Robert chuckled. "Of course."

"Aleta will be sorry she missed it."

"It would have been bittersweet for her at this time."

"I'm baking a cake this afternoon. We can have a small family celebration when you finish. Will you be done by six?"

"I'll be here at six-thirty no matter what."

At the time promised, Robert Locke entered the Praetzel house to be greeted by a crowd of people shouting "Congratulations!"

Surprised, he spun around and rushed back out the door. He was back in ten seconds. He found the whole group shocked into silence.

"Where are your cars?" he burst out.

Laughter erupted and explanations poured forth.

Aleta had been told the news when she woke and had called Lauren. It was to be a come-as-you-are surprise party with everyone bringing what they were making for supper. The counter was loaded with an odd assortment of dishes from lasagna to hot dogs. Bertha had thawed a few of the frozen dinners made previously and before the guests lay a veritable feast.

Aleta's work papers were piled on the chair in the bedroom as her table went back into service in the family room. Stanley insisted on dressing but was confined to his recliner which several early arrivals helped Aleta move into the living room.

Five of their group were still in Florida, but Aleta decided surprising her father on his big day was essential. None of the family had been able to be at the ceremony, and she sensed from Bertha that even though he understood, he was a bit disappointed.

Robert was properly overwhelmed. There were no gifts except for Stanley's, but his was enough. It was a new nameplate to hang outside the office door announcing Robert Locke, Attorney at Law. As usual, Stanley had ordered his gift well in advance.

Lauren, as usual, had worked out a way to mix everyone up. As they came through the line she randomly assigned them to tables. For Kay's mother, Eunice, this was a bit unsettling. She only knew Bessie Dobbs. Maryanne, for whom this was the second such affair, joined Kay's mother who was hanging back and told her that she knew how she felt.

"Next time you'll enjoy it," she predicted.

"This is a one-time thing," Eunice said politely. She was an attractive heavy-set older woman with hair that had been lightened to a light strawberry blonde. She had clear skin and large brown eyes.

"Don't kid yourself," Maryanne returned. "No one is here by accident. No one enters Aleta's house that she doesn't personally choose. This is a permanent group."

"I'm just a guest of Bessie's."

"Are you an artist?"

"Actually, I'm a nurse, a private duty nurse."

"Bertha is a practical nurse. She works for Aleta. She's their housekeeper and cook. Aleta hired her after she had her stroke. Aleta's had need of a nurse off and on after that."

"Really?"

"She's had four brain surgeries, which is why Dr. Taekman is a guest. He did all four along with Dr. Cook."

"Is she okay now?"

"Oh, she's fine."

"Her other parties," Eunice said. "Were they like this one? Spontaneous pot-lucks?"

""Nothing is ever the same I understand. From what I've been told we all sit down and eat, and Lauren is the hostess and directs things. And every party has its surprises. We were all shot at last time."

"Shot at!" Eunice gasped.

"Not us actually. Aleta and Stanley were shot at in their bedroom."

Eunice looked around. "Are we safe?"

"Bullet proof glass all around," Maryanne replied. "And police everywhere. I think we're pretty safe. We have all three local police chiefs in the group."

"Really?"

"And three doctors in case you get shot," Maryanne teased.

Eunice smiled. "What do all these people have in common?"

"Aleta likes them."

"That's it?"

"She has great taste in people. You'll see. There isn't a person here not worth knowing."

Eunice watched Aleta go into the living room with a full plate.

"Where is she going?" Eunice asked.

"To serve Stanley," Maryanne said. "Before you and Bessie arrived, Lauren announced that he was confined to his recliner. His doctor is here, so he doesn't dare move."

As they came to the end of the line, Lauren assigned them each their table and excused herself.

"Not much room lately," she said as she hurried toward the guest bathroom.

When Eunice sat down, Lyle, who was at her table looked around. "Where's Lauren."

"Ladies room," Eunice said.

He relaxed and went back to eating.

Aleta stayed with Stanley sharing the food on his plate.

"I'm not sure this is a good idea," Stanley cautioned.

"I'm not eating your food. Mine's on this side of the plate," she told him.

"They're touching."

"The food's not infectious. You are."

"Aleta, if you get sick, I'm going to hit you with so many I-told-you-so's, you'll wish you'd listened to me."

"I always listen to you," Aleta responded evenly. "But I don't always do what you wish. I have my own decision-making apparatus. It's called a brain."

After a few more bites, Aleta stopped.

"Stanley, I need to check on something. You wait here."

Stanley looked at her with an amused grin.

"Exactly where do you think I'll go?"

She bent over and kissed him on the forehead. "I love you."

Immediately, he knew something was up.

"You aren't coming back?" he asked.

"Not for a while."

"Aleta, what is it?"

She didn't answer, but went to Bertha and whispered in her ear. Bertha nodded and rose.

"Everyone," Aleta announced, "there's loads of food left. Please feel free to taste something you didn't have room on your plate for first time through."

As a number of people rose from their places, Aleta slipped into the laundry room and closed the door. She picked up an armload of towels and the unopened box of sterile gloves. Bertha went to Aleta's closet and selected a clean outfit of Aleta's and made her way through the people into the laundry room. Aleta shut the door behind her. Carrying the clothes Bertha followed her to the guest bathroom. Aleta knocked softly.

"Lauren, it's Aleta. I'm here to help. I have clean clothes."

The door opened. Aleta gasped. The floor was wet and bloody.

"I was praying you'd come," Lauren said. "Everything was normal until I stood at the sink to wash my hands. I've never had my water break like this. I'm so sorry."

"It's no bother, Ma'am," Bertha said, putting on her professional manner. "Are you having contractions?"

Lauren bent over and Aleta saw the pain etched on her face.

"She's having one now," Aleta said.

"I'm sure I'm not really in labor. I have these pains so far apart."

"Bertha, take her to the back bedroom and help her out of these clothes. I'll fetch Dr. Chesney."

"Don't tell Lyle," Lauren said. "He'll make a fuss. "And I'm sure this baby is a long way off. I'll go to the hospital when the party's over."

"Bertha, I'd like to clean up a bit before I climb in a clean bed."

"You stand there, Ma'am. I'll wash your legs," Bertha said. "Aleta, have Dr. Chesney wash up."

As Bertha removed Lauren's shoes, Lauren repeated her desire about Lyle not knowing.

"I'll ask him to help Stanley," Aleta said, "but he's no fool."

"Tell him I tried holding it too long," Lauren said.

Aleta did as Lauren recommended. "Bertha and I are helping her clean up and redress. She thought you might worry. Please tell Stanley what's going on. I know he's feeling abandoned."

Lyle went to Stanley immediately and Aleta spirited Dr. Chesney away from the party. She closed the laundry room door and told him he needed to wash in the laundry room. Then she explained why.

"We should call an ambulance."

"Lauren says no, but she will go with what you say. She says her contractions are far apart—twenty to thirty minutes. And some of them are not contractions at all. But the one she had when I was with her seemed strong to me."

"My bag's in the front hall," he said.

"I'll send Bertha for it right away. I told Lyle a story sort of. I'm stuck back here."

Dr. Chesney finished his wash. Aleta handed him a clean towel and led him to the guest room in the back.

"Bertha, Dr. Chesney's bag is in the front hall," Aleta said. She took Lauren's hand as a contraction took over. It passed quickly.

"Not much of a contraction," Dr. Chesney commented.

"Over half of them are like that," Lauren said.

"You should be in the hospital," Dr. Chesney said.

"Not until after Robert is served his cake," Lauren said. "I have hours of labor left. I can wait until after the party."

Dr. Chesney checked then announced. "You are probably correct. You aren't dilated enough and your contractions are too light. I agree you do have a long time to go. But you must stay in bed."

Bertha arrived with two cases and Dr. Cook came in immediately afterward.

"Is someone in labor?" Dr. Cook asked.

"Early stages," Dr. Chesney said.

"She comes quickly when she comes."

"She's less than five centimeters and her contractions are twenty minutes apart. The last one wasn't significant."

"This attention is embarrassing me," Lauren said. "Please go back to the party. I don't need to be watched."

"I'll stay," Aleta said.

"You have to take care of the party," Lauren said. "And Bertha can't stay either. It's Robert's party. He won't enjoy it without her. In fact, he won't enjoy it if either of you is missing."

"We could take turns," Dr. Chesney said.

"Can I help?" Came a soft voice from the doorway. "I'm a registered nurse."

"That's even better," Dr. Chesney said. "Twenty minutes each."

"I'll check in in twenty, Wayne you come back in forty."

When Aleta reentered the family room with the two doctors immediately behind her, the room grew quiet.

"Lauren is in labor. The contractions are far apart. She plans to have the baby well after everyone has gone home and gone to bed. At this point, both doctors agree with Lauren's assessment."

Lyle walked past Aleta, paused a moment to note that Bertha was mopping the bathroom floor and then ran to the end of the hall.

"Lauren, why didn't you tell me?"

"I thought I could get through the evening and then my water broke."

"You had Aleta tell me a lie. She never lies. She will kick herself for a long time to come over this."

"I'm sorry. It was a mistake to ask her to do that."

"She did couch it by saying 'Lauren told me to tell you she couldn't hold it.' Then she said Bertha and she were helping you change."

"All that was true."

"It was misleading. Aleta doesn't excuse herself for misleading anyone," Lyle persisted.

Lauren's eyes filled with tears.

"I hurt you and I'm so sorry," Lauren moaned softly. The tears spilled down her cheek.

Lyle ran to her and knelt beside her and kissed her. "I was too harsh. But please don't shut me out ever again."

"I won't. I promise. I'll fight and argue but I won't shut you out again," Lauren resolved aloud.

"Now tell me, how long has this been going on."

"All day."

"Did it start before I went to work?"

She hesitated. She had habitually kept her secrets secret.

"Yes," she murmured.

"Why didn't you share it?" his query was without rancor. It was simply an inquiry.

"Because I didn't want to be monitored like this," Lauren replied. "It's okay now because I'm not dealing with a twinge now and then. It's not false labor. It's the real thing. It will end in our little girl being born."

Lyle took her hand. "We'll wait together."

"I suggest you sit on a chair," Lauren said. "It's going to be a long night."

"You're sure you can't do exercises or something to hurry things along?" Lyle asked fetching a chair and setting it beside the bed.

"Honestly, Lyle, you've only been here five minutes and already you're impatient."

As if to grant him his wish, a strong contraction took hold of Lauren's body. She squeezed Lyle's hand and he watched the pain contort her face. Eunice came over and put her hand on Lauren's belly and timed the contraction. She left the room and fetched Dr. Chesney.

Dr. Chesney examined her and found she'd dilated very little. He waited for another contraction. When it came, it was a minor one and they all told him so.

He settled into a chair and told Eunice to join the party.

"I can stay a bit longer," Eunice offered.

"They're serving the cake now."

"Bring these two some," Lauren suggested.

Dr. Cook arrived with two plates of cake. "So how's it going in here?"

Dr. Taekman followed him in, carrying two more plates. Midway through their cake, Lauren tensed. All three doctors put down their plates one after the other as they realized how strong the contraction was. Dr. Cook disappeared.

"But she's not fully dilated," Dr. Chesney protested.

"Wayne's gone to wash up," Dr. Taekman said. "Maybe you should too."

Lyle looked hopeful. "You mean it's coming?"

Another contraction began. It passed quickly.

"I think it will be a while," Dr. Chesney said. "Now would be a good time for me to scrub up."

"Should I call for an ambulance?" Lyle asked.

"Please don't," Lauren said. "Please!"

Lyle looked at the anxiety wrinkling her brow. He stroked her forehead. "I'll let the doctors decide."

Lauren smiled at the fat neurosurgeon. "Ever delivered a baby, Doctor?"

"A long time ago."

"Do you remember how?" she squeezed out before a new contraction overtook her.

Dr. Taekman rushed to her side. She grinned at him. Lyle felt his hand go numb.

"Other end, Doctor," she grunted. "It's not stopping."

The words were barely spoken before another contraction hitchhiked on the first. He folded back the sheet as the head emerged.

He automatically reached down and cradled the baby's head.

The other two doctors came in as Dr. Taekman was urging Lauren to keep pushing.

"I'm a novice at this end," he said. "I need you to take a deep breath and push."

"That's all you doctors ever say," Lauren wheezed.

"Well, what you have now is half a baby. If you want a whole one, you'll have to push him out."

"It's not a 'him,'" Lyle insisted. "It's a girl."

"Right now it's a head," Dr. Taekman said.

Dr. Chesney began to more toward him when Wayne nudged him. "Give our famous neurosurgeon a minute. Let's see how he handles real doctoring."

Lauren took a deep breath and her body responded to its pre-programmed urge. She went with the overpowering urge and every fiber of her being focused on the final contraction.

Her yell could be heard in the family room.

Instant silence covered the room. Everyone waited.

The relief when the baby was fully out and began to cry lustily was tremendous. Lauren was ecstatic.

"You have a fine baby boy," Dr. Taekman announced.

"Michael, that's the cord you're looking at," Dr. Chesney commented.

"Really?" Michael said. "It did look too big for a penis."

"Someone hand the father a scissors," Dr. Taekman ordered.

"So?" Lauren asked. "Is it a girl?"

"It's a boy with only one penis."

"Michael," Chesney scolded. "Now's no time to joke."

"I'm not joking. He has only one penis."

Chesney reached in his open bag and took out a wrapped scissors. "You do remember what girls look like, don't you?"

"I'm a newlywed. I know full well what girls look like. Lauren has just given birth to a boy."

"You're serious, aren't you?" Chesney said, pulling on a pair of gloves.

Dr. Taekman grinned, "You two can finish up."

"Oh, for heaven's sake," Chesney griped. "Lauren did all the work."

"Don't all mothers?" Taekman quipped.

"That's the last time I invite you to assist me," Chesney went on. "Imagine changing the sex at the last minute on these good folks. They were hoping for a girl."

"He could have had two penises."

Lyle laughed finally. "Don't worry, guys, I'm not disappointed at all."

"You aren't?" Lauren asked, surprised.

"To have a second beautiful healthy boy? Not in the least. I'm pleased as punch!"

"You are? I thought you wanted a girl," Lauren pressed.

"He's got your red hair. How lucky can one man get?"

"He hasn't got a name."

"Sure he has. Robert Locke West."

"How'd we come up with that?"

"If he was born on St. Patrick's Day, I'd have called him Patrick," Lyle said. "I was at Robert's admission ceremony this morning and you gave birth during his celebration party this evening. It's his day."

"Well, you're lucky I love the name," Lauren said.

"You mentioned it first when we didn't know the sex."

"You remembered?"

He kissed her. "Thank you for another son."

Dr. Taekman disappeared. He washed up before reentering the family room. Again the room fell silent."

"It's a boy."

Gasps were heard all around.

"Are you sure?"

Michael laughed. "Dr. Chesney verified it. He figured I'd spent so much time operating on brains, I'd forgotten basic anatomy."

"They were expecting a girl," Ruth West commented.

"Life is full of surprises," Dr. Taekman said. "And surprisingly, they are thrilled."

"They only picked out a girl's name," Ruth went on obviously stunned.

"He's been named," came the announcement. "Robert Locke West."

He searched out Robert's face. Surprise dropped Robert's jaw and widened his eyes.

"You heard me right," Michael Taekman reported. "It was the first choice of both of them. It appears you have a namesake."

"I have a camera," Kurtz West said. "A Polaroid."

"Give it to me. I'll take photos. She's not ready to have visitors yet."

Aleta spoke up. "In the closet in that room is a bassinet with a stack of clean baby clothes and blankets."

"I planned to take one photo naked as proof that I passed basic anatomy."

"You passed that at age eight," his wife quipped. "He started playing 'doctor' at an early age."

"Practice makes perfect," Taekman retorted taking the camera.

Aleta went over and hugged her dad. "Feel better?"

"Overwhelmed doesn't begin to describe how I'm feeling."

He kissed her on the forehead. "Thanks, Aleta."

"You need to thank Lauren. She went all out to make this celebration a success."

"You can say that again. Mother will be upset she missed it."

"We can have a small family celebration when they return," Aleta said.

"No, when they return, we'll celebrate Stanley and me becoming partners. Just the nine of us. Jocelyn is going to attend one of these even if it kills her."

"Don't you remember? She did. And it did. That's when she said, 'never again.'"

"Well, she's got to get over that."

"Oh, Dad," Aleta laughed. "Will you never learn?"

Chapter 28

When Claude and Harriet arrived at Stanley and Aleta's house, it was Kurtz West who opened the door.

"Ruth and Aleta are cooking for tonight's party," he said by way of greeting. A small, slender man, he carried a presence that demanded respect.

"Aleta doesn't cook," Harriet pointed out as she stepped through the door.

"Ruth does, which is why I think we've been voted into the family," Kurtz said with a twinkle in his eye. "Tonight was to be a family dinner but... well... Lauren threw a monkey wrench into the works and we tagged along."

"Lauren?" Harriet asked as the Senior Praetzels joined them.

"Aleta and Lauren threw a surprise celebration to honor Robert upon his admission to the bar. It was a come-as-you-are and bring-your-supper affair. Robert was overwhelmed. But the surprise dinner wasn't the end of it. Lauren gave birth during dessert. Taekman actually delivered him."

"Him? You mean her!"

"That's what Chesney kept insisting. We had a lot of fun with that one."

"So are we celebrating the baby's birth?"

"I guess that's what makes this doubly exciting."

"When's Lauren coming home?" Lydia asked politely.

"She never left. She's in the guest room with Lyle and the baby. Robert Locke West."

Harriet's mouth dropped open.

"That's the same expression Robert came up with when Dr. Taekman announced the name."

"Where was Dr. Chesney?"

Kurtz smiled. "Michael said he left them to clean up. It seems Bernard and Wayne were scrubbing up when Lauren told Michael he'd just switched specialties."

"Sorry we missed all the fun," Harriet said.

"You want to see the pictures. I gave Taekman my Polaroid."

"Or maybe you'd rather see the real thing," Lyle said entering the living room cradling his newborn son wrapped in a blue blanket. Everyone rushed over.

Harriet looked at Lyle's beaming face and said, "I can see you're happy. I thought you wanted a girl."

"I wanted to have another child with Lauren. I didn't care about the sex."

"He's got reddish hair," Lydia commented.

"That's what I was hoping for. He's our first redhead."

"Ruth, does he look like Lyle as a baby?" Harriet asked.

"No, we think Locke looks like Lauren," Ruth called back, "red hair and all."

"Locke? You're calling him Locke?"

Lyle rushed in. "Josh thought since Lyle Kurtz West goes by Kurtz, Robert Locke West should be called Locke. He was pretty firm about it."

"I like it," Harriet said.

"You would," Claude teased.

The baby began to fuss. Lyle turned and headed back to Lauren.

"Why a family dinner?" Harriet asked Kurtz.

"Oh, that," Kurtz said grinning. "To celebrate the new partnership. Robert no sooner was sworn in Stanley made him partner. And gave him all the work."

"How is Stanley?" Lydia asked.

"He has to stay in bed until tonight. Aleta is firm about this. And even tonight, he can only come as far as the recliner."

"Stanley must be feeling pretty lonely," Lydia observed. "Hubert why don't you go in and tell him what we found on our trip. I'll take Aleta's place in the kitchen."

"I'll help too," Harriet said. "It'll give me a chance to catch up."

"Claude, do you want to take a stroll?" Kurtz asked. "If we stay here, we'll be roped into some kind of chore."

The men split. Hubert headed for the bedroom.

"Bring me up to date on the trial," Hubert said after Aleta joined them.

"What about our witness list?"

"We have none," Aleta said. "We will call only rebutted witnesses. That way Powell won't get his hooks into our plan."

"We have a plan?" Hubert asked.

"We will have one," Aleta replied with confidence.

"The first part, Dad, appears to be to catch Eugene Powell unprepared. That she did brilliantly."

"He's no fool. He'll be ready for her tomorrow."

"Which is why you are going in alone on Monday," Aleta said. "I have a copy of each brief I handed in for you to study. You may do whatever you think will serve our purpose in the long run."

"You don't think we should be there together?"

"I think we need you to have your turn at leading the charge," Aleta said with disarming sweetness.

"Watch out, Dad," Stanley interjected. "Aleta has something up her sleeve.

"I don't work well in tandem," Hubert said.

"And I know that and so does Eugene Powell. He will be absolutely certain that you have snatched the case from me," Aleta said. "Remember you have carte blanc when you're in charge. Just try not to drop us into too big a hole."

"Aleta!" Stanley erupted.

She tossed her head and laughed. "You are two peas in a pod. This is going to be fun."

Stanley glanced at his father's face and shook his head. He knew his father did not consider his work "fun".

Aleta hurried on. "Tell me we found the witness."

"We did. And I deposed him," Hubert said, glad to be back to a normal exchange of information. "I didn't try to break him down, just to explore his testimony. He's been prepped. Almost didn't catch it at first."

"How good a witness is he?"

"One of the best I've encountered. There's no way he's going to break down on the stand. He's going to sink our case."

"What about the third interrogator?"

"Disappeared. No trace of him."

"What about the manifesto?" Aleta asked.

"We hit a bit of luck there," Hubert explained. "The men on the impound lot will swear no one took anything from the trunk of that car."

"And the police report only shows them finding the Koran," Aleta said. "The manifesto is one of the keys.

"We know that their case is built on lies," Hubert said. "Proving it is another matter."

Stanley interjected a suggestion that they give Hawk a heads-up.

"If you give him a theory, it messes up his thinking," Aleta said.

"Who told you that?"

"Lyle."

"All he talks to me about is his baby," Stanley complained.

Hubert smirked. He knew Stanley would be worse.

"So what's Lyle's suggestion?"

"Ask Hawk a question," Aleta said. "His brain goes into high gear when he's asked a question, but it has to be a neutral question."

"I want to know if the manifesto was ever in the trunk of that car," Hubert said.

"Ask him that then," Aleta said.

"We'll go with your question whatever it is," Hubert said. "We need his brain stirred not just nudged."

"Do we have eyewitnesses to rebut the cop's story?" Aleta asked, moving on.

"One. Another prisoner," Hubert said. "I don't think he'll fare well under a hard cross."

"What about our cop witness? What do we know about him?"

"Clean."

"Can't be, if he'll lie on the witness stand," Aleta asserted.

"Ed didn't find a hint of anything."

"I've decided we need a witness list," Aleta said abruptly.

"What brought about this change?" Hubert asked. "Not that I think a few character witnesses …"

"I want to add all of the people on the prosecution list."

"All?" Hubert challenged.

"Anything less will give our plan away."

"We have a plan?"

"It's developing."

"Are we going to share?"

"When it's fully formed, I'll share," Aleta promised.

"We might be able to help," Stanley suggested.

"The idea is too naked for public view," Aleta declared.

Hubert sucked on a huge lungful of air. "You do have an expressive way of putting things!"

"Anything else?" Aleta pursued.

"We found several police officers who saw the three Feds together, so there is a third investigator. We deposed those officers."

"So we can prove the third Fed is not a figment of Shakir's imagination."

"Do we need a jury selection specialist?" Hubert asked.

"Trust Aleta with that, Dad," Stanley said.

He smiled at his wife only to discover that she'd moved on.

"I need to talk to Lydia," Aleta said. "I want her to teach me how to do something."

"What?" Stanley said curious as to what would distract Aleta in the midst of planning a case.

"I don't want to tell you," Aleta said. "You two enjoy yourselves guessing what I'm going to talk with her about. And Hubert, you stay in here. It's private!"

"But…"

Hubert stopped when Stanley shook his head.

He turned to his son, "Do you know what she's going to talk to my wife about?"

"Not a clue."

"Why did you stop me?"

"Her brain is working on a plan. Somehow Lydia can help and we can't."

"Of course, we can," Hubert declared.

"You and I think that," Stanley admitted. "But Aleta doesn't."

"I don't like distrust," Hubert declared his anger rising.

"Aleta trusts you, Dad. It's something else."

Aleta headed straight for her mother-in-law.

"Lydia, I need you."

The three women stared at Aleta with surprised puzzlement.

Lydia was the first to shake free of her surprise.

"Did Hubert offend you?"

Aleta's shocked expression told the three that he hadn't.

Lydia dried her hands on a towel and said, "Where shall we talk?"

"I told Hubert not to leave the bedroom, so anywhere is okay."

"The barn," Lydia decided.

Hubert and Stanley spotted the pair walking toward the barn from the bedroom window. Both women turned and waved.

"They're smiling," Hubert said. "What could they be talking about?"

"About puzzling us is my guess," Stanley responded.

"I'm not used to being kept in the dark," Hubert complained.

"Don't put it on my shoulders," Stanley said. "She's not my wife at this moment. She's your partner."

"We should work a plan out together."

"If you want, you and I could work up a plan and present it to her," Stanley said. "That might engage her enough to share her thinking."

"Let's get to it," Hubert said, immediately taking up the challenge, "As I see it we have two problems."

"The manifesto and the witness," Stanley agreed. "The rest is window dressing."

"The jury won't like some esoteric argument about the soil found on the floor matching the soil on the manuscript," Hubert stated. "They won't even care that the police handled both pieces of property differently."

"Because he was the only one who handled it. The interrogator used gloves."

"You'd think if it were his, there'd be other prints on it."

"Like whose?"

"His wife's when she moved it to dust or his son's when he packed his briefcase or..."

"His son packed his briefcase?" Hubert asked.

"That's why Shakir had the Koran with him."

"The Koran was inside his briefcase?" Hubert asked.

"The briefcase had opened. Its contents had spilled out."

"How did the cops know the book was the Koran?" Hubert asked.

"They didn't. They flipped through the pages and saw it was in Arabic and they arrested him."

"Why, if the manifesto was in the briefcase, weren't the son's prints on it?"

"You know, with a number of such questions," Stanley said thoughtfully, "we can make inroads into its value as a piece of evidence."

"What can those women be discussing?" Hubert asked.

"Intriguing, isn't it?" Stanley chuckled

Inside the barn, Mr. Hubbs emerged from his room and asked if a ride was planned.

"Just here to pet the horses," Aleta said. "You do keep their coats shiny and clean. They're all looking great. How's Sterling's foot?"

"I figure it'll hold the baby."

"You think Sterling will like that?"

"He's a saddle horse. And he's a gentle one."

"We'll need a special saddle," Aleta said.

"Yes Ma'am."

"Can you fashion one?"

"Yes, Ma'am."

"And don't worry," Aleta said. "It's only for the baby. Not anyone else."

"Thank you, Ma'am."

"You're going to put a baby alone on a horse?" Lydia asked flabbergasted.

"We aren't going to let him ride by himself," Aleta responded calmly as she stroked Sterling's nose. "He's such a nice horse. He will like being useful again."

Lydia found herself drawn to Jezebel. "This is a nice one too. How old is she Hubbs?"

"Coming up on twenty-one."

"Too old to ride?"

"Yes, Ma'am," Hubbs replied politely. "But it ain't just 'cause of her age. She's wore out."

"To answer your question, Aleta," Lydia said without any preamble. "You already know how."

Aleta moved to her horse and began stroking his nose. Her reply assumed that Lydia knew the question.

"But you're a master," Aleta pointed out. "I need to be that good for this case."

"Well, the way to start is with innocuous questions, the more unexceptional the better. They should be dead on relevant but nothing that would raise an objection by your opponent."

"How do you select the query to open up the witness?"

"I study the man beforehand," Lydia said.

Aleta was caught off guard. "Study?"

"Instinct needs fuel to work well. I don't look for the usual secrets he's trying to hide although I don't overlook them; but, I study his passions."

"So his passion is racing cars and he's testifying about a crime he witnessed. My mind can't connect the two."

"That's because they aren't real," Lydia responded. "You don't plan how to surprise the man. You get to know the man and then when he's on the witness stand, you let all your knowledge flood your mind, and you go with the first query that pops into your mind."

"Is there any way at all you can show me?"

"I love you, Aleta. I don't want to cause you distress."

"You feel as if you know me," Aleta said. "If you do, you will know that I am willing for you to take the gloves off as if I were on the witness stand."

"I might really hurt you."

"I will have Stanley put me back together," Aleta said. "Please, give it your best shot."

"Do you consider yourself a truthful person?"

"Yes."

"Have you ever apologized for lying in small matters occasionally?"

"Yes."

"So, you are a normally truthful person, correct?"

"Yes."

"Why then did you betray Lyle West on Friday?"

"Betray? I didn't betray... oh my God, I did, didn't I. He trusted me to tell him the truth and I lied to him."

"So is that a character trait of yours—betraying the people you love?"

Aleta grew angry. "No!"

"Then why did you betray Lauren when she needed you most?"

"Lauren? I didn't betray her. I did as she wished."

"Your very action told her a lie."

"What lie?"

"That you agreed that her husband couldn't be trusted."

"I did that?"

"You betrayed your own husband as well."

"Stanley? No. I didn't. I love Stanley. I would never betray him."

"Your action told Lauren her husband couldn't be trusted. She would assume that you were reflecting your own feeling for your husband because you couldn't possibly know her husband that well. Your lie hurt the three people you love the most. That, my dear, is betrayal."

"My Lord," Aleta burst out. "I lied when I said I was ready. I wasn't ready at all."

"How do you feel right now?" Lydia asked gently.

"Ashamed, disoriented, dissected, and exposed," came the reply from an obviously distraught young woman.

"A witness that feels exposed is as malleable as clay in a potter's hand. He will be quite pliable. Mold him carefully and your opponent will never get him back to his side."

"Where am I right now?"

"Needing Stanley. He's the first one you need to apologize to and you know it. When he forgives you, you will be halfway restored."

"I don't know if I can take people apart like that," Aleta confessed.

"You are the only one I have explained this to, the only one I have demonstrated my method to. In the hands of someone less caring, it would be a devastating tool."

"I plan to break a man using it."

"Are you broken?"

"I feel like it."

"But are you?"

Aleta thought about the question.]

"Mom, you're right. I'm in the middle of the healing process. It began the moment I acknowledged my guilt."

"Your witness has the same options," Lydia commented.

"I don't want to tell anyone what went on here," Aleta said, "except, of course to apologize."

"Just say it is not something you are prepared to discuss yet."

"That's like saying I don't trust them."

"Tell them it's a secret I've asked you to keep. Hubert won't press the issue."

"And Stanley will honor it."

"We have two good men on our side, haven't we?" Lydia said taking Aleta's arm.

When Aleta returned, she didn't head straight to Stanley's room. Seeing Lyle in the kitchen, she asked if she could talk with him and Lauren. She followed him to the guest bedroom.

Lauren had just finished nursing the baby and had him leaning over her shoulder as she gently patted him.

"My milk is in," she announced happily. "He has a full tummy now."

Aleta closed the door and the two knew that something serious was up. Lyle sat next to his wife on the bed as she cradled little Locke. They waited quietly for Aleta to speak.

They both noticed she was having difficulty; but, neither dared guess why.

"I owe you each an apology," she said. "I betrayed you both and I am so sorry. You are my best friends."

Tears began to flow. The two sat stunned.

"Betrayed?" Lyle finally queried. "How?"

Her voice trembling with emotion, Aleta went on, "You have never let me down, Lyle. You have always believed me even when it was difficult to do so. I lied to you. You trusted me to be truthful and I betrayed that trust."

Lyle turned to his wife, "I told you this would hit her hard."

Aleta, surprised by the reaction, nevertheless charged on, "And Lauren, when you asked me to prevent Lyle from learning the truth about what was happening, I didn't tell you that of all the men in this world, you had a husband who could be trusted to do the right thing. You had a husband who would listen to your fears and not dismiss them as meaningless. You had a husband, who while he would be excited and joyous and even fearful, would not override your sensitive state. He, better than me, would have cared for you and loved you. You thought I was helping. I wasn't. You trusted me to be a good friend. I failed you too. You can't know how deeply I regret having hurt each of you."

Neither of them said a word. Both were too shocked by the depth of Aleta's sorrow.

Lauren said, "Lyle, give her the baby."

Lyle took the baby and handed him to Aleta. She looked into the tiny face and smiled. "Hi, little guy. Don't worry about my tears. You did nothing wrong. You are an absolute delight."

The baby waved its hand toward Aleta's face and she kissed it.

"We want you and Stanley to be Locke's godparents," Lauren said.

"There's no one we trust more," Lyle added.

"After the way I acted?"

"It's nice to know that you make mistakes too," Lauren said. "Lyle and I have already dealt with my not trusting him and I apologized to him. He said I'd hurt you by asking you to lie to him. I didn't see it until now. I'm sorry I asked you to do that."

"You were confused and afraid," Aleta said. "People do uncharacteristic things at times like that."

"You did help us to take one step closer to each other," Lauren said. "Like you and Stanley."

"Stanley!" Aleta exclaimed. "I almost forgot. I have to apologize to him too."

"Whatever for?" Lauren blurted out.

"The same action, of course," Aleta said handing the baby back to Lyle. "You explain it to her, Lyle."

"Me?"

"You know, and you know you know," Aleta said turning the knob. "And Stanley and I would be thrilled to be Locke's godparents."

When she entered the master bedroom, she said abruptly, "Hubert, I need to apologize to Stanley privately."

"Aleta," Stanley chided her softly, "you interrupted us."

Aleta burst into tears. Hubert put his arms around her. "Don't worry, I'm not offended. I appreciate your honesty."

Aleta cried even harder.

Hubert held her close.

"Pregnancy does things to a woman's emotions," he told Stanley. "Your mother did this frequently when she was expecting you."

"Mother cried?"

"Over just about everything," Hubert said gently moving Aleta toward the bed. "Here you sit down and get that apology out of your system. You'll feel better afterward."

"Mother cried," Stanley mused softly.

"I didn't know what to do about it either," his father confessed. "I'll go see how dinner's coming. Robert and Bertha will be here soon."

Hubert handed Aleta over to Stanley and left.

"You are going to apologize?" Stanley prompted. "For what?"

Aleta burst into a new outpouring of tears and sobs.

Stanley held her close. "Whatever it is, Aleta, I forgive you."

He gently lifted her face to his and kissed her tenderly.

"I love you. I will always love you," he said softly. "And I forgive you. Please stop crying. It makes me feel as if I've let you down."

The crying increased. Stanley murmured, "Now I understand my father's words."

Aleta gulped hard and stopped. "I am so sorry. Can I explain later?"

"Apology accepted. Explain whenever you choose," Stanley said. "In fact, my acceptance covers anything you've done or imagined you've done, so take advantage of its blanket quality and when you remember some other supposed sin, know that I've already forgiven you."

Aleta hugged him. "As your mother said, we have a pair of fine men."

"My mother said that?"

"She thinks you're as wonderful as I do," Aleta said.

"I'd say it's Dad and I who are the lucky ones," Stanley said. "I assume Mother pointed something out on your walk."

"She did indeed."

"You aren't angry with her, are you?"

"She answered my question is all," Aleta said. "We are closer than ever."

"That's good," Stanley said casually, "because I can't change my mother."

"Don't even try," Aleta said. "She's perfect!"

"Like you," he said and kissed her quickly before she could burst into tears again.

When he finished she murmured, "Lyle and Lauren want us to be Locke's godparents. I said yes."

"That doesn't mean we have to change his diapers, does it?"

Aleta laughed. "Why did I know that was the first thing you'd say?"

"Because you know me," he said suddenly serious, "which means you know that I will forgive whatever you imagine you've done."

"I didn't imagine anything!" Aleta flared up. I actually broke the trust of the three people I love the most."

"This is about your lie to Lyle?"

"Yes," she replied. "Let me explain."

And she did.

Chapter 29

The following morning Stanley woke up to Aleta on the phone making an appointment with Ed Ornstein.

"I need you for a couple of hours," was all she said.

When she closed the phone, Stanley said quietly, "I order you to make mad, passionate love to me before you do anything else."

"You order me?" Aleta asked, shocked.

"Yes."

"As you wish," she agreed. I hope you're up for it."

And he was.

"I feel better," Aleta said to Stanley afterward.

She heard Bertha let Ed in.

"So do I," Stanley returned. "I like it when your good benefits me."

"You've never ordered sex before."

"And I probably never will again," he said. "But you needed to do some penance to feel completely forgiven."

"But we were going to make love anyway."

"Ordering changed it though, didn't it?"

"I gave it my all."

"I expected no less."

"You are a complicated man," Aleta said. "But, as I said, I feel better."

"I'm ready to nap now," Stanley said. "Run along."

In the study, Ed, with a fresh cinnamon roll and coffee, listened while Aleta explained what she needed.

"I need to know everything we can find out about the witness that plans to lie about our client."

"I looked him up already. He's clean as a whistle."

"He's about to lie on the witness stand," Aleta said. "I need to break him."

"I ain't gonna blow hope up your skirt," Ed said, "but there ain't nothing."

"I don't want you to look for anything bad," Aleta said. "I want to know all about him—his habits, his passions, his beliefs, his ambitions, his record of achievement, his intelligence, his family life, his duties as a police officer and his former jobs going back to high school."

"That's a tall order," Ed commented.

"I want you to teach me how to access the information I can get off the internet. If he's got a website, I want you to help me find it. After your show me how to find what I can find, then I want you to go back to your office and look up what I can't find."

"You want me to sneak into his computer, don't you?"

"I want you to uncover any information I'm too much of a novice to find."

"Okay, let's start with his website," Ed said. "People put lots of clues on their website. His is pretty dull."

"You looked it up?"

"I told you, it's a great source of information. His weren't; but you're after something different from what I was."

Three hours later, Bertha knocked on the door. "Would you like to take lunch in here?"

"Yes, please," Aleta said. "Ed's got a one o'clock appointment he can't miss. We need to keep going and he needs to eat."

"What appointment?" Ed asked.

"I don't know. But it's important," Aleta said.

A second knock was heard.

"Come in," Aleta said expecting Bertha with the food.

Lyle popped his head in. "Ed, we're having a conference at one o'clock. I'll wait for you if you'll be free in time. I'll be coming back directly to take Lauren and the baby home so you won't be stranded.

"Sure, I can go," Ed said. "Lemme finish up with Aleta."

Bertha came in through the door with two plates of food.

"Good, I get to eat!" Ed exclaimed.

"Okay if I borrow Ed, Aleta?" Lyle asked.

"She said it was important," Ed said taking the sandwich from the plate Bertha had set in front of him.

"She said...?" Lyle murmured as he left. "How did she know?"

At one o'clock, when Ed followed Chief Lyle West up the stairs of Willow Glen's police headquarters to Chief Tom Milani's office, Oakwood's Chief Alan Peets was already seated, drinking coffee and talking with Kay Rivers. Ed helped himself to a donut and sat down in one of the chairs facing the chief's desk. Lyle poured himself a cup of coffee and accepted congratulations on the birth of his son.

He pulled out several shots of Locke and passed them around.

"Locke?" Kay said. "I thought his name was Robert."

"Robert Locke West," Lyle stated. "Josh, who's six, decided since we called the last baby by his second name that we should do that with this one. We tried to explain that in that instance we didn't want two Lyles in the house; but, he didn't see that as a reason at all. He argued that this was his mother's second batch of kids and so they go by their second names to tell them apart from her first ones. It was a strange kind of logic but Lauren and I like the name Locke so we gave in."

"Second batch?"

"Josh thinks in terms of cookies," Lyle said. "Camay and Josh are from Lauren's first marriage."

"I see," Kay said.

"Well, you don't quite," Lyle said. "We thought what you're thinking so we asked him what he meant. He said that we had him and Camay and then when they were grown up we decided to have another batch."

"Grown up? At six?"

"He was four when we had Lyle Kurtz Junior." Lyle laughed. "I guess walking and talking makes one a grown-up."

Milani laughed. "Let's get down to business. Tell them Peets."

"The leader confessed to conspiracy. I couldn't get either of the men I had custody of to turn on him. I thought we were sunk and then his lawyer found him and he was visibly agitated after the lawyer left. He asked for me. Then he confessed. We offered to fetch back his lawyer, but he said no."

"Did he tell you who hired him?" West asked.

"No. That was part of the deal," Peets said. "I accepted it because without his confession he would walk."

"Why on earth would he confess?" Kay Rivers blurted out.

"It seems he's more afraid of being outside prison than being in," Peets said. "He insisted he be allowed to choose his prison."

"Tell them the rest Peets," Tom urged. "You did get more out of him than his confession."

"He named the driver of the big rig that smashed into Kay Rivers' car. He said that he has two guys he usually works with. They've done this before."

"Did you tell the Lake County Sheriff?"

"He won't testify," Peets said.

Milani jumped in, "What we thought, Kay, is what you could do is pass along the three names as an anonymous tip. I understand the sheriff has hit a blank wall."

"Why me?"

"Because if it came from Peets, the tip would be traced back to the men he has in his jail."

"I still don't understand why he confessed and then gave you the names. He's not getting anything."

"I promised him minimum for the guilty plea and for cooperating," Peets said.

"Now, for the coup d grace," Milani announced. "The contract on Aleta Praetzel has been effectively cancelled."

"By whom?"

"It seems our two fathers have been busy," Milani said. "I confirmed it with my source in the city. It's the reason for the confession. The leader was told that if he went free, he'd be dead."

"Someone threatened him?" Kay said. "His confession won't hold up if that was the case."

"It wasn't a direct threat," Milani said. "The word on the street is that Aleta Praetzel is not to be harmed."

"Wow!" Kay breathed. "Who does she know?"

Lyle grinned. "I guess I better encourage her to keep handling dogs."

Kay looked at him quizzically. "I don't follow."

"People who show dogs are very intense about winning. Aleta handles dogs with the skill of a pro. And one of the dogs she wins with belongs to, let's say, a man with mob connections."

"How do the two fathers fit in?"

"Well I imagine Robert Locke gave our bulldog owner a heads-up," Lyle replied. "And Hubert Praetzel is a criminal defense attorney. I imagine he told his clients to lay off his family. Only fathers could get away with such a move."

"Now what?" Milani asked.

"Powell could bring in outside help," Lyle replied. "Until we shut him down, she's in danger."

Hubert Praetzel arrived at his son's home shortly after one o'clock."

"Are they asleep?" he asked Bertha.

"He could be," Bertha replied, "but Mrs. Praetzel is in the study."

"I'll check on Stanley first," his father said moving toward the bedroom. "You may tell Aleta I'm here."

Stanley's face lit up at the sight of his father. Hubert was warmed by his son's smile.

"How'd it go in court today, Dad," Stanley asked.

"Judge Heard liked Aleta's brief."

"After you added a few arguments?"

"Perhaps after I reiterated a few of her arguments. Your wife was very through. It was a compelling presentation," Hubert reported. "The prosecution presented a weak-kneed argument that stated basically that tradition dictated that he be allowed to depose all defense witnesses."

"So what did the judge rule?" Aleta asked as she entered.

"That such a practice was based on the prosecution not having had a chance to thoroughly question the witness. In Mr. Aloman's case, the prosecution had thoroughly grilled the witness under the direst of circumstances without allowing him representation on the pretense that he was not yet under arrest when their intention was clearly to arrest him," Hubert said. "The judge said he considered the defendant deposed."

"And Powell wanted a ruling that he'd be given some latitude in questioning him, didn't he?" Aleta asked.

"He didn't get it," Hubert said.

"Then Judge Heard ordered the prosecution to produce the missing interrogator."

"And Powell said he couldn't," Aleta guessed.

"That's when we got a big break."

Surprised, Aleta couldn't even guess to what Hubert could possibly be referring.

"Judge Heard banned all reference to the interviews conducted by the unknown interrogator."

"That's most of them," Aleta said. "He was a master at twisting Aloman's words and attacking him with them."

"The other interrogators were allowed to refer only to their own questions and answers."

"Hubert, you take them," Aleta said. "I'll concentrate on the witness."

"Lydia taught you her method, didn't she?" Hubert guessed. "You plan to break the witness on the stand?"

"Yes."

"And you think you can do it?" he asked skeptically. "Others have tried to copy her approach and failed."

"One can't copy her method," Aleta said. "One has to learn it. She taught me well."

"But you haven't ever tried it," Hubert objected. "You don't know if you can do it."

"But I do know," Aleta proclaimed.

"How can you be sure?"

"I know myself. That's enough," Aleta affirmed with such confidence Hubert believed her.

"She's been working on it all morning," Stanley said. "Aleta has no illusions about her own ability. Mother must have told her she could do it. And Mother is no fool."

"She never would teach me," Hubert complained.

"It's a woman's method," Aleta asserted.

"She asked you not to tell," Hubert accused.

"She didn't have to," Aleta said. "She trusted me to keep it confidential."

"A woman's thing, huh?" Hubert said. "Nonsense!"

"Did you argue that the manifesto should be excluded?"

"On what grounds?" Hubert asked.

"The missing interrogator is the missing link in the evidence chain. There is no proof he found the manifesto in Aloman's car or briefcase or that it even belongs to Aloman. The fingerprints aren't proof as the manifesto wasn't examined before... you did, didn't you?"

"Yes, I did," Hubert said. "Judge Heard wants a brief on his desk first thing tomorrow."

"I guess you'll be busy tonight, won't you?" Aleta returned almost gaily.

"You don't want to do it?"

"That's your part of the case. Remember? However, if I were going to write the brief, I'd include an argument that the manifesto not only didn't go through proper channels, it appears it was actually deliberately tampered with and ask for a hearing on that matter separate from the trial."

"That's half his case," Hubert said.

"That's your half," Aleta said. "Your argument is that brief..."

Hubert interrupted.

"What brief?"

"You aren't going to petition for a separate trial without a brief to hand over?" she queried, as if such an action were unthinkable.

"That's how it's usually done. The judge may rule without a formal argument."

"Not this judge," Aleta said. "He likes his lawyers to work. He likes time to consider his rulings."

"Go ahead and tell me how I should argue this," Hubert said with a hint of facetiousness.

Aleta eyed him coolly. "Don't ask me a question unless it's an honest one.

Hubert sobered instantly. "I apologize. Please share the approach you would use."

"The main argument is that if a false piece of evidence is introduced at trial it might prejudice the jurors even if it is proven to be manufactured during the trial."

"We could use that to our advantage in the trial," Hubert said. "It could be a solid peg to hang our argument that our client is being framed."

"If it's presented and certain passages are read, it could inflame members of the jury beyond reason," Aleta said. "I need their minds clear—well, as clear as a normal person's mind can be considering the clutter of prejudices gathered over the years."

"You are the lead in this case," Hubert said. "We'll do it your way."

"Do you think I'm making a mistake?"

Stanley spoke up. "Both sides have merit; but, considering Aleta has the toughest part of the case in her court, I would vote to let her decide. Her mind is still putting things together and I think she's instinctively choosing the better course."

Hubert nodded. "I will get the pre-trial hearing. Now I need to head over to see Hawk right now. I have a couple of questions for him that need answering before the hearing."

"The briefs?" Aleta said.

This time it was Hubert who eyed Aleta coolly.

"I have two bright associates that can flesh out my ideas. I'll review their work tonight.

Aleta flushed. "I'm sorry. That question was rude and I apologize."

"Are you going to come to court with me tomorrow?" Hubert asked.

"I'd rather not," Aleta said. "I have a great deal of research to do."

"Then do it now," Hubert said. "You will need to be there for the jury selection. The prosecution and the judge need to know you're lead counsel from the start."

"What about the hearing?"

"I can handle it," Hubert said. "Actually, I'd prefer he didn't have a test run at you. That will be to our advantage later."

"We are thinking alike on this," Aleta said. "You are a brilliant attorney."

Hubert laughed. "Well, thank you."

When he left, Stanley rose from his bed and embraced his wife. "You are the brilliant attorney."

As she melted into his arms, she whispered, "I love you too."

"Don't worry about my father," Stanley assured her. "He'll hold up his end."

"And will his son hold up his?"

"It's mid-afternoon!" Stanley gasped. "And we have company."

"You said any time, any place," she reminded him.

"Did it ever occur to you I might not be up for it?"

"Nonsense! You're a man."

"A sick man."

"There is that," she said. "Get back in bed. I'll be in the study."

"You're giving up?"

"You actually are sick," she said. "And I want you to get well. I'll take a rain check. First rainy day after you're well, you'll come home mid-afternoon."

"I could be in court!" Stanley wailed.

"Better not schedule a court appearance for a rainy day then," she suggested. There was no compromise in her tone. She meant to hold him to it.

"That's impossible!" he declared, knowing full well what her response would be. He was gratified when she said,

"You'll figure out a way."

Chapter 30

One day melted into the next. Aleta had a second computer connection put in the bedroom so she could spend more time with Stanley.

Because she was working, Stanley couldn't watch television during her long periods of silence. He tried reading but the books were heavy, so when sitting tired him, he napped or lay awake and watch Aleta.

More and more he grew determined that he would be in court to watch her try this case. He read less and less and lay still more and more, willing his body to recover.

No one could figure out why he had stopped fighting to rise out of bed and do things. They would have worried had he not been cheerful during his enforced recovery period.

Robert visited every day and summarized the cases he was handling. Such was the nature of their field, that none of the cases could be postponed for as long as it would take for Stanley to recover. Robert was plunged into a full work load the day after being sworn in.

Claude visited Stanley every day and talked with him about the statistician's most recent report.

Only Stanley knew that it was Claude funding Kay Rivers's suit against Eugene Powell, so his was more than idle conversation. He was depending on Stanley to tell him when the statistician had compiled enough clear evidence to influence a jury.

These visits took place when Harriet interrupted Aleta for their daily dog training session. Afternoons Aleta rode. She found that her mind worked best when she switched to an activity that called for the expenditure of physical energy. She avoided taxing Stanley during the daytime hours; but, each night she approached him with a demureness which he found appealing. Their lovemaking was more reserved and Stanley's tired body settled into it happily.

All this came to a halt the first day of jury selection. Hubert Praetzel had successfully managed to have the manifesto declared inadmissible as evidence based on the absence of the interrogator who was the finder. Powell had spent the week telling the government that the man was essential to the case only to be told to rely on the witness whom they believed had been prepped thoroughly. Powell himself had thrown everything he could at the man and Richard Young hadn't faltered. He became the prosecutions entire case.

Since Hubert Praetzel had been so active the ten days prior to the jury selection, Powell had assumed he would continue in the lead role. When he saw Aleta sitting in the courtroom, he discounted her as a major force. This would be a battle between experienced lawyers with each vying for jury members that leaned toward their side.

The first two the judge excused for cause after the prosecution asked a few questions. The third was about to go the same route when Aleta stood up and declared, "We accept this juror, Your Honor."

Powell couldn't believe his good fortune. He instantly said that he also accepted the juror.

Hubert pointed to the jury list. Aleta recognized the mark as being one meant to designate those the defense should use a challenge for.

Aleta leaned over. "He's honest."

Hubert mulled over her statement. The fourth juror Aleta questioned, "Do you believe a man is innocent until proven guilty?"

"Yes, I do," the fat man said.

"Do you have any particular prejudices against other races?"

"No," the man declared.

"You consider yourself to be open-minded?"

"Yes," came the reply.

"We reject this juror, Your Honor."

Again Powell was shocked. He planned to use one of his challenges because he was too pro-defense.

Aleta leaned over and whispered in Hubert's ear, "He's a liar. He's as prejudiced as they come."

"How do you know?"

"When he came in, he left a seat between him and the black woman who's next."

Aleta rose to question the next juror and smiled at her. "You are a parent, are you not?"

"Yes, Ma'am," the woman said politely.

"Your son is in the army, isn't he?"

"Yes," the woman said proudly.

"We accept this juror, Your Honor."

"Approach the bench," Judge Heard ordered.

Aleta and Hubert approached as did Eugene Powell and his two associates.

"I was going to dismiss this juror for cause," Judge Heard said.

"Are you planning to excuse all the jurors I want?"

Judge Heard winced. The woman had a sharp tongue.

"Mr. Praetzel, perhaps you should guide Mrs. Praetzel in the selection of a juror."

"She has given me appropriate reasons for her choices," Hubert stated resolutely. "She needs no coaching from the likes of me."

His statement startled the judge.

Powell was inwardly delighted. Praetzel was going to allow his daughter-in-law's stupidity rather than admit that the defense wasn't united.

Foolish man, Powell thought.

"Well, I need a reason," the judge declared.

"The woman is a patriot," Aleta explained. "She is proud of her son. She hates terrorists. But she understands prejudice, that is, she understands being judged on appearance alone. She will be fair."

"You have convinced me," Judge Heard declared. "She will make a good juror. Don't you agree, Mr. Powell?"

"Yes, Your Honor, we accept this juror."

Aleta allowed the prosecutor to take over the questioning. She watched the Asian man's face as the prosecution questioned him. When her turn came, she asked bluntly. "Are you prejudiced, Sir?"

"I must admit that I am," he replied politely. "I try not to be but I am."

"Does your prejudice extend to Arabs?"

"It does."

"We accept this juror, Your Honor," Aleta said.

"Approach," Judge Heard said.

The other lawyers scraped back their chairs and moved forward.

"Explain," Judge Heard demanded.

"You cannot ask me to do that," Aleta declared. "I am accepting this juror."

"One I was about to excuse for cause," Judge Heard said.

"Everybody is prejudiced, Your Honor. The man is hiding nothing. Mr. Powell said he would accept him. You didn't ask him to explain."

The Asian man was seated.

Several jurors were rejected for cause by the judge. Aleta didn't object. Two more were seated, a man and a woman, a pharmacist and a dental assistant. Both sides found them acceptable.

The next jury candidate was an Arabian man considerably older than Shakir Aloman.

Aleta rose and questioned him.

"You are a naturalized citizen, correct?" she asked.

"Yes."

"You have many family members in this country?"

"Yes."

"You consider this your home because your family is here, correct?"

"Yes."

"You are a Muslim, are you not?"

"Yes."

"Thank you for answering my questions honestly. Please forgive me. Your Honor, we are using one of our challenges."

Hubert looked as bewildered as Powell.

"I will explain later," Aleta said.

"Powell was going to reject him," Hubert said. "We wasted a challenge."

"Oh no, we didn't," Aleta whispered. "Trust me. Now you accept the next two witnesses."

"We don't know anything about them."

"I do," Aleta said. "And we need the jury to like you too."

"My God, Aleta," Hubert hissed. "This is crazy!"

"And don't look at me for confirmation. Just accept them."

"Can I ask them some questions?" Hubert asked.

"Of course. I don't want you not to appear reasonable. By now you know what I want in a juror."

Hubert rose after Powell finished his questioning. It was obvious that Powell liked this juror.

He decided if he was going to go down as an idiot, he might as well ask some hard questions.

"You were in the service, I believe."

"Yes, Sir. I served in Vietnam."

"So you have no sympathy for anyone who would threaten this country."

"No, Sir."

"We accept this juror, Your Honor," Hubert said. He saw approval on the faces of several jurors. When he returned to sit beside Aleta, he saw a smirk on Powell's face.

The next juror called was a tall, thin man of considerable age. The prosecution asked a few simple questions and sat down, saying that he accepted the juror.

Hubert rose. What in the world did Powell see in this gentleman? He decided to find out.

"I believe you're at an age where people are automatically excused from jury duty. Why did you choose to accept the task?"

"Because I can."

"Your cognitive skills are intact?"

"Some days."

Hubert was startled. "And on other days?"

"I forget things. I am unaware of my surroundings. I make mistakes like letting the meat burn. I lose a lot of frying pans on those days."

"What makes you do those things?"

"I get involved in some mathematical theory and my mind shoves aside everything else."

"Will you absent your mind from theorizing and concentrate on the case when necessary."

"Lawyers blather a lot; but, I do intend to pay attention. The man on trial deserves that much."

Hubert said happily, "The defense accepts this juror, Your Honor."

Hubert smiled at Aleta as he sat down, "Thanks."

Two male candidates were accepted after a few cursory queries by each lawyer. While both were marked as ones to reject, Aleta accepted both. Hubert didn't protest. They seemed like ordinary conservatives. They could do worse.

The next juror was a young married woman whom Aleta rejected without asking a single question. The woman scowled fiercely at Aleta as she left the jury box.

How did she know? Hubert asked himself.

"We only have one challenge left," Hubert told her. "Powell has two."

"Don't worry," Aleta said. "The judge has some."

"He might not use them," Hubert said.

"He'll reject the next one," Aleta predicted.

"How can you be so sure?"

Aleta just smiled at him.

Powell questioned the gentleman first. He was a thin man with spectacles and a trim beard. He elicited the fact that the man was an accountant, was married and had two children.

The man seemed innocuous enough. Hubert couldn't see a problem.

Aleta rose. "This is your second marriage, is it not?"

"Yes," the man said. Hubert saw his eye twitch.

"You were a widower when you remarried, true?"

"Yes," the man replied. The twitch disappeared.

"Your wife and unborn child died on September 11 when the Towers were hit, correct?"

The twitch returned.

"Yes," came the reluctant reply.

"Your former wife was as pregnant as I am, wasn't she?"

"Yes, but that won't keep me from doing a good job as a juror," the man insisted.

Aleta turned to the judge. "I'm willing to accept your ruling on this juror."

"Juror is excused," Judge Heard said.

Powell jumped to his feet, but a glare from the bench forced him to reseat himself without uttering a word.

The next juror was a young pregnant woman.

"How far along are you?"

"Five months," the woman said.

"Closer to six, aren't you?"

"Yes," came the quiet response.

"A trial is a very stressful event," Aleta said. "I think you shouldn't be tempting fate."

"But you're farther along than I am," she protested.

"Our circumstances are different," Aleta responded evenly. "Your Honor, we will use our last challenge to excuse this juror and wish her well."

When she sat down, Hubert whispered, "Why remind Powell we are out of challenges?"

"I was reminding the judge."

"He keeps track."

"But he may not believe I have."

Powell was ecstatic. Two jurors to go and the opposition had no challenges left. His jury advisor had already marked the two he definitely wanted.

The next juror was a young black man who was on his list to accept. Aleta rose and began her questioning.

"You are a college student, aren't you?"

"A graduate student," the man said.

"You are a member of an anti-terrorist group on campus, aren't you?"

"I am," he replied.

"We accept this juror, Your Honor," Aleta said.

"As if she had a choice," Powell murmured to his partner. "Do I have to take this one?"

The young black man was looking at Powell when he made the whispered comment. While the grad student couldn't read lips, he'd seen that facial expression too often not to know what was being said.

Powell was listening to the response without expression, his eyes finally resting on the young black man whose face was now blank of expression.

"We accept this juror, Your Honor," Powell announced with seeming magnanimity.

Aleta winked surreptitiously at the young grad student—a slight nod was his response. Hubert, aware of the subtle exchange realized Aleta had actually chosen this man.

A young mother was seated when Powell's associates told him not to reject another woman.

"She can be led," they advised.

The final candidate was questioned by Powell who rejected her after Aleta declined to ask any questions.

"One of ours," Hubert said.

"We knew that would happen," Aleta responded.

The next candidate was a mannish-appearing woman whom Aleta knew was on Powell's list to take. She rose to question her first.

"Do you think a woman can deliver justice as tough as a man can mete out?"

"There ain't no man what's stronger than me when it comes to that," she declared. "I can send a man to death what deserves it."

"Would you be sympathetic to a man with a family?"

"Not if he was guilty. I ain't sentimental."

"If a man told you something and a woman told you something, which one would you believe?"

"The woman, of course. Men is liars."

"Thank you. We find this juror acceptable, Your Honor."

Powell rejected her outright despite whispered protests from his jury consultant.

The final candidate was one Powell attacked with a series of questions designed to make the man seem unworthy to the judge. He was a huge, black man a laborer by trade. He replied politely but was obviously upset by the questions. Powell goaded and just before he exploded in an angry outburst, Aleta rose and said, "Your Honor, we gladly accept this juror. He is obviously a man of honor and integrity."

It was an unprecedented action and took both Judge Heard and Powell by surprise. The huge laborer looked at

Aleta gratefully. Hubert caught the look and acknowledged it.

Aleta, however, was looking at the judge and immediately knew he was furious. Her manner was instantly apologetic, her words softly spoken.

"I spoke out of turn, Your Honor. I apologize both to Mr. Powell, who has conducted himself in a proper fashion during this entire process and never once interrupted me, and to Your Honor. I have no excuse for my bad behavior. I am truly sorry. It will not happen again."

Powell saw the scowl on the judge's face disappear. This woman was going to get away with this travesty. His ire mounted. He was momentarily speechless.

Aleta stepped in.

"Please continue, Mr. Powell," she urged. "You were accusing his man of unpatriotic thoughts to which he was about to respond. I imagine he was about to tell you that he was wounded in the Gulf War and lost his foot as a result of a terrorist bombing."

Powell's rage reached the boiling point when he glanced at his partner and was waved over. Powell swallowed his biting retort and walked to his table. A quick consultation resulted in Powell turning around and smilingly accepting the laborer as juror number twelve.

"Alternates are critical," Hubert reminded Aleta.

Aleta's question to the first alternate juror candidate was, "Are you willing to pay attention through a trial knowing you may never get to voice your opinion?"

"No," the first man said, "but do I gotta choice?"

Judge Heard lectured him, but didn't dismiss him. Instead, he warned him to pay attention or face contempt of court charges.

Aleta sat down. "I like him."

"You set him up," Hubert said.

"Yep."

A young Japanese-American woman was next.

Aleta questioned her first.

"Will you listen to the evidence intently even though you may never get to voice an opinion? It is a difficult task."

"I will," the young woman said.

Abruptly, Aleta told the judge that this person was acceptable and then sat down.

Powell's associates were discussing her heatedly in quiet whispers. Aleta sat down quickly.

"Accept her," she heard an associate whisper. "She's only an alternate, for God's sake."

The young Asian was accepted as the final alternate.

The lawyers left immediately. The trial would begin the following morning.

Driving home, Hubert said. "Explanation time."

"You want to know why I rejected the Arabian as a juror."

Surprised that she remembered, he nevertheless pressed for an explanation. "He was a sure vote."

"For the opposition."

"He was an Arabian naturalized citizen."

"He was a Muslim. Our client is Roman Catholic."

"You think he would hold that against him?"

"Shakir's entire family shunned him for years. Doesn't that tell you something?"

"Still, they're both naturalized citizens," Hubert argued.

"But our juror-to-be had his whole extended family here, Shakir doesn't. I didn't know how he would react to Shakir's rushing to see a cousin from home."

"I understand," Hubert said. "So what about the other explanation you owe me."

"You mean why did I set up the first alternate for a scolding? I needed him to pay attention during the trial," Aleta said.

"You might have lost him."

"If you remember to address him as part of the jury once or twice, you'll win him back."

"Stanley was right. You have great instincts. I'm afraid I thought you'd done us all in when you interrupted Powell. Your apology was well-timed."

"And honest," Aleta added. "Judge Heard wouldn't have responded to anything less. I was truly sorry after I did it, but Powell was baiting the man. It bordered on the abusive. I felt impelled to stop it!"

"You won that man's gratitude; but, not necessarily his vote."

"Powell was attacking him because he was black. Our young grad student will see that he knows that."

"Who do you think our jury foreman will be?"

"I vote for the Vietnam vet you approved."

"He's on the wrong side."

"The jury likes him," Aleta said. "He will be fair."

"This has been the strangest jury selection I've ever been involved with," Hubert said. "Thanks for the ride."

"You want to tell Stanley, don't you?" Aleta asked. "You won't do yourself justice."

"Be my guest," Aleta said. "I have work to do."

"You are coming tomorrow?" Hubert inquired, suddenly concerned.

"I thought you could handle it. Powell won't start with his primary witness," Aleta said.

"He might if you're not there," Hubert returned. "You've rattled him."

"Then I'm coming," Aleta decided. "I don't need to over study this."

"Over study what?" Hubert asked.

"My part in our case," Aleta replied.

Judge Aramis Heard called his old friend Roy Lutz and told him about what had happened during the jury selection.

"She challenged my rulings three times and she was so determined and reasonable I had to back down," Aramis Heard remarked. "She managed to get every juror she wanted. At least I assume she wanted them because she did tear down a couple I would have taken were I her."

"Tell me what happened in detail," Roy Lutz said.

And Aramis Heard did.

"So what was she looking for?"

"I'm not sure. I could see from the expression on Hubert Praetzel's face that he didn't know either, but he never stopped backing her."

"What did you expect?"

"I expected him to take over," Judge Heard chuckled. "And he did, but when he did she gave him directions. Can you remember when Hubert Praetzel was second chair to anyone?"

"Never."

"He is in this trial."

"Why do you say that?"

"When he questioned the two jurors she gave him— and yes, she assigned him two prospective jurors—he asked her type of question. Both of these were Powell choices and even though they answered in a fashion absolutely guaranteed to result in a challenge from the old Hubert, the new Hubert accepted them both. It was something to witness."

"So you saw nothing strange in her actions?"

"Roy, she's brilliant. This poor Arab has the best defense lawyer in the state at his side."

"Powell is dead set against her admission."

"She's running rings around him. He's going to fight against her even harder when this is over. He could win."

"He doesn't have to. She withdrew her name from consideration."

"She doesn't want to be a lawyer?" the judge probed. "She is so adept."

"She said her pregnancy was precarious and she couldn't handle the stress at this time."

"No wonder she's been absent," Judge Heard said. "Interesting that she chose her client's welfare over her own. She doesn't sound like someone we don't want."

"She accused Eugene of being a racist."

"She accused him outright?"

"Says she can prove it," Roy said. "When she withdrew it made me wonder if she really could prove it."

"From my experience, I would say she can," Aramis Heard commented. "And from what I saw today, she's right."

"What do you mean?"

"In my description of the events I left out a detail which now appears relevant. The mother of the soldier was black; the grad student was black; the laborer Powell goaded was black."

"Did she swing the other way?" Roy asked. "You know, take anyone who was a minority?"

"She dismissed an Arab which surprised me," the judge said. "I still don't understand that one. But the minorities she accepted were good, sensible people."

"Powell claims she'll prophesy in court and disrupt the judicial process."

"Well, she did excuse a pregnant juror who was less pregnant than she is. She said the trial would be too stressful. The woman protested, but Mrs. Praetzel was firm. If she foresaw anything, she was discreet about it. Hubert was angry with her about that one."

"I wish I'd been there."

"You would have enjoyed the show."

Chapter 31

The next morning as Stanley watched Aleta dress for court, he wanted desperately to tell her how proud he was of her. His father's account had been glowing. He'd drunk in every word. He wanted to share all with Aleta; but, he'd fallen asleep before she slipped in beside him. His father and mother had shared supper with him while Aleta was holed up in the study.

"You're doing the opening today," Stanley said.

"No. I'm along for the ride."

"Does Dad know that? I don't think Dad knows that."

"I told him he was in charge."

"I think he thought you meant of the witnesses."

"Why would he think that?"

"Lead counsel usually opens and closes."

"Then I guess I'd better think of something to say."

"Aleta, an opening statement is important," Stanley charged. "Haven't you given it any thought at all?"

"I thought your dad was going to do it. Does that count?"

"You can't wing it!"

"Really?"

"You had a great day yesterday because you were prepared. You can't let up," Stanley scolded. He scowled at her.

Aleta kissed him on the forehead. "You are so intense."

"I'm worried."

"I know, and it's not good for you," Aleta said. "Bertha is going to drive you to court and you can sit in the back. I will have reserved a place for you. You will stay no more than one hour and then Bertha will drive you home."

"But I won't know when to go in," Stanley muttered. "I should be there from the start."

"Then you'd better hurry," Aleta said. "But I'd give Powell a chance to warm up."

"He might cut it short."

"Not a chance."

"You purposely didn't give me enough time to make it there early."

"You are so right."

"I have to shower and shave."

She kissed him and murmured, "I know. I love you."

Stanley thought about the plans she's made and realized she planned to make the opening statement all along.

"Where is my brain?" he muttered as he turned on the water. It was always set at a temperature they both liked. This morning, however, a shower of cold water hit him.

"Darn you, Aleta!" he cried as he danced away from the cold spray and turned the knob. He was thoroughly cold when he finally had the water the right temperature.

"Aleta you knew I wouldn't step out, you little vixen. Well, I'm awake now. You'd better be good!"

He walked into the courtroom as Powell was plowing into the meat of his speech. Stanley sat down. Aleta was right. Powell was going to bore them all with a long-winded address.

Stanley studied the jurors. He felt as if he knew each one. It was a varied group. He yawned a couple of times and found a juror's eyes fastened on him. He put his hand over his mouth and the juror smiled. Stanley was grateful he hadn't started an epidemic of yawning.

The first thing Aleta did when she rose was arch her back and stretch a bit. She looked at the jury.

"What I'm going to say is important. Suppose all of you stand up. A seventh inning stretch, so to speak," she said. "Come on. You've been sitting still for an hour. Your muscles need it."

"Mr. Lincoln," she said looking into the eyes of the young black grad student, "are you brave enough or should I ask Professor Micken or Mr. Morrison to lead the way. Both are used to standing in front of groups."

The three men rose simultaneously.

"Mr. McGowan, we want you wide awake during my boring address, my blather as Professor Micken calls it. Mrs. Roberts you're brave enough to lead the women to their feet. You raised a son brave enough to fight for our freedom."

Slowly, Mrs. Roberts rose.

"Mrs. Thurman, you aren't going to let a fellow mother stand alone."

The young woman shot up.

The rest of the group rose.

"Now, Ladies and Gentlemen of the Jury, my opening remarks are going to be brief. Why don't you sit down so I can see all your faces? If anyone yawns, I will stop. You have all been polite long enough.

"You were all chosen especially to pass judgment on the man seated next to my vacant chair. You were not lightly chosen. You each have the one special quality that makes a good juror. You each have an open mind.

"I see a yawn," Aleta said. "Thank you for your attention. Mrs. Birkenstock, I apologize by not recognizing you before."

Abruptly, she whirled around and returned to her seat. The jurors glared at the young dental assistant.

"I didn't think she'd do it," the young woman said.

"Judge," Mr. Morrison said standing stiffly as if at attention. "May we respectfully request that the lawyer continue."

The young black grad student stood up. "I vote to hear her out."

The professor stood up. "Her blather was better than most."

One by one the other jurors rose, including the young dental assistant asking if they could hear her out.

"The jury will please be seated," Judge Heard ordered.

The veteran sat immediately and the others followed his lead.

"Mrs. Praetzel, the court requests that you complete your opening statement."

"Yes, Your Honor," Aleta said politely.

"To continue, you all have another special quality I need--intelligence. It's that simple. I need a smart jury, one that will find the truth buried in the web of deceit the prosecution will weave around my client. As for the other stuff—you know, honesty, patriotism, common sense and bravery. You all have those qualities as well. You are a unique jury and it gives me great pleasure to appear before you.

"I see a quizzical look on Mrs. Birkenstock's face. Have I failed you again? I see you have read up on things lawyers can and cannot say in a trial.

"I see Mr. Morrison nodding as well as Mr. Lincoln and Professor Micken. Before the rest of you join in, let me say what you want to hear me say. As you know, I cannot lie in court.

"Mr. Shakir Aloman is innocent of the charge levied against him."

Aleta paused for just a moment and then added. "And I will prove it."

In the back row, Stanley wanted to stand and clap. Instead he left when the judge told the prosecution to call its first witness.

"Bertha, do you know what a fantastic job Mrs. Praetzel did in that courtroom?"

He heard two men walking up behind him.

"Talk about an opening!" one exclaimed.

"It was worth taking in. How many others were here?"

"I saw five."

"Are you sure she isn't examining witnesses today?"

"Hubert's taking the first ones."

The men brushed past the slow moving pair.

Stanley and Bertha walked on silently.

A little before noon, Hubert pulled into the drive with Aleta and Bertha took one look out the window and immediately scooped some ice cream and milk in a blender and whipped up a thick milk shake.

Aleta walked to her room slowly.

"She doesn't have to go back," Hubert announced.

"Lunch will be ready in a few minutes. Robert is coming."

"My guess is she's too tired to eat," Hubert reported.

Bertha plucked the shake from the blender and poured it into a large glass. "Help yourself to coffee, Sir. I will be back shortly."

Bertha knocked on the door gently and then went in. She told Stanley his father wanted to see him in the kitchen. Stanley rose and pulling on his robe left the room. Aleta came out of the bathroom and Bertha handed her the shake and began to help her out of her clothes.

Before Aleta could protest, "The baby needs to eat and you need to rest. Mr. Praetzel is lunching with his father and Mr. Locke."

Aleta gave herself into Bertha's care.

"Why am I so tired?"

"You can't handle a night without rest and day without food. You're pregnant, Ma'am. You cannot do this again."

Aleta was too tired to even respond. Bertha made her drink the entire shake before she'd let her lay her head on the pillow. As Bertha drew the sheet over her, Aleta realized she was naked.

"My pajamas," she murmured.

"You may put them on when you wake up. They're right here on the chair," Bertha said matter-of-factly.

Aleta's eyes closed and sleep came quickly.

When Bertha reentered the kitchen, the three men were chatting amiably.

"Sirs," she said in her most serious tone, "you are never to drive her to exhaustion again."

The protests came swiftly. Bertha paid no heed but finished lunch preparation until the men stopped telling her that no one could control Aleta.

As their plates appeared in front of them, Bertha glared at her employer, "You, Sir, can order her to get at least eight hours of sleep a night if you can't persuade her. You can stop asking her to be your nurse. A trial is enough of a burden for a pregnant woman to carry."

"Nurse?" Stanley asked bewildered. "I don't ask her to be my nurse."

"Of course, you do—subtly, of course. If you want to go out, you make arrangements with me. You stop expecting her to make sure you have company when you're awake. You tell her you like quiet times to think and then you think about how you can take the load off her shoulders without hurting your own recovery."

The two fathers were smirking when Bertha was scolding Stanley. She caught them at it and turned on them.

"You two are no better."

"Us?" they chorused.

"You, Mr. Praetzel, Sir, need not to burden her with so much work. Urge her to use your associates and yourself.

Make sure she doesn't take any more of the case. You're a competent lawyer. Act like it!"

Robert Locke swallowed his smirk because Bertha eyed him next. "And you, Mr. Locke. Remember that you are allowed to practice in this state and your daughter is not. Much as she is pleased for you, she is mourning the loss of her dream. She has this one case and after that nothing. She is too good for that to happen to her. There are three of you sitting here secure in your chosen profession and the woman you all profess to love is suffering from the 'slings and arrows of outrageous fortune.' You are letting a hateful man destroy her dream. You need to fight him for her."

Suddenly, Bertha burst into tears and ran from the room. The three men stared at each other.

"We do think of Aleta as indestructible sometimes," Hubert commented. "She is so strong."

"She would hate to be helped openly," Stanley put in.

"But, Hubert, you and I put a kink in Powell's plan to kill her," Robert Locke said. "What can we do to see that he doesn't succeed in killing her dream?"

"She should never have come before a committee in the first place," Stanley said. "Her religious beliefs are not harmful to a living soul. She has never acted irrationally in court or out."

"But the process has begun," Hubert said.

"Then we should reverse it!" Robert declared.

"There were seven lawyers in the courtroom today besides me watching her," Stanley reported.

"What if we formed an ad hoc committee to promote her admission," Hubert said. "My wife and Kurtz West would join in such an effort.

"Don't forget Professor Burrows," Stanley said. "He's been an advocate all along."

"We'll meet at my house tonight," Hubert said.

"I'll be there," Stanley said. "If I rest the remainder of the day, I shouldn't set my recovery back at all."

"I'll pick you up," Robert said. "Bertha and Jocelyn can keep Aleta company."

Bertha returned. Stanley told her he was going to his father's house that evening. He asked her to stay with Aleta.

"I will be going too," Robert said. "We listened to you."

Bertha acknowledged him with a small nod, and then in her usual, detached, professional manner she said, "I baked a pie this morning. Apple. Would any of you gentlemen care for a piece?"

Three plates were held out.

As they were leaving the house, Hubert said to Robert, "You've picked quite a woman to be your wife."

Robert smiled. He had indeed.

After court the following day, Melvin Hillers took Eugene Powell aside and told him an ad hoc committee had been formed to fight for Aleta Praetzel's admission to the bar.

"Who formed this committee?" Powell asked.

"Her father, the Praetzels and a couple of friends including Kurtz West and Professor Burrows.

"How do you know about this?"

"Roy Lutz called. He thought you should know."

"Is he on the committee?"

"He's staying neutral."

"As always!" Powell spat out.

He scowled as he considered what this might mean. Finally, he snapped, "So what! She's withdrawn her application... Or has she reapplied."

"She isn't aware of the effort being made on her behalf."

"How could she not be aware of it?" Powell asserted.

"That's what I was told."

"Well, tomorrow I'm putting my main witness on the stand. That should just about finish this case and then I'll deal with Mrs. Aleta Praetzel."

"Why not just let this go?" Hillers suggested. "We don't want to take on half the lawyers in Northern Illinois."

"You're exaggerating. Only a small handful, mostly relatives are involved. I can counter that pathetic sentimental effort," Powell proclaimed. "Is the Kay Rivers affair buried for good?"

"She doesn't have a new lawyer and I haven't heard that she's made any inquiries. Apparently she's given up."

"When I take care of Aleta Praetzel, I'll take Rivers out at the same time."

"I thought the locals told you no one would touch Aleta."

"Outside talent will do the job better and it'll be much cleaner. There'll be no connection to me at all."

"You're going to wait until the trial is over, aren't you?"

"I intend to."

"Maybe defeating her will be enough."

"I want her gone. Defeating her will be my alibi. No one will point a finger at me. Victors don't kill the defeated."

"Except in war."

"Only you and I realize that war is what this is."

Chapter 32

Aleta, who had left at noon on the first day of the trial, had not shown up at all on the second day, appeared on the third day to the jury's delight. She received multiple smiles and nods from the jury members as they filed in and took their seats. She returned each silent greeting with eye contact and a slight nod.

So intent was she on the jury, she didn't notice the people dressed in business suits filing in to the rows behind her. She didn't even notice that Stanley and Bertha were there as well. The two had entered quietly and placed themselves in the back row directly behind her where even if she looked around, she probably wouldn't spot them.

Hubert didn't survey the crowd either for to do so would have called Aleta's attention to its presence, but he was aware that the number of people had increased five-fold from when he was in charge of the defense the day before.

Justin Conway was the sole representative of the press in the courtroom that day, but he didn't care. There would be no reports but his. What few reporters that appeared on the first couple of days had enjoyed Aleta's outrageous performance, but grew weary when she left at noon on the first day and didn't return for Eugene Powell. Without Aleta Praetzel there was no story.

Justin, however, knew that Aleta, who'd opened on the first day, was lead attorney. That she had left the grunt work to one of the area's most prestigious attorneys bespoke how seriously she and he took this case. Aleta would show up again. And as Justin had watched the courtroom fill, he knew this was the day. It wasn't the day the verdict would come in. It was the day the verdict would be decided.

Eugene Powell called Richard Young as his final witness. The man was in plain clothes but he was nevertheless impressive. Tall, muscular with a blonde crew-cut and neatly trimmed mustache, Young stated his name in a pleasant baritone voice.

Plus for the prosecution, Justin thought. The man exuded confidence and authority.

Powell carefully led Richard Young through his assignment as an undercover officer placed in the jail cell next to the one the defendant was incarcerated in. Step by step Powell led Young through his damning testimony.

He had talked at length with the defendant Shakir Aloman during the five days he was in the Clearwater, Florida jail. Government agents had repeatedly interrogated Shakir Aloman and the defendant had spoken to Richard Young at length about the questions they had asked and the answers he given.

Young claimed Aloman had gloated over his cleverness in hiding the truth.

As Young was testifying, Aleta could feel the rage building up in the man seated beside her. When her sensibilities told her he was ready to burst out and call the man a liar she whispered, "The bigger the lie, the better."

Shakir had pondered that thought through most of the remainder of the testimony.

Eugene Powell asked him to sum up what he had been told. Richard Young, looking straight at the jury declared in no uncertain terms, "Shakir Aloman confessed to me that he was part of the terrorist group responsible for the 9/11 attacks."

On that note, Eugene Powell turned the witness over to the defense.

To everyone's gratification, Aleta rose from her chair. She leaned over and whispered a stern warning to her client.

"Say nothing. Do nothing but watch. Your life and honor are in my hands. I intend to preserve both. Trust me."

Shakir leaned over toward Hubert Praetzel. "Sir, help me comply."

Hubert said. "Trust her. Don't act surprised or upset by anything she says."

"Would you?" he asked as a man whose fate was riding on the slim shoulders of a young, inexperienced, pregnant, woman lawyer.

"With my life," Hubert said firmly.

"Mr. Young," Aleta began, "you have an outstanding record as a police officer. You are known for being meticulous in your attention to technical detail. In fact this trait of yours has made you a favorite officer in the eyes of the prosecutors in your area. Is this correct?"

"Yes," he said matter-of-factly. She was going to do the butter-up technique. Powell has practiced that one with him, nevertheless Young tensed slightly.

"You've tensed up, Officer Young," Aleta observed. "Have I said something that frightened you?"

"No, Ma'am," Young replied quickly, forcing himself to relax.

"That's better," Aleta said. "I need you to answer a few simple questions for me. First, do you believe in telling the truth?"

"Yes."

"You're married, aren't you?"

"Yes."

"Do you love your wife?"

"Yes."

"Two young children, I believe."

"Yes," Young replied. Suddenly, he couldn't see where she was going.

"And you love them too?"

"Yes."

"You're a racing enthusiast. You've loved cars since high school when you got a number of speeding tickets and then began using a race track to test your skill behind the wheel at high speeds. You've won quite a bit in the amateur circuit, haven't you?"

"Yes," he replied, a touch of pride in his voice. Back to buttering him up. He was ready for this approach.

"You've wanted to turn pro, but your wife said she'd leave you if you did, didn't she?"

"Yes," Young replied. This was getting too personal. He glanced at Eugene Powell.

"I would too if you were my husband," Aleta remarked. "Mess up that handsome face and possibly a few other vital parts."

There was a murmur of laughter.

"But she supports you engaging in both police work and amateur racing, doesn't she?"

"Yes, she does."

"Courageous woman," Aleta remarked, and then turned, "Mr. Powell you may object at any time."

Powell was too surprised at the aside directed at him.

"I will object when you're objectionable," he burst out.

Again a titter of laughter was heard.

Judge Heard banged his gavel.

Before he could speak, Aleta apologized. Order was restored and the judge relaxed.

Aleta turned back to the witness, "So, Mr. Young you are a truthful man?"

"Yes," he replied. She was back on track.

"Tell me have you been truthful about your homosexual tendencies?"

Powell was on his feet bellowing his objection.

"Irrelevant," he screeched.

"My, he does get worked up over the simplest of inquiries," Aleta remarked. "Judge, a little latitude here. Please."

"Overruled," Heard declared.

"You may reply," Aleta said to Young. "Do you remember the question?"

"I'm not a homosexual!" Young declared.

"So you don't remember the question," Aleta remarked. "Let me repeat it."

Young glared at her.

"Are you always truthful with regard to your homosexual tendencies?"

"Let me repeat myself," Young said, his anger rising. "I am not a homosexual."

"That isn't my question," Aleta said. "For a man so meticulous in his work and with his words, you keep misunderstanding me. Did you misunderstand Mr. Aloman likewise?"

"No!" Young bellowed. "I understood him perfectly. And I understand you perfectly."

"Then please answer the question asked," Aleta reiterated. "For the third time, are you always truthful with regard to your homosexual tendencies?"

"Asked and answered!" Powell bellowed.

Aleta turned to the jury. "This is why I needed a smart jury."

"Mrs. Praetzel," Judge Heard warned.

"Well, if the witness could be instructed to answer the question properly yes or no, we could proceed."

"The witness will answer the question yes or no," Judge Heard ordered.

"No!" Richard Young shot out.

"Is that your answer? Because if it is I can sit down."

Young looked puzzled. "No, I am not a homosexual."

"Whoever said you were?" Aleta gasped. "Not me! Besides I wouldn't care if you were or weren't. It wouldn't be relevant to this case."

"That's what you asked!" Young declared.

"What I asked is whether you were always truthful—emphasis on truthful—about your homosexual tendencies. In other words do you always tell the truth about your sexual orientation?"

"Yes."

"Mr. Young, may I remind you that perjury is a serious offense."

"I'm not a homo and I never told anyone I was."

Aleta smiled. "Mr. Young, may I draw your attention to the rear of the courtroom."

For the first time Aleta turned around. Her surprise was real. "Where'd all these people come from?" she uttered. "Strike that, Your Honor."

"Mr. Jocko Mooney, please rise," Aleta ordered.

An ordinary man in a rumpled suit rose.

"Mr. Mooney is willing to testify that you not only told him you were homosexual but you engaged in certain sexual acts which sexually gratified both of you."

"I was undercover!" Young protested.

"Did you or did you not misrepresent your homosexual tendencies to Mr. Mooney, unless, of course you are, in fact, a homosexual, in which case you've lied under oath."

"Undercover means you lie," Young explained.

"When does the lying stop...? Never mind, we'll get to that. I want to understand this clearly. You lied to Mr. Mooney because you were undercover and it's allowed when you're undercover, is that correct?"

"Yes, it is," Young said firmly. "You have to lie. It's part of the job."

"Does your wife know about these undercover assignments?"

"No. That's part of the deal."

"So you lie to the person you're trying to trap into a confession. And you lie to your wife as well. That's a lot of lying for a man to do. Must be hard to know where to draw the line."

"No, it's not. I don't tell my wife because she'd worry."

"But you race cars. And that doesn't worry her?"

"That's different."

"Let's move on," Aleta said. "Your lies are confined to your whereabouts and activities while you're undercover, correct?"

"Yes."

"What happens if it spills over?"

"Nothing spills over."

"You busted a prostitution ring recently, didn't you?"

"Yes."

"It was your eleventh successful undercover case wasn't it?"

"Yes."

"Did you share that one with your wife?"

"No."

"None of it? The case made the headlines."

"None of it."

"Where is the line between lie and truth in your world?"

"What do you mean?"

"Would you tell the truth if a man's life depended on it?"

"Yes."

"I suggest you'd lie even then."

"No, I wouldn't."

"You didn't tell your wife you contracted an STD on your last assignment, did you?"

"No."

"You became infected with a sexually transmitted disease and you went to the police physician and he told you not to engage in sex, did he not?"

"I'm careful."

"Really?" Aleta scoffed. "I assume you think using a condom is enough. Oh, wait, you can't use a condom. Your wife wants another child, doesn't she?"

Young didn't respond. How had she dug this up? Only the police physician knew. And he'd been assured the blood had gone in for analysis under an assumed name.

"Is this one of those times that a lie is called for?"

Young remained mute.

"Judge, order the witness to respond.

"Yes!" Young burst out. "I couldn't tell her because then I'd have to tell her about the undercover work."

"And have you abstained from sex since contracting this disease?"

"No," came the response in a small voice.

"So you are putting her at risk regularly?"

"Yes."

"At this point in time, you are violating your marriage vows, assuming you got married."

"Of course, we got married," he came back loudly. "You just don't understand."

"Oh, I understand quite well. When I was in a medically fragile condition, my husband took a vow of celibacy so as not to harm me in anyway. I don't believe he's the only husband to love his wife that deeply. I can't imagine him deliberately passing along a sexually transmitted disease. He allowed himself to be shot to save me."

"I'd do the same thing."

"Only you won't tell your wife the truth so she can live disease free. Are you punishing her for not letting you die in a car wreck on the race track?"

"Don't meddle in stuff that doesn't belong in this trial."

"I'm meddling, as you call it, in your tendency to lie any time it suits you."

"I don't do that!" Young declared.

"Why should we believe a man who would hand his wife a sexually transmitted disease, and lie about it?"

"Because I wouldn't lie about something like this. Not when I'm under oath on a witness stand."

"Wouldn't you?"

"You can't pull up anyone out of that magic hat of yours that can prove I'm lying."

"What about my client?"

"He's the one who's lying. He's a sonofabitch who deserves to go to prison."

"So you sent him there without benefit of a trial?"

"I didn't do it."

"Didn't the government man ask you what you found out?"

"One did."

"The one that hasn't testified, right?"

"Yes."

"And you told him what he wanted to hear?"

"That's my job."

"Which is?"

"To tell him what I found out."

"Oh, I thought maybe it was to tell him what he wanted to hear."

"Well, what I found out was what he wanted to hear," Young said, again confident.

"You have a surprising track record for an undercover cop," Aleta commented. "How do you explain that?"

"Just good at my job, I guess," Young boasted.

"So you're an accomplished liar."

Young took the bait. "I do my job well."

"You're very believable both in the field when you're masquerading as someone else and on the witness stand, true?"

"Yes."

"So believable you could lie and get away with it? Yes or no?"

"I'm not lying now."

"You mean today, under oath?"

"Yes."

"Well, I'm glad there's one time you don't lie."

"Undercover and to my wife, that's all."

"Never on the witness stand? I mean apart from the lies you told us today. I assume you want us to ignore those."

"I don't lie under oath."

"So you have never lied on the stand, except for today?"

"Stop saying except for today!" he snapped.

"I have to say it because you lied to us today and what I want to know is have you lied before today."

"Never under oath."

"May I remind you again that the penalty for perjury is severe."

"I've never lied on the stand under oath," Young declared.

"Before today."

"Yes, before today."

"Mr. Todd Jamison, will you please stand," Aleta said.

A tall, thin blonde man stood.

Richard Young blanched.

"You testified under oath that Mr. Jamison had confessed to you that he'd robbed a liquor store. Mr. Jamison was convicted on your testimony. He claimed he hadn't done it; but, he couldn't prove he was home alone at the time. Later that robbery was linked to several others and the perpetrator confessed. Mr. Jamison is ready to testify that you befriended him in jail and he told you repeatedly he was innocent. You lied on the witness stand."

"I made a mistake that time. I thought I heard something I didn't. That was a long time ago."

"So long ago you forgot about it completely?"

"Yes."

"The question is can we trust you today?"

"I'm an honest man. I wouldn't lie about something really serious."

"Mr. Young, you already have."

Aleta went back to her table, took a sip of water and leaned over to hear what Hubert had to say. She shook her head.

Richard Young fidgeted on the stand.

She turned and faced the witness. The courtroom, which had buzzed during the brief break, fell silent.

"Mr. Young, when the government promised to take care of you how did they plan to do it?"

Young, still spinning from the blows dealt by this woman, thought about the question several minutes.

"It's not a trick question, Mr. Young. "What did the government offer?"

"Nothing. I would never take a bribe to lie."

"That's nice to know," Aleta said calmly. "Only I wasn't asking if you were bribed. Am I to assume that you agreed to testify about a terrorist's activities without any guarantee of safety?"

"Yes!" Young spat out quickly. "I didn't take anything. It's part of the job."

He glanced at Eugene Powell and caught his nod of approval. All was not lost. All he had to do was stick to his story. That's what Eugene Powell had hammered into him.

"Mr. Young, if you're telling me the truth, you are dumber than dumb."

"Don't use that phrase," Young snapped.

"I only said you were dumber than dumb if you honestly thought you'd bagged a terrorist and came to his trial without any protection. You'll notice I arrived with four armed guards because I've been threatened."

"I haven't been threatened."

"Nobody in the group of terrorists to which this man supposedly belongs threatened to harm you or your family if you testified?"

"No."

"Did you ever consider that they might?"

"Never thought about it."

"Hmm," Aleta murmured. "You had just heard a man confess he was part of a group responsible for one of the most devastating terrorist acts in history and you weren't afraid of retaliation?"

"No."

"People who inform on the mob in this country are put in witness protection. That wasn't offered to you?"

"No."

"Well, either you and your family are unimportant, which I have difficulty accepting, or my client wasn't deemed dangerous. Which is it?"

"Mr. Aloman was in custody. He wasn't considered dangerous."

"You don't know much about terrorists, do you?"

"I know a fair amount," Young blustered.

"Terrorists are inherently dangerous," Aleta explained, as if he hadn't spoken. "They kill without remorse and have no problem killing women and children. They are people who strike terror in the hearts of most people. I suggest that you weren't afraid of Mr. Aloman because he wasn't a terrorist."

"He said he was," Young insisted.

"Words in the absence of action possess an inherent frailty, Mr. Young. Let me leave philosophizing until later. My next question is, as far as you know were any guns or explosives found on the person or in the vehicle of Mr. Shakir Aloman?"

"No."

"Insofar as you are aware, did he resist arrest?"

"No."

"From your prospective in jail, did you ever see him attack a guard?"

"No."

"Did he ever use foul language or call his captors unsuitable names?"

"No."

"Did he attempt to escape, talk about escaping or plan to escape?"

"No."

"Did he at any time threaten you or anyone in your hearing?"

"No."

"Did he ever recite inflammatory words from the Koran or any other source?"

"No."

"Actually you did hear him recite certain phrases, didn't you?"

"Yes."

"The rosary, I believe."

"It could have been."

"You are Catholic, are you not?"

"Yes."

"And you don't know the words of the rosary?"

"It was the rosary."

"So he prayed as a Catholic in his time of need."

"It was an act."

"Isn't that the basis on which you formed the so-called friendship?"

"Yes."

"And did he appear knowledgeable about Catholicism?"

"Yes, but he's a smart man. He could've studied up."

"Actually, I believe that's exactly what he did do. And he was tutoring his son in comparative religion as well. Do you believe he chose to be a Catholic because that faith preaches terrorism?"

"Catholics aren't terrorists!" Young proclaimed without thinking.

"Mr. Aloman is a Catholic."

"He's an exception," Young stated.

"So you believe there can be exceptions to a rule?" Aleta asked matter-of-factly.

"That's what I said," Young alleged.

"So do you believe that a large number of people could share the same name and one be a terrorist and another not be one?"

"Yes. It's possible."

"Possible, but not probable?"

"Yes.

"Did you know there are a number of convicted felons named Young?"

"It's a common name."

"Aloman is a common Arabic name," Aleta said. "Let's move on. The federal agent to whom you reported your findings is not present today, is he?"

"No."

"Nor yesterday?"

"No."

"When he sent you into that jail cell, did he tell you that he'd gotten a confession?"

"He said Aloman almost confessed, but became frightened and I was to go in and be friendly and maybe he'd confess to me."

"That's what you say he said," Aleta quipped.

"It's the truth!" Young declared.

Aleta smiled. "Curiously, enough I believe every word you have just spoken."

Richard Young smiled.

"Did you know that many of the convicted felons named Young are black?"

"Yes."

"Are you?"

"Am I what?" Young asked bewildered.

"Part Negro?"

Young exploded. "You have got to be the stupidest woman on the planet. What you see is what I am. One hundred percent white Caucasian, just like you!"

Aleta smiled as she turned toward the jury. "But I'm not. I'm part Negro."

"That's a lie!" Young yelled at the back of her head. "You're trying to trick me."

"I'm a lawyer. A lawyer can't lie in court. Did you know that? The jury knows that. I'm surprised you don't know that."

"I know that," Young confessed calming down. "But why would you admit it? That's a stupid thing to do."

"I believe the phrase you want is dumber-then-dumb, isn't it?"

"Yes."

"What if I told you Mr. Powell was planning to use that fact in his closing argument?"

"Then it would be smart."

Aleta moved back to the subject of the federal agent so smoothly it was as if she hadn't taken the inexplicable detour she had.

"This mysterious federal agent you were dealing with," Aleta posed. "Did you assess him to be a smart man?"

"Yes."

"A man who knew what he was doing?"

"Yes."

"He knew he couldn't go into court with a partial confession, true?"

"Yes."

"So you were sent in, right?"

"Yes," Young said a trifle impatiently.

"Bear with me, Mr. Young, for just a couple more questions," Aleta begged. "And he was pleased with your report, correct?"

"Yes."

"And you think he believed you?"

"Yes."

"And you think he could tell you were the type of witness that could convince a jury you were telling the truth, true?"

"Yes."

"Then why didn't he go to trial?"

"I don't know."

"Well, we're in trial now, three years later and he refuses to participate. Why is that do you suppose?"

"I don't know."

"We're talking about convicting an alleged terrorist and he hides from witnessing. Do you have any idea why?"

"No."

"May I suggest one," Aleta said. "There was no partial confession or even a hint of one. He sent you in knowing you would fail and then when you came out he coached you so your story would coincide with his. He was supposed to testify, wasn't he?"

Young hesitated.

"Let me clarify my question. The federal agent you were working with told you he was going to testify, didn't he?"

"Yes."

"But he's a smart man. He didn't want to be caught committing perjury. He did report the confession, however, and told whoever makes such decisions that a good lawyer might get Aloman off and so Aloman was shipped off to prison without a trial. Either the agent didn't believe you had gotten a confession or he knew you didn't get one because the two of you manufactured one. Which is it?"

"I guess he didn't believe me."

"Why not?"

"I don't know."

"Maybe because he knew Aloman had never confessed to you. It that possible?"

"No."

"Did it ever occur to you that the agent would send someone in to monitor you?"

"Why would he do that?"

"Answer my question please," Aleta said firmly.

"No, it didn't cross my mind."

"Why didn't he, do you suppose?"

"Because he trusted me."

"That was a foolish move for a smart man."

"I'm an honest man," Young retorted.

Aleta smiled. "Let's not go there. Since you insist on misreading my inquiries let's take this one piece at a time. You were in jail cell separate from the one the defendant was in, correct?"

"I'm not a dumb kid! Stop treating me as one," Young snarled.

"Answer the question yes or no!" Aleta insisted.

Young swallowed hard. "Yes," he sputtered angrily.

"He could not touch you, correct?"

"Yes," he said slightly bewildered.

"You could wear a wire and he wouldn't know, correct?"

"Yes."

"So, why weren't you?"

"I...," Young hesitated. "I was going to be there several days.

"Did you pack a suitcase?"

"No, of course not."

"So you weren't planning to change clothes, were you?"

"No, of course not."

"So there'd be no way Mr. Aloman would know you were wearing a wire."

"I'd run out of tape," Young said with a smug smile. "It'd be useless after a couple hours."

"How about a transmitter with a recorder in another room?" Aleta posed.

"We don't have that sort of equipment," Young said.

"The federal government doesn't have that kind of equipment?"

"It wasn't necessary," Young said. "I'm a good witness. I can convince a jury of anything."

"Even an outright lie I would assume," Aleta commented. "Shall I suggest an alternate explanation?"

"You're going to do it anyway," Young said bitterly.

"Either the conversations were recorded and there was no confession and so the tapes were destroyed, or no tapes were made because then there'd be no evidence to prove he didn't confess. So which is it?"

"Neither. None. No tapes were made. It wasn't thought of."

"It's common procedure," Aleta said. "Why deviate?"

"It isn't all that common. It wasn't thought of. That's it."

"Hadn't the federal government taken over Aloman's case?"

"Yes."

"Didn't you ask about using a recorder?"

"Didn't think about it?"

"Oh, Mr. Young," Aleta said. "How many counts of perjury are you going for?"

"What do you mean?"

"You told a fellow officer you thought you should have a transmitter."

"Shit!" Young exclaimed. He caught himself almost immediately. "I forgot. That's all."

"So, I'm going to return to a version of a former question now that your memory is back," Aleta said matter-of-factly. "What reason did the federal agent give you for not outfitting you with a transmitter?"

"He said a clever lawyer would use the tapes against us."

"A lawyer could only do that if the tapes contained no confession, true or false?"

"False. Lawyers twist stuff around."

"You mean when a man says he's not guilty on a tape, the lawyer might twist that around to prove he was innocent."

"Yeah," Young said only half listening to the question. "Like you're doing to me. I tell you the man confessed and you make it about me and whether I lied to my wife and what the hell has that got to do with anything and about a mistake I make once and stuff I did as an undercover cop which I've got to do to get convictions and here we've got a terrorist that lands in our jail and you don't think we're going to let him go free. Hell, we do what's necessary to do."

"Include lie on the witness stand?"

"Objection!" Powell bellowed. "Asked and answered."

His voice startled Young out of the somnolent state into which he had fallen.

"I withdraw the question, Your Honor," Aleta said. She walked back to her table and took a sip of water. She glanced at the audience and her eyes fell on Stanley. He smiled at her. She let her eyes swing back to the two seated at the table and raised a brow at Hubert. He nodded almost imperceptibly and the lawyers in the gallery who were watching every move grew silent. She had tried to break the man, but despite all her efforts he'd remained glued to his story that the defendant had confessed to him. Powell still had a case.

What the lawyers didn't know was that Hubert was merely affirming that Aloman was under control. She remembered that Lydia had told her to let her mind put it all together and to go with what it generated. The idea that came to her was a wild one. And, inexplicably, she knew she had the answer. Everything fell into place, including the warning she'd felt impelled to give Aloman when she began.

"Mr. Young, we're almost done. I must admit you have been a remarkable staunch witness for the prosecution."

"That's because...," Young began.

Aleta interrupted him. "I haven't gotten to the question."

Young closed his mouth.

"Your very stubbornness tells me that you have a personal issue here. No one puts as much on the line as you have today without some motivation stronger than anyone here has guessed.

"You've risked your job; but, actually you don't much care. You want to race cars.

"You risked your marriage; but, free of your wife, you'd be free to race cars.

"You're risked jail time; but, a good lawyer will get you a minimum sentence and the exchange was worth it.

"Now before we delve into the force that is driving you to lie about Mr. Aloman, would you like to recant your statement that he confessed to being a terrorist?"

"No."

"I have two witnesses to the event you are trying to hide."

Shakir started to rise. Hubert caught him and hissed at him to sit down and be quiet.

Young glared at Aloman. The forty year old defendant shook his head. Fear rode his expression.

Hubert took hold of Shakir's arm and whispered at him to keep it together. The man eyed his lawyer angrily.

"But....," he began when Hubert hissed at him to trust in God and Aleta.

Aleta saw the direction of Young's gaze. "Mr. Aloman didn't break his promise. He didn't tell me."

"There weren't nothing to tell. Nothing happened."

Aloman began to rise again.

"That's...," he began.

Again Hubert grabbed him and hauled him back into his seat.

Aleta heard the scuffling behind her. She spun around. "Mr. Aloman, if you don't sit down and be quiet, Judge Heard will sanction me. Do you understand?"

Aloman melted under her stern gaze and sunk into his seat. He bent over as if expecting a beating.

Was this what Aleta was threatening Young with—abusing a prisoner? The lawyers in the gallery wondered. Not much of a punch line.

Eugene Powell smirked. She'd overreached herself. She was about to crash and burn.

Richard Young caught the smirk and immediately he concluded that Aleta was bluffing. He sat back and let a sneer twist the corners of his mouth.

"You're sneering," Aleta said.

"You've nothing because there is nothing. You've uncovered all the skeletons in my closet."

"Well, I will admit that we've uncovered quite a few—the net result which will probably mean dismissal from the force, a divorce and prison time. Still you stick with your testimony."

"That's because it's..."

Aleta interrupted harshly. "Do not speak until I ask a question."

Young fluttered his hands and snorted, "My we are touchy, aren't we? I'd say it's that time of the month; but, it's obvious you were knocked up long ago."

Judge Heard banged his gavel. As he was about to speak, Aleta said evenly. "Forgive the witness, Your Honor. Please let me continue without interruption."

The court grew silent once more.

"How did you keep the young boy quiet while you raped him?"

Young blanched. She did know. The stinking Arab had told. Well, he'd pay.

"I didn't rape him!"

"That wasn't the question," Aleta said icily. "I know you raped him. I have two witnesses. How did you keep him quiet?"

"It's a lie conjured up by the defendant in a feeble attempt to blacken my good name."

"On the third day you were in prison, did you not share your cell for one night with a young black male?"

"Yes, but nothing happened."

"Judge Heard, please instruct the witness to only answer my question."

"Mr. Young, consider yourself warned," the judge ordered.

"The young man was a minor, was he not?"

"Yes."

"Twelve years old?"

"He was big for his age."

"But you knew he was twelve, didn't you?"

"They told me he was a minor and they wanted to put him in with someone they could trust."

Aleta's next questions were purposely rapid fire.

"Did you have him stick a sock in his mouth or was it his endurance? Did you explain what you were going to do to him or did you just force him to bend over? How did you frighten him into compliance? Threaten his mother? Threaten his younger brother? Threaten both? And after each harrowing experience, did you make him stay gagged so no one would be awakened by his crying? And from the adjoining cell, Mr. Aloman, a father of a young boy, begged you to stop, did you tell him if he breathed a word to anyone you would hunt up that precious son of his and rape him?"

Shakir shouted out before Hubert could stop him. "I didn't tell her! Honest!"

Hubert grabbed his arm and hissed at him to be quiet. Judge Heard banged his gavel.

Aleta immediately apologized for her client. "Please forgive him. He will not do that again."

"He was warned," Judge Heard reminded her. "I heard you tell him to be quiet."

"Hold me in contempt then. I did not properly prepare him. I surprised him. He didn't know I knew about the threat. I am the one at fault."

"Then you will spend one day in jail for contempt.

"Thank you, Your Honor."

"No!" shouted Aloman.

Hubert tightened his grip and hissed at him to be silent again.

"Two days," Judge Heard ordered.

"Yes, Your Honor," Aleta responded evenly, bowing her head.

Hubert squeezed Aloman's arm, "One more sound out of you and I will personally throttle you!"

"But..."

Hubert clapped his hand over his client's mouth. "Shut the hell up!" he hissed.

Hubert didn't remove his hand until he felt Shakir got the message. Every word out of his mouth Aleta would pay for.

Aleta sensed when Hubert finally had control of Shakir. The court room was rife with whispering. The lawyers watched the jury's faces at the judge meted out his sentence. They knew Aleta knew that Judge Heard was harsh when it came to outbursts. She had pointedly warned her client. Obviously it wasn't for show. The consensus was, however, that she was earning sympathy points with the jury.

When the court grew silent, Aleta spoke with obvious respect. "Again, I apologize for my client's outbursts. May I please continue?"

"Proceed," Judge Heard said, satisfied that he again had order in his court.

"Mr. Young, I don't expect you to answer the questions put to you before the outburst. Let us start over with the first one. "Did you use the boy's sock to gag him?"

"No."

"His underwear?"

"No."

"You do realize there is no such thing as consensual sex between an adult and a child?"

"I know the law," Young said. "I didn't rape him."

"His name was Samuel Jackson, not the movie star, of course. That's why I looked him up. I was curious. That's how I found out his age and where he went after he left your cell. Do you know?"

"No."

"Really?" Aleta commented. "He was committed to a youth psychiatric ward."

"I didn't know."

"I'd be careful what I say at this point. When I finish here—if ever I get out of jail, that is, I will look up young Mr. Jackson and represent him in a suit against you. I will be subpoenaing these records you may be sure."

"He hasn't any money to pay you and I don't have any money either. You're bluffing."

Aleta eyed him coldly. "I don't bluff."

She waited a long moment.

"Did you think you could repeatedly rape a young boy in the presence of others and get away with it?"

Richard Young realized the question had no answer, but she would keep hounding him until she got one. Without too much thought he invoked the Fifth.

Powell's groan was almost audible.

"Thank you, Mr. Young. I am finished with my questions," Aleta said politely. She then went to her chair and sat down.

The witness was excused.

Powell announced, "The prosecution rests."

"Court is adjourned until Monday morning," Judge Heard declared banging his gavel.

The jury stood up to leave when they heard the judge tell the bailiff to take Mrs. Praetzel into custody. Shocked, they stood with their mouths gaping as the bailiff cuffed the young lawyer in front of her desk.

Not a lawyer in the courtroom moved until Aleta was escorted to the side door leading to the holding cells.

Just as she reached the door, unexpectedly the lawyers burst into spontaneous applause.

The bailiff halted mid-stride. Aleta turned and nodded her acknowledgement. She then disappeared through the door.

A second bailiff came and took the defendant away in cuffs.

Stanley stayed pinned to his seat, scarcely able to cope with what his wife's arrest might mean for her safety. He was furious with the harsh punishment meted out for a stupid action on the part of a defendant which in his mind wasn't serious enough to warrant one day, let alone two.

And where was his father. He was the one who was supposed to control Aloman. He knew this wasn't a charade. His father would never have agreed to anything like that. This was spontaneous.

Right, he told himself, Aleta surprised them all. His father didn't dream she'd offer herself to stand in her client's stead. Not in her condition. He probably expected Heard to accept Aleta's apology and issue a warning. Only Aleta didn't seem shocked. She took the sentence with uncommon grace.

Heard was touched, Stanley realized as his mind continued to mull over the event. The judge had adjourned the court until Monday.

But what about Aleta, he wondered. It was a tough cross. She'd caught the witness at every turn. And she'd finally exposed the reason he was clinging to his story. He had to put Aloman away.

Who was Aleta's second witness?"

His father approached and put his hand on Stanley's shoulder. "I will see to Aleta. You need to go home and rest."

"Dad, I can't leave her."

"You have no choice," Hubert said. "Please trust me."

"It's not that. She must feel so alone."

"Ah, Stanley, didn't you hear the applause of approval her fellow lawyers gave her? Don't you think that will warm her heart for a while?"

Bertha spoke up. "It's time to go, Sir. You promised me you would go right after."

"Mother taught her well, didn't she?" Stanley said rising.

"Aleta added a few twists of her own," his father replied. "Now I have to go and let her allow me to take charge of our client's testimony. We absolutely need her for the concluding statement. The jury dotes on her."

"You need to see if you can get her out of there."

"That was a given," his father smiled. "I was telling you what you didn't know."

Chapter 33

Hubert debated whom to visit first and decided that their client, Shakir Aloman, needed to see his lawyer. It was important that in the throes of guilt, he wouldn't say anything compromising. On top of that if he had thought that Aleta would stop representing him, he might plunge into despair and do something foolish. What he did need was a stern reprimand. Hubert couldn't deliver one if Aleta were free. Besides he wanted to take her home personally.

When he'd left the courtroom, he noticed Milani's men were gone. He hoped they'd gone with her to the county jail.

After he'd delivered his lecture to Shakir Aloman, he journeyed over to the county jail. Judge Heard took long lunches on Friday and he did not like to be interrupted when he was eating, but he'd finish up afterward in his office before departing for the weekend. There was time.

Hubert found Aleta sitting alone in a bare cell at the end of the two. She was hugging a pillow, eating a chocolate bar.

"Well, you acquired some perks quickly."

"A couple lawyers who'd been in the courtroom stopped by. Their wives suggested a pillow and chocolate. I hope I can remember their names. They took everything away from me. I don't have a scrap of paper to write a note on. Of course, I don't have a pen either. And look."

She held out her hand. Her wedding ring was missing.

Hubert sat down next to her and put his arm around her. "I'm so sorry."

"Tell Stanley not to worry and to stay in bed."

Footsteps made Hubert turn. He smiled at a longtime acquaintance. The gentleman had white hair, long bony fingers and a slight stoop. He carried a cane with a gold knob.

"Sorry to interrupt. My wife said an extra blanket might be welcome. She sent her favorite."

"How gracious of her," Aleta said. "It is most welcome."

Hubert got up and took the hand-off through the bars.

"That was a brilliant cross," the gentleman said. "Reminds me of those your wife did, Hubert."

Aleta flushed.

The elderly gentleman caught the blush. "So she finally let go of her secret. And to a woman! Leave it to Lydia. Wait until I tell Beverly. She'll get a kick out of this."

He had been gone less than a minute when another lawyer showed up with another blanket.

Aleta squealed with delight as she spread the blanket on the cot. "I can lay on something soft. You have no idea how hard this bench is to lie on."

Hubert started to speak half a dozen times but men who'd been spectators came bearing gifts and praise. Aleta glowed under the plaudits and received each gift with unbridled enthusiasm. Candy and fruit, pillows and blankets, a robe and slippers and a mystery book to read.

After an hour Hubert stood up. "I'm not discussing the case now because I can't get a word in edgewise."

"You want to take over Shakir's testimony," Aleta said knowingly. "Do it. You'll be perfect after me. And poor Shakir needs a calm reasonable presence."

"You aren't done!" Hubert exclaimed. "You must close."

"I know," Aleta replied. "I'll be okay by Tuesday."

After Hubert left, Aleta padded her bench with all the gift blankets but one and lay down. She took the soft white blanket that was the old gentleman's wife's favorite and covered herself with it. She barely fit on the bench sideways, but she was too tired to care. Sleep came quickly.

A soft voice woke her an hour later. The cell opened and Chief Lyle West walked in carrying a bullet proof vest. He went over to her and told her he wanted her to wear it.

"I'm in the middle of a dream," she said.

"You're in danger," he said quietly.

Aleta eyed the vest.

"If anyone sees this they'll just shoot me in the head," Aleta quipped and then relented and added sleepily, "But leave the vest. I'll put it on later."

With that she rolled over and faced the wall.

Lyle took the blanket and laid it across her body.

"My head too," Aleta said. "It's drafty in here."

"Go to sleep, Aleta," Lyle said covering her head. "I'll let myself out."

Aleta giggled. "As if I have a key."

"Go to sleep."

He stood against the bars, watching her as her eyes closed. On the floor next to the hard bed that served as a place to sit as well, lay the vest.

Lyle picked up the vest and tucked it under the blanket long ways. It stretched from her head to just below her waist.

"You're in God's hands now, Aleta," he murmured.

Day faded into night and Aleta slept on. Her supper tray was set down and half an hour later removed with the food untouched.

"You don't suppose she's sick?"

"She's breathing, ain't she?"

"Yeah, but..."

"And she's got all the comforts of home in there. Bet she gorged herself on that candy so she just ain't hungry."

"Yeah. You're probably right," the first guard said a trace of concern lingering in his voice.

"Stop worrying. With whole basket of fruit in there, she ain't gonna starve."

"You're right."

The stream of lawyers slowed to a trickle after the evening meal. Thus, the appearance of a nattily dressed man with a thick briefcase and a pillow tucked under one arm was no surprise.

"Lost track of time," Hugh Blackman said, adjusting his horn rimmed glasses. "Look I've got some sensitive film in my case. Can I just leave it here while I say hi?"

"She's asleep," the guard stated.

"Others have just pushed their gifts through the bars," offered the other guard as the man set the pillow on the belt that traveled through the X-ray machine. Blackman set down his briefcase and put his key ring with the small automatic car door opener attached. He also set a gold pen and a nail clipper on the tray.

"We'll keep these for you," one of the guards said pointing to the nail clipper and the pen on the tray.

Blackman picked up his keys and pocketed them. Then he reached into his pocket and pulled out a plastic asthma inhaler and inhaled. "Jails make me nervous."

"You?" the two guards laughed. "A lawyer?"

"Mostly I deal in wills and estates," he replied. "Which cell?"

"The cell at the end. The one with all the stuff."

Blackman pressed the smooth oval fob on the key ring in his pocket. He turned and walked down the corridor, his heels clicking loudly on the hard floor.

The guards watched him. Neither noticed the gas escaping from the slight opening in the briefcase sitting behind them.

The guards saw him bend over and push the pillow through the bars. One guard sank into his chair.

"Do you smell something funny?" he asked.

"No, but I'm a bit dizzy."

"Sit down. It'll pass," the first guard said. Those were the last words he spoke. His head lolled to one side. His eyes closed and he lost consciousness.

The second guard was too busy trying to stand up and walk to notice what had happened to his partner. He kept staring down the corridor. The man had left the cell and was hurrying back.

His last thought was that the man was using that inhaler a whole lot. He collapsed where he stood.

The gas, by now, had begun to fill the corridor that ran past the cells. One by one the inmates fell asleep.

Blackman slipped on a mask and extracted his gun from under the gas canister in his briefcase. He moved quickly down the corridor to the cell where Aleta lay sleeping.

She stirred as he approached and rolled over onto her back. She lay fully exposed for a few minutes. The man raised his gun but realized that her stomach was too large. It blocked both her heart and her head.

He moved around the corner.

Aleta, finding the weight of the baby too much, wriggled around so she could sleep on her other side. She now lay facing Blackman, completely uncovered.

Blackman lifted the gun and realized at once that the silencer wasn't attached.

"Damn!" he exclaimed. The shot would alert the guards on the men's level one floor above.

Unsettled, he walked back around the corner of the cell, reached through the bars and snagged a pillow.

Happy with his solution, he turned his attention back to the woman on the cot. She was still facing him only she'd pulled her blanket over her head and upper torso. Her hands were holding the blanket as one would hold a child.

He looked behind him and realized the corridor light was shining directly into her eyes or would be if she hadn't covered her face with the blanket. She probably wouldn't move again and he was running out of time. He could no longer hear the hissing of the canister.

She grunted with the first shot and her body twitched. The second and third shots produced no reaction.

Hugh Blackman was sure she was dead. He'd hit her heart with the first shot. That's why the next two shots didn't elicit any reactions. Still the fourth round left the gun's chamber and buried itself beneath the blanket covering her head.

That there was no blood satisfied him completely. Dead bodies don't bleed. The blood flow stops when the heart stops. Blood would seep through the blanket eventually. If he was lucky, it wouldn't be noticeable right away.

He hurried back the way he came. He picked up his briefcase and walked away leaving his gold pen and nail clippers on the tray.

Roger Kuchera, the beefy head of security at the county jail, was visibly upset. Two guards down. Aleta Praetzel shot. A huge error in judgment worsened by the fact that the Chief of the Arborville Police had warned him. He vowed no more errors would be made. Accordingly, after he called the paramedics, he called in Hawkins Monroe, the best forensic man in the area.

Kuchera personally went to Aleta's cell when the guards told him she wanted to make a deal. Her deal shocked him.

She insisted no one be told. Kuchera protested that Judge Heard would have his head if he didn't tell him.

"And I'll have your head if you do," Aleta declared. "It's my life on the line and I'm not about to risk it again because of your foolishness."

West was in Aleta's cell in twenty minutes. Dr. Cook was with him.

"West is not your doctor," Wayne Cook said. "I am."

"It's only a scratch."

"That's for me to say."

Aleta held out her arm. "Then say it."

Wayne turned to Lyle, "You're right. It needs stitches."

"Go on, Doctor, stitch," Aleta said.

"I have anesthetic with me," Dr. Cook said, opening his bag.

"No. I want to know what Stanley went through," Aleta declared.

The stitching was as painful as she had imagined. She wanted to yell at him to stop but didn't. Each stitch she thought was the last and then there was another. Finally she heard the snip of the scissor and Dr. Cook announced, "That's it!"

Relief flooded Aleta's whole being. It was followed by anger.

"I think you took extra stitches," Aleta accused. "I figured one, maybe two."

"You wanted me to do a good job, didn't you?" he replied pleasantly.

"Not that good!" Aleta quipped. "I counted five. That was three too many." She turned her attention to the Arborville police chief.

"Lyle, go see Kuchera and see to it nobody else kills me tonight," she ordered peevishly.

"You weren't killed," he returned miffed.

"You weren't on the receiving end of Dr. Cook's needlework," Aleta quipped. "He took more than twice the stitches required."

"They're very nice stitches," Lyle said. "Very professional."

"Don't praise him. It'll go to his head."

"Are you sure you want to stay here?" Lyle asked.

"I have to finish at least one day. Anything less would hurt the case. In fact, anything less than two would hurt our case."

"Well, I can probably protect you as well here as anywhere. I only have to add a few men," Lyle said. "But I have to tell Stanley."

"Tell him everything," Aleta said, "and ask him to honor my decision."

"I don't get any of this," Lyle said.

"I just wanted to taste the bitter pill Stanley had to swallow. I honestly thought there'd only be one stitch. And I hate needles."

"That makes a little more sense," Lyle chuckled.

Aleta laughed lightly. "Boy, have I ever replaced my hatred of needles!"

Chapter 34

If Aleta thought what happened wouldn't be found out, she was mistaken. Justin was at the hospital when the guards were brought in. He saw Chief West and Dr. Cook take off and he followed them to the county jail. He pieced together what had happened. The only prisoner that could have been hurt and would have enough clout so the doctor would come to her was Aleta Praetzel.

When Hawkins Monroe left the county jail, Justin cornered him and got him to talk.

"She was in jail for contempt," Justin opened.

"What on earth did she do?" Hawk asked curious.

"Her client wouldn't shut up. She took his punishment."

"That sounds like her," Hawk remarked.

Justin Conway called his TV contact.

"Aleta Praetzel who was so spectacular in court this morning..."

"Not her again," came the moan.

"She was shot in jail this evening. You want it or not?"

"Where do I send the cameraman?"

Lyle West was talking to Stanley when the ten o'clock news came on.

"How'd Justin find out?" Stanley asked.

"Hawk," Lyle said.

Stanley watched as Justin caught Lyle coming out of the county jail.

"You're in uniform there," Stanley noted pointing to the television screen. "I thought you were on leave."

"French needed a day off."

"You're substituting for your substitute?"

Lyle grinned. "Something like that."

Stanley's attention returned to the screen. "Why are you defending Kuchera?"

"The jail was guarded. His guards were very careful about whom they let through."

"He'd put a key on the tray."

"A ring of keys, you mean," Stanley surmised.

"That too. Only this was a single key. The guards noticed it because it wasn't on the key ring. He picked all his keys up right away."

A single key," Stanley pondered. "To what I wonder."

"A locker is my guess," Lyle surmised.

"That's a good way to hand over the payment," Stanley agreed.

"I've got men on two banks of lockers nearest Powell's office," Lyle said. "We could be too late."

Stanley shook his head.

"Powell wouldn't put the money in a locker until the deed was done," Stanley reasoned.

"You think there are two keys?"

"Well, I know he wouldn't put that kind of money in a locker before the deed was done. He doesn't trust anyone."

"Except his partner," Lyle said.

"You know," Stanley said, "even if Hillers is Powell's attorney he could be in trouble. A lawyer is liable if he has advanced knowledge of a crime."

"I have no proof," Lyle said.

"But you could question him," Stanley said. "You're closing in on Powell. Hillers could be getting nervous."

Lyle nodded, and then said, "Judge Heard could release Aleta."

"Heard goes to his cabin on weekends. No phone. No TV. No radio. He likes his privacy," Stanley countered.

"So Aleta stays in jail."

"Can you set a no visitors policy for Aleta?" Stanley asked. "Just my dad."

"You sure?"

"It's the safest way."

"Okay," Lyle agreed.

By late Saturday morning, Aleta, despite the physical evidence of sympathy of her compatriots, was feeling bereft. Two extra guards were stationed across from her cell in full riot gear, still that didn't dispel her deep sense of loneliness.

When her father-in-law arrived, her joy at seeing him was dashed by his news that Stanley had asked that no visitors other than he be allowed.

Seeing her crestfallen expression, he was prompted to ask, "I can get Stanley to change his order if you want."

"No. Don't. He knows what he's doing."

"He doesn't know how badly you're feeling."

Aleta managed a wry smile. "Oh, he knows."

"I'm afraid he doesn't realize how pregnancy affects a woman. Your feelings are less under your control."

"He knows," Aleta reiterated. "And he cares; but, he's thinking if there's a ban on all relatives, then no one can try to sneak in as one."

"That's pretty unlikely," Hubert protested.

"I would have said yesterday's attack was unlikely," Aleta smiled.

"Oh, I almost forgot," Hubert said. "Kay Rivers sent you a little present. Open it when I'm gone. It'll give you something to do."

He handed her a small box. As she took it, she saw her father-in-law sitting exactly as he was now only he was wearing a different tie and his face was drawn.

His words chilled her. "Kay Rivers was shot dead this afternoon outside Bessie Dobbins house. She was going to visit her mother."

"What did you say?" Aleta asked.

"I said if you open the box when I'm gone..."

Aleta interrupted.

"Not that!"

Hubert's brow wrinkled in confusion.

"It's the last thing I said."

Aleta elaborated, "You said Kay Rivers was shot to death this afternoon."

"How could I? It's not even afternoon yet."

"On her way to visit her mother," Aleta averred. "Outside Bessie Dobbin's house."

"When did I say that?" Hubert asked more confused than ever.

"Just now. Only your tie was different."

Hubert looked down at his tie. "What's my tie got to do with it?"

"Nothing," Aleta remarked. "And everything. I must have received a vision."

"You mean right now?" Hubert gasped. "But you didn't..."

"What?" Aleta laughed. "Turn purple? Or faint? Or look weird?"

"Something like that," Hubert confessed sheepishly.

"I think it would help if I didn't think they were commonplace occurrences, except for the messages, of course."

"So what do we do?"

"We tell Lyle right away. He'll know what to do."

"Lyle's on leave."

Aleta smiled wickedly. "Wanna bet?"

"He's home helping Lauren with the baby."

"Guard," Aleta called. "Radio Chief West. Tell him I need to talk with him here now."

"I could have called him," Hubert protested.

"No, you stay here," Aleta said. "Maybe you'll say something else helpful. You're my muse."

The guard reported back. "Chief West will be here in ten minutes."

Aleta smiled at her father-in-law. "He's using his siren."

"You're enjoying this, aren't you?"

"That's what Stanley always accuses me of doing," Aleta said. "It is true. But, I never cry 'wolf' unless there is one."

When Lyle West walked in, Aleta was surprised to see him in uniform.

"You're supposed to be on leave."

"Stanley gave me a clue as to how to talk with Lauren and I'm not on leave anymore."

Aleta giggled. "Stanley is giving marital advice?"

"No. He just helped me figure out what Lauren wanted. I had it wrong. That's all."

"Does he discuss me with you?"

"Boy, am I ever sorry I said anything," Lyle retorted perturbed. "I merely made a casual remark and Stanley responded. That's all."

"So he is giving marital advice?"

"You called," Lyle reminded her querulously.

"Kay Rivers is going to be shot this afternoon on her way into Bessie Dobbins' house."

"And Hubert couldn't have called me?"

"He told me," Aleta explained. "Only he doesn't know he told me. But I kept him here to see if he'd say anything else. But he hasn't."

"I don't remember saying any of this," Hubert clarified. "I don't understand what's happening. I mean I understand Aleta had a vision only I'm having trouble with my part in it."

"The vision was of him telling me about Kay's death."

"So I wasn't some sort of puppet," Hubert inquired, hopefully.

"No, I just saw a future conversation. That's all."

"I can deal with that," Hubert said relieved.

"Rifle or handgun?" Lyle asked.

"Rifle," Hubert said without thinking.

Aleta said nothing.

"Thank you both," Lyle said.

"I didn't do anything," Hubert objected.

Lyle glanced at Aleta who shook her head so slightly Hubert didn't notice. Lyle left without another word, stopping just long enough to say a few words to each of his men.

"What will he do?" Hubert asked.

"Take care of it," Aleta responded calmly, realizing her father-in-law was still a bit shaken.

"Suppose there is no shooting?"

"I should hope there wouldn't be!" Aleta proclaimed.

"I'm sorry, my dear," he said, patting her hand. "I don't know why I said that."

"He has to tell the truth," Aleta said abruptly. "Shakir has to be made to understand that."

Hubert stared at her. When had their focus changed?

"Why would he lie?" Hubert asked uncertainly.

"To save his son," Aleta responded.

"His son's in no danger," Hubert protested.

"If he lies, Powell will put his son on the stand and Shakir will go to jail for perjury," Aleta said. "On top of that we could lose. No matter how much trouble Shakir thinks telling the truth will be, convince him a lie will be worse."

"I wish you could be there. He listens to you better than me."

"Right," Aleta scoffed. "That's why I'm sitting here."

"Point taken," Hubert conceded. "I know you don't plan to be in court Monday; but, I think we may need you to patch up our case after Eugene Powell gets done with Mr. Aloman.

Aleta grew quiet. Her hands lay folded on her lap and her head was bowed. Hubert had never seen her pray; but, he guessed that's what she was doing. He sat quietly until she opened her eyes and looked at him.

"Were you praying?" he asked inanely, not able to ask a sensible question at the moment.

"I was arguing with God," she said.

"You argue with Him?"

"All the prophets did. None of them ever wanted to do what He asked. We humans are a headstrong, inflexible, stubborn species. The bull, pig and mule are weak imitations when it comes to possessing a truly obdurate character trait."

"Who won?"

"He did," she said simply.

"What were you arguing about?"

"Whether or not to go to court with you Monday."

"Oh, my God!" Hubert exclaimed.

Aleta smiled broadly. "Evidently, He is. He agrees with you. I will be in court on Monday."

"Oh, Aleta," Hubert said. "I don't want to pressure you."

"You didn't. God did."

"I'm sure I can handle it."

"He wants me there."

"Why didn't you want to be there?"

"I didn't want to give my hired assassin another shot at me."

"Neither do I!" Hubert said firmly. "I will handle whatever Powell throws at us Monday. I have two days to prep our client. That should be enough."

"You have no choice anymore. I have to be there

Hubert's mouth set in a grim line.

"Aleta, you are not risking your life. I won't allow it! I'll tell Stanley; he'll order you to stay home."

"He would never counter an order from God."

"Not even to save your life?"

"No."

Shortly after leaving Aleta, Hubert dropped in on his son. Bertha let him in.

"You're working," Hubert Praetzel inquired, surprised. It was her day off.

"Yes, Sir," Bertha replied. "Mr. Praetzel is asleep; but, you can go in. He's been wanting news of his wife."

Hubert entered the room and watched his son sleeping as he used to when he was a child. He wavered between letting him sleep and waking him.

Stanley, however, sensed a presence. He awoke with a start.

Hubert apologized and then related the events that had occurred when he visited Aleta, ending with, "I thought I'd call Kay and warn her, maybe have her meet me at the office until police protection can be arranged."

"Don't!" Stanley charged. "You'll mess up Lyle's plan."

"Suppose he doesn't have one. I'd never forgive myself if she died because I didn't speak."

"It wasn't your vision. It was Aleta's. She knew exactly what to do."

"She was playing the puppet master pulling Lyle's strings and enjoying it."

"She does that; but, Lyle allows it," Stanley returned. "It's a game—a private game between them."

"Well, Kay's life is not something to be toyed with!" Hubert scolded.

"If Kay was supposed to be warned, Aleta would have done it. She's saved her life twice before."

"She can't call. She's in jail."

"She would have gotten permission from Lyle if that was the route to take."

"What do you mean? Of course, it's what should be done!"

"I think the problem is that the killer is stalking Kay. If you change where she plans to go, Lyle's men won't be where they need to be to save her."

"We should do something."

"We are.   We're letting the expert handle the situation."

"How can you sit by and do nothing?"

"Now you know how Shakir felt in court," Stanley said.

"Speaking of court, I asked Aleta to be my back-up on Monday. When I found out her reluctance was based on her fear of being a target, I withdrew my request and..."

"She said no."

"She said God wanted her there. But I don't want to put her in danger. I thought maybe you could... you know... order her."

"I only do that for her own protection."

"I'm asking this for her protection," Hubert insisted irritably.

"If God directs her, I leave her protection in His hands."

"She could die!" Hubert exploded.

"That's true," Stanley responded with uncommon calm. "But God's love is even greater than mine."

"So you'll do nothing?"

"God reads my heart."

"You never used to talk like this."

"Dad, I'm married to a prophet."

Uncomfortable, Hubert switched to his next concern. "She is certain Shakir will lie on the stand and nothing I will say will dissuade him."

"We need to prep him together," Stanley said.

"But you can't."

"If we go right now, I'll be fine. My strength is returning."

"But you'll set your recovery back."

"I'm not doing this lightly, Dad. Aleta is in jail. And she's worried. That's reason enough for me. I don't want her risking a trip to the Arborville jail on Sunday to see Shakir with a killer on the loose."

As the two Praetzel men were preparing to visit their client in jail, the partner of Eugene Powell was alone in the office with Powell making a call. Melvin Hillers asked young Basil Aloman to call his mother to the phone.

Sadah answered warily.

The voice that came on was not Melvin Hillers' but Eugene Powell's. She sat down, a chill racing up her spine robbing her of words. She needn't have worried. Powell intended to do all the talking.

He told her to give her husband a message. Sadah didn't understand it.

"Why should he lie?" she asked when Powell finished. "He will go to jail."

"If he doesn't, I will put your son on the stand."

"Basil is not afraid," Sadah claimed without much conviction.

"It's your husband's choice."

"You can't touch my son. His lawyer will protect him."

"You mean the one who can't get herself out of jail?"

Sadah was silent. Aleta had forbidden her to come to court, so she didn't know why Aleta was jailed. All Shakir would tell her was that it was his fault. He'd cried out the truth and the judge had thrown her in jail for contempt.

"But she didn't do anything," Sadah puzzled aloud. "Why was she punished because you talked out of turn?"

Shakir refused to tell his wife that he'd let a woman take his punishment. That would be demeaning. Even the remembrance cowed his sense of manhood. So he lied.

"They do that here just like in the old country."

When Sadah didn't respond, Powell knew he had her. He then warned her that if she told anyone but her husband about his call, her husband would have to be retried. He assured her that the Praetzels would not defend her husband a second time.

Shortly afterward, Shakir listened to his wife intently then asked, "Is he offering me a deal?"

Powell says that if you lie, he will put Basil on the stand to prove you lied. Then he will drop all charges of treason because the Koran wasn't, in fact, your book. You will go to jail for perjury, but not for treason."

"But if I tell the truth then I won't have to go to jail at all."

"But he'll have Basil arrested for treason right there in the courtroom. Powell said to tell you Basil will spend a night in jail. He says he will arrange his accommodations," Sadah said. "What does all that mean? Do you know?"

Shakir slumped in his chair. "I know."

"So what will you do?"

"I will do as he asks," Shakir responded. "Tell Basil he is to tell the truth to every question asked. He is not to lie."

"I will do that," Sadah promised. "Will you tell your lawyers?"

"No."

Chapter 35

Chief Lyle West was out of uniform. He was in hunting camouflage lying on the roof top of the horse barn of Bessie Dobbins' neighbor. Two of his men were hidden in Bessie's barn, two were in the house and a road block waited on the road out of sight of Dobbins' house.

Kay passed a car on the road. Its hood was up. Just as she passed, Hugh Blackman slammed down the hood. His action precluded her needing to stop to offer help. She drove straight on to the gravel road leading to Bessie's farmhouse.

It was a sunny spring day and the jonquils were in full bloom along the side of Bessie's newly restored homestead. Kay opened her car door.

On the rooftop, Lyle followed the movements of the man after he slammed down the hood of his car. He had told his men that when they heard the crack of his rifle shot, they were to appear and demand the man surrender.

"But won't you give him a warning before shooting?" Peter French had asked.

"I'll be too far away to be heard," his chief had replied. "That's why I'll be aiming for his rifle."

"No one can shoot that well!" a new man piped up.

Several glares had shut him up.

Lyle kept his focus on the car the would-be assassin had disappeared behind. He couldn't see the rifle.

He lifted his head and looked around.

Where was the man?

He wasn't in the car. And Lyle couldn't see his head through the car windows.

Kay had stopped her car and opened the door. Lyle searched the road on the other side of the car. Just as Kay rose, the assassin's rifle barrel glinted in the sun.

The man was lying in the grassy ditch further down the road. Lyle realized at once what had happened. The man had discovered that one of the huge trees surrounding Bessie's house interfered with his having an extended line of fire, so he'd moved down the ditch.

The rifle was in place. Lyle knew the man's finger was on the trigger. He was too late to take aim.

The crack of two rifle shots shattered the quiet of the spring afternoon.

Kay spun around and fell to the ground.

West's men rushed from the house. One, crouching low, headed straight for Kay; the other, using a broad tree trunk as a shield shouted for the shooter to drop his weapon. Both men had their guns trained on the car believing that the shooter was hidden behind it.

Lyle saw the rifleman swing his gun toward the officer hiding behind the tree. Lyle's eye followed the rifle's movement.

Two shots startled the officers crouched in front of the house.

The cop behind the tree felt a bullet whiz past his ear. His eye caught the flash from the rifle. He dropped instantaneously. Two more shots rang out. He heard one round hit the wall of the house behind him. He didn't know where the other shot went. He lay flat waiting, afraid to move.

"Arrest him!" Came the order over his radio.

The cop lying on the ground stayed prone; however, French left Kay Rivers, after telling her to stay down, and ran forward, calling to the shooter to raise his hands.

"I can't," Blackman shouted.

"I will shoot you in the head if you don't," French said with a confidence that bespoke authority.

Two men came running from the barn, guns drawn. Slowly, the cop on the ground rose, his gun aimed directly at the chest of the man who'd just shot at him.

Hugh Blackman slowly lifted one hand to the side. The wrist was fractured and bloody. The hand was obviously useless. Blackman gauged the intent of three cops backing up the man closest to him. The men were advancing slowly now their guns carefully aimed at him. Theirs would not be wild shots that would miss their mark. These men would bring him down.

Blackman let his rifle drop from the bloody fingers of his other hand. Then he lifted that hand as well.

"Chief," Blackman heard the nearest man say into his radio, "Both hands are bleeding."

"Cuff the one that was holding the rifle to his leg," came the answer. "Put a tourniquet on the other arm. I'm on my way."

French motioned to the officers and ordered them to do as the chief suggested. Blackman's nearly useable hand was cuffed first. A tourniquet was applied to the other. An ambulance was called for. The injured man was read his rights, but not once were the guns withdrawn.

A man in a hunter's camouflage walked up the road, a rifle in his hand. Blackman noted that the men with their guns trained on him didn't turn away.

These men have been well-trained, Blackman thought.

The man walking toward them was short-statured and slender. Blackman assumed he was the marksman who'd nailed him. He wondered where the chief was.

Chapter 36

Aleta arrived home Sunday afternoon. She fell into Stanley's waiting arms and began to cry.

"It's a good thing I don't believe in surprise parties," he quipped, undone by her obvious misery.

"Don't ever leave me," she begged.

Shocked, Stanley gasped. "Whatever gave you the idea I had even considered that for a fraction of a millisecond?"

As she wiped her eyes with the back of her hand, she sniffed, "That frequently, huh?"

"I have good news for you," he remarked.

"Besides the fact that you aren't thinking of leaving me?"

"Oh hell, Aleta!" he exclaimed. "I missed you every second you were gone. I love you more than life itself."

She kissed him passionately.

"There is no one like you," she whispered. "No one!"

"That's a generic statement if ever I heard one," he remarked wryly.

"You don't want me to regurgitate your words do you?"

"I don't think I'd mind," Stanley teased. "They're good words."

"Okay, I love you."

"How much?"

"A whole lot," Aleta replied. "And I am going to court on Monday. And I know it's risky, but God wants me there. And, no, I have no idea why."

"It's okay," Stanley responded. "The killer who was after Kay is in jail. Lyle thinks he's the man who shot at you. You should be safe enough."

"Maybe," Aleta said.

"Okay, spill it. What do you see?"

"Nothing," Aleta said.

"You see something. Tell me," Stanley urged.

Aleta, however, didn't.

She just hugged her husband. Finally, he gave in, led her to the couch and sat with her, holding her as she began to cry again.

"Did something terrible happen in jail?" he asked.

Abruptly, she drew back and stared aghast at her husband. "You mean besides being shot at?"

"Yeah, besides that."

"You mean besides Dr. Cook taking five stitches in my arm without any anesthetic?"

"Yeah, besides that."

"You mean besides having a vision that one of my friends was going to be shot to death?"

"Yeah, besides that."

"You mean besides not having you there?"

"Yes, besides that."

"There is no 'besides that'. That was the worst."

"Can't be."

"Why not?"

"I'm here now and you're crying."

"Just kiss me and stop asking questions," Aleta said.

"Why?"

"That's a question."

"I know," Stanley said. "I want to know why you're crying. You're home. You stuck out two days in jail without complaint. You did us all proud by your brave demeanor under pressure. So why are you crying?"

"I wish I could lie to you," Aleta said, "but I can't. All we have done for Shakir has been tossed aside. He is listening to someone evil. And he doesn't see it. And his wife doesn't see it. They are going to make dreadful errors in an attempt to protect their son and, if they do, he will be lost forever."

"We can talk to him again," Stanley said.

"He is too shortsighted to listen. He is taking away his son's future, the very future he is trying to preserve."

"He's an intelligent man," Stanley argued. "We can reason with him."

"His heart is filled with fear. He can't think straight."

"How is Powell communicating with him?"

"My guess is Powell managed to persuade Sadah that he is stronger than we are."

"But ownership of a book is not proof of a crime or even of intention. It is, after all, a religious text," Stanley asserted. "We spent a lot of time with him, Dad and I. He seemed to understand that."

"Evil frequently appears more powerful than good," Aleta maintained. "And that is what is happening now. By the time Shakir figures this out, it will be too late."

"Is that the weight you're carrying?" Stanley asked.

She nodded.

"Did God give you this burden?" Stanley queried.

Aleta shook her head slowly.

"You believe He takes burdens, don't you?"

Aleta nodded, still looking at the floor.

"So why aren't you letting Him take this one?"

Aleta's head shot up. "Why did He give me knowledge of it if I wasn't to carry it?"

"So you'd be prepared to do battle," Stanley suggested. "He can't use you if you are wallowing in the pit of despair.

You now understand the feeling that has enveloped your client."

"He may refuse to let me pull him out."

"He is an adult. He has choices."

"He is afraid."

"Then attack his fear."

"How?"

"The same way you attack your own."

"I cry on your shoulder," she remarked.

"Well, that one's out," Stanley quipped, "I suggest that you search through your own experiences. You'll find an answer there."

"I need to go to bed," Aleta said suddenly.

"To bed?" Stanley gasped.

"I need you to come with me."

"Whatever for?"

"I need to feel safe and loved while I delve into my most fearful moments."

"Can't we do that sitting here?"

"Ordinarily, we can," Aleta admitted. "But I've spent two days sitting and sleeping on a hard bench. My body needs to sink into a soft mattress. And you need to rest."

"I'm not tired."

"Of course, you're tired," Aleta stated. "I'm tired, so you're tired."

"That reasoning doesn't compute."

"Don't say that in front of our children. I plan to use it regularly."

"It'll only work until they're old enough to reason."

"And what age will they be?" Aleta asked.

"If they have our genes, I'd guess age one and a half."

"That late, huh? I figured it'd be good until their first birthday."

"Pretty short-lived reason," Stanley observed.

"Not if we have one child a year."

"You're kidding, aren't you?"

"Oh, I plan on stopping as soon as I have the whole passel of you trained."

"If we produce a little Aleta, that will never happen," Stanley said half-seriously.

"We are having all 'Stanleys'," Aleta stated unequivocally.

"Now that you're back to normal, we can go to bed."

"Go to bed? It's the middle of the day!"

"I need to rest," Stanley said, wondering at the sudden emotional switch.

"You rest then. I'm taking a shower," Aleta announced. "I need to shed these clothes."

"I didn't plan a party, Aleta," Stanley said. "I wanted you to myself."

"I'm not disappointed," she returned with a pleasant smile. "An evening alone with you sounds wonderful to me."

When she emerged from her shower, she found Stanley sound asleep in their bed. Without dressing she slipped in beside him reveling in the feel of clean sheets and a padded mattress. She reached over and took her husband's hand in hers and began to ponder how she'd shed her fear in dangerous situations.

Soon she stopped squeezing Stanley's hand every time she resurrected an old memory of a perilous experience.

An hour later, she rolled on her side and fell asleep. Stanley was awakened by the movement of her hand to its favorite resting place.

"Well, at least you're comfortable," he murmured softly, glad she'd fallen into her old habit. He closed his eyes.

The afternoon faded into evening.

A soft knock on the bedroom door woke both of them. Stanley rose at once and donned his robe.

Aleta assumed that he was as surprised as she. Had Stanley expected company, he would have been dressed, she reasoned as she watched him slip through the door.

He was gone for what to her was a long time. Since he was not alone, she pulled on her sweats, shoved her feet into slippers and left the bedroom, which put her in the living room.

The number of people that shouted "surprise" took her aback. She looked around for Stanley. He emerged from the guest room hallway fully dressed. He was smiling broadly.

"You didn't think you'd escape, did you?"

She spotted her best friend. "Lauren, how could you!"

Lauren laughed gaily. "We brought supper. I kept it down to just family and adopted family and a few close friends."

Aleta looked around. "You invited everyone!

"Of course!"

"I'm not dressed," Aleta declared.

Lauren disagreed. "Yes you are!"

"I'm in sweats."

"We don't care," Lauren said as she came over and hugged her. "We're so glad you're alive!"

The murmurs of ascent told Aleta that was the reason for the celebration. Aleta relaxed. It wasn't about her being in jail. It was about her escaping an attempt on her life.

"You all make my life fun. Thank you for coming. When do we eat?"

The responding laughter set a festive tone and the party came alive.

Chapter 37

Monday, ten minutes before the case was scheduled to start Aleta entered the courtroom, took one look around and left. She sought out the bailiff and asked him to save two seats and the headed straight for the ladies room.

Two women were standing at the wash basins chatting. Aleta ducked into the first stall and let go of her breakfast.

"Are you alright in there?" one of the women asked.

"Just a bit of morning sickness," Aleta responded, which was true insofar as it was morning and she was sick. She knew it was the sight of the crowd.

As she turned and sat down to recover her equilibrium, Aleta heard snatches of the conversation at the washbasin.

"I hear she won't be here," said a high-pitched voice.

"It's just as well," returned a pleasanter voice. "Judge Heard doesn't take kindly to being castigated by the press. Her presence would be a thorn in his side today."

"I can't believe she'd leave her client to face Powell alone," the high-pitched voice criticized.

"Hubert Praetzel will be there," her companion put in.

"Powell has a vendetta going. The man needs someone who can pull a few rabbits out of the hat again."

"There's no hope of that. Hubert will be brilliant, but predictable."

"What would you do?"

"I have no idea. I almost feel sorry for Hubert. There's no way he could prep this man to withstand the assault of an angry Powell."

Aleta waited until the two women left. Then she went to the basin and slapped water on her face. She accidentally splashed some water on the front of her blouse. She looked in the mirror and cringed. Hurriedly, she dabbed at her blouse with a towel. It didn't help at all.

She glanced at her watch. Too late to do anything. She pulled her jacket closed even though it was a bit too tight. It did, however, hide the stain on the front of her blouse.

She breezed through the door and straight to the table, her face carrying the concern over her blouse, which Powell interpreted as dismay over his being the aggressor today.

Aleta rose with the others when the judge entered. He scowled at her because she remained standing.

"Your Honor," she said politely. "I wish to apologize for any inappropriate remarks made by members of the press with regard to your ruling on Friday. I believe the sentence was a just one and deserved by the defense. I apologize again for each disruption caused by my client and myself last Friday."

"You were injured in prison," Judge Heard said, his words inviting comment.

"Which was not Your Honor's fault and which you had no way of foretelling. I'm a prophet and I didn't know the attack was going to occur. No blame should be assigned to anyone other than the shooter and the man who hired him."

"You refused to go to the hospital. Why?"

"The injury was minor."

"It required stitches."

"Yes, it did."

"Were you trying to embarrass me?"

"No, Your Honor. Frankly, I was afraid to leave the jail. The hospital cannot be so well guarded. I'm sorry I didn't think of what repercussion might result from my decision. I simply wanted to stay alive. I assumed Your Honor is glad for that outcome as well."

Judge Heard smiled. "Your apology is accepted."

"Thank you, Your Honor," Aleta said and sat down. She took a sip of water and kept her eyes from straying. The judge was watching she knew. Her decorum told him this wasn't a trick but an honest apology.

Hubert rose and called the defense's only witness. The forty-year-old accused terrorist took the stand. Hubert led Shakir Aloman through his decision to become a U.S. citizen, his conversion to Catholicism, his graduation with honors from the University of Chicago, his marriage and the birth of his children. He had him talk about his children's fascination with the English language and their prowess in spelling competitions.

Hubert led him through what sacrifices his conversion to Catholicism had brought about insofar as family relationships. Then Hubert led him to speak of the pain of losing all contact with his family resulting from his choices.

Bit by bit Hubert completed the picture of a man whose choices had isolated himself from the family of his birth and from the Muslim community as a group, a group that might have provided companionship and friendship in a strange land. His wife and he were an island in the middle of the ocean. Over the years a yearning for contact with his family increased.

Thus he had been overjoyed when his cousin contacted him. He had eagerly headed to Florida to meet him and get news of the family he'd not heard from for twenty years.

"Let's move on to the day you were stopped," Hubert said.

Suddenly the breaking of glass split the silence of the courtroom. It was followed by Hubert turning and rushing over to Aleta.

"Are you alright?" he asked deeply concerned.

"Dad, loan me your handkerchief and apologize for me. The glass slipped," Aleta said softly, but loudly enough to be heard in the still courtroom.

Aleta held out her left hand and Hubert glanced at the message beneath it as he pulled his embroidered handkerchief from his coat pocket. Aleta immediately dabbed the water that had spilled down the front of her blouse earlier.

Hubert apologized on her behalf and asked permission to continue. Aleta continued to pat her wet blouse with the handkerchief, seemingly oblivious to Hubert's next question. The courtroom soon lost interest in her.

She listened to Hubert follow the first of three suggestions on the paper her hand had drawn his attention to. Hubert moved to the second phase of inquiry, she flipped the paper over inside the folder and moved two written pages on top of it.

Fifteen minutes later when Hubert had completed the third of the three tasks Aleta had set forth on the paper, he announced that he was turning the remainder of the examination over to his colleague, Aleta Praetzel.

A murmur of excitement permeated the quiet. Judge Heard raised his gavel and the courtroom fell silent.

Aleta rose, smiled at the jury and began her questioning.

"Mr. Aloman, when you were in jail, you were interrogated extensively, that is for more than a few hours, correct?"

"Yes," Shakir replied still wondering why Aleta had taken over. Hubert had been doing a good job he felt.

"At times the language was a bit harsh, was it not?" Aleta asked. "That is, the voices grew louder, the words, angry; the attitude, hostile, correct?"

Reluctantly, Shakir replied affirmatively.

"I'd be surprised if they weren't," Aleta remarked smiling.

Shakir relaxed slightly. Aleta took a step forward.

"Last Friday you heard testimony about the rape of a young boy in the cell next to yours."

Shakir was about to speak when Aleta raised her hand. "Wait for the question, Sir."

Shakir leaned back as Aleta continued. "Had you discussed this incident with any of your attorneys before Friday's testimony?"

Shakir shook his head vigorously. "No."

"I object!" Powell burst forth.

Aleta spun around and stared at him, surprised. She said nothing knowing full well the judge was equally surprised.

"On what grounds?" Judge Heard asked.

"Irrelevant."

"It will become relevant shortly," Aleta continued. "Besides he's my witness."

"Overruled," came the decision.

"After Friday did you discuss the incident with any of your attorneys?"

Shakir looked puzzled. Aleta hastened to break down her query.

"Did any of your lawyers ask you about the incident?"

"Yes."

"Did you refuse to discuss it?"

"Yes," Shakir said emphatically. She had effectively freed him of suspicion of having broken his promise.

"Was the reason for this because you felt guilty about your participation in the rape of that twelve-year-old boy?"

Shakir's mouth dropped open. His shock was obvious to every person in the courtroom. The impact of the unexpected question caused Shakir to stammer out his response in broken bits.

"I... I didn't... I never took part... I tried to get him to stop... I couldn't have... I was in the next cell... I wouldn't..."

"I suggest you participated repeatedly in the rape of that child by that brute of a man."

"Objection!" yelled Powell. "Counsel is... I don't know what... attacking her own witness."

"Your Honor, may I please treat this witness as hostile," Aleta said.

"It appears you already are," Judge Heard commented. "If you continue in this vein, I will ask you to stand down."

"If you ask me to stand down, this man will suffer consequences he cannot even envision so wrapped up is he in fear of our system of justice."

The gavel banged. "I will not have this court insulted. You will apologize or serve time for contempt."

"How much time?"

Startled Judge Heard replied, "One day for each hostile question."

"Thank you, Your Honor. I accept the judgment of the court as to which of my queries qualifies. May I continue?"

Surprised at her response which was, to say the least, unusual, Judge Heard allowed her to continue, certain in his own mind that he had effectively curtailed her tendency to move beyond the boundaries of proper treatment of one's own client. One did not roast one's client in open court.

"Mr. Aloman, you just said that you tried to get Richard Young to stop what he was doing, do you recall saying that?"

"Objection!" Powell shouted. "Irrelevant."

"If Mr. Powell could manage to keep his pants on," Aleta retorted, "I will show the relevance of this line of query in exactly seven questions several of which will earn me jail time."

The courtroom drew in its collective breath and stifled its desire to laugh. This would be too delicious to miss. Heard had been known to clear a courtroom that didn't keep still.

"Overruled," Judge Heard said. "Try to look a little less like a jack-in-the-box."

"Mr. Aloman, how did you try to stop Mr. Young?" Aleta asked.

"I told him to quit."

"Through the bars, correct?"

"Yes."

"Did you yell for the guard?"

"No."

"Did you report his action at any time?"

"No."

"Did you know that your silence has condemned the young man to spend three years in a prison as horrible as the one you were in?"

Judge Heard banged his gavel. "One day."

Aleta nodded.

"Answer the question," she demanded.

"He was put in a mental institution," Shakir responded. "That's not a prison."

"He's not insane. You did to a young boy what was done to you. You are an adult who, by his silence, visited unspeakable mental anguish on a boy the same age as your own son. You would have protected your own son with your life, but someone else's son doesn't have any value in your eyes, does it?"

"Day two," Judge Heard announced.

"Answer the question," Aleta demanded. "Was this child not worthy of your protection?"

"He was worthy," Shakir said. "He was innocent."

"When a person sees a crime and does nothing to stop its occurring, isn't that participation by inaction? Weren't you, in fact, guilty of letting your fear of a future possibility override the current horror you were witnessing? Weren't you, if fact, being a coward?"

"Day three," Judge Heard proclaimed.

"Answer my question," Aleta said. "Did you, in fact, not lift a finger to aid a young boy who was being subjected to one of the worst experiences that can befall a child?"

"I couldn't let that happen to my son," Shakir said.

"Is that what you believe this judge will do?"

The courtroom burst forth in loud exclamation.

"Day four, five and six, Mrs. Praetzel! One more query like that this court will begin assigning months."

"Answer the question," Aleta demanded.

"Will he really put you in jail?" Shakir Aloman asked.

"He has done it before," Aleta said harshly. "He will do it again. I have six days of jail to look forward to. You may not think that is much; but to me in my condition, it is severe punishment. Now answer my question."

"He will put me in jail if I answer."

Aleta turned to the judge. "Please, Your Honor, explain to my client that the court only punishes witnesses for lying."

Judge Heard cleared his throat. "Mr. Aloman, there are rules governing a lawyer's conduct in court. Mrs. Praetzel has broken those rules."

"She has failed to properly respect the judicial process, correct?" Shakir asked.

"You are correct," Judge Heard replied a bit surprised.

"And if I say something disrespectful, will I also be sentenced to months in jail?"

"Mr. Aloman, I grant you a blanket immunity covering any expression about the legal system in this country. You are an American citizen and, as such, allowed to speak freely."

"Now answer the question," Aleta demanded. "Do you remember it?"

"I remember my answer," Shakir said. "Yes, I am afraid this judge will send my son to jail and he will be thrown in with a man like Young or, even if he is not, a guard will be assigned to him that will molest him. I do not trust this country's whole legal system."

"And that includes your own attorneys, does it not?"

"Yes."

"You know what I want you to do, don't you?"

"Yes," Shakir said. "To tell only the truth."

"And you are afraid that if you tell the truth horrible things will happen to your son and, if you lie, they will happen to you and not to him."

"Yes, I believe that."

"Have you lied thus far in this trial?"

"No."

"Mr. Aloman, if you go to jail what will happen to your son?"

"Nothing."

"How would you feel if he chose to go to jail in your place?"

"I wouldn't let him."

"Has he broken any law?"

"No."

"Have you?"

"No."

"So it is your belief that one innocent person is going to jail today and you intend that that person be you." Aleta began then stopped. "Wait. Strike all that."

She paused as if to gather herself. Shakir, however, saw a twinge of pain cross her brow. "Let's take a step back. How guilty do you feel about not helping Sam Jackson?"

Shakir was puzzled. If she was in pain, why was she not sitting down?

"Should I repeat the question?" Aleta asked firmly.

Shakir shook himself awake. "No. The answer is I feel very guilty."

"Do you suppose your son would feel that way too if he were forced to stand by helpless while you took upon yourself prison time you didn't deserve in exchange for his well-being?"

"He would feel nothing because he will know nothing."

"This trial is playing big in newspapers and on television. He will be asked how he feels."

"Can't you stop that?"

"No," she replied evenly. "I'll be in jail, remember?"

"He shouldn't be made to feel guilty," Shakir responded, her calmness calming him.

"The press will be as merciless as I was to you just now," Aleta predicted. "So what will he do with his guilt?"

"Confess to a priest," the father replied. "That's what Catholics do."

"And that will assuage him?"

"I expect he will be sad for a while."

"You are underestimating how strongly a son loves his father," Aleta countered gruffly. "He will be devastated. He will try to escape the pain. There are several ways a child tries to escape such a burden of shame. Do you know what they are?"

"I guess," Shakir replied. "I mean I know some ways."

Aleta raised a brow.

"You want me to name them?"

"Yes," Aleta said, gritting her teeth as another spasm caused extreme discomfort.

"Alcohol, drugs, pills, other things like that."

Aleta couldn't speak so she raised her eyebrow again.

"And they could get rebellious or depressed," Shakir finished.

The pain dissipated and Aleta asked a single word question.

"Suicide?"

"Never!" cane the shouted response. "Catholics don't commit suicide. Besides he's too young."

"Suicide is one of the leading causes of death among teenagers," Aleta put forth. "Do you want to know how to stop him from making that choice?"

"He would never make it."

"Reply to these next questions honestly and you will see what I see."

"The Koran that was found in the trunk of your car had marks on the pages. You and he made them. Why?"

Unknown to Shakir, she'd made an assumption and asked a question based on it.

"I had come to Catholicism in a comparative religion course. I wanted Basil to understand my choice."

"So you were tutoring him in both religions?"

"Yes."

"And which way were you leaning?"

"Catholicism, of course."

"And which way was Basil leaning"

"He was curious. I'm not certain he'd made a decision at that time."

"He was thirteen then. Has he made a choice in the three years you were away?"

"He claims to be an agnostic. My imprisonment soured him."

"So he has cut himself off from Catholicism and its mandate against suicide, has he not?"

Shakir hesitated and Aleta turned and walked back to her table. She searched for her glass of water. Hubert offered her his. She took a sip, set the glass down, and slowly turned back to face her witness.

"Has he decided God has forsaken you and your family?"

"Yes."

"To whom will he turn when you are in prison?"

"His mother."

"Then would it not be better for her to say, 'Your father is an honorable man who told the truth'? Is not that the legacy you want to leave your son? Or would you rather she say, 'your father told a lie for your sake.' He's in prison because he trusted none of his friends to help you. Instead, your father trusted his enemy who told him to lie."

Powell was on his feet. "Objection! She's at it again, Your Honor."

"Withdrawn," Aleta said quickly.

"Mr. Aloman, did you know your son is sitting outside these doors, waiting to be called to testify?"

"Yes."

"Who told you?"

"My wife."

"Did she beg you to save your son?"

"Yes."

"Does your son have a lawyer?"

"Yes."

"Is he in court today?"

"No."

"So, you feel that there is no one but you to take care of him?"

"Yes."

"Who is your son's lawyer?"

"Stanley Praetzel."

"Will Mr. Stanley Praetzel please rise?"

Stanley stood up.

"It seems, Mr. Aloman, that your son's lawyer is present and ready to represent Basil, should he be called to testify. He will protect him. He knows how."

A spasm of pain hit Aleta and prompted her client to challenge her. "And if you are rushed off to the hospital to have your baby, will he stay here and protect my son?"

Aleta smiled at Stanley. "If that should happen, Mr. Stanley Praetzel will stay here. You have my word."

Stanley sat down and whispered in Bertha's ear. "Is she in labor?"

Bertha nodded.

"It's too early!" he hissed, upset to the core. "How dare she make such a promise!"

"Sshhh," Bertha whispered putting her hand on Stanley's arm. "Be still."

"Mr. Aloman three more questions and I'm done," Aleta promised. "Whose Koran was found in the trunk of your car?"

"My son, Basil's."

"Have you ever been a member of any group that perpetrated any terrorist activity against the United States?"

"No."

"Have you individually ever perpetuated any terrorist activity against the United States or any of its citizens?"

"No."

"Thank you, Mr. Aloman," Aleta said and quietly took her seat.

The crowd murmured its approval of her handling of the questioning. Stanley squirmed in his seat because he was worried about Aleta.

"Do you want to leave?" Bertha whispered.

"No," he muttered. "She's pinned me down as usual."

Bertha swallowed a smile.

Eugene Powell rose from his seat. He scowled at Shakir Aloman. His voice was rough and angry when it lashed out at the man in the witness chair.

"Are you telling me you are not a terrorist?"

"Objection!" Aleta said in a firm voice rising. "Asked and answered."

"Sustained," Judge Heard ruled.

"Are you claiming the Koran found in your car belonged to your then thirteen-year-old child?"

"Objection," Aleta said, rising. "Asked and answered."

"What thirteen-year-old is interested in comparing religions?"

"Objection," Aleta cried. "Irrelevant."

"Sustained," Judge Heard ruled.

"Did you give him the book?"

"No."

"Did he buy it?"

"No."

"Did one of your terrorist relatives send it to him?"

"Objection!" Aleta said, rising. "The defense will stipulate that the book was a gift from Basil's uncle; however, his political views are irrelevant."

"Irrelevant!" Powell exploded. "He's sent a book by a terrorist and you consider such communication irrelevant?"

"Objection!" Aleta persisted. "Prosecution is attesting to facts not in evidence."

"Sustained," Judge Heard ruled. "Strike the entire discourse including the last question asked of the witness."

"Did you not tell the interrogators in Florida the book was yours?"

"Yes, I did," Aloman replied. He wanted to explain but Hubert was busy writing and he remembered him warning him to explain nothing. Answer all questions yes or no. We will call for an explanation later if one is necessary."

"So were you lying then or are you lying now?"

"Then."

"Why?"

"Please be more explicit?"

"You know a lot of fancy words for a foreigner, don't you?"

"Yes," Aloman said, refusing to take the bait.

"Do you consider yourself superior to the men and women on the jury?"

"Perhaps in spelling, certainly not in common sense or I never would have travelled to Florida at such a time."

Powell smiled slyly, "And why not?"

"The country was still reeling from the horror of the 9/11 attacks and all people of Arabian descent were suspect. If I had been wise, I would have stayed where I was known and respected."

"So you lied to the interrogators in Florida about the book?"

"Objection!" Aleta said rising. "Asked and answered."

"Sustained."

"Didn't you also lie about being a terrorist?"

"No."

"Wasn't the reason you didn't want them questioning your son was because he was and is a terrorist?"

"Objection!" Aleta shouted, rising. "Purporting facts not in evidence."

When she sat down, she leaned over and whispered to her father-in-law to take over.

"Are you alright?" he asked, a worried frown covering his forehead.

"I'm okay, but the jumping up and down is wearing me out."

Hubert objected to Powell's next five questions. All his objections were sustained. Aleta had managed to steal Powell's thunder in her rough examination of their client. Powell's frustration had evolved into rage. He could barely hold in his contempt for his opponents and their client; however, Hubert icily refused to let him badger Shakir Aloman. Powell didn't know there were so many ways an opposing attorney could object. Aloman hadn't answered a question in the last ten minutes.

Finally, when Hubert objected for the sixth consecutive time, Powell exploded. "I object to defense counsel's constant objecting."

Hubert responded icily. "Then stop asking silly questions."

"Your Honor, I object," Powell reiterated.

"Move on," Judge Heard ordered.

Powell huffed and charged angrily.

"Mr. Aloman, do you know whether or not your son is a terrorist?"

"Yes."

"Is he?"

"No."

Powell smirked. "That's all. Prosecution calls Basil Aloman to the stand as a rebuttal witness."

Shakir blanched. White faced he returned to his seat. He was visibly shaking as he sat down.

Stanley rose from his seat and shot through the door.

"I'm your lawyer," Stanley said, speaking rapidly. "Tell the truth, but pause before you answer, so I can object if it's a trick question. You learned how to be careful and deliberate in spelling contests. Use that knowledge here. If I tell you not to answer, don't. You don't know what went on to this point. I do. Trust me."

Stanley walked with young Basil down the aisle alone. He had told Basil's mother she might be used as a witness later. The truth was he needed her to wait outside. He didn't want her coaching from the sidelines.

Stanley placed himself beside young Basil. Stanley's reputation as a child advocate was well known. He'd long ago won the battle to stand at the child's side when the child testified. He never coached. Nor prompted. Nor even urged the child to answer. If the question appeared to be one that would violate the child's rights, he first asked for his answer and then the child either answered or he didn't. Judge Heard did not want a child hung out to dry in his courtroom. He was pleased that Stanley was there.

The first query warned Stanley that this was not about whether or not Basil was a terrorist and whether or not his father knew it or whether or not Shakir had lied on the stand. Powell was going for a mistrial. In a mistrial there were no winners or losers. Why would he sacrifice himself, Stanley wondered. Almost at once he dismissed the idea. Powell wouldn't.

He must have some sort of back door, some way to get himself off the hook, Stanley thought. That he would want a mistrial was understandable. Aleta had whipped him soundly. But there was a piece to the puzzle he was missing.

He looked at his wife and realized how important this trial was to her. She'd lived in fear for her life for months, still she'd persisted. She not only wanted Shakir freed, but declared innocent.

She wanted a verdict so he could never be charged for this crime again. She wanted him completely exonerated.

Did Powell hate her so much he'd temporarily put his own head on the chopping block just to rob her of her victory? He shook the thought from his mind.

And then it occurred to him that Powell would deny it was him and charge the defense with malfeasance. He was planning to put Aleta on trial. He must have testimony lined up.

Stanley realized suddenly that Aleta wasn't prepared for a sneak attack on herself. And he had no way to warn her.

While his mind was running through the purpose behind the simple question, he listened to Basil Aloman's carefully formed response.

"At that time we received a call from a man who purported to be Mr. Hillers."

"Purported to be?" Powell scoffed. "Didn't you recognize his voice?"

"No."

Stanley was astounded at the boy's acumen. He was pleased he had been still.

"Who did he say he was calling for?"

"He asked to speak to my mother."

"Did you hear their conversation?"

Aleta was on her feet. "Objection. Hearsay."

"Sustained."

"When she finished her conversation, what did you mother say?"

Stanley put his hand on the boy's arm and asked what his reply was going to be. When he told him, Stanley said, "You may answer."

Powell frowned. He didn't want Stanley standing in the middle of the road he was racing down.

"My mother said I might be called to testify and that I was to tell the truth."

"What else did she say?" Powell prompted.

"Objection!" Aleta said. "Relevance? I mean I realize that counseling a boy to be truthful is important but could we move on to why this boy was called to rebut his father's testimony."

Basil looked at Stanley, who immediately bent over and whispered, "That was the pretense Powell used. You are here for another purpose. Your father told the truth. Don't worry about him."

Basil nodded. He turned toward Powell and waited for the next question.

"I understand you are no longer a Catholic. Is this true?"

"No."

His reply electrified Powell. He couldn't figure why Shakir would lie about this; but, the reality is that he'd caught Shakir Aloman in a lie.

"Your father stated that you were an agnostic," Powell said. "Is this untrue?"

"I was," Basil said, "until last night when I decided that I really did believe in God. I was just angry with Him. No, that doesn't explain my feelings fully. I was exasperated. More than that really. Incensed and indignant. Outraged is closer to the truth."

As he spoke Basil grew heated. He raced on.

"I blamed God for taking away my father, for putting stupid men in this world who would put an innocent man in prison on the basis of his race, for letting them get away with it. The point is how can one be an agnostic and be angry at God simultaneously? The two are dichotomous."

Powell scowled fiercely.

"Sir, I don't mean to use words you don't understand," Basil said with a touch of facetiousness.

"You arrogant little prick!" Powell blurted out.

Aleta's objection was shouted out before Powell could go on.

The gavel banged. "Mr. Powell, you will refrain from such outbursts," Judge Heard stated. "One more display of temper and I will cite you for contempt."

"I want the witness's response stricken as unresponsive"! Powell shouted.

"You will not shout at me," Judge Heard declared. "One day for contempt."

"Preposterous!" Powell yelled. "I won't be sanctioned!"

"Two days!" Judge Heard said glaring at the irate man. "Care to try for three?"

"You can't do this!" Powell ranted.

"Six days!" the judge declared with a gavel bang.

One of Powell's assistants rose from his seat and hissed in his ear. Whatever he said calmed him.

Powell adjusted his tie, straightened out his jacket and cleared his throat.

"This conversion of yours," Powell began his tone dripping with sarcasm. "It came at a convenient moment, did it not?"

"Yes," Basil said calmly.

Powell waited. He needed more. He hated to ask another question he didn't know the answer to; however, part of his brain reasoned that if the boy gave another impassioned response, he would use it rather than react to it.

"Please explain," he said as calmly as possible.

"You remind me of a cat lying in the grass waiting for the bird to light," Basil said.

Stanley smiled inwardly.

"The truth is that this trial made me want to do something to help my father."

The boy watched Powell's eyes light up. Basil continued wondering if he'd regret his words. Stanley's touch on his shoulder told him to continue.

"I couldn't think of anything I could do. You do know, don't you that an agnostic isn't like an atheist. An agnostic sits on the fence, not committing himself to either side. All by myself I was pretty helpless. So I apologized to God for my anger and asked Him to help my dad. I must admit I'm testing Him right now. You aren't supposed to test God, but

I can't help it. But I really do believe in Him. I'm just not sure He cares about what happens to me."

"You didn't answer my question," Powell began. "Unresponsive, Your Honor."

Before the judge could rule, Basil piped up, "You are pretty rigid in your interpretation of responsiveness Mr. Powell. I didn't use whatever words you were looking for, but I did respond. To put it more simply, I was confused and frightened. My father could possibly be taken from me for the rest of my life. Doesn't everyone make big decisions in crisis situations? You used the word convenient which means 'fitting in with a person's needs.' I tried to explain that I found God because I needed Him."

"Unresponsive," Powell insisted.

"Mr. Powell, you asked for an explanation," Judge Heard ruled. "That's what you received."

Powell charged ahead, determined to break this boy down.

"Are you not fabricating this story to disguise the fact that you are angry at your father's incarceration, so angry, in fact, that you are planning to revenge this injustice?"

"No."

"You are not angry with the men who imprisoned your father?"

"Yes," Basil said without explanation.

"I suggest you are so angry at such injustice and that you are right now planning to lash out in a terrorist-type activity."

"You mean load a car with explosives and ram a building with it. Is that what you're asking?"

"Yes!" replied Powell eagerly.

"Perhaps that type of vengeance would appeal to you. To me it's foolish. Terrorists are single minded. They shut off the reasoning part of their brain. They let evil take over their hearts. I have neither abandoned my reason nor chosen evil as my master. I am not a terrorist."

"You have smart answers," Powell commented. "We are not fooled."

Stanley put his hand on the boy's shoulder and gave it another squeeze.

"You're excused."

"You may step down," the judge said.

"Can I stay?" the boy asked Stanley.

"Take my seat," Stanley said pointing. He turned and joined his father and wife at the defense table.

Aleta rose. "The defense rests and requests that they be allowed to make a short concluding statement immediately."

Judge Heard looked at his watch. "It's quarter to twelve. I was going to break for lunch."

"If it please the court, now would be better. I can keep my summation to seven minutes."

Judge Heard smiled. "You have seven minutes."

The courtroom buzzed with excitement.

The gavel banged.

Aleta approached the jury. "Now it's your turn. The judge will give you instructions later. Later the prosecution will inundate you with words. Try to relax and float on top of the deluge. Don't drown in it.

"The facts are simple. The Koran is a religious text, a sacred book in the Muslim world, the equivalent of the Bible in the Christian world. And just as some of you mark favorite passages in your Bible so you can find them when you need them, Shakir Aloman marked both his son's Koran and his own Bible as a lesson in comparative religion. It is natural for a parent to take a child down a path that led to his own enlightenment. There is nothing sinister in marking lines in a sacred text.

"Moving on, the prosecution relied solely on the testimony of a single witness. Unfortunately, they chose a man who has lied on the witness stand before. The prosecution will make a big point of the fact that Mr. Young did not waver in his testimony. And for good reason. Mr. Young is a pedophile and until this trial, that wasn't known. Imagine his fury at being uncovered. A man of such loathsome passions would seek vengeance upon the man on trial and his lawyers. He had nothing to lose to lock himself into his story. His hatred would give him the power to remain unyielding.

"Hatred is a powerful emotion. Most of you know its strength first-hand. Love is the antidote; but, it is a slow acting antidote.

"That fear and hate caused Shakir Aloman to be detained after he'd been stopped for a minor traffic violation is understandable. That Richard Young, so immersed in the evil pleasure of his own perversion, lied to hide his secret and found in his compatriots enough anger of 9/11 to deafen them to a single man's cries of innocence is understandable. Not forgivable, but understandable. Guilty men all scream that they are innocent. They are actually believed more than innocent men. They have more experience at protesting their innocence. They are adept. So it is no wonder Mr. Aloman's feeble protestations were not heeded.

"A grave injustice was done when Mr. Aloman was imprisoned without a trial. That, however, is not what this trial is about. This trial's goal is to determine whether Shakir Aloman is guilty of treason.

"Keep your anger against the perpetrators of the 9/11 attacks, but don't convict an innocent man. Don't kill the dolphin caught in the tuna net. He may be swimming in the same waters; but, he isn't the same.

"The defendant is one of us—an American citizen, horrified and furious at the loss of innocent life in those earth-shaking attacks. He is no more a terrorist than you or I. He is an innocent man caught in a net meant to sweep up potentially dangerous citizens whose loyalties are suspect. His are not.

"Keep this country's honor intact. Mistakes were made by officials but that is not unusual. The final judgment belongs to you, the people."

"Finally, a word to the alternates, Mrs. Nakayama and Mr. McGowan. While we were fortunate that no tragedy or illness struck a member of the panel, I personally appreciate your attention to every part of this trial.

"You are also to consider yourselves included when I tell the jury; I will probably never find a group of citizens I trust more. You are honest, open-minded people whom I know have set aside whatever prejudices you have in order to deliver a just verdict.

"Mr. Wynkoski I trust your honesty; Mrs. Roberts, your patriotism; Professor Micken, your intelligence; Mr. Morrison your leadership; Mr. Lincoln, your sense of justice; Mr. Jones, your deep understanding of prejudice; Mr. Thurman, your understanding of parenting; Mrs. Berginstock, your outspokenness; Mr. Wong, your forthrightness; Mr. Walberg, your learned ability to differentiate between two pills that look alike; Mr. Schneider, your business sense; and Mr. Blanchett, your ability to judge people. Each of you brings to this deliberation a valuable trait.

"An innocent man's fate is in your hands.

"I thank you in advance for your time and patience.

"My seven minutes are up. I will not be here to hear Mr. Powell's closing argument and I apologize to him, to you and to the court. It does appear that I am in labor. I am hoping the doctors can halt it as it is too early. Take care of my client for me."

Having said that, Aleta walked to the defense table and sat down.

"Court will reconvene at two o'clock," Judge Heard announced. The people stood at the judge exited.

Aleta turned. "Dad, take care of things, please. Stanley, get me to the hospital fast!"

Chapter 38

The first ten minutes after Aleta left, Hubert Praetzel spent calming Mrs. Aloman who'd seen Bertha rush from the courtroom and heard her call the doctor.

"Premature labor," Bertha had said over the phone. "And she's in court... She will come straight to the hospital... She has four police officers guarding her. I think they can scare up one squad car. It'll be faster!"

Sadah had watched one of the men split to ready the patrol car while the other two stood at the door ready to rush down the aisle the minute the gavel banged.

The officers didn't have to clear the way. The spectators at the aisle openings held those behind them in check. Aleta was escorted directly to the patrol car and with sirens screaming, the two patrol cars sped toward the hospital.

Dr. Chesney and Dr. Cook were both standing beside the waiting gurney. Aleta was taken straight up to the maternity ward.

Stanley paced outside the door to the room where nurses were removing her clothes and dressing her in a hospital gown.

"If you don't sit down," Dr. Cook warned, "I'll send you home. You're still recovering. I gather you were in court this morning without my permission."

Stanley looked around for a chair.

"Aleta asked me to come. She didn't tell me why."

"She must have sensed something was wrong early," Dr. Chesney remarked to Dr. Cook as one of the guards fetched a chair.

"Can the baby even survive if it's born this early?" Stanley asked as he allowed himself to be waved into the chair.

"Let us examine her first and then we can talk about options." Dr. Chesney said.

"Options?" Stanley shot back. "No options. You take care of Aleta first. That's my option."

"That's not quite the option I was thinking about," Dr. Chesney said. "I was thinking of hospitalization or home care."

"Which will be better?"

"Well, you do have an in home nurse and Aleta hates hospitals...," Dr. Chesney said, "so that's a viable option."

"Which is safer?"

"If she's here, we will have everything we need at hand."

"Then she stays," Stanley said.

"Unhappy mothers are not a good idea," Dr. Chesney postulated.

"She will be happy," Stanley declared firmly.

"We will see how she feels about it," Dr. Chesney remarked. Dr. Cook smiled. Bernard was about to get a lesson in who ran the family.

"No, we won't ask her," Stanley said. "You may tell her the options, but I will choose."

Dr. Chesney swallowed his smirk. Aleta was one of the most iron-willed women he'd ever met. She would do what she wanted to do.

The nurse called the doctors in. Stanley rose, to accompany them.

"Sit!" Dr. Cook ordered. "Stay!"

Stanley sat like a chastised child, head down, hands folded between his knees. Why hadn't he insisted she stop when Aloman said something? He thought back to that moment. Aleta's smile had reassured him.

He sat and fretted for what seemed like an interminably long time. The more the minutes stretched on, the more his level of anxiety rose.

That a hand roused him startled him.

"You can come in now," Dr. Cook said.

Aleta was smiling.

"The baby's heart is strong," she said. "He is no longer under stress. We think the labor has stopped. Isn't that wonderful?"

"All that in a few minutes?"

"It's been a bit longer than that," Dr. Cook said kindly. "But since you were stuck in the hospital hallway, I'm glad you napped."

"Stanley, Dr. Chesney said that I could go home since Bertha's there."

"But not this monitoring equipment," Stanley said. "Which one of these monitors the baby's heartbeat?"

"This one," Dr. Chesney said. "And you are correct. You won't have any monitors at home, but Bertha can listen to the heartbeat regularly."

"But this machine keeps track every minute, right?"

"That's true."

"And the baby was in distress when we arrived, wasn't it?"

"Yes."

"Aleta, we live almost twenty minutes from the hospital. The baby could be in distress forty or fifty minutes before we even know it. That hour could be the difference between life and death."

"I don't want to spend a month lying in a hospital waiting," Aleta protested. "I just spent two days in jail. I'm not up for a repeat performance."

She turned to Dr. Chesney. "Tell him I'll be okay at home."

"I can't promise that," Dr. Chesney said.

"But it's not foolish to choose home, is it?"

"No, it's not foolish. It's not preferable, however, in an uncertain pregnancy such as yours."

"Stanley, think positive. I'll come back at the slightest twinge," Aleta pleaded. "I'll be lonely and useless here."

"You don't want to stay?"

"Absolutely not!"

"You will hate it?"

"Yes, every minute."

"You know what that means, don't you?"

"Stanley, please don't! I'll stay for a couple of days and then go home. Okay?"

"You'll stay until the baby is born," Stanley said with authority.

"You're ordering me to?" Aleta wailed. "Do you hate me?"

Stanley took Aleta's hand and kissed it. "I love you with all my heart and yes I'm not only ordering you to stay, but to obey every order of Dr. Chesney's exactly as he wants it obeyed."

"You'll find that part particularly useful," Dr. Cook mentioned. "Aleta is very creative in her interpretation of doctor's orders."

"No chance of a reprieve, Stanley?" Aleta inquired meekly.

"Absolutely none," Stanley said. "I need to go back to court now and sleep through Powell's summation. Tonight I'll bring news and chocolates."

"Have Bertha pack me a bag and bring me my robe," Aleta said pleasantly.

Dr. Chesney spoke up. "You aren't getting out of bed for anything. We're taking no chances."

"No robe, I guess," Aleta said, disappointed, but not querulous. "Maybe Bertha could bake me some cookies. Those oatmeal, chocolate chip, nut ones."

She looked at Dr. Chesney. "Okay?"

"A few extra pounds now will probably be good for both you and the baby. I think she should include some of those lemon squares to assuage hungry doctors who visit."

"Am I getting a phone?" Aleta queried.

"No phone," Stanley decided. "No television."

"I assume you have a reason?"

"I don't want you excited or upset."

"Books, maybe?" Aleta asked deferentially.

"Anything in particular?"

"Just bring me a mix."

When the two doctors and Stanley left the room, Stanley drew them aside.

"I don't know if you know it, but Judge Heard handed Aleta a seven day sentence for contempt."

"She can't go to jail!" Dr. Chesney objected, shocked.

"Won't he excuse her?" Dr. Cook asked.

"He might postpone it, but he won't excuse her. So what I plan to do is offer to serve the time in her place. That means I'll get plenty of rest."

"You're going to do it now?" Dr. Chesney gasped.

"I can't do it at my convenience," Stanley said. "And not a word of this to Aleta. She'd forbid it."

"She's expecting you to visit this evening," Dr. Chesney put in, wondering who exactly was in charge in this family.

"I'll send Lyle. The guards will let him through."

"She'll worry," Dr. Chesney said.

"He'll tell her I'm away on business."

"I don't want her in jail afterward either," Dr. Chesney remarked. "The baby will need her. Could she really stop you from doing this?"

"Yes."

Chapter 39

As soon as Eugene Powell completed his closing argument, and the jury was dispatched to deliberate, Stanley presented himself to Judge Heard and politely suggested he be allowed to serve Aleta's contempt sentence. Hubert stood beside his son.

"It was her punishment, not yours," Heard objected.

"We are a team. She did nothing without my knowledge and permission," Stanley countered.

"If I may, Your Honor," Hubert insisted, "Aleta will be punished with Stanley's absence at this time. She will think twice before repeating today's performance."

"I'm not sure I want that," Judge Heard said. "However, I'll allow it. You do realize I intended to send her to jail immediately after Powell's closing."

"I assumed you would, Your Honor," Stanley said stoically. "Six days I believe starting right now."

"Bailiff, cuff Mr. Praetzel and put him in a holding cell for transport to the county jail."

"Then return and take Mr. Powell as well."

Powell who'd been smirking when Stanley was cuffed, exploded, "The trial's not over! Tradition says I get to wait until the verdict is in."

"As you wish," Judge heard ruled. "Seven days after the jury returns the verdict."

"Seven? It was six. And that's all I'll serve," Powell declared arrogantly, whispering to his colleagues, "Keep your numbers straight old man."

"Ten days," Judge Heard ordered. "In case you haven't noticed, the court is still in session. Your disrespect is on the court records."

"What disrespect?" Powell challenged.

"Read Mr. Powell's last comment, please," Judge Heard instructed his clerk.

"Keep your numbers straight, old man," the clerk read.

Powell reddened. "She wasn't supposed to hear that."

Judge Heard banged his gavel. "Court's adjourned."

That evening at the hospital, Aleta's eyes lit up when three visitors walked into her room.

"Mom, Dad you're early. Lyle, where's Stanley? He's okay, isn't he?"

"He's fine, dear," Lydia said. "The question is, 'How are you?'"

"I'm okay. The baby's okay. Will Stanley be coming later?"

Lydia turned to Lyle. "You tell her."

Lyle looked into Aleta's eyes and hesitated.

"What is it?"

"Stanley's in jail."

"Lyle!" Hubert exclaimed. "He didn't want her to know."

"What did he do?" Aleta asked, more curious than dismayed.

Hubert spoke up. "He took your place. He's serving your six days for contempt."

Suddenly, Aleta was angry. The beeps on the monitor sped up.

"He can't do that!" Aleta exclaimed. "They're my six days!"

"Stanley was very persuasive," Hubert said calmly. "The judge locked him up as soon as the jury was dispatched to reach a verdict."

"He didn't get to hear it?" Aleta groaned. "How am I going to know?"

Hubert laughed heartily and the others joined him.

Aleta immediately realized her faux pas and joined in the merriment. "Dad, I'm sorry. Is the jury still out?"

Her heart rhythm slowed down.

"They were back within the hour," Hubert replied. "Powell was carted off for his ten days right afterward."

"Ten days?"

"He insulted the judge. He was so intrigued with Stanley being handcuffed that he forgot the judge was still sitting," Hubert said grinning. "At least he can't use your contempt charge against you. He got a stiffer sentence under the same judge during the same trial."

"So what was the verdict?"

"Aleta, they deliberated for only an hour," Hubert said. "After your closing, did you have any doubt?"

"Of course, I had doubt."

"You'd pulled the teeth out of all Powell's arguments by the time you finished. He had nothing left to say.

"So what did they get hung up on?"

"An hour's a quick verdict."

"They talked about something," Aleta insisted.

"They examined Powell's charge that the character traits you assigned to each were bogus."

"I didn't mean for that to happen," Aleta said. "I wanted them to focus on the trial."

"They were focused," Hubert said. "Each one was convinced by a different combination of arguments. The decision was unanimous. Aleta, you did a super job!"

"Dad, you are going to visit Stanley, aren't you?"

"Every day," Hubert said.

"He will be more lonely than I."

Chapter 40

The remainder of the week was quiet and Aleta managed to read almost a book a day. While she was an extremely fast reader of fiction, she slowed her pace to give her imagination exercise. However, on the day Stanley was due to be released, she could think of little else but seeing him again.

Dr. Chesney was called in when her heart rate increased. He sat down and talked with her after lunch was over. He teased her about her accelerated heartbeat and said it looked as if he might have to ban Stanley for the duration of her stay.

Her heart skipped a beat when she protested vociferously, "You wouldn't."

He took her hand. "Of course not!"

Her heart rate dropped instantly.

"I need you to relax. What is worrying you? You must have sent ten messages the last two days that he was to come straight here. Where else would he go?"

"Home to shower and change, the office to check on things, to see Lyle and find out how he's progressing, to a hundred different places."

"Would you relax if I can guarantee he will come here?"

"You can't," she stated unequivocally.

"Oh, I can. You relax. I need to make a phone call."

"You won't lie and tell him I'm dying?"

"I would never do that!" Dr. Chesney said. He stepped outside and made two calls.

He was smiling when he returned. "Guaranteed. Stanley will be here immediately after he's discharged. I sent someone to fetch him."

"Who?"

"Why the chief of police."

"Lyle has other things to do."

"Not at three thirty this afternoon."

Hugh Blackman had been confined to a lower floor of the hospital until after Eugene Powell was released from the county jail. By that time two weeks had passed. His fractured wrist was still in a cast, his other hand had fared no better as several bones were smashed. It had been operated on and was now wrapped in a huge bandage with wire splints to keep his fingers extended. He, however, had limited use of the fingers on the hand attached to the wrist in the cast and so he had been moved to the county jail.

His lawyer, Melvin Hillers, visited him regularly and assured Eugene Powell that Hugh Blackman had no intention of naming his employer. He planned to plead guilty to attempted murder; but, wanted the attempted manslaughter charge on the police officer reduced to assault with a deadly weapon.

Kay Rivers was upset at the thought that in less than ten years he could be out of jail and intent on finishing the job.

"He won't want to give back the money he's already been paid," Kay had argued. "He'll come back for us both."

Lyle wasn't happy at the prospect, but he had no bargaining power, especially as Blackman's lawyer was Melvin Hillers. Blackman wouldn't say a word without his lawyer present.

Blackman waived a preliminary hearing the first day out of the hospital. A trial date was set and both sides met repeatedly to argue the sentencing recommendation. Blackman kept offering bits of information; but Lyle West only wanted one thing--the name of the man who hired him.

Later, Lyle sought out Stanley and dejectedly told him that the prosecutor insisted he couldn't charge Powell with conspiracy without more evidence.

"It all seems so logical to me," he finished. "We actually found bills in Blackman's wallet that matched bills in the lot that Powell withdrew from his bank. The prosecutor said that could be mere happenstance."

"What's next?" Stanley asked.

"If any food is delivered—candy, nuts, fruit, donuts, anything—call me and let me test it."

"You think he'll try poison?" Aleta asked.

"Why not? You and I keep shooting the men he sends armed with guns," Lyle rejoined with a wry smile.

He signaled Stanley to follow him into the hallway. Before he had a chance to run his latest idea by Stanley, one of the guards hailed him.

"Chief," his man said, "there's a stab wound coming in from the county lock-up. It's Blackman."

Lyle's face was grave. "If Powell is behind this, he's getting desperate."

He opened his phone and called his lieutenant and spat out orders as he hurried toward the elevator.

Chief West waited at the emergency entrance with Dr. Cook. He'd already been told the wound was superficial. How it happened was still a mystery. All he'd been told is that there'd been a fight and someone pushed Blackman against the bars and one of the men in the next cell had stabbed him.

When Dr. Cook pulled back the blanket covering Blackman, he said, "Superficial, my eye! Prep him for surgery. An artery's been nicked."

Blackman spotted Chief West. "I need to see you," he whispered. "Alone. Now."

"Afterward," Dr. Cook said firmly.

"Now or I won't let you operate."

The room was cleared in seconds. Dr. Cook said in parting that the tourniquet was only good for five more minutes.

"The man you want is Eugene Powell," Blackman started.

"If you don't let them operate, you won't live to testify."

"I'm not testifying," Blackman said. "You're going to find evidence."

"Where?"

"My wallet has a note that was left in the first locker."

"We searched your wallet."

"Look again."

"Where's the one hundred twenty-five thousand?"

"He'll deny giving it to me."

"I can already connect him to several bills in your wallet. If I have the rest, I can nail him."

"The key you found…" Blackman began.

"The locker was empty."

"It's a bottom locker. Look on its roof," Blackman said. "And you found this stuff by yourself, okay?"

"Okay," West said puzzled.

"I was warned," Blackman said. "I hit a family member. Powell knew it—the sonofabitch. I'm a marked man unless you nail him."

"Are you angling for a reduced sentence?"

"No. The family said that if I pleaded guilty to the max they'd know I was cooperating and I wouldn't die in prison."

"You'll testify if I need you?"

"Try not to need me."

"I'll get Dr. Cook to keep you here for a couple of days, so we can talk."

"A family member," Blackman stated. "How many people has she killed?"

"A fair number," Lyle replied solemnly.

"Okay, tell the doc he can save my leg now," Blackman said.

That night Lyle told the Praetzels about his arrest of both Eugene Powell and Melvin Hillers.

"Hillers' fingerprints were on the note. It seems Powell had written it and asked Hillers to put it in the locker. When he discovered he was being charged with conspiracy and as an accessory before and after the fact, he folded and turned state's evidence."

"Did Powell deliberately set him up?" Aleta asked.

"Powell's admitting nothing," Lyle replied. "Blackman's agreed to testify as well."

"Why did Blackman change his mind?"

"A visit from a family member."

"And you let him in?" Aleta gasped.

"He didn't show up with guns or knives or blackjacks, Aleta. It turns out Blackman has a new lawyer. He wasn't too happy to see him but when he urged Blackman to cooperate fully Blackman took it as a threat. I don't think the lawyer knew what that meant exactly. Blackman was taking no chances. He admitted to the attempt on you in jail. That added a couple more charges."

"So we're safe?" Aleta asked almost not daring to put her hope into words.

"I'm keeping the guards in place," Lyle said. "Both Powell and Hiller will make bail."

A nurse walked into the room. "I was told Dr. Chesney sent this up."

Stanley took the box and opened it. He took a piece and handed the box to Lyle who took several seconds to choose as Aleta watched impatiently. He handed the box to Aleta and took a bite of his chocolate.

Suddenly, Aleta yelled. "Spit it out! Both of you! Now!"

The two men spit their half chewed chocolate into their hands.

"Wash out your mouths," she ordered. "Hurry!"

The two rushed to the sink and turned the water on full force. Using their hands as cups rinsed out their mouths. Stanley grabbed his toothbrush and handed his spare to Lyle. Both brushed away the residual chocolate, rinsed several more times and wiping their mouths on towels, reappeared.

"This wasn't a joke, was it?" Lyle asked.

Aleta eyed them with disdain.

"Get those half pieces analyzed, so you'll know whether you need an antidote," she ordered.

Lyle turned to Stanley. "Did you swallow any?"

Stanley shook his head.

"Guards!" Aleta yelled.

Puzzled, the guards dashed into the room.

"Rich, call French. Get Dr. Cook up here," Aleta ordered. "Garrett, get this down to the lab. Have them first test the two half pieces for poison. Sit on them until you get an answer."

Lyle nodded his approval. Both guards moved quickly.

Lyle turned to Aleta, "Do you have any idea whether it was fast or slow acting?"

"No," Aleta responded.

"If it were fast-acting we should be dead," Lyle concluded.

"It would seem so," Aleta agreed.

"And we're not," Lyle responded.

"Talk about the obvious, Lyle," Stanley joked.

"You won't laugh when Dr. Cook orders your stomach pumped."

"You're kidding!" Stanley shot back.

"First thing on the list," Dr. Cook said walking in.

"I didn't swallow any," Stanley protested.

"It was in your mouth, wasn't it?"

"How do you know that?" Stanley shot back.

"That's why I'm here, isn't it? You don't call a doctor when you're only looking at the poison."

He moved over to the bed and lifted Aleta's wrist.

"I'm on the monitor," she quipped.

He half-turned. "So, you are. Well let's just see if it's working."

"You're kidding!" Aleta breathed.

He dropped her wrist. "Tell me you didn't eat any of whatever they ate."

"I didn't. When I took the box I saw them dead."

"Next time, get me a few symptoms, will you?"

"Don't we want to wait for the lab results," Stanley asked plaintively.

"He goes first," Lyle decided.

"Why me first?"

"Because you don't know what you're in for and you might not go through with it after you see me."

"You're hoping the lab results will come back and you'll get out of it, aren't you?"

"You're still going first."

Dr. Cook received the lab report shortly after both men had had their stomachs pumped.

"What's Haloperidol?" Stanley asked.

"A central nervous system depressant," Dr. Cook replied. "There wasn't enough in any piece of candy to cause immediate death. The drug, however, is cumulative. Four pieces would kill you, even if they were spaced hours apart."

"It was meant for Aleta," Stanley breathed. "How come she saw us die?"

"Remember we were each talking about which piece we wanted next," Lyle remarked.

"And she said she can't see her own death," Stanley reminded them.

"It has a strange side effect," Dr. Cook said.

"Death isn't a strange side effect?" Lyle asked.

"This one will make a normal sane person psychotic," Dr. Cook said. "That's not the worst of it."

"Turning one crazy sounds pretty bad to me," Stanley commented.

"If we discovered that you'd had a heavy dose and stopped the drug which is the only way to counteract its effects, the sudden withdrawal results in either psychosis or death."

"So did pumping our stomachs do any good at all?" Stanley asked.

"Sorry, no."

"No?" Stanley cried. "That was for nothing?"

"If any slipped down your throat it was absorbed on the way down."

"So what can we expect?"

"Haloperidol is a major tranquilizer. It's used to calm agitated psychotics. Too bad neither of you qualify. I don't think you got enough to even be drowsy."

"I plan to get a good night's sleep myself," Lyle said. "Which reminds me; the guards have been telling me Aleta has seemed down to them."

"Down?" Dr. Cook asked. "How?"

"Depressed."

"It's the monitors. The beeping is wearing on her," Stanley explained.

"I think we could try a night without them. She seems to relax at night," Dr. Cook said.

"She likes the quiet."

"Then we'll give it to her."

"No interruptions if I stay the night?" Stanley asked.

"I'll arrange it."

After Dr. Cook and Lyle left and the door was closed, Stanley began to undress.

"You don't have any pajamas," Aleta said.

"It wouldn't be fair."

"What wouldn't be?"

"Me being dressed and you not being dressed."

"I have on a hospital gown."

Stanley completed the folding of his last piece of clothing. "Hand me your gown please."

"Why?"

"So I can fold it, of course."

"Stanley, we can't have sex."

"This isn't about sex. It's about us being together all night as man and wife."

"In separate beds?"

"We sometimes fit a huge Labrador in our bed. He takes twice as much room as any human."

"But this is a single bed."

"Our Labrador is at home." Stanley grinned. "Can you sleep on your side?"

Aleta laughed, "In case you hadn't noticed, that's the only way I can sleep.

"Suppose we don't fit," Aleta worried turning on her side.

"We will fit. I will not spend another night alone in bed," Stanley vowed.

Aleta smiled happily as he squeezed in behind her and folded his arms around her. She curled up inside his embrace and sighed with pleasure. "I've missed you too."

They both slept soundly until morning.

When Dr. Chesney checked on Aleta early the next morning, he commented on how much better she looked, "Whatever you did last night, do it again."

The two laughed. "We didn't do anything."

"Well, do it again tonight," he said, listening to the sounds inside Aleta's womb. "I like the sounds I'm getting."

"There's a difference?" Aleta said.

"All I can say is the baby is not in any distress. If you could keep him in this state, he might not come early."

"We slept together," Aleta said. "Without the monitor."

"The last part Dr. Cook wrote on the chart," Dr. Chesney said as he read aloud, "No monitor. Privacy relaxes the patient. But I see no note about you sleeping together. Are you talking about sex?"

"No," Aleta replied. "Just sleeping together."

"That's a single bed."

"We sleep close."

"I'll say."

"So we can do it again?"

"I'd recommend it," Dr. Chesney said. "But no intercourse."

Aleta blushed. Her heart increased its beat.

It was Stanley who responded evenly. "Whatever you say, Dr. Chesney."

Aleta's heartbeat slowed.

"I heard about the stomach pumping," Dr. Chesney said. "I'm sorry."

"It's not your fault."

"I have the box packed just for you. The clerk knows just what I want. She must have told someone."

"Don't fret. Chief West told me he's got good leads on this one," Dr. Stanley said. "He sounded very positive."

"I wish it were Powell," Aleta said. "One enemy is all I can handle right now."

"You got your wish," Lyle West said, walking into the room. "It was him."

"But he's in jail."

"He left the box on his desk at the office with a note that it was to Aleta from Dr. Chesney. His secretary didn't realize the note was to prevent her from helping herself. She thought it was a directive and so she delivered the box. She gave us the note.

"We got a search warrant and found the syringes and the drug in his office safe. He had been granted bail again despite the prosecutor's strong objection seeing as how his case was stronger now with Hillers' and Blackman's testimonies. We caught him coming out of the courthouse and arrested him on the new charges. He won't get out on bail this time."

Aleta relaxed visibly. "So I'm safe."

West nodded. "I believe so. You will understand if I leave protection in place for a while longer. Blackman is, after all, still in the hospital."

"You don't think..."

"No, but his presence makes guards on your door standard protocol."

"I rather like having them here," Aleta said.

"It's a great training ground," Lyle remarked. "Things keep happening."

"Nothing happened last night, did it?" Aleta asked.

"They turned away two nurses, a lab tech and three reporters. The lab tech turned out to be a reporter as well."

"You do know," Aleta said, "in any other place but here, I'd be dead by now. I think you should all know I know this."

"I'll pass it on," Lyle said. "Have a good day."

The days melted into weeks and in mid-May Aleta's doctors relaxed. She was still confined to bed because both doctors were certain that is what was holding back premature labor.

Then in mid-May when Dr. Cook arrived at her room a few minutes before noon with a wheelchair, both Aleta and Stanley were surprised.

"My grandmother is throwing a party in the new physical therapy wing. I told her it would be okay for you to come," Wayne Cook said. "I think everyone's hoping you'll have the baby there, but I told Grams that if you went into labor, you weren't staying."

Aleta eyed her husband who shrugged his shoulders.

"What's the occasion?" she asked.

"I'm not supposed to tell you. It's a surprise."

"Will you give me a hint?"

"Not a chance. Lauren would kill me."

"Not your wife?"

"She'd just make my life miserable."

"Dead and miserable, huh?" Aleta giggled. "Can't have that, can we?"

As the three entered the tunnel, Dr. Chesney joined them.

"Under no circumstances are you to get out of that wheelchair," he said.

"That's an order," Stanley said as he opened the door into the new wing. The cacophony of sound drifting down from the floor above them told Stanley there were more than two dozen people up there.

"What makes any of you think I plan to stand up dressed as I am?" Aleta asked, concerned with Stanley's order.

"We know you!" the three chorused.

"Oh, for heaven's sake!" Aleta rejoined indignantly. "I'm not about to show the world my backside although if you thought I was, Wayne, you should have given me a robe."

"We don't want your legs buckling," Dr. Cook said.

"Or your water breaking," Dr. Chesney added.

"Or labor pains to rob you of your party," Stanley said.

Aleta turned and eyed him squarely as the four entered the elevator. "You've figured out what this is all about, haven't you?"

"You'll know too in a minute," he said smiling.

It was only when the door opened that Aleta became aware that the floor held not two dozen of her closest friends but a horde of people. The throng parted to let her through and then closed in behind her.

Aleta found herself wheeled to the far end of the room where Judge Aramis Heard and her mother-in-law, Judge Lydia Davis, both robed, were standing.

Judge Heard spoke.

"It is our pleasure to inform you that your application to practice law in the State of Illinois has been approved by the Illinois Supreme Court. Are you ready to be sworn in?"

Stanley put his hand on Aleta's shoulder and now she knew why.

"Yes," she said. "May I take the oath sitting down?"

"You may," Judge Davis said smiling. "Raise your right hand."

Aleta raised her hand. The words floated into her ears, but, her brain, befuddled by the suddenness with which her dream had become a reality, didn't process them immediately.

Stanley squeezed her shoulder and she responded appropriately.

People then rushed to congratulate her. To everyone's amazement, when each introduced himself, she thanked him for the gift he left when she was in jail. The first one that wasn't part of the gift giving community was treated to Aleta's wit.

"Next time I'm incarcerated for contempt of court, I expect a pillow from you."

The man laughingly stepped aside only to hear her tell the next one that he was to bring a book.

"Do you expect to be jailed for contempt again?" a third asked boldly.

"I'm not looking forward to it," Aleta confessed. "And I hope it never happens. But I'm a realist. I'm a transplanted Californian. I come complete with some outrageous ideas."

"I'm from California. Don't believe her!"

"Dad!" Aleta cried. "You're here!"

"Everyone's here," he replied, then introduced her to the ad hoc committee members whose efforts pushed for her acceptance without further ado.

Justin Conway presented her with that afternoon's paper fresh off the press. "We tried to get in last night to get a photo but your guards couldn't be persuaded to let us in."

Aleta blushed.

Justin grinned. "That's what they hinted at."

"You knew about this?"

"Mrs. Cook called me."

"Some of the quotes from the letters are in the article," Justin said.

Aleta scanned the article. "Electrifying. Brilliant. Bold. Who said that?"

"It was the theme of a number of letters." He pointed to a quote. "This one's my favorite."

With some encouragement, Justin read it aloud in his rich voice. The crowd silenced to listen.

"She seemed to have a personal vendetta against lying in her court. And make no mistake, it was her court. With a rapier wit she slashed away at every form of subterfuge employed by the witness who dared to hide behind such a shield. When she finished, she'd been bloodied by repeated contempt charges; but, the truth was uncovered and deceit lay dead at her feet."

The applause was thunderous.

When it finished, she asked. "Who wrote that?"

"I did," Judge Heard said. "I was going to excuse the contempt charges, but then your husband stepped up. It was such a noble act; I couldn't not let it play out."

"He needed the rest," Aleta said graciously. "Thank you."

"I beg to differ," Stanley said. "I didn't need that much rest!"

The group roared and the party continued until just before two when that afternoon's court sessions beckoned.

At about that time, Stanley who hadn't left his wife's side, mentioned being hungry. Aleta told him she was still too excited to eat.

"I'll make up a plate for you to eat later," he said and he left her in the company of Lauren and Martha Cook Taekman.

"You made it through," Lauren said. "Martha and I were worried you wouldn't."

Aleta simply grinned at the two of them.

"The baby is on the way," she said.

"Should I alert Wayne?" Martha asked looking around.

"I see Dr. Chesney," Lauren said. "I can do this quietly. Trust me."

"I don't really want to be rushed out of here. And Stanley should eat. He'll be too upset later."

Martha patted Aleta's hand. "Here comes Stanley. Let me go scare up Wayne."

Stanley sat down and asked Aleta if she wanted anything from his plate. She shook her head.

"This was a wonderful surprise, wasn't it?"

"I honestly didn't know, Aleta," Stanley said, taking a bite of food. "I knew our fathers had formed an ad hoc committee but I lost track of the project completely."

"I'll never live up to the hype," Aleta said.

"The words weren't hype, Aleta. They were history," Stanley said. "This is a day you'll never forget."

"And one you won't forget either," Aleta smiled. "It's the day you're going to become a father."

Stanley paused in his eating

Dr. Chesney joined them. He pulled up a nearby chair and sat down. "I hear you've been in labor for several hours."

"Hours?" Stanley gasped.

"Stanley, eat!" Aleta ordered. "You'll be too nervous to eat later."

"I'm too nervous to eat now."

Dr. Cook joined them. "I see Stanley's been told."

"You knew?" Stanley queried.

"I suspected."

"You let her come," Stanley accused.

"I was ready to take her right back too."

Dr. Chesney spoke up. "Women in labor often deny it for hours, especially, the first time."

"You knew too?"

"I'm not a mind reader. No, I didn't know."

"What are you doing?" Stanley asked, upset. "You better not have an appointment."

Dr. Chesney smiled. "I'm timing her contractions."

"You're not touching her," Stanley declared.

"Her neck muscles tense," Dr. Chesney explained. "Ten minutes and they're getting stronger. I'm afraid the party is over for you, Aleta."

"I agree," she grunted.

Dr. Cook took hold of Aleta's wheelchair and began pushing it.

"We'd better hurry," Dr. Chesney said. "Straight to delivery."

"What's that mean?" Stanley asked as they entered the elevator. Aleta took his hand and squeezed it hard.

"Hang on," Dr. Chesney said. "Try not to push."

Another labor pain assaulted her as they neared the tunnel. Her nails dug into Stanley's palm.

"I can't help it," Aleta grunted.

"Stanley run ahead and grab a gurney," Dr. Cook ordered.

Aleta released his hand and he raced through the tunnel and entered the hall. He ran to the intersecting hall and saw a gurney at the far end. He raced toward it and snatched it from the hands of the technician.

"I need this!" Stanley said.

The tech held on. "So do I."

"Dr. Cook told me to get it."

"Not this one. It belongs to the morgue."

"As of right now, it belongs to obstetrics," Stanley said yanking it away and retracing his steps.

The three men lifted Aleta from the chair and put her on the gurney. Aleta grabbed Stanley's hand.

"Don't leave me," she said as the group squeezed into the service elevator.

Aleta sunk into the throes of a new contraction as the elevator ascended. Stanley offered her both his hands and she squeezed them both. Her cry filled the elevator.

"She's tearing," Dr. Chesney said. "It's coming too fast."

The contraction stopped; the elevator doors opened; the group raced toward the delivery room, shouting for nurses as they sped down the hall.

Once inside the delivery room, the doctors began to wash up as the nurses had Aleta scoot onto the delivery table.

Minutes later, Aleta screamed as the baby pushed its way through the birth canal. The sound tore through Stanley's eardrums and embedded itself in his brain. He was shocked at its volume.

The yells increased as the baby's shoulders tore down the birth canal and Stanley vowed that this was their last child.

Suddenly, it was over. The baby cried as soon as its legs were out. It was a high-pitched wail the like of which caused every mother within hearing range to feel a response in her womb.

Dr. Chesney laid the baby prone on top of Aleta's stomach. Aleta's hands let go of Stanley's and stroked the wet head of the baby lying on the outside of her womb.

"Is it a boy?" she asked.

"Of course. A fine, beautiful big baby boy," Dr. Chesney said.

Dr. Cook slapped a pair of scissors into Stanley's hand.

"Cut the cord," he said pointing.

Stanley cut the cord and then followed Dr. Cook and his baby to the table and watched as he was cleaned and weighed.

"Our one and only," Stanley announced, bringing the baby to his wife. He put him in her arms.

"Gerard Aramis Praetzel," Aleta said.

"Where'd that middle name come from?"

"From Judge Heard. I want our son to know he was named for an honorable judge," Aleta replied. "And he's our first, but not our last."

"I won't put us through that again," Stanley said adamantly.

"Of course you will. Your hands will heal."

"I was thinking about you."

"Me?" Aleta queried. "This has been the best day of my life. Besides the second baby will be easier. Isn't that right, Dr. Chesney?"

"Usually is," Chesney replied not stopping his work.

"And you promised me one that looks like you," Aleta reminded her husband. "Gerard is a redhead. On top of that, he looks like me."

"My parents, your father, your grandmother will all be as ecstatic as I am right now. Aleta, you did it! You did everything you needed to do to give our son a chance to live. I can never thank you enough."

"A second child will do it," Aleta said quietly.

"Can we enjoy this one for a few years first?"

"A few months anyway."

"Aleta!" Stanley gasped. "You're still being stitched up."

"I know," Aleta said. "The anesthetic wore off two stitches ago."

"You're not yelping?"

"Then you'd really never let me have another," Aleta said. "If I talk to you now, you'll know how much I want another baby."

"You are so right," he said. "You do know how to frame an argument. You win."

"Done!" Dr. Chesney said pulling off his gloves and trotting around the draped stirrups to take a look at the baby. "You're been a good patient, Aleta."

"Can we go home now?" Aleta asked abruptly.

Dr. Chesney's eyebrows shot up.

"Right now?'

"You're done, aren't you?"

"I've never had anyone leave straight from the delivery room."

"I have a nurse at home," Aleta said.

"There is that," Dr. Chesney responded. He turned. "Dr. Cook, how's the baby?"

"He can go home," Dr. Cook said. "Bertha will help Aleta take good care of him."

Reluctantly, Dr. Chesney agreed. "You can go. Just remember your spirit may be soaring, but your body needs rest."

When Aleta was transferred back to her hospital bed, Stanley asked her if she was sure she was up to going home.

"What I'm not up for is staying here," Aleta said as the baby was placed in her arms. "Isn't he beautiful?"

"He's so tiny."

"He's eight pounds!" Aleta rejoined.

"Okay, he's big for someone so tiny."

"You haven't been around enough puppy births," Aleta remarked.

Stanley groaned. "I'm sure you're planning to see that that changes."

"You can kiss me now," Aleta said. "I'll take a congratulatory kiss, a job-well-done kiss, a..."

He stopped her recitation with a tender kiss. "How about just a plain old I-love-you kiss?"

"Mmm," she murmured. "That too."

He kissed her again and she knew his passion for her was still alive. She would have more children, arguments notwithstanding.

She relaxed inside the circle of love he enveloped her with. The baby in her arms slept peacefully.

The Prophet Series